RIPTIDE

ALEERA ANAYA CERES

D1569172

RIPTIDE

Book design by Dark Imaginarium Art & Design

Editing by Lisa Nieves-Taylor

To the sea.
You will always have my heart.

"Why do we love the sea? It is because it has some potent power to make us think things we like to think."
-Robert Henri

TRIGGER WARNING

This book contains dark materials, such as the mention of rape, abuse, and dubious consent, that may be triggering for some readers.

THE SINKING

She never imagined she'd die like this. With the weight of crushing water pressing up against her chest, threatening to cave it in. She had tried to stay afloat for as long as she could, but the sinking of the boat had caused vicious whirlpools around her. It was as if the water itself had unforgiving arms that dragged her under... under... under...

She flailed her arms in a panic through the endless void until her hands came in contact with something solid. She grabbed without seeing, kicked her legs in a powerful thrust. Swimming upwards, she breached the surface and gasped for breath.

Her lungs burned as she swallowed gulps of fresh air, but when she realized what exactly was keeping her up, she let out a shrill scream, jerking back and falling away from the upturned corpse.

Soon, even that drifted away, and she had absolutely nothing to hold onto; she was left suspended on the surface for hours, listening desperately for any sound of help. There was nothing but the lonely cries of gulls overhead and the violent crashing of waves.

Her strength and determination lasted a while, but even that eventually dissipated. She could no longer move her legs, her arms; her head, suddenly leaden, bobbed below the water, and she gave no further struggle as she sank.

It was then that the miserable thought flooded through her mind.

I never thought I'd die like this.

In fact, the thought of her own death had never before crossed her mind. It wasn't something any sane person contemplated, really. But now that she was in this situation, she found that drowning in the ocean was a terrible way to go.

The air that inhabited her lungs was replaced with the burn of salt water. She swallowed mouthfuls of it; her very chest was on fire; her nostrils, mouth, and insides fighting back against the violation of it into her body. It was a feeble attempt to keep her lungs from bursting against the pressure they found themselves under. She physically fought back, as if convulsing in trepidation could have saved her. It did little good.

She sunk deeper towards the darkness. Her body would become a feast for the fishes. She pondered the thought as she said a quick farewell to the light of the sun breaching the surface.

It would be the last she ever saw of the light. The last she ever saw of the sky before she became one entirely with the ocean.

She was just about to close her eyes to fate when the quick motion of something bright and blurry caught her eye. Panic was now a familiar emotion to her, but even as the sentiment buried itself in her chest, her body didn't have the energy to fight back whatever creature had come for her.

A long, scaly fin in a scintillating blue and green camouflage of color curled against her legs. Then a figure appeared before her. She tried to scream, wanted to, but couldn't. Not with the lack of air in her system and certainly not at this fantasy sprung to life before her.

Her brain was probably deprived of oxygen and that's why she was imagining things. Because she knew in her mind that mermen did *not* exist.

Certainly not one as beautiful as this one.

He leaned forward, taking her face in his scaly hands and, in a startling move, pressed surprisingly warm lips against hers. She wondered if he was trying to breathe oxygen into her. If so, she felt nothing but warm water slide down her throat.

And then nothing at all.

gone, Coral sunk back into her chair and leaned her forehead against the cool wood of the desk.

She tried not to take what Olivia had said to heart. Usually, her friend was so overly dramatic that most of what she muttered about could fly over Coral's head, but in this instance, could she really be upset with her friend when she was *right*? She was overworked, sure, but Coral enjoyed working at the library. She loved being surrounded by books. It was like living a fantasy. When she surrounded herself by the crinkling pages, she was *home*. In books, she would not find ever-lasting heartache. In books, the characters did not leave her in the dust with a lonely, broken soul.

Coral shook that thought out of her head and sat back up, staring at the blank pages of her unfinished novel. For months it had been this way. It didn't matter what she did, the writer's block wouldn't go away. Some days, she'd sit at her desk for hours, fingers tracing lightly over the keys of her computer, but no words would flow.

Maybe it was because her brain *was* on overload. If Coral was honest with herself, the idea of a vacation did seem appealing to her, but... a *cruise*? She couldn't imagine herself getting on one ever again, since just the thought of them brought up painful memories.

Coral hadn't always been this way. She used to be fun. She used to laugh without restraint and find joy in the smallest of things, but then...

No.

Her thoughts screeched to a halt. She wouldn't think of him now. It was one thing to have him in her subconscious thoughts, preventing her from even wanting to step foot on a boat or near the ocean ever again, but to actually have his name in the front of her mind was unacceptable.

She groaned and tugged at the ends of her dark twin braids. Why had she let him haunt her this way? Why had she allowed him to sink himself so deep into her mind that she could hardly continue on with the life she'd led before?

But she knew the answer to that well enough.

He'd irrevocably damaged her.

And maybe that's why she couldn't write a single, freaking word! Because he was still *there* in her mind and she needed to get him *out*.

And how was she supposed to do that when he'd been implanted into her mind for so long, leaving her bereft of joy?

The first step would be to go near the ocean again, a tiny voice in her mind urged. *What better way to get over it than to face your fears?*

Coral shot to her feet, not caring that she'd toppled over her chair with the brusque movement. She had nothing to prove, certainly not to Olivia, but the urge was there. The urge to demonstrate to herself, to the *world,* that he'd no longer have a hold on her. That she was normal. That she wasn't *broken.* So, without knocking, Coral barged straight into her friend's room and declared, "Fine! I'll go!"

Olivia was sprawled on her stomach, looking nonchalant, passing a brush over her fingernails. She didn't even look up at Coral's entrance. She smiled as if she'd known what the result would be this entire time. "Good," she replied. "Best start packing. We leave tomorrow."

ABOARD

THEY'D HOPPED FROM PLANE TO PLANE TO PLANE, THEN from a taxi, to the hotel, to another taxi, and now an enormous cruise ship stationed at the docks in Neo Limani, Greece. The minute Coral set foot on the deck, she tugged self-consciously at one of her braids, then at the bikini top Olivia had so *graciously* lent her. Generous amounts of boob nearly toppled out of its small size, making Coral wonder why she had even accepted borrowing it in the first place. Anxiety clawed at her throat at the feeling of being so exposed.

She looked around, palm splayed over her chest as if that could cover her almost-nudity, only to notice that a lot of the female passengers were dressed in light tank tops despite the heat. She shot Olivia a look, but the other girl didn't notice. She was busy ogling a passing man in a speedo.

"Take a whiff." Olivia placed her fist on her hip and inhaled deeply through her nose. "You smell that?" She nudged Coral, nearly knocking her into a man next to her. "It smells like we're not in Kansas anymore!"

"We're from Colorado..."

"Don't be a party shitter. Now come on!" She grabbed

Coral's elbow and tugged her forward, nudging through the crowd of vacationers on board *The Siren*. There was chaos all around, and it sent Coral's frigid and orderly nerves into a frenzy.

The cruise ship still hadn't taken off yet, presumably waiting for the last passengers or doing last minute engine checks. Coral assumed the latter. She also wondered if it was too late to turn tail and run.

Stepping onto the ship and trying not to think of the past was probably the hardest thing she'd ever done. But a steady elation built in the pounding of her chest at the sight of the water and the smell of crisp ocean air. Despite those awful memories that threatened to plague her, her heart still thundered at the sight of the crystal blue water.

"I can't believe how beautiful this place is!" Olivia was saying as she dragged Coral along behind her.

Considering Olivia had barely glanced around at the Grecian scenery, too rushed to get on board before Coral decided to change her mind, Coral shot her a disbelieving look. Sure, the inside of the ship was beautiful, but she didn't think anything could compare to the outside.

But Coral didn't want to put out the flame of her friend's optimism, so she dutifully followed her down and through hallways, below deck until they reached their shared bedroom.

The interior was opulent—it *was* the honeymoon suite, after all—with an enormous king-sized bed littered with flower petals and chocolates in a way that leaned towards frivolous. The walls were set in a latticework of glittering golds and pink patterns; two windows spread adjacently across the wall, giving them the perfect view of miles of cerulean ocean.

Olivia, ignoring the beautiful setup of the bed, hurried in and threw her bags on top of it with surprising strength.

Inside, she looked around and again, took a giant whiff of the air. "Look." She pointed at the windows. "An ocean view!"

Coral rolled her eyes, closing the door and coming in to claim the right side of the bed. She placed her bags down in a much gentler manner, opening them to start unpacking. First thing she planned on doing was changing out of the ridiculous swimsuit for a new, more comfortable one. A one piece would do nicely. Or maybe board shorts and a t-shirt.

Beside her, Oliva began jumping on the bed.

"You're going to break it," Coral berated sternly.

"We're on vacation! All exclusive, everything paid for! I will jump on this bed if I damn well please." She giggled between words and finally flopped back down onto the mattress, wincing when her head hit the box of chocolate. She pulled it out to look at it absently. "In a way, I'm kind of glad he couldn't come on this trip." She tossed the candy to the floor with a single, distracted flick of her fingers. "It gives me and you a chance to hang out and reconnect."

Coral nodded solemnly in agreement.

The mysterious 'he' was Olivia's boyfriend. He was as rich as he was handsome and old enough to be Olivia's father. Coral had never met him, but her best friend talked about him enough that she felt as though she knew him already. He sponsored everything from sports to wildlife research campaigns with his billions. Coral didn't really understand his job. All she knew was that he'd cancelled this trip on Olivia at the last minute but had given her leave to invite whoever she wanted.

"We're going to have a blast!"

"I'm sure we will," Coral replied, taking out her own one-piece swimsuit and letting it unfold. She'd be more comfortable in it as it showed less cleavage. Smiling, Coral set the swimwear down and began to strip. She dropped her shorts and swim bottoms first, then reached behind her neck, untying the string and letting the top drop.

Humming absently to herself, she picked up her own swimsuit and stepped one leg in, then another. She was interrupted mid-task by Olivia's low, appreciative whistle. Coral looked up in surprise to find Olivia staring at her with wide eyes.

"I'm so jealous of your tits." She sighed, still staring.

Coral blushed a deep shade of red, then stared down at her boobs. They were bigger than she liked and made her self-conscious, even more so now. Hands trembling, anxiety clogging her throat, she tugged up the swimsuit quickly, securing the straps against her shoulders.

"I don't understand why you have to hide them. I'd kill to have curves like yours."

Olivia was tall and willowy. She had wide hips, but that was pretty much where all curviness ended. Olivia was everything Coral was not. Tall to Coral's short. Thin to Coral's curves. Olivia had blonde hair and eyes the color of copper, but Coral had hair as dark as ink and eyes as blue as the sea.

"Now that you're marrying a rich man, maybe he can buy them for you," Coral joked, earning herself a swift pillow to the face. She laughed, surprised by how easy it was to suddenly fall back into that banter with her best friend. With a start, she realized how much she missed that. She hadn't been herself at all. She'd been going through life like a phantom of her old self, uncomfortable in her own skin, dreading almost every second of every day.

Well, she decided with firm determination, that was going to change.

~

THEY STARTED AT THE SPA, then headed off to the buffet. When they finished eating, they sat on deck beside the pool and took in the sun. More accurately, Olivia took in the sun; she even untied the strings to her thin bikini, claiming to hate tan lines. Coral just sat a little further in the shade wearing sunglasses and a sunhat, a novel propped up on her knees.

The spa had relaxed her immensely. After pushing past the discomfort of having a stranger's hands on her and once the woman began kneading at the knots in her neck, it left her forgetting she'd even had problems in the first place. Why had she objected to a vacation, again? She couldn't even remember. All she knew was that she was finally having a good time.

"This is the life," Olivia echoed Coral's thoughts aloud. "I could stay here forever."

Though Olivia couldn't see with her eyes closed, Coral nodded her agreement. It felt good to finally let go, to feel the tension of the previous year slowly release from her body.

"All you need now is to find a man to help rattle your sheets."

Coral snorted at the same time anxiety exploded in her chest. She took a breath and tried for levity. "Yeah, right. With you creeping on the other side of the bed?" *No, thanks.* As far as she was concerned, a man was what had gotten her into that situation in the first place. She didn't need another one. Ever.

Coral licked the tip of her finger and changed the page.

"Are you going to read this whole vacation?" Olivia demanded.

Coral shrugged. "Probably." She was able to read two whole paragraphs before Olivia interrupted her again.

"Can you please not?"

"Is my sitting here quietly bothering you?"

"Yes. You should be doing something. Like swimming. You should be swimming instead of reading."

Coral slammed her book closed with a frustrated sigh, knowing that if she even tried to continue, her friend wouldn't let her. Since murdering her friend with a book was illegal in any country, Coral decided to concede. "Fine!" She stood up, clutching the novel tightly between her fingers. "Let me go drop this off in the room. I'll be back up in a bit."

"Don't dawdle down there. Hurry back."

"Yeah, yeah," Coral waved her off and headed down to the room. When she arrived, she put her book away and made quick work of using the restroom and fixing her swimsuit in the mirror. Before leaving the room, however, she peered out the window. She found herself looking out of them often. The ship seemed practically anchored at the slow pace it was moving, and Coral liked to watch ocean life swim past the window.

Just that morning she'd seen a school of fish rush by. It was like having an aquarium right outside her window. Coral sighed, pressing her nose against the cool glass to stare at the bubbly water. She squinted, hoping to catch a glimpse of *something* before she had to resurface. When nothing passed by for a few minutes, she was about to turn in defeat, but froze when movement caught her eye. It had passed so abruptly, she may have imagined it, but for a brief second, it had looked like a large tailfin—the size of an entire body—had zipped past.

She gave a startled yelp and fell back, tripping to the floor when the shadowed silhouette of a massive hand pressed against a corner of the glass.

A second later, it was gone.

Scrambling to a standing position, Coral rubbed a hand across her eyes before looking out the window once more. Had she imagined it? Coral pressed against the thick panes, hoping to catch sight of it again, but there was nothing. No sign of any creatures swimming through the blue depths.

The water was empty.

Convinced she'd only taken in too much sun and was starting to hallucinate, she laughed nervously to herself. But she couldn't shake the feeling that someone had been watching her. That someone was still watching her even as she left.

THE ACCIDENT

THE NEXT MORNING, CORAL WAS UP EARLY, RISING BEFORE Olivia even stirred. She'd spent most of her night downing margaritas and dancing wildly on the bar while Coral spent most of the night trying to get Olivia *off*. Olivia had tried convincing Coral to drink tequila shots, which she vehemently refused. Looking at her friend now, Coral certainly didn't regret her decision. Olivia moaned in her sleep. Just in case, Coral hunted down a bucket and placed it next to her bed before leaving the room behind, novel in hand.

On deck, the sun was already shining, and people were walking around in vacation bliss. Parents watched after their children as they jumped into the pool and ran about. Coral smiled at the sight as she made her way to the railing. It was tall, taller than her at least. Probably made so that children— and drunken idiots—didn't fall over to their deaths.

Coral was neither drunk nor a child, and she was curious, the image of the palm pressed tightly against glass haunting her. She placed her forearms against the railing and using all her strength, pulled herself up so she dangled in order to peek over the edge at the ocean below.

The white and blue waves splashed almost violently against the bottom of the boat. The whole imagery of it was rather relaxing, to see the water bubble on the surface and splash like waves crashing on a shoreline. The whooshing sounds of it filled her veins, thrummed through her blood. It seemed like the very threads of the crystal surface was calling out to her, beckoning her to jump in.

She relinquished all feeling, falling victim to the magical call of the sea. She focused on seeing just below the surface at the creatures underneath. Even now, how many sea animals were swimming away from the massive ship as it tore through their path? Was that the gray tail of a shark she saw? Were there groups of dolphins under there even now? It was amazing to think of a whole world living just beneath her.

Coral sighed contentedly, leaning her cheek against her arm, still gazing at the water. It hypnotized her, left her *wanting*. Wanting what, she wasn't sure. But she *wanted* with every fiber in her being something more. She watched the colors dance across the surface. Blue, white and green, even the yellow of sunlight shining down on it. Then, a flash of red passed through the water—

"Lady! You can't be up there!"

Coral startled, hopped from the rail, and turned with a blush, face to face with a security guard. His expression was angry, stern, and it sent her apologizing ferociously. He warned her away from the railing and didn't leave until she found herself a seat in a shaded area on deck.

She'd brought her book to read in peace before Olivia came up to interrupt her. Coral knew she probably should have socialized with other passengers, but she felt content enough alone. People were *ew* in her opinion.

It'd been a long while since she'd actually read for pleasure. Sure, she worked in a library, but she didn't spend work hours laying around reading. She shelved books, charged late fees, tutored children, etc. There was a lot more to her job than just spending the day reading. It felt nice to finally be able to bury herself in words and a fantasy world.

She was halfway through her novel when she was interrupted by someone clearing their throat. She looked up from her page to find a bright orange speedo pointed straight at her face. She flushed three different shades of red at the sight. Her eyes darted up to the man standing confidently before her, fists on his hips, pelvis jutted forward.

"Hullo." He smiled down at her, his very bright tan nearly burning holes through her eyes.

"Hi." Coral's voice came out scratchy, so she cleared her throat, feeling the sudden tightness there. She couldn't help the burst of fear at his proximity. She wanted to close her eyes, but they were wide, hyper focused on his every move.

You're safe, she told herself. *There's people around, you're safe.*

"I saw you sitting all alone and wanted to ask you a question."

"Oookay..." Coral gripped her book tighter, discreetly holding it up against her chest when she noticed his beady little eyes looking in that direction. His tan really was rather ridiculous. His coloring was a mixture of orange and brown, a spray tan gone wrong, while his eyelids and surrounding area were pale. She wondered what question he meant to ask, but at the same time dreaded its arrival.

He smiled, revealing wide horse teeth. "Did it hurt?"

"Excuse me?"

"Did it hurt when you fell from heaven?"

Oh Jesus, he did not just ask me that. She wanted to blush, sigh, roll her eyes, flee from him, and laugh at him all at once. How was she even supposed to respond to that? Was she supposed to thank him? Cuss him out? She did neither. Instead, she re-buried her face in her novel, trying to pick up where she left off. Maybe he'd take a hint.

But he didn't. He stood and stared down at her as if expectant of a response.

"Um..." She fiddled with the edges of the book anxiously. "No."

Coral jerked up at the sight of Olivia suddenly beside the man. Relief coursed through her almost instantly. She had on enormous sunglasses, a hat, and her bikini. Coral didn't have to see her eyes to know she glared mutinously at the man. The wonderful result of her hangover.

The man turned to Olivia with surprise. "No?"

"No," Olivia repeated. "Get lost. She's not interested."

The man sputtered. "I—I think that's for the lady to decide. Not you."

Olivia snorted, and in a swift, elegant movement, pulled the sunglasses from her face. Yes, Coral had been right. She looked mutinous. Her brown eyes seemed to blaze. "You look like a greasy, hairless oompa loompa. If that doesn't automatically disqualify you, then that stupid pick-up line and your leering eyes did. Now get lost before I knee you in the nuts."

His face flamed brightly beneath his ruddy tan. Coral almost felt sorry for him. "*Bitch!*" he spat. Well, almost. With that said, he turned on his heel and walked away.

"What a pig," Olivia complained before flopping down into a seat next to Coral, wincing as she did so. "God, can't they shut their kids up?" She threw her arm over her forehead and whined a low groan. "I'm never drinking again."

"You say that every time you drink," Coral reminded her gently. "And it's never true."

"Shut up."

"Thanks for saving me."

"I got your back, Jack."

Coral chuckled at that truth. They'd been friends for years, practically since childhood. Olivia was always standing up for Coral, always fighting her battles when she lost her voice to do so. Theirs was a true friendship that would last forever.

"Coral," Olivia groaned unpleasantly, "why is the boat spinning?"

"It's not spinning," Coral mumbled as she lazily flipped a page. "It's moving forward. It's a boat, not a merry-go-round."

"It feels like it's spinning."

Coral sat back in her chair, ready to bury herself in her book again. "That's just your hangover."

"No. I swear, it's *spinning!*"

Olivia shot up in her seat, hands gripping tightly at its sides. Her face had gone a pale, sickly green. Coral dropped her book with alarm at the sudden movement and reached out to comfort her, to push away sweaty, blonde tresses. She wondered if she'd need to run and find a bucket for her to puke in, but when she threw her legs over the side of the chair, she felt it too.

The world was twirling. More specifically, the boat.

Shouts of alarm rang out on the deck, parents calling out to their kids to run to them, surprise and confusion resonating around them. Coral stood on wobbling legs. Yes, the world was definitely going in a circle.

"What's going on?" Olivia asked in a panicked voice. "Is it a tsunami or something?"

"I don't know." Coral tried taking a step and nearly fell. She righted herself and looked around. They weren't the only one's feeling the vertigo. The floor suddenly lurched beneath them. There was a near deafening screeching sound like metal scraping metal, and then the boat came to a halt.

There was a pause as if the air itself stilled. Coral took a few steps, slowly because she was afraid even the slightest of movement might send the boat into a frenzy again. But nothing happened.

"What was that?" Olivia demanded. She still clutched tightly the sides of her seat.

Security guards rushed on deck. "Don't worry," one of them reassured in a voice that didn't convince Coral. "We're experiencing engineering difficulties." Then they began droning on and on, reminding them about ship safety regulations, emergency exits, lifeboats, life vests, and emergency protocol. Coral drowned them out and walked over to the ledge again. She heard Olivia cry out to her to be careful. She knew there was a special stupidity in leaning over the railing *now* after what had just happened, but something was calling to her, a hypnotizing song that only she could hear, beckoning her to the water.

She reached the railing, traced her fingers lightly against it. If she looked over now, would she fall? It didn't seem to matter anymore. She wanted to look. Just a peek to quench her curiosity.

But that's when chaos broke loose.

There was that sound again first. Metal crunching harshly against metal. The boat gave a violent lurch that sent Coral toppling onto her hands and knees. A jolt of pain ricocheted through her nerves. She gave a cry and looked up. Olivia was still in the chair and it was wobbling side to side. Her hands were frozen at her sides in fear. Her gaze found Coral's from across the ship, and she opened her mouth to call out to her...

Then there was a splintering shriek just before the deck split down the middle, leaving a gaping aperture along the floor, tearing the ship in half.

Coral screamed as the boat seemed to tear from the inside. Wood and metal and bodies flew up. Flying debris rained down, cutting into her face, causing the glasses to fall from her nose and the world to become a blur. Coral threw her hands up to protect herself, but it did little good.

The ship tilted and groaned, but there was little she could

hear over the screams of other passengers. When her world tilted to the side, she tilted with it, sliding unwillingly as the ship tore itself apart.

Coral's back slammed against the railing, knocking the scream from her lips. Desperately, she gripped for the bars and held on, praying she wouldn't fall but knew what a useless chore it was.

Debris flew through every direction. Bodies were hurled through the air from impact, cries and shrieks rose in a terrifying crescendo. When Coral regained her breath, her own voice joined in on the song. She shrieked Olivia's name, hoping her friend could hear her above the chaos. Her eyes frantically searched for her friend, the desire to save her from this nightmare pushing against her limbs. It seemed a useless hope. So useless. She couldn't see her behind the curtain of smoke or the rising water.

Wood and steel still flew. Coral barely had time to react as a large bit of wood aimed straight at her and hit her body with an intensifying jolt. The pain sent awareness shocking her awake. She cried out from the impact, forgetting that she was holding on for dear life.

And then the boat was tilting

And Coral fell backwards into the water.

THE MERMAN

PAIN STABBED THROUGH HER UNCONSCIOUSNESS. WAKING was an agonizing feat, her mind sluggish in its attempt at waking. It wasn't just the bones in her legs and feet, which felt as though they'd been pounded by a very large hammer, but the pain in her chest was nearly unbearable. It was the crushing weight of fire, burning holes through her lungs.

She rolled over in what felt like soft sand as she recalled the accident, recalled the panic as the waves of the ocean yanked her under, the water forcing a path down her throat. There had been that last kiss of light as the darkness dragged her down and then...

Coral heaved a shuddering breath, but there was no air. She gasped, coughed, sputtered, and panicked. There was no press of oxygen or breeze around her. There was nothing but cold liquid invading open crevices. Water shot into her nostrils and down her throat. She spat it back out, held her breath until she could no longer and wheezed. It was agony. It was like drowning all over again. She gripped at her throat, clawed at the pain there. As if that could help her. As if that could bring air into her lungs.

"Calm down."

Coral shot her eyes opened and winced at the first sting, only to ignore it and look towards the voice that spoke and gape.

"Take a deep breath. Relax," the deep, masculine voice continued. His chant was a hypnotic melody, but she shook off his voice and stared at *him*. At the most beautiful man she'd ever seen. She may have had bad eyesight on a typical day, but she saw him clearly enough. In fact, nothing was blurry, as if she'd somehow been cured for this moment alone.

His skin was a light brown, pulled tightly against the bulge of muscles and ridges and bumps of his upper body; an upper body decorated in shells and strange black leather material that looked mysteriously like armor. There was a belt at his waist, knives with black blades holstered there. Reddish-brown hair floated against the hard lines of his face, and blue-green eyes nearly penetrated deep into her soul.

But what had her staring with disbelief was what was below the waist. Just beneath the hem of his strange jacket, embroidered along the edges was flowing fabric. Fabric that did not hide a tail. A tail in dark green and blue with scales that shimmered like an iridescent rainbow.

Oh Jesus, she thought. *Mermen aren't real.*

The stranger frowned at her. "You are not breathing," he said in perfect English. At least, she thought it was English. The sound seemed warped and strange, below the words a melodic cadence she found hypnotic. She couldn't get over the sound of it, flowing towards her like a pretty, echoing song. One she'd give anything to hear again.

Slowly, she opened her mouth and sucked in a breath only to have water invade. She sputtered and tried coughing it out, tightening her hand around her throat.

"Do not fight it!" he scolded. "Let the water flow into your gills and lungs. Let your body get used to the change!"

Change? What change? She wanted to demand what brand of crack he was smoking. Instead, she found herself following his instructions. Tentatively, she breathed in. This time, when the water came into her mouth, she tried to relax, tried not to push it back out as every instinct in her body wanted her to. She let it circulate through her system. It was painful, but it was even more painful to fight it. She took another breath. And another. And another. The pain slowly receded to a dull throb; she was breathing almost normally again.

"Good," the stranger continued. "Very good. Let your body take its natural course. The change is painful at first. You will grow accustomed to it."

Coral just stared and breathed. She'd thought this was a hallucination, that his tail was just a figment of her wild imagination. She stared at it, waiting for the mirage to disappear. But it didn't. It floated before her. Floated? She looked around in a panic. *Oh, Jesus on a cracker.* She swooned. She was underwater! She was breathing underwater and talking to a merman. Okay, she thought, taking a deep, water-filled breath. There had to be a logical explanation for this kind of hallucination. Like she was in a sun-induced coma because the weather was just too hot for her pasty ass. Or maybe she fell asleep on the deck and was dreaming and none of that titanic class sinkage nonsense really happened.

Or maybe she was fished out of the water and strung up on the top-shelf hospital drugs. Yeah, that had to be it.

"I'm dreaming," she whispered reassuringly to herself. "You aren't real." She looked at the merman who gave no indication whatsoever if the words were true or not. He merely stared at her with penetrative eyes. She smiled and his eyebrows rose. "You're just a figment of my imagination, aren't you?" She reached a hand out—he was close enough to touch—and pressed her palm against the hard decorations of his jacket.

The merman seemed to still at her touch, his whole body freezing unpleasantly. She smiled wider, not sure why, not sure why she felt the sudden need to put her hands on him. If this was a dream, she might as well get the full experience, right? Besides, it was a far cry from the nightmares she'd been suffering for the past year. Maybe this was her mind's way of reaching that point where her past trauma met normalcy. Maybe this was a way to heal.

After all, mermen were always such a fascinating subject. Particularly, their cocks. Mercocks? Merdicks? Fish sticks? Fish dicks? That sounded like something Olivia would say.

Chuckling softly at her train of thought, she slipped her hand inside the lapels of his jacket to press her fingertips against his warm skin. He flinched, then held still. Coral looked up into that pretty face. His hair curled and floated against his forehead. His eyes seemed to burn her own, causing her to blush despite herself. And his mouth... she'd never seen anything more inviting in her entire life. Bottom lip slightly fuller than the top with a cupid's bow.

She reached her other hand out on impulse and ran her thumb against his bottom lip. He closed his eyes at the movement as if praying. Maybe he was. She knew that the sight of his dark lashes, curling at the top curve of his rounded cheekbones was something short of heavenly.

She kept the pad of her thumb against his lip, gently sliding her fingernail across, daring his tongue to dart out and...

The merman suddenly had her wrist in his tight grip. "Don't," he warned in a deadly voice.

"But this is a dream," she argued.

"No, it is not."

"But mermen aren't real."

He released her hand and she let it fall gently to her naked chest. Wait, she startled. Naked? Coral looked down at her chest to find it white and bared. Her breasts floated and bobbed in the water, entirely on display.

She let out a small squeak and covered her chest with her arms, pressing them down tightly. Heat crept up her cheeks, burning her face brightly. Where was her swimsuit? Why was she naked? She made a move to stand up, but she didn't move an inch. Her lower body felt numb. Coral looked down.

And screamed.

"My legs! What did you do to my legs?" They were gone, and in their place... a fishtail. "What have you done?!" Coral shrieked. She reached a hand to touch the deep blue tail she now possessed. It was smooth with blue and silver shining scales, thick and... foreign.

Hysteria rose up to her throat. She couldn't have a tail any more than she could be a mermaid. It wasn't possible. It was all the more proof that this was a dream. She sat up straight and tried moving the thing. It merely twitched.

Surely, if this was a dream, she'd be swimming laps around him by now, right?

She tried again, pretending it was a pair of legs, forcing it up. It moved in an undulating motion, sending silt swirling up in a cloud of smoke. *Am I really a mermaid?*

"Listen, human," the merman said. His voice had a sudden urgency to it. When she looked up at him, he wasn't looking at her but behind her. Probably giving her some privacy to observe her new body. "I need you to get up slowly."

She eyed him suspiciously. He still wasn't looking at her. "Why?"

"Just do what I tell you."

Coral frowned but tried doing what he said anyway, using all of her strength and muscles to get up. She wiggled her lower body, undulated her tail and used her arms as aid, moving them about as if she were swimming. She floated upwards, kicked her tail and stayed afloat for a few seconds before her muscles gave way to pain and she fell back to the ground in a cloud of smoky sand.

"You must hurry," the merman urged.

"What's the rush?" she demanded, feeling embarrassment and anger show on her features.

"Hurry!" he snapped. His hand gripped her upper arm and pulled her up. Her every muscle screamed in protest. The pain was excruciating, and the fire in her chest hadn't completely ceased either.

"What's wrong?" She tried yanking her arm away, but his grip was adamant.

"We need to leave at once." His eyes were still glued behind her.

"What are you looking at?" Coral started to turn, but his hand was suddenly on the back of her head, keeping her in place. Her heart thundered rapidly. Fear began rising to the center of her chest.

"Do not turn around, human."

"Wh—what's wrong?"

"Do not make a sound or any sudden movements. There is a group of tiger sharks behind you, waiting to attack."

Her stomach lurched. Sharks? This time, hysteria stuck tightly in her throat. *Oh, Jesus.* She really was going to be food for the sharks! She was going to die. Her heart beat a wild rhythm against her ribcage, and she trembled against his touch.

"You need to swim, human."

"I can't." Her tail and limbs felt leaden, weighed down against the silt.

She was as good as dead.

"Please," she sobbed helplessly.

"Stop crying," he commanded, giving her a sharp shake. "I will carry you, but you must calm down." She didn't feel like she could, but for both of their lives, she would try. Coral stilled against him. "Lift your tail up," he commanded. It was a struggle, but she did what he said and as soon as she did, his strong arms were under her tail and pulling her closer to his body into a protective circle. "Wrap your arms around me." She did as he asked, clasping her hands together at the back of his neck. "Hold tight, human. And do exactly as I say."

Coral gave a brusque nod, biting her bottom lip in order to avoid crying out again. He held her tightly in his arms, and she felt the muscles of his body harden beneath his jacket. Later, if she survived this, she would marvel at the fact that she'd put her arms around a man for the first time in a year. Later, her mind would process the fact that she didn't recoil from him, that her body curled into his for protection instead of flinching away in fear.

She felt him brace himself, and then he spun quickly in the water and *swam*. His tail moved with strong grace behind them and so did his upper body. Coral clung to him and dared a peek behind his shoulder. The sight beyond had her heart lurching and dropping to the pit of her stomach.

He hadn't lied. A dozen sharks were hot on their fins. Each one was about six feet long with angry eyes and row after row of deadly-looking teeth. Coral feared there was no way the merman could outswim them when they glided through the water with harrying speed. Jaws snapped near blue-green fins, and Coral gave a shriek and clung tighter to his body. He wasn't deterred by her fear. The merman kept swimming, his powerful tail pushing them even faster.

Coral felt tears of fear burn like acid behind her eyelids. A cynical part of her wondered if she'd even be able to feel them fall now. Another part of her felt a sudden burst of clarity. They would die. There was no way they could survive this. Even with the merman zigzagging and swimming with all of his might, he couldn't escape this. She could feel his heart beating wildly against her own body, the heavy thuds like bullets to the heart. He'd be faster without her. If he put her down and left, then at least one of them would make it out alive.

She didn't want to die. She didn't want to be mauled by sharks; it'd be such a shitty way to go. No shittier than drowning. And the merman had saved her from it, so now it was her turn to save him from this.

"Put me down," she shouted in his ear.

He ignored her and kept swimming. His breaths were coming out in pants now as he soared through open water. It was no use. She looked back at the sharks. They were still following, still catching up. Two sharks broke off from the group and swam to their left, two more did the same on the right. They were circling them, herding around them in a tight formation so they'd have nowhere to swim to. They'd both die if she didn't do something fast.

"Let go of me!" she demanded of him again. "Save yourself. I'm only holding you back." She dropped her arms from his neck and let herself go slack in his arms. Hopefully he'd drop her and just leave without her. A part of her wished it with all her might. The other part hoped he wouldn't.

Slacking in his arms seemed to work. He grunted and seemed to trip on his own tail. He let out a low curse as they went tumbling through empty water, and then Coral twisted and held out her hands as she fell to the sand. It flew up into a smoky cloud, invading her nostrils. She coughed briefly before turning on her back. A shark was swimming straight for her. She screamed and prepared to feel the bite of unforgiving teeth, but the merman was suddenly in front of her. The shark's jaws gripped him tightly. Blood flowed from his wound and curled through the water in red tendrils.

The scent of it sent the other sharks into a frenzy. They all rushed towards the merman at once. Coral screamed and tried to get up, willing her tail muscles to comply. She floated up, moved her tail back and forth like she'd seen him do. It wasn't perfect or graceful, but it kept her upright enough that she was level eyed with the shark latched onto his arm.

In an almost instinctive move, Coral reached for the blade at the merman's waist, unsheathing it quickly. With a cry, she drove it into the shark's eye. It let out a roar, releasing the merman's arm, as blood oozed from the wound she had caused. The merman wasted no time. He gave a twirl, whacking the shark away with the fins of his tail. Then, he surprised Coral by lifting his hand up and closing it in a fist.

The open waters around them became as violent as a riptide. It was like standing in a storm and feeling wind and water slapping from every direction. Coral shielded her eyes as sand flew from the ground and became a stormy whirlwind. Rocks and glass hit her skin, slicing her flesh open in tiny little cuts. Her hair whipped across her face, blinding her briefly. She pushed it aside and saw as the sharks were caught in the maelstrom.

The merman flexed his knuckles, and the small water tornado whirled and whirled, twirling the sharks within it. It was dizzying to watch, but Coral couldn't look away. The merman swept his hand through the water in one violent motion and the storm copied his movements, jerking and taking the sharks away with it. Coral watched them disappear until they were nothing but a speck of black against blue and then turned to look up at the merman.

His hand slowly lowered, and he winced at the pain. His ugly jacket was in tatters, and there was a large gash along the length of his forearm, the skin split open in ugly flabs. Blood still swirled from the wound to cloud the blue waters. Coral's heart gave a painful thud at the sight.

She should apologize. She knew she should, because it was her fault. If she hadn't slacked her weight, he wouldn't have fallen and the shark wouldn't have gotten him. But when she opened her mouth, an apology wasn't what came forth.

"You should have left me behind," she accused, unsure where the reprimand had come from. "I told you to leave me."

The merman looked at her. Really looked at her, as if he could see into the very depths of her heart and burn it to ash. He may as well have, she thought. "I was not going to leave you," he simply said, cradling his injured arm with the other.

Coral put her hands on her fists. "You should have. It was my decision. There was no way you could have outswam them. Not with me as deadweight. You should have left me and saved yourself."

A small bit of emotion passed over his face, finally. He stared at her incredulously for a second before anger replaced his features. "If you had not tripped me, we would have made it. I would have used my magic on them eventually, but at the right time. This," he gestured to his injured arm, "is entirely your fault. I believe you owe me an apology."

Coral felt anger flare up in her chest. Anger that distracted her from the real pain of her situation. It turned her into something else, burning away the meek person she'd become into something, someone, else. Into what she'd been, once upon a time.

"*I* owe *you* an apology?" she asked disbelievingly. "I won't apologize for trying to save your life!"

"Is that what you were trying to do?" He scoffed. "It was nothing but a stupid, reckless decision that could have gotten both of us killed. Were it not for me, you would have been their next meal."

"Were it not for you, I would have drowned like I was supposed to."

"Am I supposed to apologize for saving you from the ship-wreck as well?" he asked sarcastically, his lip quirking up in the tiniest hint of a smile. "You are the most ungrateful little human I have ever encountered."

"Then maybe you should have let me die!" Coral sobbed, her situation finally hitting her with full force. She could have died and Olivia—oh God—Olivia! Her best friend had been on that shipwreck. Her best friend had been on the other side of the boat when it had split in half. Coral started to fall to the seafloor, but the merman was suddenly there to hold her upright as she cried. She gripped tightly to the lapels of his jacket, bunching them into whitening fists.

She'd never sought comfort in another before. Not on that day, and not afterwards, either. She found it surprisingly easy to reach for him now, to let him hold her up while she broke apart.

"Human?" A breath of bubbles blew on the top of her head.

"Did—did you save anyone else from the wreck?" she managed to choke out from between tears and gasps. She looked up into his eyes. She had to know the truth. Slowly, he shook his head. "But could they still be—" He shook his head again.

"There was no one," he said softly. "And if there were, the sharks got them."

A sob wrenched itself free from her throat. "No!" she cried, and just because she could, she punched her fists into his chest. He took the blow without comment, and so she did it again and again. Who was *he* to decide who should have been saved? Why couldn't he have just let her die with her best friend? She had no family, no parents, no one else. All she'd had was Olivia. And now her best friend was gone.

"I should be dead! It should have been me!" Coral struck him, this stranger, this merman who had decided she was worthy of saving, and he received every blow she dished out. He let her hit him until her knuckles felt raw and aching.

Throughout it all, he held her with one hand clasped tightly behind her head and the other around her waist.

"I am sorry, human," he whispered against her hair. The echoing sound of heartbreak in his voice was the softest dirge. "I know your pain. I am so sorry."

Coral sniffled, pressing herself tighter against his chest. "I'm sorry, too. You saved my life and I—" A lump formed in her throat and she swallowed past it. "I'm just sorry. I thought I was helping you."

"I know, human." He rubbed his hand against her head in soothing motions. As if he was physically telling her that it was alright. That he understood. She believed he did, even if she didn't know how. She heard it in his voice when he spoke, felt it in the comforting touch of his fingers against her body. He would never know how much those motions meant to her. He'd never know that he was the first man to press his fingers against her broken body, and it was like he was picking up the pieces another had left behind.

"Why did you save me?" she whispered. The question had him tensing and releasing her almost cautiously. He looked at her, his face already becoming a mask of indifference.

"Does it matter?" he asked.

"Yes." It mattered. It mattered a lot.

He just shrugged and turned, obviously done with the conversation. Coral let it drop. For now. Later, she would ask him again. If there was a later.

What did he plan on doing with her now that the sharks were gone? Was he going to leave her alone without even the basic knowledge of swimming? Sure, she was floating upright *now*, but the earlier adrenaline had been an easy push to get that accomplished. Surely he didn't plan on leaving her alone? She was his responsibility now, whether he liked it or not. He needed to help her. Maybe he could take her to some shoreline and turn her back into a human. He had to.

The merman brought his thumb and forefinger to his mouth and whistled. The sound reverberated through the water. What was he doing? She didn't ask. She watched as he turned back to her.

"We need to leave. Sharks scavenge through shipwrecks. The site is not too far from here and trust me when I say, more will come." He turned back to the direction in which he whistled and waited a few moments. There was a violent stirring in the water. Coral tensed when she saw an enormous creature that seemed to gallop on fins towards them.

A scream caught in her throat as the creature came closer. It roared back, its fins slapping higher waters before it lowered itself. The merman swam up to the giant thing and reached a trusting hand out to stroke its face. The creature let out low noises of contentment. The merman chuckled deeply.

Coral could only stare at the creature. It was as big as an orca with an enormous head and wide, long back. It had many fins on either side of its body, a long serpentine tail and an elongated snout. Gills and red and orange scales covered the animal over every inch of its body.

The merman turned to look at Coral. "Human, this is Redwave. He's my hippo—"

"Hippocampus," Coral interrupted with awe, looking up at the creature. It resembled a horse in certain ways.

"You know of hippocampi?" the merman asked, accusation in his tone and glare.

Coral ignored him and swam slowly and painfully towards Redwave. "I'm a librarian—I read," she replied. She'd read all sorts of books on mythological creatures. Not only were mermaids real, but hippocampi were as well. It was fascinating. She was beside the merman now and in front of Redwave. Redwave eyed her uncertainly and flapped his fins, rearing back. The merman went to grab for his reins to hold him steady, but Coral put her hand on his arm.

"Don't," she said to him. He stopped, and she could feel his heavy gaze on her. It made her all the more determined to prove herself. "It's okay," she whispered to Redwave. She held out her hand, palm towards him. "I won't hurt you. I promise."

Redwave eyed her palm with big, brown eyes. Then slowly, cautiously, he nudged his nose forward, bumping it against her palm. She stilled, waiting for him to trust her. He bumped against her hand again, and then his tongue darted out to lick her fingers. The feel of his rough tongue had Coral laughing gleefully. Redwave snorted with happiness and repeated the action. Coral rubbed her hand across the length of his nose and ran her hand against his mane.

"He's beautiful," she whispered. And he was smooth. Something about him calmed her aching heart.

"I have cared for him since he was nothing but a guppy." He gave the hippocampus an affectionate pat on his rear. "It is time for us to go."

Coral turned to look at him sharply. "Go where? We can't go. I have to bind your wound and then you have to take me to shore and turn me back into a human. I need to let the authorities know that the boat was destroyed if they don't already know."

The merman's lips formed a thin, disapproving line. "I can bind my own wound." As if to prove his point, he bent to tear a strip off his flowing garment. He barely wiped down at the blood of his wound before using only one hand and his teeth, binding his arm and tightening it into a strong knot. "Now, we must leave, human." He made his way to the side of Redwave and waited for her to follow. She did but frowned.

"Didn't you hear me? I asked where you planned on taking me?"

"I am taking you to the Dark Waters, the Black Kingdom. To the land of mer. I am taking you to my home."

The Dark Waters? That sounded ominous, not to mention dangerous. Coral frowned at him. "You have to take me back to shore. I need to go back to my own kind."

The merman had become suddenly busy with the bags saddled to Redwave's side. She noticed that he had barely looked at her since declaring they leave.

"What aren't you telling me?" A sudden foreboding tickled the back of her mind.

The merman sighed and finally turned to look at her. "I cannot take you to the humans because the merfolk are forbidden to go near them. Besides, I cannot change you back into a human."

Coral jerked at that last part. "What do you mean you can't change me back? You changed me *into* a mermaid, surely you can unmake me, right?"

"I am afraid I do not have that kind of power."

"What do you mean you don't have that kind of power?" she nearly shrieked, hysteria rising once more. "You're lying!"

"I am not. Even my magic has limits, and I fear I have exhausted them extensively already. The only one with the magic to change you back to your original state is the Queen of the Dark Waters. We will go to see her and you will beg for your legs."

Coral gaped at him. None of what he said made any sense! He could change her into a mermaid, but changing her back into a human was beyond him? He would take her to see his queen? She had to *beg* to get her legs back? What the actual fuck was going on?

"I may not be from the Dark Waters, but won't it be a tad bit difficult to just waltz up to Her Majesty and ask for favors?"

The merman smiled. "It is a good thing, then, that I am of

Her Majesty's Personal Guard." He held his hand out to her in invitation and waited.

Coral stared at it. Did she really have any other choice but to go with him? He'd saved her life twice, had taken a shark bite for her. Obviously, she could trust him, but she'd trusted the wrong person before and that had ended in wretched disaster. Did she really want to go with him? If she stayed, she was as good as dead. She didn't know where she was or even how to swim. If he left without her, she would probably be dead within minutes.

With a weary sigh, she made her decision, placing her hand in his own. She would go with him and meet the Queen of the Dark Waters and she would convince her to give Coral her legs back. And then Coral would go home.

The merman wrapped an arm around her waist and the other beneath her tail and hoisted her up, placing her on the strong back of Redwave. Her tail hung off the side of his body rather uncomfortably. She snuggled tightly onto the saddle, and when the merman hoisted up and settled behind her, she tentatively placed her hands on Redwave's mane.

"Let us be off then, human."

She tightened her fingers. "My name is Coral," she said.

The merman paused. "Coral," he whispered. He did not offer up his own name. Instead, he dug his tail into Redwave's side. The hippocampus reared back with a cry and began their journey forward. To the Dark Waters.

Coral dared one last glance back towards the direction the shipwreck lay. She could see it no longer, but somehow she knew it was back there. She'd floated too far away from it and they'd swum even further with the sharks after them. That ship hadn't meant anything to her; she hadn't even wanted to be there at first. But she was leaving Olivia behind. Her best friend was gone, and Coral was all alone in a world she knew nothing about.

Tears filled her eyes once more, but she braved them, not letting them fall. The heartbreaking feeling that she was leaving behind her home nestled in her chest, and she knew it'd stay with her forever.

Closing her eyes, Coral turned back around and buried her face into Redwave's strong neck. She gripped him tightly as they pounded through the water. Behind her, the merman caged her in protectively. He would be her lifeline now in this strange world that hadn't even existed hours before.

Keeping her face tight and the tears at bay, Coral whispered her final goodbye as they left her friend and the world she knew behind...

A LESSON IN HISTORY

They traveled for what felt like hours without resting, and Coral was beginning to feel saddle sore. Her butt and back muscles ached like the devil and her tail was tingling with numbness. The discomfort in her chest had receded completely as her lungs and body had finally gotten used to inhaling water instead of air. Her head had started bobbing from exhaustion, but she jerked awake before she could fall off the hippocampus.

After a while, she started feeling fatigued, and the merman finally pulled Redwave to a stop when her stomach gave out a deafening growl.

"We should rest here for a moment before continuing. It is still a long way to the Dark Waters." He hopped off Redwave with an ease she envied, then reached his hands up, gripping Coral by the waist and pulling her down. The minute he let her go, she sank involuntarily to the ocean floor below, her muscles cramping with spasms.

She let out a curse and tried moving her tail in undulating movements, but she seized up in pain. Crying out, she fell back into the sand, puffs of it clouding around her vision before settling back against the ocean floor. The merman sighed at her inability to swim but didn't rush to help her. He tended to Redwave first, feeding him strange looking food from the saddlebag then letting him rest. Only then did he swim down with the saddlebag to sit next to Coral.

He reached inside the bag and pulled out a plump looking green round... *thing* and handed it to her. She took it carefully. It was squishy in her hands.

"What is this?" she asked, bringing it up to her nose to sniff it.

She was surprised when a sweet scent hit her nostrils. She never imagined there could be scents beneath the water, yet there were. They were all so vivid, the colors so bright. It made her senses feel *hyper stimulated*. Like she was taking in so much at once and her mind felt dizzy and overwhelmed.

He took out one for himself and bit into it. Juices spilt from the fruit, thick and frothy and bright; it reminded Coral of those art videos where they swirled paint underwater. The color stained the tips of his fingers before swirling like a cloud that slowly disappeared in wisps.

The inside of the strange food was pink with large, black seeds. He chewed and swallowed, the strong muscles of his throat bobbing up and down. He wiped his mouth with the back of his hand before answering. "Jelly fruit."

Coral looked down at the fruit in her hand. It certainly felt like jelly. It was bouncy and smooth. When her stomach gave another unforgiving growl, she decided to stop dawdling and took a small bite. Sweet flavors and juices burst inside her mouth and swirled around her tongue. It was surprisingly delicious and soft in her mouth. She let out an appreciative moan low in her throat. Either she was starving or the jelly fruit was just that good.

When she opened her eyes to take another bite, she found the merman was staring at her, jelly fruit near his opened mouth. Coral swallowed and licked the stray juices that fell down the side of her mouth. His eyes followed the movement of her tongue, and she closed her mouth self-consciously.

"So," she began nervously, suddenly very aware once again that she was still naked. After all of the excitement she'd forgotten to ask him for something to wear. She crossed her arms over her chest. "Do you think I could have a shirt or something?"

His dark cheeks colored, but he gave a terse nod and reached inside the saddlebag, emerging with a black wrap. "Will this do?" He handed it to her. Coral took it from him, blushing when she had to uncover her breasts, but she looked closely at the fabric. It appeared to have been weaved with what looked like tendrils of hair. Probably some weird mermaid material, threaded through with tiny silver pearls. The piece of fabric looked similar to Olivia's many head-scarves.

"This will do fine." She smiled, setting her jelly fruit to the ground. "Could you—turn around?" He complied without argument or raised brows, giving her the privacy she needed to wrap the thin fabric around herself. She invented a dress, wrapping and tying it tightly just above her breasts and taking another strip of the fabric to fashion a strap over one shoulder. The garment flowed down her waist, a little over her tail.

Coral took a moment to study that newly formed part of her anatomy. Every part of it was iridescent, shining back and forth between colors of blue and silver and gold. Like what she imagined sapphires would look gleaming against the sunlight. It was wide and long, with spanning fins on the sides and bottom in much lighter shades of blue. The scales were hard and smooth and, weirdest of all, right down the middle of her tail, where the spaces between her legs should have been, looked like thick nerve endings that connected the space together. Like thin ropes keeping legs firmly closed.

She ran her fingers down the center of it, over the curve that should have been her knees. The touch seemed to make the ropey nerve endings move, and a flutter coiled deep in her gut.

The black dress billowed against her scales and she gave a sigh, settling it over her in a way so it wouldn't float back up.

"You can turn around now." She picked up the fruit as he turned around and took another bite of it, relishing in its taste.

"So," she began after chewing, "what's your name?" It felt awkward thinking of him as 'the merman' in her head.

He gave pause, as if debating whether or not he should answer. Then, "Matthias," he replied slowly.

Matthias.

She rolled the name around in her mind then nodded. "Matthias," she said, and he tensed. "Right. Okay." Feeling awkward, she took another bite of fruit, spitting out the hard, black seeds as she went. When she finished with the fruit, Matthias was placing another one in her hands. She ate obediently in silence for a while, lost in her thoughts. They kept traveling back to that moment on the ship. Feeling a pull towards the water, seeing flashes of color beneath the surface, and then that earsplitting creak that forever changed her life.

Her heart felt heavy and weighed down by Olivia's image. Had she suffered? Had she drowned as Coral had started to, or had a shark gotten to her? Maybe she'd managed to escape on a lifeboat and there were other survivors.

Damn it, Coral cursed. She should have checked! She should have begged Matthias to take her back to the site. She should have torn everything apart to find her best friend. In her grief and hysteria, everything had flown from her mind.

Olivia wouldn't have forgotten about *her*. Even if Matthias had told her there were no survivors, she should have checked for herself.

Coral felt her chest lurch with that invisible grief that easily started to become a tangible thing. She could feel it on her like a ghost waiting to suck the life and happiness from her.

Her parents had died when she was eighteen in a car crash. Olivia had been there with her through it all. She'd been there to hold her at night when the nightmares became too much to bear, when she was so overcome by loss that she sat there in numbing pain, even when the tears wouldn't come. Olivia had brought her back to reality. Olivia had helped her move on.

And now Coral truly had no one.

A silent sob rose painfully in her chest. Coral hung her head low, burying it in her lap. It was all suddenly too much, too surreal. Hours ago, she'd been laughing with her best friend and now she was gone. Olivia was too *lively* to really be gone. Coral couldn't imagine her any other way besides alive. This couldn't be real. It couldn't be true. *It couldn't.*

Coral tugged at her floating tendrils of hair and yanked at them painfully. Maybe this would wake her up from this terrible dream, she thought. She pulled hard enough to hurt and then again, hard enough to pull a few strands from her scalp. This pain was less than what she deserved. Why did Coral get to live while Olivia died? Olivia had so much more to live for. She had many friends, a doting boyfriend, while Coral had nothing but books and a broken heart and a sad excuse for a life she never lived.

"What is a librarian?" Matthias asked abruptly, his deep, rumbling voice cutting through her own agonizing thoughts. Coral looked at him, trying to push aside her grief, but all she saw was her own pain reflected deep in his eyes. His eyes strayed to her fingers, gripping tightly at her hair. She couldn't help but feel scrutinized, or like the question somehow served as a distraction to her emotions. "You said you were a librarian," he pointed.

Before she answered, she forced herself to take a breath. It was surreal to expect to inhale air and instead feel the slide of water through the gills now at her neck, and focusing on that new oddness of her life distracted her from the wrenching agony.

"Ah! Yes. I suppose you wouldn't have libraries here in the ocean? I work in a building shelving books and tutoring kids." At his blank look, she tried to specify. "Books are... objects... that people can read. They contain information and stories in all subjects on them. I take care of these objects, and I learn from them and teach children and adults."

Matthias looked at her curiously, eyes slightly widened before his expression closed to her completely. There was something indecipherable about his expression. It was dark, edged with a soft hint of mystery. Like, she could spend a lifetime of getting to know him and would still never scratch the surface of his secrets, his soul.

"If you are rested enough, we will be on our way," he said after a moment, stretching his body up to marvelous height. He threw the saddlebag over his shoulder and turned around to go secure it on a waiting Redwave. Coral watched him work, his powerful tail swaying from beneath the flowing material of his clothes. Scaled, green, and covered in the slightest crisscrossing of scars. He prowled through the water, a powerful specimen, every move calculated and in command. It had Coral wondering why he'd decided to save her, of all people, and why he hadn't saved anyone else.

If there'd been anyone else left to save.

After tying the saddlebag tightly, he swam back to where Coral was sitting and without waiting for permission, bent to take her in his arms. He gripped her tightly, though his hands never roamed or stroked her, it still felt strangely intimate everywhere they touched, making her feel breathless and overwhelmed. He heaved her up onto Redwave's back, and she held on before she toppled off to the side. He followed up after her and clicked his tongue, sending Redwave into a gallop.

His hooves beat against the water like a horse's did against the ground, powerful serpentine tail swishing behind them, propelling them forward. Coral leaned back against Matthias, her stomach rolling with nerves the faster the hippocampus moved.

"We will arrive at the Dark Waters in four hours."

Coral didn't respond. Instead, she gripped the hem of his jacket in tight fingers absently. Her mind was elsewhere. It was still on the ship. It was on the opposite side of the deck, reaching for the railing as a sudden earsplitting creak tore wood and metal in half. She was at the heart of screams and blood and pain as chunks tore through flesh and tossed bodies into unforgiving water.

"I will be requesting an audience with Her Majesty. It will be granted, and we will be escorted to the throne room. There is specific etiquette you must be aware of before being presented to the queen."

Coral's brain left the dark thoughts behind momentarily to catch up with what Matthias was saying. Royal etiquette. Meeting the queen. Getting her legs back. Right.

"You will sink to the floor with your palms splayed on it and your head bowed low. The queen is very powerful, and any sign of disrespect may very well get you beheaded for insolence. Do you understand?"

Coral's fingers gripped Redwave's mane tighter out of fear. "I understand," she whispered.

"You will not get up unless she gives you leave to do so.

You will say, 'Greetings your Royal Majesty, Queen Ulla Magissa of the Dark Waters and the Atlantean Kingdom, Commandress of the Royal *Stratia*, rightful ruler and heiress of the throne.'"

Coral found herself snorting, if only to break through the tension of his words. "That sure is a mouthful."

If she expected Matthias to laugh, he didn't. His body went taut around her, and he seemed to grip the reins tighter. "Show her disrespect and you die."

Coral swallowed her own laugh. Either he was terrified of his queen or very defensive of her. Either way, she made a strong mental note to heed what he said. He'd gone through great lengths to save her; it'd be an insult if she got herself killed the minute she swam into the throne room.

"What else do I need to know?"

"After you speak those words, you will *stay silent* until she orders you to speak your purpose. You will beg her in the most amiable and humble of ways to offer you the favor of your legs back. Let us hope she is in a fortuitous enough mood to grant your wish."

"And if she isn't?" Coral dared to ask. Matthias didn't answer. But his silence was answer enough.

Queen Ulla Magissa sounded ruthless and dangerous. This woman—mermaid?—held Coral's future in her hands. She could either set her free or break her entirely. "So... *Atlantean?*" Coral asked. "As in, Atlantis?"

Matthias tensed again—he seemed to do a lot of that—as if debating what exactly he should tell her. A human. An outsider. She felt a little hurt by that. Even if he didn't outright say it, she could feel his disdain well enough.

Finally, he answered, "Atlantis was the original home of the merfolk, but when it fell to ruins, they rebuilt the city and named it Atlantica in its honor."

"So is that where we are going now?" She'd read about

Atlantis and had watched a few documentaries, not to mention her all-time favorite Disney film. Legend said it was a super advanced society that had sunk to the bottom of the ocean after natural disasters struck. Scientists had tried and exhausted resources looking for the make-believe city.

Now he was telling her it wasn't as make-believe as they thought, but it was still a desolate ruin, rebuilt anew. Excitement thrummed through Coral at the thought of seeing it when no one else had.

"We will be going to the Dark Waters."

"Is that not the same thing?"

"No. Queen Magissa resides in a Royal Palace of the Black Kingdom, the capitol of the Dark Waters—her original home —while Atlantica is further away. The Atlantean Kingdom used to be its own sovereign kingdom, separate from the Dark Waters, but now Her Majesty rules over them both."

"Who *used* to rule over Atlantica?"

Matthias sighed in what seemed like exasperation. "This is not a history lesson, Coral and do not presume me a teacher when I am not one. You are an outsider to the realm. A *human*. If Her Majesty thinks you know too much, then she will not grant you your legs. You will be a threat to our existence."

Fear, a now familiar friend, rose once again. "You're saying she could kill me if she thought I'd take your secrets to the humans?"

"She would."

"I would never do that," Coral said firmly. "You saved my life. I wouldn't betray you that way." She realized what his fear was, and it was warranted. If humans knew of mermaids existing, they would scour the waters looking for them. They would take them from their homes and use them as scientific experiments. Coral imagined Matthias strapped to an operating table, being poked and prodded and interrogated in a torturous way. The image didn't sit well and made it hard for her to swallow. No, she would take this secret to her grave.

"That is comforting to know, Coral." There was equal parts mirth and bitterness in his voice. "But I can tell you nothing else."

Coral let loose a breath. "It's okay. I understand. I won't ask anything else about your home." Though she itched to do so, she'd respect his wishes. His and his peoples.

"Tell me, Coral, what were you doing on that ship?"

His question caught her off guard and had a lump forming tightly in her throat. "To be honest, I didn't even want to be on that ship at first," she whispered. The words felt like truth and lies packed together. "I was just there because Olivia—" She choked on her friend's name, tears already forming at the back of her eyelids. She pushed them away and continued, "Olivia was supposed to go on the cruise with her boyfriend, but he cancelled last minute so she invited me. Actually, she manipulated me into going." Coral recalled the way she hadn't even been surprised when Coral burst through her room, claiming she would go on the cruise. Typical Olivia.

"Who is Olivia? What is a boyfriend?"

"Olivia is—" Coral sucked in a painful breath. "*Was* my closest friend. We were practically sisters." It hurt to speak of Olivia in past tense. It hurt to accept that she was dead. "And a boyfriend is..." How would she explain that to Matthias? She blushed and went on. "It's like a friend but *more*. A boyfriend is someone you can share secrets and jokes with, and it's someone you can kiss and do... other things with. It's someone you can love." She beat herself against a wall mentally for getting so sentimental with him when he seemed like a brick wall in comparison.

"A boyfriend is like a mate?" Matthias asked.

Coral blushed even more deeply at the word 'mate'. It

seemed more primal, animalistic. "Yeah. A boyfriend is like a mate."

"And do you..." Matthias cleared his throat, and she noticed his knuckles tightening white as he gripped the reins harder. "Do you have a boyfriend?" he asked awkwardly.

"No. Not anymore."

"Why not?"

An image of Trent slowly appeared in her mind. Of distorted memories and rough hands. Of a yacht swaying above water. Of pain and blood between her legs. Of cruel laughter and a body that didn't feel like her own.

She pushed them away. That seemed so long ago now, after everything that had recently happened. It didn't even seem to hold any bearing over this moment. She said as much. "It doesn't matter."

Matthias nodded, as if that were all the answer he needed, and they went the rest of the way in silence.

THE BLACK KINGDOM

CORAL DIDN'T KNOW WHEN SHE DOZED OFF, AND SHE didn't know when Matthias accommodated her, using his arms around her as a barrier to keep her from falling. When she awoke, Matthias's strong muscles were pressed tightly up against her and her head was lying comfortably in the crook of his neck.

Her foggy brain seemed to command her movements. Instead of forcing her away from him, she stayed, her nose tickling his skin. The scents of the underwater world were foreign to her, but if she had to describe his, it would be golden. Coral wasn't even sure if gold had a smell, but his was rich and glittering and exotic. Like champagne and sunlight.

The sharp point of her nose pressed against the three lines of gills against his neck. They opened and closed in fascinating movements that she itched to touch with the tips of her fingers. She didn't realize that was exactly what she'd raised her hand to do before Matthias stiffened, making her all too aware of what her addled brain was making her do.

"Sorry," she mumbled, sitting up straight and stretching her arms over her head. She yawned, arching her back and accidentally bumping the back of her head into Matthias's lip. "Sorry," she apologized again, leaning forward as far as she could. She was all too aware of his warm body and breath on her, and it made her want to curl up in a ball and shy away. She blamed it on his presence. Demanding and *kingly*. It didn't repulse her, but it was rather calming.

She forced herself to look away, her gaze snagging on her surroundings.

They'd been in open waters before with nothing but the expanse of ocean sand and the occasional fish or two. Now, they were passing coral reefs and, to Coral's surprise, homes. The homes looked like small, underwater cabins made with driftwood, rocks, sea glass, and coral. They didn't look much different from human houses. There were doors and windows, and there were even cute little knick-knacks, shells and jewelry hanging from seaweed like wind chimes and were blowing along with the flow of the current.

Coral couldn't keep her gaze away from the amazement. It was an actual underwater village. More homes lined up, all of them plain and dilapidated, but none of that took away from her bewilderment. They were riding Redwave at a steady, slow pace down what looked like an underwater road, a pathway marked with rocks, conches, and broken bits of coral, and houses framed either side of them.

Everything was quiet. Too quiet. All Coral could hear was the steady breathing of Redwave and Matthias. And Coral realized with a start why that was.

The place was abandoned.

Desolate.

There were no fish swimming in and out of their coral homes, and neither were there any merfolk. Coral squinted to look through the opened windows, but all was dark and silent inside. Chills went down her bare arms at the abandoned village and questions rose to her mind. She was itching to ask them, itching to get answers, but judging by the tight posture of Matthias's arms, she knew he wouldn't want to answer them.

The whole place felt *wrong* somehow. It felt cursed, *evil*, and she couldn't exactly explain that sentiment. It wasn't just because there was no one around to reassure her, but it was as if the barren waters exuded darkness. The hairs on the back of her neck prickled; she swiped at her skin absently in an attempt to shake off that feeling.

Noise seemed forbidden and she was too afraid to break the silence, so she held her breath. They rode on for minutes longer and the passing scenery was all the same. Just long lines of crumbling, spectral phantasms of where merfolk once lived, their ghosts a pulsing echo against her skin.

When Matthias finally pulled Redwave to a stop, it was above a ledge of sand. Coral held her breath as Matthias nodded towards the enormous drop below. "Welcome," he said darkly, "to the Black Kingdom."

And a black kingdom it was indeed.

It was a city entirely in black and blue that stretched out for miles and miles. Buildings carved of obsidian and tourmaline spiraled high in the water, their windows glowing in electric blue light. Black houses surrounded the terrain, carved of the same smooth stone as the gargantuan castle beyond. The lights were dimmed to a low glow, making the entirety of the floor below look encased in shadows.

Like an image straight from hell. Coral imagined the shadows reaching wispy fingers at her fins, threatening to drag her below.

"The Dark Waters." Even as shivers raked down her spine at the terrifying picture the kingdom made, she couldn't hold back the whisper of awe in her voice. The place was amazing, but it was also eerie and sinister. It looked like the catacombs where the dead resided, and she could see where it had gotten its name. She wondered if the queen was dangerous in the same way her kingdom projected. She must have been, to rule over something as dark as this.

"The queen's castle is the largest one over there." He pointed a finger down at the city. "The one with the triple spires." The castle in question was overwhelming to look at. Even from a distance, it was easy to make out the intricate grandiose of it. It cut high through the water, like a gothic building of old. Its spires twisted and curled, the tips ending in sharp, knife like peaks. Like a threat that chilled Coral down to the marrow of her bones.

"Of course, it is," she breathed, a little overwhelmed.

Matthias dug his tail into Redwave's side and pulled the reins. Redwave turned and began a slow swim down the slope and towards the city. The way there, Coral ran over what she was going to say to the queen. How could she best word it? Should she tell her the whole story? Would the queen be compassionate and give her legs? She hoped so. Everything depended on this. Her *life* depended on this.

Every stroke through the water brought her closer to her fate. When they finally reached the outskirts of the city, her fears melded into awe until both sensations were prominent in her chest. Here, there were merfolk swimming about. Merfolk of all kind.

There were mermaids with long and beautiful tails in all sorts of colors, some that were female from the waist up with the lower bodies of crabs and lobsters. There were mermen that had the heads of hammerhead sharks or the elongated faces of swordfish. Some had scrunched up, flabby faces and others had long, razor-sharp teeth. Mer with dorsal fins, tiny mer with dozens of thin limbs like shrimp, and even mer with tusks and barbed tails. Merfolk darted through water, and Coral's eyes seemed to go everywhere at once. From the mermaid with the lower body of a jellyfish to the merman with shark fins.

And the buildings! From far away they'd looked like shadow incarnate, but up close she had the urge to run her hands against the smooth stone. It was a dark blue-purple, a color so deep it looked black. And the blue lights emanating from the opened windows shone down on the walls, giving it an almost mysterious glow.

The stone was embedded deep into the ocean floor. Deeply eroded, it looked as though it had grown there like tree roots and they'd merely carved the stone hollow to make their homes. These ones were grander than the one's outside of the city, but Coral noticed that these had little personality to them. All of them were the same carbon copies of obsidian structures.

Redwave swam slowly through the city roads, and Coral immediately became aware that the surrounding merfolk stopped to stare. At her. She felt her face flush at their penetrating gazes, body tensing. That same feeling of foreboding she had when first passing through that abandoned village returned with full force. Goosebumps, hairs prickling, a strange tingle down her spine.

She dared a glance backwards, beyond Matthias's chest. A crowd had gathered behind them. And they seemed to be following them. She whipped back to the front. The crowd was thickening, all whispering harshly to one another and glaring at her.

"Matthias..." she whispered, a stabbing sense of foreboding tearing through her.

"Be quiet!" he hissed in her ear. She got chills and knots in her stomach from his tone alone. Was the crowd going to turn against them? The thought came quickly and as violently as the harsh, rising voices behind them.

"Matthias..." This time, her voice trembled.

"I said shut up!" He dug his fingernails into her side, causing her to flinch and clamp her teeth down onto her bottom lip. She dug her own fingers into Redwave's mane. Fear was crawling up her tail at the sight of the merfolk gathering in what was so obviously a lynching crowd.

Some of them carried what looked like small pitch forks and knives and even swords. They openly glared at her and then began calling out to her, shouting angry things in languages she didn't understand.

"Anthropos!"

When she looked cluelessly at them, they began their slurs in English, their accents garbled, not at all musical like when she'd first heard Matthias'.

"Down with the human!"

"Kill her!"

"She must be punished for her sins!"

Coral trembled at the words she did understand, gripping tightly to Redwave. They hated her. They hated her and didn't even know her! And how had they known she was human? Was it that obvious by looking at her that she wasn't one of them?

"Matthias." Her nails dug into his jacket as if she could somehow ground herself, but it was useless. She was afraid. Afraid of what these merfolk would do. Matthias hadn't said anything to her except to be quiet. Was he as afraid as she was like when they'd faced the sharks? His body was tense and rigid, arms locking her in. "I'm scared," she confessed.

Matthias eased his grip from the reins and placed his heavy hands on top of her trembling ones. The action reassured her, gave her faith that everything was going to be alright. He gripped her hands tightly and leaned forward until his chest was tight against her back. She almost shivered at his nearness. Matthias bent down, his lips against the lobe of her ear and he whispered, "I am sorry." And then he pushed her off the hippocampus.

The heavy weight of her body and the uselessness of her tail was enough to sink her. With a cry, Coral fell to the ground, swallowing silt in the process. Coughing, she sat up only to find herself surrounded by merfolk and their weapons. Their angry, alien-like faces sneered down at hers, and before she knew it, they were pummeling their fists onto her body. Instinct had her throwing her hands up to protect herself, but it did little good against their blows.

Pain came at her from nearly every angle, and when she felt something sharp scrape her tailfin, she screamed.

"Move aside!" Coral looked up to see Matthias pushing past the crowd to get to her. They parted ways after hearing the commanding tone in his voice. Demanding. *Kingly.* In his hands, he carried thick green rope. "This *anthropos* has been brought to the Dark Waters to be taken and tried before the queen and the royal courts!"

Coral could only stare at her savior in shock. He'd been so gentle, so caring all of this time they'd been together. This person before her was someone else entirely. There was fire in his eyes and something else there as well. Something vile when he looked at her. Hatred.

Or maybe it had been there all along. Maybe the flashing in his eyes had been violence, not mystery. She'd just been too blind to see it.

He bent down to Coral, and she flinched at his nearness where earlier she'd nearly swooned. How quickly things could change. He ignored her and jerked her arms behind her back. She bit the inside of her lip to avoid crying out at the wrenching pain it caused her shoulders. Then, he was tying the rope around her wrists. The material of it was rough and bit into her skin. He gave it one last tight yank to ensure she couldn't wriggle out of it and whispered to her. "We have to go to the palace now." He pulled on the rope, tugging her as well.

She felt her own hatred rising up to lash out at him. She ground her teeth together. "I can't swim."

"If you do not swim then I will drag you through the streets." His eyes were the violent color of a blue fire, his voice venomous. This was the same handsome merman who had saved her life? Who had gently grabbed her hips to lift her on top of his beloved hippocampus?

Coral spat in his face.

Matthias wiped away the bubbles that blew from her mouth, and his beautiful, full lips quirked up into a vicious smile that revealed white teeth. "Then I shall drag you." He straightened and gave a sharp yank of the rope, sending her falling to her back. She bit the inside of her mouth to not scream in pain. When he pulled, she slid against the silt and cried out. It felt like her arms would pop out of their sockets. He pulled harder and was true to his word. He dragged her through the streets.

All around them, voices of the merfolk cheered and cried out as he dragged her. She felt the pokes and probes of their weapons against her body, the sharp ends of their knives tearing at the material covering her.

Warm squishy things splattered against her skin, and she tried not to think about what it could be, instead focusing on the waters above. No light shone through these parts except the dull blue glow in the windows of houses. This part of the ocean seemed entirely encased in darkness. This time, there was no light at the end of a tunnel she could look at. No hope she could reach forward and grab. This time there was nothing but blackness and despair pressing around her.

Tears sprang to her eyes but were chased away by the jabs of pain that kept repeating over and over against her flesh. Things were thrown, fists connected against her tail, her sides. And throughout it all, Matthias just pulled her with little remorse. She didn't even think he looked back.

Coral tried drowning out what they were saying, but it all eventually became an endless loop in her mind.

"Anthropos!"

"Kill the human!"

"Disgusting!"

And more vile things. Things she tried to push from her mind, but they kept shouting them and they kept *hurting* her. How long had he been pulling her through the streets? How many more mer had joined in on her humiliating drag across the city?

When it finally stopped, Coral could have cried out with relief. She blinked when she was suddenly hauled up by the arm by Matthias. He sneered into her face. "You are taking too long. At this pace, the mer will lynch you to death before we make it to the palace. Come on." He pulled her by his side. The crowd booed, but Matthias ignored them, pulling her alongside. Anytime she tripped over her tail and nearly fell, he'd haul her up before that happened. *"Come on,"* he'd growl low in her ear, low enough that no one could hear. "Bear with it, Coral. Without fear and without tears, for the worst has yet to come."

She wasn't sure if it was a warning or a threat, but she took those words and tucked them deep into her heart, for she was sure she would need them later.

She would need them to survive within the massive spiraling palace that came into view.

She would need them to survive the Queen of the Dark Waters.

Twin guards were standing watch with spears in front the looming gates. They took one look at Matthias, at Coral, and then at the crowd that had followed behind them. They didn't even ask Matthias what his purpose was or who Coral was. They just opened the tall creaking gates and stepped aside to let them pass. The crowd stayed behind, and when the guards closed the gates, they pressed themselves up against the bars to sneer their last insults in Coral's direction.

Though she was glad they were no longer behind her to taunt, Coral still felt a nervous fear freeze her insides. They were in the palace now, Matthias swimming and keeping her upright through massive halls. Even these were black, the color starting to bleed into her soul. This was the queen's home.

The material she'd used as a dress was tattered and torn in places, rendering her wrap useless. Her skin was already bruised, the marks on her flesh an angry red and mottling purple. Her shoulders ached, and she had cuts and slashes on her arms and waist; she was even missing a few scales.

Why had he done this to her? Had he pretended to care only to get her to come to this wretched city? If he'd wanted to kill her, he could have easily done so before. He could have let her drown. He could have let the sharks maul her inch by painful inch. He could have left her behind without a clue how to swim and she would have been dead within hours—minutes. Why go through such lengths to save her and then bring her here to be tortured? It didn't make sense.

"Why are you doing this?" she croaked. Her voice was scratchy from screaming and her tongue hurt from biting heavily on it in a weak attempt to stave off the pain.

He squeezed her upper arm. "Be *quiet*," he commanded.

Coral looked at his profile. His nose was slightly rounded, his lips full and pink. His jaw was perfectly square, throat curving, traveling down to a nicely corded neck. He was beautiful. But his lips were forming a too-thin line, his jaw flexed enough that she could see the veins beneath the muscles on his skin. His shoulders were bunched tight and nearly up to his ears. He'd been tight before on the journey, but it'd only incremented the closer they got to the city. The closer they got to *her*.

"You're afraid of her," Coral surmised. The words hit their mark. Matthias growled low and dug his nails deeper into her arm.

"Of course, I am. You would do well to be, too. Bravery is rarely rewarded with anything other than death. Now *be quiet* and *move*." He shoved her ahead of him—hard—and she flapped her tail a bit to keep her balance. It wouldn't do good to fall in here. Not with the hard marble floors. There would be no sand to cushion her, and Coral didn't need any more bruises.

"So, it's the cowards who are rewarded here?" Coral asked defiantly. She knew she should have shut up, should have held her tongue. Under any other circumstances she would have. She was the quiet one, always had been. But everything around her had suddenly changed. She was faced with a new challenge, one she didn't know how to handle. Matthias brought out a fire in her, and she wanted him to burn.

"I told you to be quiet."

"You're a coward, Matthias. And I hate you. I wish you would have just let me drown."

Her words nearly had him tripping, but he righted himself and kept on as if she hadn't said a word. Still, Coral didn't miss the final squeeze he gave her or how his grip on her arm loosened while the rest of his posture tightened. She didn't miss the look of anger flare up in his eyes at her comment or his mask of hatred that fell into place at the right time. Right as they swam up to a set of double doors flanked by guards. They nodded once at Matthias and opened the doors for him and Coral to pass through.

Coral had barely gotten a look around before Matthias had barged them into the place and threw her to the ground. She let out an awkward grunt when her chin hit the smooth floors, causing her teeth and head to rattle. Her hands were still tied behind her back unpleasantly, and it hurt to even try and slip out of her bindings. She accommodated her body, wiggled around a bit to get into a more comfortable position, and lifted her head up from where she lay.

Only to find herself looking into the eyes of the Queen of the Dark Waters.

ULLA MAGISSA

"YOUR MAJESTY, QUEEN ULLA MAGISSA OF THE DARK Waters and Atlantean Kingdom, it is my greatest honor to stand in your presence once more."

Beside her, Matthias bowed low, his long green-blue tail sweeping gallantly across the perfectly polished ground with the gesture. But Coral's eyes weren't on him. They were glued to the throne in front of her. A throne made of the same obsidian as the palace, carved in intricate detail. The high back of it rose up to loom over her in the gargantuan image of a two headed eel, jaws gaping to reveal sharp, shining teeth poised to strike.

And just below those gaping jaws, looking as though she'd be swallowed by them, was Queen Ulla Magissa. If Coral had conjured up an image of the queen in her mind, the real vision of her swept that away in an instant. No image or thought of this mermaid could ever compare.

She lounged on her throne in a comfortable, lazy manner, elbow poised with grace on the arm rest. Her chin was propped up on her hand and a slow smile curled on her beautiful mouth. Looking at the queen made it hard for Coral to believe that perfection did not exist, for there was not a flaw on her.

Her skin was as smooth and as pink as a pearl, hair like white snow that was braided and coiled, neatly tucked behind an enormous silver crown. The crown looked like rows of icicles, jagged and razor sharp, studded at the base with black and blue gems. The queen wore a beautiful flowing gown in a color that matched her crown. It was silver all over, diaphanous and threaded through with black pearls and small bits of blue diamonds.

Coral couldn't help but admire her beauty. And her tail... Well, her tail wasn't a tail at all. Queen Magissa had the lower body of an octopus. Her tentacles were black with a strawberry, purplish underside, eight of them lounging as lazily as the rest of her, curling and uncurling, sliding up and down against her obsidian throne.

"What pretty words," she said in a voice that was both powerful and sweet, young and ancient, amused and chastising. A song of life and the low timbres of a dirge. "Flattery has always been your favorite form of art, and I must say, my little merman, you have perfected it."

Matthias chuckled, the sound so natural coming from his throat, and one Coral hadn't heard before now. "I must say, my queen, it is now you who flatter me, for I speak only the truth."

"I am sure." She pursed her lips, and then her gaze flickered to Coral, as if noticing her for the first time. Her interest seemed to pike; she unfurled herself from her lazy position and straightened, her back regal and her gaze penetratingly stern. "Who, pray tell, is this insolent beggar you have brought to my throne room?" She full-out glared now, her long fingers and sharp black nails digging into her chair.

Coral made a pathetic attempt to sit up, but her hands were tightly secured behind her back and her tail was nothing but a useless, dead weight behind her. Instead of sitting then, she lifted her head up to stare at the queen.

"Your Royal Majesty," Coral began. Her voice trembled with fear and pain and tears. "My name is Coral Bennett. I am a human from Colorado, and I was traveling on a cruise ship in Greece when it sunk. I've come to beg you to give me my legs back and allow me to return home. Please."

The queen smiled. It wasn't the same type of smile she'd given Matthias when they'd first entered. This one was cruel and spiteful. "An *anthropos* in my palace. Really, my little merman?" Though she directed the question to Matthias, she didn't even glance his way. She stared at Coral in a way that made her want to curl up and hide. "A human dressed in tattered rags, brought before me in chains like a common criminal, in the royal palace, lying before the Royal Queen, and she has the *audacity* to ask for favors? My dear, you have not even bowed to me yet."

Coral gulped past the lump in her throat. "My apologies, Your Majesty. I didn't think."

She snorted and flicked an invisible speck of dust from the arm of her throne. "You humans never do."

Coral bowed her head low, pressing her forehead against the cool ground. She fumbled for the words that Matthias told her she must memorize. "Greetings Royal Majesty, Queen Ulla Magissa of the Dark Waters and Atlantica." What else had he called her? She couldn't remember. It had been such a mouthful.

"That is it?" the queen asked incredulously. "You belittle my titles, human. Tell me, my little merman, did you inform her on how she was to address me?"

"I did, Your Majesty," he replied somberly.

"Then tell me, human, is my merman lying or are you simply stupid?"

"H-he isn't lying, Your Majesty."

"I did not think he would. So, you are stupid, then?" Her voice was all cruel amusement. It sent a stab of humiliation through Coral.

"No, Your Majesty."

"You obviously must be." She looked at her with such obvious disdain that Coral's face flamed an unattractive shade of red. "Oftentimes one must admit to their own failings in order to swim ahead in life. So..." She curled her fingers in front of her face, examining the movement closely. "Admit to your failings, human." She smiled widely and stared at Coral expectantly.

"Your Majesty?" She trembled at the devilish look in her eyes. It wasn't a pleasant one and Coral knew that this would not end happily.

"I want to hear you admit it, *anthropos*. I want to hear you admit to your own stupidity."

Coral's heart flew up to her throat, her pulse thrumming an erratic rhythm. It wasn't enough humiliation to drag her through the city to be lynched, but she had to insult herself for this evil queen to satisfy her sadistic nature?

Ulla wanted to see her begging. She wanted to see her bleeding and broken in body and spirit. She didn't know why this queen hated her so much. Was it because she was human? If that was the case, then Coral knew that her legs were a lost cause anyway. These people wanted to see her break.

And she just might.

"I am waiting..." the queen said haughtily.

"If I admit to it, will you give me my legs back and let me leave?"

"You *insolent* little..."

All of a sudden, Coral felt a tug on the ropes, pulling her backwards. She gave a startled cry when she was pulled into a floating position by the hair. Matthias tugged at the roots painfully, inciting another cry of pain from her. He bent his face down to hers to murmur in her ear, loud enough for even the queen to hear.

"Do not be an insolent wench, human. Apologize to Her Majesty at once." As if he'd known Coral was going to refuse, he pulled at her hair, hard enough to rip it from its roots. She cried out. "I am sorry, I do not think I heard you correctly." He smiled into her face. There was so much cruelty there. She'd been so ignorant to it before. Why had she imagined that his touch had meant anything? That he'd allowed her to cry into his chest for her friend out of the goodness in his heart? He'd been manipulating her the entire time. She despised him for it, but Coral hated herself even more.

"I apologize, Your Majesty. I am stupid," Coral ground out painfully. The words were like acid on her tongue. They shouldn't have been spoken, for she didn't deserve them at all.

Matthias straightened, hand still clutched tightly in her hair, nails digging painfully into her scalp. "Does the apology please Her Majesty?"

The queen smiled sultrily in his direction. "It pleases me greatly indeed. Now..." She flicked her wrist with disinterest in Coral's direction. "Have the guards send this *anthropos* into the *calabozo*. On the west end, I think. I will call on her when I next feel like it." Then she turned her dark gaze to Coral and her upper lip quirked up in a sneer. "Hopefully next time we meet you will have learned some manners. Guards!"

The doors to the throne room opened behind them. There were no stamping feet to alert Coral of the guards' arrival but there was an unusual stirring in the water as they swam towards her.

The queen smiled sweetly—as sweetly as a venomous snake could smile—in Matthias' direction. "You have been gone from my side for far too long, my little merman. I wish to speak with you alone."

At the queen's words, Matthias' fingers tightened a fraction into her scalp, like a tensing of his body that felt almost involuntary. But it was gone a second later, and he released his hold on her slowly. Before she could gently float to the floor, the guards were at her sides, lifting her up by the upper arms, pulling her from Matthias. They hauled her away, her tail floating like some dead thing in front of her. She was slack in their arms as they led her out of the throne room. All the while, she kept her eyes glued to the front, glued to Matthias as he gave her one last look before turning around to swim up to the throne and press his palm to Ulla's cheek. The queen smiled as if she'd won some imaginary game of chess that no one knew they'd been playing.

And then the doors slammed in Coral's face.

Even as the guards glided her through the halls, speaking in what she now assumed was Greek or Atlantean or some other mermish language, Coral could not shake Matthias' face from her mind, that last look he'd given her before turning around to pleasure his queen.

There was something about his eyes that she couldn't quite decipher. Even when the guards swam her down a flight of barnacle-covered stairs where the water around her felt cold and smelt musky and dirty, she tried to pick apart what she'd seen, as if she could somehow make sense of it.

When they turned the key within an iron cage and threw her inside and she fell, hitting her chin and elbows—as they'd refused to untie her—she didn't think of the pain anymore. Instead, she thought of Matthias.

And when the guards finally left her alone to take in her dark surroundings, she didn't think of the skeleton companions chained to the bars, faces covered in algae, barnacles, and silt. She didn't wonder that maybe they had been human once too and had been left there to rot. She didn't shiver with disgust or nausea as fish darted in and out of empty eye sockets.

Coral didn't recall crying that night. Maybe she did, but she was too busy translating the message Matthias had been trying to convey to her in the severity of his expression. It wasn't until later that night when Coral was at the brim with exhaustion, did she realize what it had been. As she drifted into a cold and lonely sleep, Coral realized the emotion that swelled within Matthias' eyes had been a mirrored image of her own.

What she'd seen in him had reflected the depths of her own soul.

In Matthias' eyes, she saw sorrow.

THE TRIAL

THEY WERE STARVING HER. IT'D BEEN DAYS; AT LEAST, Coral assumed it had been days. Without light or an open ocean above her, she had no idea how long had passed. It could have been hours. It could have been days. It could have been *weeks*. To Coral, it felt like the latter. Her stomach had gone into a pattern of growling, lurching, and heaving. It had lasted a while and had weakened Coral. She could barely move in her vaulted cage, staying in the corner opposite of her skeletal prison mates.

The hunger didn't bother her as much as the loneliness did. She was going crazy here. And the occasional, distant sound of singing and wailing didn't help her sanity, either. She half wondered if she was imagining it or if she'd gone mad without even realizing it.

Her thoughts kept rewinding to everything. To every moment that had led her up to here, locked away in a cage like a common animal. Trent and the whirlwind affair that made her believe he cared. Waking up with memories clouded through smoke and an unmistakable pain between her legs. Falling into depression. Nearly a year of losing herself. The cruise. Olivia. The accident. Sinking. Waking up in a different body. Meeting a merman. *Losing* Olivia... Everything piled up and replayed in an endless circle in her mind.

When they'd first dropped her into that cell, she'd spent for what felt like hours thinking of nothing and no one but Matthias. His eyes had been full of sadness, a look so heartbreaking that had been gone in an instant. She'd replayed his image over and over until the exact expression was etched into her mind. When she had that image memorized, she replayed another. The image of him swimming obediently up to the queen's throne and placing his hand reverently on her face. It had made her blood boil at first, but she'd expelled that sentiment from her body. Why should she feel the least bit angry? He was a manipulative asshole and the queen was a sadistic bitch. They deserved each other.

With that thought, she'd given Matthias' face an enormous shove out of her mind. When she successfully banished him from her thoughts—at least for a little while—she'd tried moving her tail, lifting it up and down. She attempted simple things first like staying afloat, upright in the water. It hurt her muscles to stay upright for long lengths of time, especially with her hands tied behind her back and so little space to move around in, and she was forced to rest. She'd considered trying to pick the lock, prying off a rib or something from one of the skeletons, but even if she could open her cage, where would she go? She didn't know her way around the palace, much less the ocean. Besides, she still didn't know how to swim like a true mermaid. It would have been hopeless to even try.

She was leaning against the bars, imagining trailing her fingers against her tail. It was like smooth sapphire when she'd first seen it but now the scales were dull and dirty. Silt stuck to her, and the algae that dirtied the cage was spreading onto her fins. How could she be underwater and feel like she was in dire need of a bath? It was ridiculous. The underwater world was a strange, foreign place.

The sound of a door squeaking open caught her attention. Her head snapped up. Had someone finally come to put her out of her misery? Two guards swam into view, both of them wearing black jackets with silly adornments over the breasts. They didn't speak to her. They just swam forward and unlocked the door to her cage and opened it. One of them swam in and hauled her up, pulling her out with him towards the other guard. Together, they led her out of her cell without a word and through many more hallways. She tried memorizing the way, but her mind was so muddled from all that time without company, sunlight, and food that she couldn't keep up with the heavy strokes of their tails.

Their destination was the throne room. When they arrived inside, it wasn't like the last time she'd been there. It wasn't just the queen in her frivolous dress and crown. Yes, *she* was there, sitting straight backed and regal beneath the canopied gaping jaws of eels. She wore a black crown sharply shaped like stars, studded at the base with silver scales, diamonds, and bright red rubies. Her dress this time around was a high-necked crimson that was tight against her generous chest and waist, but flowed and floated over her curling tentacles.

There were other merfolk in the throne room as well. Chairs had been set on either side of the queen, each one occupied by a different mer. All of them were dressed in vibrant colors that set off the parlor either of their skin or tails. They all looked rich, as if that fact hadn't been obvious the minute she swam in. The queen seemed the type who would never allow commoners to sit beside her in her throne room.

There was an audience there as well, though Coral didn't get a chance to get a good look at them because the guards swam forward and deposited her on the floor, where she slowly sank onto her stomach. It was uncomfortable and her shoulders were aching non-stop, but she had to pretend to be strong, even if she didn't feel it. And wasn't that the mantra of her life? *Pretending.*

She pressed her forehead against the floor and made sure her voice rang out across the room. Words she'd stupidly forgotten before but had come back to her in her prison cell. "Many greetings to Her Majesty, Queen Ulla Magissa of the Dark Waters and the Atlantean Kingdom, Commandress of the Royal *Stratia,* rightful heiress to the throne. It is an honor to be in your presence once more." The words hurt as they exited her throat, but they were a necessary evil.

"I knew a week in the *calabozo* would instill in you much needed manners, *anthropos.*" The queen sounded as though she were smiling. It was a good thing Coral couldn't see her face or she would have glared at her. "You may rise now."

Coral's face flamed. The queen had done that on purpose. She would have Coral make a total fool of herself for the benefit of her menagerie. Groaning, Coral rolled to her back, very hard to do without an actual sense gravity pulling her to the ground. Sure, her weight kept her anchored for brief moments sometimes, but luck wasn't on her side. She floated in awkward circles through the water, earning herself laughter from everyone present.

"For the love of Neptune, will someone help the *anthropos?*" The queen's icy voice cut through the water, and a guard was immediately at Coral's side, adjusting her so she was in a kneeling position before them all. It was awkward to stay afloat, but she finally managed after planting her tail fin firmly against the floor, anchoring herself steadily. Apparently, that was the trick to it.

Queen Ulla glared at her. Her fingers stroked the armrests of her throne, fingernails scraping at the stone lightly. Coral tried not to look at her too long and instead did a sweep of the merfolk currently present. There were many of different kinds, all of them with beautiful upper bodies and faces, their tails were what varied. Some had regular mertails, others had legs with webbed feet and fins on their calves, and others had the lower bodies of sharks, clown fish, and manta rays. None but the queen, she noticed, had the lower body of an octopus.

Coral's gaze stopped on Matthias. She hadn't seen him when she first came in because he was behind Ulla, hidden slightly behind her throne. He was as handsome as ever, his dark red hair curling above his head, dark skin hidden behind the same black jacket that the guards wore. This one, though, was decorated differently. There was a bulbous squid stuck to his shoulder, the tentacles stretching long across his chest as if securing the jacket in place. There were other mermen near him as well, all bearing the same clothing.

"Let us begin," the queen called out. She turned to the merman closest to her and nodded her head.

He bowed his head low to his queen and swam up straight. He was an old merman, with wrinkles and saggy skin, black dress robes clasped together at the throat by an oyster shell.

He cleared his throat.

"The royal court will now come to order." Silence rang out and he continued. "On this day, the fiftieth year of the year of the Magissa, I declare that the trial now come to session." He looked straight at Coral. "State your name for the courts, *anthropos.*"

She gulped. "Coral Bennett."

He nodded and continued. "It is by my power as Magistrate to Queen Ulla Magissa, her Royal Majesty and heiress of the throne of the Dark Waters and rightful ruler of the Atlantean Kingdom, Commandress of the Royal *Stratia,* defender or the merfolk and savior of the realm, that Coral

Bennett stand trial on this day for the crimes of: endangering the kingdoms, mass murders of the merfolk, and ocean pollution. These offenses are of the severest nature and are punishable by death at the queen's command. How plead you?"

Coral's head spun with the ridiculous accusations. She looked up, hoping that maybe this was some kind of a joke, but a sweep across the room told her that this was not. They all looked at her like she was already guilty. "Not guilty!" Coral cried out. "Those accusations are outrageous. I've done no such thing in my life!"

The magistrate turned to the queen, waiting for her instruction.

The queen was looking at Coral, her eyes boring into hers. "You tell me, *human*, that you are absolute of all sin against the merfolk and my kingdom?"

Coral nodded. "Yes."

The queen then let out a trill of laughter. A bone-chilling, sinister sound. When it subsided, she scraped her nails against her throne, causing Coral to flinch.

"Do not act so innocent. You stand before my royal court in representation of the *human race* for the crimes they've committed against *my oceans*. So, I will repeat the magistrate's question: *How plead you?*"

"Not guilty," Coral repeated firmly. "It's completely unfair for me to stand trial on behalf of the entire human race! I've done nothing wrong! I'm just a librarian!"

"Oh, it is completely fair," the queen replied with venom in her words. "And I will remind you that this is *my* court and *my* kingdom. You will be tried in accordance to our laws and customs. I do not know what savagery goes on up top, but *here* there are strict rules. Your kind has broken them, and you will pay for their crimes." She flicked a finger at her Magistrate. "Proceed with the evidence."

The magistrate nodded. "The royal court calls forth our

first witness on the first charge of endangering the king-doms." He gestured towards the audience. At his signal, a mermaid swam forward trailed by a guard.

Coral noticed two things about the pair. She noticed the mermaid didn't swim like the other ones she'd seen so far, with grace and elegance and the practice of years. She swam crookedly, swinging her tail in short jerking motions much like someone who had legs walked with a limp. And the second was that the guard was carrying a large, jagged chunk of metal. "State your name for the royal court."

"M-my name is Lily Yellowtail."

"Please tell the courts of the crimes the *anthropos* have committed against you," the magistrate coaxed. By now, Coral had realized that the word 'anthropos' meant human or humans. They spat the word out like it had some vile meaning.

Lily's shoulders shook as she sobbed into her hands. The court gave her a minute to compose herself. She sniffled. "I lived in a small village with my mate and our children. We had two boys and a baby mergirl. We were a humble family.

"My mate farmed sea cucumbers; we would send them to the city. We had no enemies. We were good mer." She broke off to sob again. Coral saw that her grief was very real. Her voice was heartbreaking. "Then one day, the waters darkened out of nowhere. We are far enough from the surface that ships do nothing to us usually, but this was different. We looked up and there it was. A sinking ship. We tried swimming out of the way, but we were too late. The ship crushed our home. We were all inside. Parts of the ship were buried inside my children; I was too late to save them.

"I did not receive the impact in full force, but my tail caught in the infernal metal. I was able to get out, but I'd lost everything. I have no home and no family because of the humans." As she said this, she turned to glare at Coral. There was pure, raw hatred in that stare.

"Just to clarify, what is it the soldier is carrying in his arms?" the magistrate inquired, pointing to the large chunk of metal that the merman was carrying.

Lily turned to face him again. "After our home was crushed, her most gracious Majesty, Queen Ulla Magissa sent her Personal Guard to save us from the wreckage. The soldier is carrying evidence of that wreckage."

The magistrate and the court gasped when the soldier held the chunk of metal higher above his head so they could all see it. After they all got done staring at it like some artifact in a museum, the magistrate turned to the queen.

Ulla nodded. "You have my permission to retake your seat Lily Yellowtail. Let it be known that the crown is on your side. My Personal Guard will rebuild your home. It may not bring back the lives needlessly lost, but we will spare no expense. May Neptune bless you in this time of hardship, and may the Gods and Goddesses of the deepest depths seek out vengeance and justice on your behalf."

"Blessings, Your Majesty, my most gracious queen. Blessings." Lily bowed low and crookedly, the movement jerky and awkward because of her injured tail. When she straightened, she turned with the soldier and swam back to her seat.

"Do you see, *anthropos?*" the queen asked Coral. "Humans have little regard for us and our homes. Where you go, chaos follows. Will you continue to plead innocent of these crimes?"

Coral took in a shaky breath. "Yes," she replied. The courts gasped in angry disbelief and began murmuring at her audacity. "I am very sorry about the Yellowtail family. I truly am. But I did not wreck that ship. I didn't crash it on top of her home. I'm not a ship builder or even an engineer. I'm a librarian! I've done nothing wrong!" Her desperation was beginning to seep through, and she tried to rein it back, but it was hard, so hard when these mer obviously wanted to see her pay for crimes that she didn't commit. That meant nothing to them. All they could see was that she was part of the human race and that automatically made her guilty.

The queen's eyebrows drew together, lips turning in a tight look of displeasure. "Then proceed with the trial, Magistrate."

The magistrate cleared his throat and did as his queen commanded. "The second and third charges against the *anthropos* Coral Bennett are the mass murders of merfolk and ocean pollution. May our next witnesses please swim before the royal court?"

This time, a family of mer swam up to bow before their queen. They all wore cloths over the lower half of their faces, tied securely behind their heads. When they rose, the magistrate asked them to relay their stories.

It was a merman who spoke first. There was something about his voice that was odd. It was scratchy and he coughed after every other word. "Your Majesty and the royal court. We are from the small village of *Joolau*, just east of Atlantica. We dedicated ourselves to the breeding of hippocampi. Then, two full moons ago, the waters suddenly darkened into what we thought were clouds of silt." He paused and coughed heavily. "A ship was passing overhead dropping human *excrements* into our homes." He hacked again. "It polluted the waters and invaded our systems. Our hippocampi fell ill immediately. We tried to save them, but our livestock died. We fell ill as well." He coughed into his scarf. "The healers say there is no cure for our ailment. And it is all because of the *anthropos* not caring where they pollute."

They were dismissed, and the magistrate called more witnesses before the courts. One by one, they pleaded their case against Coral and the human race. The evidence was solid, all of it. Mer brought in children and sea creatures with deformities caused by fishhooks, scarred turtles who had found themselves caught in snares, a giant net filled with plastic and trash so carelessly discarded. One by one they proved just how cruel and careless the human race was. One by one the mer signed her death warrant.

Coral didn't bother to defend herself anymore. She could plead innocence until she was blue in the face and no one would listen to her. She was human. She was guilty. Whether she had anything to do with it personally or not. She was *anthropos*, an outsider, a murderer.

She was as good as dead.

"The royal courts will call one last witness to the stand before deliberating."

Coral didn't think it mattered who else they brought to the stage. It wouldn't make a difference.

"The court calls Caspian de la Magissa as our final witness."

A hush went through the room and Coral saw why. Matthias detached himself from the side of Ulla's throne and swam to the center of the room. He swept into a low bow then straightened. His large tail gliding against the edge of the floor. Coral stared incredulously at him. They'd called on Caspian, not him.

"State your name and profession for the royal court's official records, please."

Matthias' hands clasped behind his back. "My name is Caspian de la Magissa, and I am Personal Guard to Her Majesty, Queen Ulla Magissa."

Coral started. Caspian? His name was *Caspian*? A surge of anger rushed through her blood. He hadn't even been honest about his name. That felt like even more of a betrayal than anything else he'd done.

"And you know the *anthropos,* Coral Bennett?"

"We spent time together, yes."

"In your previous statement given, you claimed you found the *anthropos*. Where did you find her?" the magistrate inquired.

"I found her drowning three leagues south of here near the coast of the human realm they call 'Greece'."

"Do you know why she was drowning, Caspian?"

"She was aboard a cruise ship, traveling to the human kingdom 'Italy'. The ship sunk and she sunk with it." His replies were short and tense. There was no emotion in his voice as he recounted the incident that pierced her heart and changed her life erratically. It made her want to punch him until he bled.

"Just to clarify, what were you doing so far from the queen's side? As a *Personal* Guard, you are to be with her always."

Coral didn't miss the way he sneered the word *personal* or the whispered snickers other members of the court gave out. She didn't have time or energy to wonder what that was about.

"We all know Her Majesty cares deeply for her subjects. With all the unfortunate and barbaric attacks against the merfolk from the *anthropos*, she grew worried that more tragedy would strike. Our beloved queen knew the cruise ship would be passing over a village—thanks to her reliable sentries—and sent us of the Personal Guard to track the ship and protect the merfolk. It was there I saw the shipwreck and the *anthropos* drowning."

"And how was it, Caspian, that Coral Bennett became one of the merfolk?" the magistrate asked suspiciously.

"Because I made her as such."

Surprised gasps penetrated the silence. The royal court fretted in their seats, whispered to each other behind webbed hands with disdain in their eyes. They looked from him to

Coral with disdain. She felt the same way about them, so it didn't matter. They'd been looking at her that way since she'd arrived.

"Why would you do such a thing?"

Coral watched his back as he answered the questions. His posture was rigid straight and his hands behind his back tightened harder with every question they asked him. She watched his knuckles go white. "I believed she possessed valuable information regarding the human world that would be useful in our battle against them."

Coral's hands tightened into fists, causing her wrists to dig painfully into her bindings. She gritted her teeth against it, but still felt the painful sting of betrayal in her throat. She'd *asked* him why he'd saved her, and he'd looked away. He'd said it didn't matter! Now she knew why. She'd been his pawn the entire time. And she knew it, she'd known he was a traitor since the moment he threw her off his hippocampus, but each new discovery was a fresh wound.

"Humans are worthless," the magistrate replied with disinterest. "I doubt this one has much information to begin with." He then ignored Caspian and turned to Coral. "Human, is it true what he says? You were on a cruise ship?"

Coral found her voice. "I was."

His fins flared at her declaration. "And yet you deny culpability in the crimes against mer. That cruise ship destroyed a village. The cruise ship *you* boarded. That ship killed dozens of merfolk. Merfolk with *children*. Yet you claim innocence and ignorance to the violence humans inflict every day. You may claim to have not constructed the ship, but you were still aboard it and someone must pay for these crimes. The sentence is death!"

Coral's heart dropped like dead weight to her stomach as the cries of agreement went up. Her pulse quickened, and her insides became liquid. This was it. They would kill her. It shouldn't have mattered to her, considering she was supposed to be dead and shark food anyway, but somehow it did. It mattered a lot.

Coral's thoughts went to her life in Colorado, to the depths she'd fallen and tried to rise out of, to Olivia and finally, her gaze found Matthias—no, *Caspian*—and somehow, he made her heart hurt all the more. She'd trusted him. Her first and last mistake as a mermaid.

"If I may be so bold as to comment, my most gracious and beautiful queen?" Caspian interrupted the shouts. The court shushed to hear what he had to say.

Queen Ulla looked at him with annoyed curiosity. "What is it, Caspian?" she asked with irritation. "I think you have said enough."

"I must disagree, Your Majesty. You see, I spoke with the *anthropos* of her human life, and it is my opinion that she would be of more use to us alive rather than dead."

The queen didn't bother hiding the angry look that slashed across her face. "And why do you think that, Caspian?"

"I know justice and revenge is what we seek against the *anthropos* for all of their crimes, but how is justice not sweeter when the other party is aware that we have won? The humans do not know that we exist. Their ships will keep sailing through our waters, and they will keep polluting our homes with their trash and plastics and excrements. We can kill each and every human that dares accidentally fall into our waters and the humans will remain oblivious to it. They will keep sending ships and fishermen to us. Maybe killing this *anthropos* will satisfy our need for justice, but it will not save us indefinitely."

The queen tightened her hands into fists on her armrest. "So," she began slowly, "what would you suggest, Caspian?"

"I spoke with the human on our journey. In the human world, she is a Keeper of Knowledge."

The whole court turned to look at Coral. The queen snorted. "*Her?* A Keeper of Knowledge? Do not be ignorant, Caspian. She clearly lied to you."

"I do not believe she did. She knew of hippocampi and Atlantis. That knowledge is of our oldest secrets. She knows things she should not. I think it would be beneficial to keep her alive as a source against the humans. Use their own as a weapon against them."

The queen contemplated this, stroking her long finger-nails against her chin. "Hmm..."

The magistrate ruffled his fins. "Your Majesty, you cannot be considering this absurd idea? Someone must pay for their crimes!"

"All those on the ship have died," Caspian pointed out. "They have paid for the crime. But if you must have this human pay, then make her pay through work. Let her see the damage her kind has done. Make her clean the oceans and cure the sick. As a Knowledge Keeper, it should not be difficult."

"You speak of letting a human swim among us. It has never been done before!" The magistrate's wrinkly face went red with rage. "She cannot even swim. What use will she be in cleaning up the mess of her race?"

"I will teach her."

There was silence and then angry shouting, shouts of disbelief and accusations thrown against Caspian. Even Coral stared at him, not believing her ears. Why was he doing this? Why didn't he just let her die? The answer was simple enough. He wanted her to suffer. He wanted to use her against the humans.

"You would waste your time with this *anthropos?* And for what?" the queen demanded.

Caspian loosened his hands from his back and pounded a fist against his chest. "For my love of the ocean, of the kingdoms and your reign, my queen. For my hatred of the inconsiderate humans. I will sacrifice anything for our home, even if it means wasting time with land-scum."

Coral's face flamed at that declaration, but she bit the inside of her mouth.

"Hmm..." The queen considered what he was saying. It felt like hours of waiting for her response, hours of waiting for the queen to decide her fate. Finally, she curled her lips and smiled. "I can see the benefits of keeping the *anthropos* alive and how it will aid our cause." She stroked her chin. "Fine! I agree to this sentence. Let the *anthropos* see the damage her kind has wrought against us. Let her clean up their mess. She will help us with information on her kind and be at our beck and call. *But...*" She held up a finger and Coral held her breath. "I have conditions. Caspian, you will teach her the ways of our kind, let her see what it is to swim among the dark mer. You will care and provide for her as you see fit, but any misconduct, any attempt to escape or anything *illegal* will be punishable by immediate death. For the both of you." She smiled like a snake getting ready to strike. "She will be supervised at all times and chained to your arm during her service. *And* she will no longer stay within the *calabozo*. The *anthropos* from now on will live with you."

If anyone disagreed with the conditions, they didn't dare voice them to their queen. Coral was afraid to do so as well. Caspian had managed to gain her time. Time she was already planning on using to learn all she could and escape when the chance arose. Her mind already raced with the possibilities.

The queen was staring from Coral to Caspian. If Coral didn't know better, she'd say the queen was plotting as well. What, Coral didn't know, but the look of pure mischief on

Ulla's face frightened her more than facing the jaws of deadly sharks had. It curled her tail and made her fins tremble.

"Take heed, Coral Bennett," the queen said slowly. The sound of Coral's name on her lips instilled raw fear inside her. "You have escaped the jaws of death, but *this* is not a permanent arrangement. Anger me, molest my people, try to escape, or disobey my laws and command and you will wish you had died on that ship."

Coral could only give a small nod of assent. The queen sneered at her and then was rising from her throne. The moment she did, the royal court and audience rose as well and bowed before her. Her tentacles curled and unfurled against the throne and floor, everywhere at once. It was both fascinating and frightening.

"You may all leave. Caspian, once you deposit this filth into your home, come to my chambers. I will have a few words with you." And with that being said, the audience cleared, and the queen swam away, trailed by the Personal Guards that had crowded around the throne.

CASPIAN

HE TOOK HER FROM THE PALACE, PULLING HER ALONG HIS side by the upper arm, as he hadn't even bothered to untie her wrists. She tried memorizing the hallways he jerked her down, but the zigzag pattern melded with her fear and anger made her forget every turn. It was nothing but an endless expanse of dark marble and bubbles of light floating across the water like flying lanterns. Salamanders scuttled across the walls, baring hissing teeth and swatting in their direction with vicious claws.

Coral yelped and cringed, only to earn herself a hard squeeze in the arm from Caspian.

He led her out what appeared to be a back door. She could no longer hear shouting crowds demanding her death in their spitting language. She was grateful for that reprieve, at least. There was, however, a young merboy waiting with Redwave. The moment they swam down the front steps, the child handed Matthias—no, she reminded herself, *Caspian*— the reins, giving Coral a curious once-over.

Caspian picked her up by the waist and dropped her onto

Redwave's back, climbing on behind her. With a click of his tongue, Redwave shot through the polished streets of the kingdom. There was no furious crowd of alien creatures, no cruel ceremony as they left. As they darted through water, it was like they didn't even exist at all. At the speed they were going, Coral fought not to topple off and not to cringe at the hand Caspian laid on her waist to keep her from falling over.

When they finally arrived at their destination minutes later, Redwave pulled to a stop. Caspian hopped off the hippocampus' back and reached up to pull Coral down from the animal. She glared at him, but the glare disappeared when she saw where they were.

Even despite the terrifying coil in her stomach and violent lurching that made her want to vomit, she still found a sliver of awe at the home before them.

It was as big as a mansion, domed and made out of the same black obsidian as the rest of the city, but this place seemed different somehow. Maybe because at the base of the home, the black stone appeared to be chipped and cracked. Underneath it glowed electric blue light, spreading out like a latticework of veins over the entirety of the outside of the home. The design looked like the crisscrossing of a spider web, sparkling against a dark night.

Caspian tossed Redwave's reins to a waiting groom and pulled at Coral's arm. There were massive steps that twisted up to a vast, open entryway that he hauled her towards. Since she didn't want any more help from him than was necessary, she made the attempt of the upward swim alone. Her tail flapped awkwardly behind her and only seemed to slow them both down. Caspian sighed a breath of impatience and tugged her to the top.

An open door with gilded edges of sapphire and gold with a curved top loomed in front of them. She caught glimpses of a foyer inside, a five-tier chandelier made of glittering rubies and coins like they'd been pilfered from a pirate's treasure chest, little balls of blue light flickering like fire from candles.

Three mermaids came into focus in front of her, perfectly aligned in a row with their heads bowed. Their submissive gestures made them easy to overlook, which was exactly what Coral had done. She stared at them then.

They were all surprisingly similar in bright pink tails and hair—if what Coral was staring at could even be *called* hair. Instead of having pretty, floating tresses of silk like the queen and some of the other merfolk she'd already seen, they had the curling tendrils of fat tentacles on their heads. The tentacles moved about of their own volition, twining around the mermaids' faces, necks, and arms as if caressing them gently. That was where similarities ended. Where two of the mermaids had skin flushed in a color between red and pink, the third had skin as brown as Caspian's.

"Welcome back, Lord Caspian," they said in unison.

Lord? He was a *lord* now? Coral tried not to frown at that. Caspian ignored their greeting, and with an imperious swish of his tail, swam past them into the open doorway. As soon as the doors were closed behind them, Caspian whipped Coral around. She let out a small shriek of surprise and flinched when he raised his hands up. She closed her eyes and waited for the blow that was sure to come, but instead she felt a tugging at her wrists and then... freedom.

Coral blinked and brought her hands to her face. He'd cut off her bindings. The relief of it nearly had her sobbing. She rubbed across her raw, aching wrists. They were bright red and mottled with bruises, the flesh swollen and painful. She didn't bother thanking him when he was the one who had tied them together in the first place. Every wound against her flesh, every scar she would bear because of her vicious drag through the city, would remind her of this. Of him.

Caspian said nothing to her, though. He barely looked at her for more than a fragment of a second. He turned to the three mermaids and began ordering them about. "Go fix a warm bath for our guest. You go fix a warm meal, and you go find something for her to wear."

The mermaids murmured something inaudible and swam hurriedly away. When they were gone, they took all sort of security Coral had felt with them there. She was now alone with Caspian.

And he was finally looking at her.

Coral crossed her arms against her chest to cover the skin exposed through the tatters and tears of the cloth he'd given her. That seemed like so long ago now. He had seemed a different merman back then. Not quite friendly, but protective. If she would have known then his plans for her now, she would have gladly let the sharks devour her.

The strangest thing was, Coral didn't feel afraid of him. Frightened of the situation, yes. But she wasn't afraid of *him*. Perhaps it was because he'd protected her previously. Or maybe it was because all her fear had melted to make room for her anger. It burned so hotly she thought she might explode.

"I would think you owe me your gratitude," Caspian said suddenly, breaking through her thoughts.

Coral gaped at him. "What?" *Was this fucker serious?* She could practically hear Olivia shouting in her ear, fueling Coral's own bravery.

"I did save your life."

"Only to condemn me to slavery!" Her chest heaved an irate breath as she screamed. Her fins seemed to respond to her mood, flaring at her sides.

Caspian just stared at her with lowered eyelids. He didn't blink; he was almost apathetic in the way he carried himself and *that* was what finally made fear crawl icily up her spine.

Coral found herself caught in the web of his gaze. Never before had she felt so much like prey as she did in that moment.

His eyes were a multitude of colors, like the scales on an iridescent fish. Blue, green, and the tiniest flecks of gold. The brightness seemed dull somehow. Bereft of warmth, of *life*.

As if her gaze was hurting him—because she saw the truth, or something else, she wasn't sure—he turned away brusquely. "There are worse things," he said softly. So softly, she almost didn't hear him.

It wasn't the type of thing that warranted a response, if only because she couldn't fathom what could be worse than what had already happened to her, but Coral found herself asking, "What could be worse?"

Caspian seemed startled that she'd even answered him. He jerked his gaze back to hers, his eyes wide with a strange look in them, a look she couldn't quite describe or understand. It was a long while before he answered. "To be condemned to slavery *and* be alone in the world."

Conveniently, Coral was both. At least he wasn't alone. He had his *queen*. "Why did you speak out for me at the trial?"

Caspian shrugged his shoulder, and with a powerful push of his tail and the wave of his arms, swam back a few strokes. "Does it matter?"

"You know it does."

Caspian swam in low, lazy circles around her, eyeing her from head to tailfin as if studying her so that he might understand how she worked—like some object. "I said as much in the royal court. You should clean up the mess made by your people."

Coral wasn't sure if she believed that, but it didn't seem like he'd be willing to tell her the truth anyway.

"Why did you lie about your name?"

He stopped swimming, causing a swirl of bubbles to form around his jerking arms and tailfin. "Because I did not trust you," he answered after a while.

"Why? Because I'm human?"

"Because I do not trust anybody."

Coral frowned at him. "You seem to trust your queen well enough."

The mention of the queen had his tense mask locking into place at once. His full lips formed a tight line, his eyes flaring before dying down to a dull color, and he floated erectly. Coral would have felt sorry she'd mentioned it if she hadn't been so curious about his reaction.

Caspian didn't have a reply to her comment. He just looked over her shoulder and nodded. "Take her. Do not let her out of your sight. I must see to the queen." And with that, he turned on his tail and swam back the way they'd came.

Coral turned jerkily in the water to find one of the mermaids in front of her. Her pretty brown skin was hidden beneath a drab gray dress, layered over with a fishing net. Hooks were twisted together to form a belt that swung low on her wide hips.

"Your bath is ready, Miss Bennett," she said in a saccharin sweet voice. She looked at Coral with an upturned chin, curiosity dancing behind her dark eyes. She didn't look frightened at all, as if she dealt with humans-turned-mermaids on a regular basis. At least she didn't look like she wanted to kill her like all those on the outskirts of the city had tried to do.

Coral nodded and leaned forward then began flapping her tail the way she'd seen Caspian do it, moving her arms as though she were in a swimming pool and started forward in the water. The mermaid made a chortled sound of gentle amusement, but Coral ignored her and kept at it. Thrusting tail. Moving arms. Repeat. The strain swimming had on her already injured shoulders was painful. After having them tied for a week behind her back they were sore and it hurt to move them, but Coral would be damned if she let these merfolk pull her through the water again.

She followed the mermaid into a brightly colored bathroom. It was grand in comparison to her meager lodgings back in Colorado. It wasn't in that dreadful black color either. This bathroom was white with gold trimming and splotches of blue, green, and red. There was a human bathtub in the middle of the room that looked like an antique. The room had shelves made of white shell and coral. Aligned on it were a variety of clear bottles filled with colorful sand, sea sponges in all shapes sizes and colors, dozens of golden trimmed mirrors covered in algae, decorative shells, and brightly colored tubeworms. A low chandelier made of sea glass swung along with the water current on the ceiling, where a blue and white light seemed to actually burn from it.

The mermaid led Coral to the tub. It was claw footed and rusted at the bottom but perfectly polished on the inside. Coral stared at it longingly and when she felt a touch on her shoulders, she jumped, tripping over her fins somehow and crashing back to the edge of the tub.

"Sorry," the mermaid apologized, holding her hands up in a gesture of surrender. Coral didn't mistake the flash of inquiry in her eyes. "We need to get those rags off and bathe you."

"I can bathe myself," Coral said defensively, pushing herself up and crossing her arms against her chest. The movement tilted her off balance and nearly sent her toppling again.

"I am sure you can," the mermaid replied, her eyes flickering over Coral's wobbly figure. "But I cannot leave you to your own. And this is my job. Come on, lest we both face his wrath." With strong fingers, she began prying away at the cloth covering Coral's upper body.

As it peeled from her skin, she felt exposed. Not just because of her nudity, but like her skin was flayed open for all to see. Half the time, she felt like a rotting infection that had festered for too long. Sometimes, she could still feel the phantom hands bruising her flesh. Now any touch felt painful, even when it was anything but. At least, at one point it had felt that way. Coral wondered if her body was starting to just grow numb to it, while her quintessentially fucked up mind bore the brunt of those memories.

The maid dropped the tattered material to the floor with a sound of disgust.

Coral floated naked in the middle of the room and covered her arms over her breasts, the feeling of discomfort amplified in the presence of this mermaid she didn't know. It prevented her own curiosity from taking hold and studying her new form like she hadn't had a chance to before. She just wasn't interested in exploring every aspect of her new body in front of someone else.

The mermaid clucked and fussed like a mother hen, pushing Coral's hair back from her face and checking her wounds and bruises. "Barbaric way to treat a lady," she grumbled with genuine offense. "Even if you *are* an *anthropos*. Now, what scent would you like?"

Coral stared at her, a little bewildered by her reactions. "Scent?"

The mermaid nodded, the tentacles around her head curling against her cheek. She pushed at them away impatiently. Coral tried not to stare at the way they moved over her shoulders eerily. "For the bath. What scrub would you like? We have many."

"Oh." Coral blushed. "Well, um, whichever is fine."

The mermaid clucked and went over to the shelf, her

fingers flickering over the jars. "So many options..." she hummed to herself. Finally, she carefully chose a bottle filled with red and white sand and turned to smile at Coral. "Sand scrub from Bora Bora with a hint of wild sea berries." She pulled the lid off and the smell pierced through Coral's nostrils. It was a scent that reminded her of the kiddie shampoo she used as a child, the kind with the fish bottle, the kind she always wanted to swallow. "Smells good enough to eat. Now, let me help you into the tub."

Coral allowed herself to be settled into tub. Cold porcelain met her back, making goosebumps kiss along her naked flesh. Her gaze focused on the smattering of scales against her forearms. In the light, with fear gone, she noticed details about herself that she hadn't before.

Details that she suddenly pushed away for later examination as the mermaid leaned over the tub and dumped the warm sand over her body.

"You smell like the very dead," the mermaid observed, causing Coral to flush.

She had the urge to reply that *maybe* she smelt and looked bad because she'd been locked up for days, but before she knew it, the mermaid was practically assaulting her, pulling her arm out and dropping sand onto her and began scrubbing. The sand was coarse against her skin or maybe it was just because of the vigorous way the mermaid rubbed it across her body.

The mermaid's movements were precise and fast. She finished one arm and went to the other, lathering the sand onto her body and massaging. Without a hint of shyness, she repeated the motion against her chest, her back, and then she reached down for Coral's tail. The sand lathered away any dirt and smell that had accumulated during that hard week she'd been in a prison cell.

When the mermaid finished her task, she swam over to

the shelf, tapping her chin in thought before she grabbed a squishy-looking tube and came back to Coral's side. She barely got a glimpse of the thing before the mermaid was squeezing it and a sweet-smelling, thick, frothy cream was poured onto her head. Fingers dug into her scalp and began pulling through the tangled tresses of her dark hair. Within moments, all the grime and algae Coral had been covered with was gone and she felt clean.

"Up you go, Miss Bennett." Coral's arms were caught in her firm grip and she was guided up and out. "Here, put this on." She seemed to produce a spongy towel out of nowhere and wrapped it around Coral's shoulders. "Come now, let us get you into some comfortable clothing."

There was a door, not the one they entered through, that the mermaid opened. It led into a massive bedroom. A monstrous clam shell against the wall with a spongy middle, and bright anemones flowing along the edges, taking up the entire center of the room. There was shelving in the room attached to the walls made of driftwood and another, richer material. It shone brightly like mother of pearl, but it was bare of things. A full-length mirror rested in a corner of the room, the gild rusting away beneath the water, though through the cracks, Coral could make out a golden color.

Coral caught sight of herself in the thing. Empty eyes stared back, and she had to quickly look away from her reflection before she burst into tears like a large part of her so desperately wanted to do and had avoided.

The mermaid brought her back to reality with her mutterings as she went to the end of the clam shell bed and picked up a folded cloth, letting it unfurl and sway with the current of the room. It was a dark purple dress that looked as smooth as silk.

As if reading her thoughts, the mermaid said, "Seaworm silk. There is nothing smoother in the ocean. Come."

Coral swam forward, dropped the robe, and managed to stay afloat while the mermaid slipped the smooth gown over her body. It felt weird to be without a bra, but the outfit was so comfortable, and it had felt like too long since she'd last worn anything decent that she didn't complain about it. Besides, she didn't exactly sag in the water; she just looked... perkier, her nipples piercing the thin material of the dress. The seaworm silk was a little loose in the waist but tight around her chest. She seemed to have lost a little weight in places she didn't want and kept the heavy boob weight. What a nuisance.

"You have a strange figure," the mermaid observed. "Not like the mer. You are all fat and curves." She trailed a hand against the side of her hip, causing Coral to jump. The mermaid's expression softened along with her voice. "You also fright very easily. Rest easy, human. You are safe now."

Coral snorted. "Safe? Yeah, right." She smoothed the silk down the front of her tail. It really was a pretty color. After all she'd been through, at least she could appreciate the fine make of everything that surrounded her for a moment.

"You will be safe from harm here. It could have been much worse for you, you know. You have Caspian to thank for that."

Again, Coral snorted and swam over to the clamshell bed, sitting tentatively on it. The anemones sucked at her tail when she went through them, creating a stinging, clean sensation against her scales. The bed was soft and bouncy. She lay still but her body floated up a fraction above the bed.

"Now, there is a matter of dinner. Shall I escort you to the dining room or will you take a tray here?"

The answer was poised on the tip of her tongue, but she held herself back instead to ask, "Will his *lordship* be joining us for dinner?"

The mermaid did not reply right away. Coral sat up to

look at her, wondering why she was taking so long to answer. The mermaid turned to her and replied stiffly, "Lord Caspian will not be joining us. He will be busy with the queen tonight."

Coral dropped her head back to the cushioned sponge and thought to herself, *Of course he will be.*

"I know how hard this must be for you, Miss Bennett. You find yourself in a strange world, surrounded by strange creatures, and if rumors are to be believed, you have been treated too callously."

"If you call being dragged through the streets, abused, then locked away to starve, then yes. Callously."

"Forgive me for being so forward, Miss Bennett, but it seems you have a predilection for danger."

At this, Coral sat up in bed. A blustering reply came to her lips, but what she shrieked instead was, "What?!"

The mermaid was smirking, though it was obvious she was trying very hard not to do so. "You have quite the mouth on you."

That was funny, Coral thought. She'd never been accused of being anything other than demure before. Quiet. Reserved.

Broken.

Mouthy was Olivia's descriptor.

"Please do not take this the wrong way," the mermaid continued. "As, since you are to live here, I had hoped we could become friends. And if you permit it, then I just want the best for you. But, if you keep it up, you will find yourself suffering."

As if she wasn't already suffering. She blew out a slow, watery breath. "Because Caspian will punish me?" she demanded.

The mermaid stared at her. "It is not Caspian you have to worry about, miss." Her gaze went distant, like she was lost in the vestiges of a memory that Coral couldn't see. "There are worse things to fear than the one who gave you a second chance at life."

Coral wanted to reply. Truly, she did. But as she opened her mouth to speak, it was too late.

The mermaid was already gone.

THE CRUEL QUEEN

QUEEN ULLA LOUNGED AGAINST HER GLAMOROUS CLAM shell bed in nothing but a white silk robe. It was belted loosely around the waist, the folds of the material slipping from the sinuous curves of her shoulders. The pink of her skin was on display, from the high arch of her neck, the sharp blades of her collarbones, down to the high curves of full breasts. Her hair was unbound, free of the heavy restraints of her extravagant crowns, white tresses floating around her face.

On any other occasion, he would have reached out to push them out of the way in a romantic gesture that would leave her almost breathless and him disgusted in a gut-clenching way he would never dare show.

This was not any other occasion.

The queen glared at him as she sat up. It was a vicious look, one that cracked like a whip, seared like a knife, and sent lesser merfolk swimming away. The tentacles of her lower body began creeping towards him; one of them snapping out to catch his wrist in a tight grip. He did not dare pull it away. He stood still as she used him as leverage to pull herself up and swim in front of him. The shoulders of her robe fell down to pool at her elbows, though she made no move to fix herself.

"My little merman," she purred with an angry smile. "What tricks are you playing?"

Caspian forced his eyebrows to furrow in confusion as he asked, "Tricks, my queen?"

It was apparently the wrong thing to say. Her grip on his wrist tightened enough to break his bones. He did not cry out in pain, for he had suffered much worse than this, and she had tortured him with more than the tightness of a grip. The queen's fingers danced across his arm until they found his cheek. She tapped the razor-sharp nails against his flesh.

"Do not play coy with me, Caspian." She dug her fingernail into his cheek, and he felt the sting of his flesh being opened and felt the warm trickle of blood flowing from the wound. She brought her blood-stained nail away from his face and pressed it sensually against her tongue quickly before it wisped away in clouds through the water. The queen closed her eyes in ecstasy as she tasted Caspian. "You spent some time with the *anthropos* on the way back from your mission." There was accusation when she opened her eyes.

"Only a few hours, Your Majesty."

Her white brows drew together, lips turning down into a frown. "A few hours is enough to fall under a spell."

Caspian quirked his lip to the side and brought the queen's hand up to his lips but felt the touch like an agonizing brand. "The only spell I am under is yours, my queen." He kissed her knuckles. "For how can anyone else enchant me when you are the image of delectable perfection?" He kissed the back of her hand. "So smooth..." He kissed her forearm. "So soft..." He pulled her closer to kiss the exposed pink flesh of her shoulder. She shuddered under his touch. "So beauti-ful..." He kissed her neck, touching his tongue to the most sensitive part of her skin. "I could never want for more." He pressed open-mouthed kisses to the base of her throat, listening as she started to come apart in his arms with need.

Caspian swallowed the rising emotions that threatened to swell up to his throat at her moans and murmurs. He forced it down and concentrated on her, on pleasing the queen in his arms. A queen who was smooth all over, a queen with magic stronger than Neptune's, and as lovely and alluring as a siren.

A queen with the power to destroy him with the wave of her hand.

A thick tentacle pressed against the back of Caspian's exposed neck. He shuddered and not for the reasons Queen Ulla thought, though he would be a fool to tell her that. Another tentacle wrapped around the bottom of his tail.

He groaned against her throat.

She trilled with laughter and pushed him away to look into his eyes. Her hands slid up the sides of his face, fingers tracing patterns on his skin. He smiled at his queen, and then cringed when he felt her razor-sharp claws dig deeply into him.

"Do not ever seek to embarrass me again, Caspian." She dug them in deeper and he groaned at the pain, even if he didn't want to. "If you do, you know what will happen to her."

Caspian swallowed the lump in his throat and nodded slowly. "Forgive me, my queen. I meant no insult. I was only thinking of your realm and our future."

"*Our* future?" She snorted. "You will not be in any future much longer if you anger me again." She pulled her fingers out with a loud sucking noise and watched the blood leave her fingers and swirl with the water above her. "Now, have a servant fetch me Matthias and Zalyn. They arrived back from their mission a few hours ago, and I will have need of you all." She gave him a sultry smile and swam back to her enormous bed.

Caspian bit the inside of his cheek and did her bidding. When Zalyn and Matthias—the *real* Matthias—arrived, they sneered at him before bowing low to the queen.

Zalyn and Matthias were also a part of Queen Ulla's Personal Guard, and thus wore the same uniform as Caspian. A black coat secured together by the tentacles of a squid that rested on their shoulders.

Zalyn and Matthias rose without waiting for the queen's permission. That insolence would have gone noticed if it had been anyone other than them. But they were her *Personal* Guards. In every sense of the words.

"My queen," Zalyn drawled in his soft, deadly voice. "To what do we owe this pleasure?"

"Zalyn, Matthias..." The queen leaned back against her sponge cushions, letting her robe slip from her arms, completely exposing her.

Caspian stared, and in his mind, he heard another voice and saw another face. A face with white skin and sapphire eyes. *"Matthias."* He had cringed every time she had said that name. It physically hurt to hear her call him by a name that was not even his, and he could not even fathom why. Just like he could not fathom why he longed to hear her call him by his true name, just to hear the word escape her lips.

"My queen, how you tempt me," Matthias said, placing a hand to his chest in mock flattery. When he pulled it away, he'd ripped away the squid with it, tearing open the lapels of his jacket. There was a primal savagery about his movements, something wild and untamed inside of him. Zalyn was the quieter of them, but it made him all the more violent and dangerous, because the merfolk could not see it. The murderous gleam of his eyes.

Beside Matthias, Zalyn was slowly prying off the squid that held together his jacket, never taking his eyes off the queen. She looked from merman to merman until her eyes finally rested on Caspian.

"What are you waiting for, my little merman?" Queen Ulla smiled. Her hand slowly and sensually began to stroke her own flesh. Her hip, her stomach, and up her breast. She squeezed and molded herself in her palm, taking her thumb and forefinger to squeeze her nipple and gasp aloud, all the while staring at Caspian. "I told you I had need of you," she gasped, her voice rising in desperation as she worked herself to pleasure.

Caspian smiled at his cruel queen and began stripping himself, pulling the uniform jacket from his shoulders and tossing it off to the side. This, this was familiar. The lust in her eyes, the wanting. None of it was real and he took no joy in it, yet it did not matter how disgusting he always felt afterwards or how he wished he could change out of his own skin and wear one the witch had not touched.

He would live this a thousand times over if only to serve his true purpose. It did not matter what she used him for.

Because he was using her, too.

SWIMMING LESSONS

CORAL SLEPT SOUNDLY THAT NIGHT, DESPITE THE MEMORIES
that plagued her dreams. Memories of every moment leading
up to this. First, she dreamt of Olivia, of the fear on her pale
face just before debris of the ship flew up to block her out
entirely. She dreamt of flying through air before sinking into
the water. All of the images rolled through her unconsciousness. Sound became a tangible thing, given life and form.
Metal screeching against metal became a kraken-like monster,
pushing limbs against the ship until it exploded. There was
the beautiful song that beckoned her from the darkness and
she followed, stopping face-to-face before a circular window.
Coral stared out of it, not daring to even blink. Her heart
beat faster when a hand thumped against the glass and stayed
there.

When she opened her eyes the next morning, the images
eluded her. All she knew when she awoke was that she was no
longer tired or in pain. Her wrists were still a little sore, but it
was just a dull pang. More than anything, she was weary.
Weary of what the day would bring.

Caspian had told the queen he would watch over her

while she was cleaning up the mess of humans, that he'd be the one to teach her the ways of the dark merfolk. Even worse, the queen had ordered them to be tied together anytime they left his house. Coral dreaded it with every fiber of her being. She didn't think she'd be able to stand being so near him, dealing with the odd mixture of everything he was. The arrogance and tension, the aloofness and...

Coral groaned and fell back to the bed, her hair floating wildly over her face. She pushed it back with a frustrating motion. She really was going to have to ask one of the mermaid servants—whose names she hadn't even bothered asking, she realized—to find her some hair ties. Having her hair in her face and floating in her mouth wasn't very pleasant and she was itching to put them into twin braids.

"Are all *anthropos* this lazy?" a deep voice said from the doorway.

Coral gasped and shot up in the bed, only to wince when her head hit the top part of the canopy. She'd put too much force on her tail and had shot up like a rocket. Relaxing it now, she gently floated back on the sponge and sent a glare at Caspian where he floated.

He was leaning against the colorful frame, his tail curled leisurely under him. His arms were crossed against his chest and gone was his ridiculous personal guard uniform. Instead, he was wearing armor composed of overlapping scales in light blue and silver. On his shoulders, he sported large golden plates that had edges as sharp as shark teeth. Maybe they *were* shark teeth; Coral wouldn't be surprised. The scales of the armor appeared to be made of metal, covering his torso and waist. The attire was tight against his chest and high-lighted the bulging muscles of his body. And it was a *lot* of muscle...

Coral glared at him. She didn't trust anyone as spectacu-larly built as him. There was something wrong with men who worked out religiously and cared more about chasing a tread-mill to nowhere instead of opening a library book. She'd trusted Trent despite her misgivings about him being a rich gym junkie. *Never again.* She'd trusted *Matthias* and that had led to her enslavement. She would not trust the Caspian floating before her, *whoever he really was.*

"What do *you* want?" she demanded, a bite of vehemence lacing the question. The conversation she'd had with the mermaid the night before was at the forefront of her mind, and there was a fearful, daring part of her that wanted to test the theory out and prove that he really was a danger to her.

He unfurled his massive body from the doorway and swam slowly and deliberately towards Coral. She flinched and tried sinking deeper into the soft sponge of the bed. He took note of her discomfort but made no move to stop inching closer to her. Caspian helped himself to a seat on the edge of the bed, ignoring at the anemones clinging to his body.

Coral pulled the thin, silk blanket over herself as he edged closer and closer... She used it as a barrier between them; even realizing that it was futile against this massive merman, it still gave her comfort. She pulled it up to her chin as he edged closer until they were face to face. Up close she noticed he had tracings of pink fleshy scars on his cheeks, obviously newly inflicted, as he hadn't had them the day before.

The tip of his round nose touched hers softly. She didn't know why but her hands started moving by their own voli-tion, lowering the blanket from the secure place at her chin. Caspian's eyes followed the movement then darted back up to stare into her own.

He opened his mouth and growled, "Get. Up."

"Wha—?"

"Get up, *anthropos.* The hour is late, and we have much to do today."

Coral's mind must have been groggy with sleep still. She

stared at him with confusion, any earlier fluttering she'd felt in her stomach dissipating at the sight of his now frowning face. "What do you mean?"

Caspian let out an exasperated sigh. "Neptune take me! I thought Knowledge Keepers were smarter than this."

"I'm a *librarian*—"

"Did you forget all about the trial and the queen's orders? Get up. Now, or I will drag you downstairs by your pretty little fins." As if to accentuate his point, he tugged the covers all the way off her and flicked his fingers against her exposed fins. They flared and fluttered, sending a tingling jolt through Coral's body. The action had seemed shockingly intimate. Maybe he had felt it too, because he'd paused and was staring with wide eyes at her sapphire blue tail. She wondered why he looked so fascinated. He'd been the one to make it. Her fins flared again under his gaze. Caspian cleared his throat and shot back quickly from the bed. "Hurry up, *anthropos*. I will not warn you again." He turned and began to swim away.

"Wait," Coral cried out. She'd promised herself she wouldn't trust him, and she didn't want to, but her body ached and longed to keep him near her if only a bit longer. It didn't make sense. She hated him, she hated what he'd done to her. But in this strange world, he was the only thing that was familiar, and that's what she was holding onto. Not him and his confusing hot and cold emotions. "What are we doing today?"

Caspian looked over his shoulder. "Today, I will teach you to swim." And then he exited the room.

As soon as he was gone, the mermaid who had helped her bathe the night before swam in. She still wore the fishing net over dull cloth. Her tail flicked as she swam over to the window and threw open draperies. Specks flew across the water with her movements and bright, fluffy tubeworms bloomed around the windows like flowers. No light seeped through the glass panes and that could have been because of the dark kingdom. Like they didn't want any happiness to get in.

As if reading her thoughts, the mermaid let out a song note, high-pitched and beautifully sung. Immediately, a bright ray of yellow shone through the window to illuminate the room in scintillating hues.

"How did you do that?" Coral asked in amazement.

The mermaid didn't stop her duties as she answered, "All mer have magic. I happen to project mine using my voice." She made her way to the bed and began pulling off spongy pillows.

"Are you a siren?" Coral sat up, throwing her tail over the edge of the bed. She braced her hands on the edge of the bed, ready to use them to make a jump-swim.

The mermaid laughed. "If I were a siren, I would not be working here. Let me tell you." She chuckled again and pulled off the blankets.

"But there are sirens? I mean, they do exist? Not all mermaids are sirens?"

"Of course not all mermaids are sirens. Thank your lucky moon for that. I imagine you would have suffered a great deal more if sirens would have found you at that shipwreck. Nasty creatures. But very beautiful. Meaner than sharks with teeth ten times as sharp. Now..." She clapped her hands suddenly. "We must get you dressed. Caspian will be tutoring you on your new body that way you will not be as helpless as a guppy."

The thought of finally being able to swim for herself was appealing and had Coral anxious for the day ahead.

The mermaid helped her out of her night dress and brought in a whole different style clothing. This was a plain medieval-looking tunic in black. It was long enough to go past her waist and cover the top of her tail. The mermaid belted a gray-brown leather belt at her waist and crisscrossed another set of belts across her chest and back.

"Are you preparing me for battle?" Coral eyed herself in the full-length mirror curiously.

Her skin looked extra pale in the black clothing, but it really made her eyes and tail stand out prominently. Her tail was the same sapphire as her eyes, if a little darker, and when the yellow of the light caught on her scales, they shone silver. The clinging tendons down the middle were a darker color than the rest of her plump tail. She still hadn't explored that particular part of herself and was curious to do so once she had a moment to herself. Scales covered her arms, shoulders, torso and the backs of her hands, a scattering of blue dots like freckles across a face.

Though her body was still bruised and covered in scratches, her skin pale and eyes dark and tired, her mermaid body was incredible.

"What is this made of?" Her hands ran across the front of the tunic. "It's so different from human clothing. The texture feels... different. And what about those lights in the chandelier? It looks like fire. How do the clothes stay in place and not float up like human clothes would?"

"Training with Caspian is likely to be a battle in itself," the mermaid replied. There was a hint of amusement in her tone at the barrage of questions. "He will be very strict with you in every matter. Best to dress you like a training soldier. No use in wearing dresses that your tail will get caught in while you swim. As for the rest..." She cocked her head to the side. A tentacle wrapping around her neck, as if choking her, and Coral barely repressed a shiver. "Garments here are made from materials of the sea. That would explain why they don't react in the water the same way your human clothes would. Just like the red fire of humans, we have blue water fire here that burns just as bright and just as hot. Does that answer your questions? Now, we must hurry for your swimming lesson."

"I suppose..." Coral said a little reluctantly. "Is he even qualified to teach me to swim?"

The mermaid laughed as she began running an amethyst studded comb through her hair. "Caspian is *very* capable of teaching you to swim. He used to be a leading commander in the Royal *Stratia,* you know."

"He was?" Coral wasn't entirely sure what the word *Stratia* meant yet, but she was positive it had something to do with an army.

"He was the best in the Atlantean kingdom." She smiled like a proud mother boasting about her son's accomplishments. Funny, she didn't look old enough to be his mother. Coral guessed her to be in her late twenties, if that. Then she wondered if the mer aged like the humans or if they were like dogs, or immortal fairies in legends.

"So, he's not from the Dark Waters? He's from Atlantica? Why is he part of the queen's Personal Guard then, if he was the best soldier?"

The mermaid paused, comb halfway through her hair. Coral tried reading her face in the mirror, but her tentacles curled around her cheeks, hiding her expression. A moment later, she resumed her brushing and the tentacles curled away to reveal her sad smile. "That is not my place to say." She began clipping up her hair with an assortment of shells and thin rope.

Coral watched her work in silence, but her brain was running miles. Something was going on here; there was something about Caspian that she wasn't telling her. Of course, it wasn't any of Coral's business anyway. She shouldn't even care about his past. All she wanted to do was get out of the Dark Waters and make it home, but to do that she needed to bide her time, gain information, and gain trust.

"I never asked you your name," Coral said.

The mermaid smiled as she tugged gently at her last floating tendril of hair. "Zenara."

"That's a pretty name. Do you think I could learn magic, Zenara?"

Zenara put the last pin in place. "Anything is possible, Miss Bennett."

She hoped. For learning magic seemed to be her only hope at freedom at this point. *Trust,* something whispered through her mind. She wanted to, but it was hard to know who was friend and who was foe.

She really hoped Zenara was the former.

"Zenara?"

"Yes, Miss Bennett?"

Their eyes met in the mirror. "Can we be friends?"

Zenara's expression softened, and the smile she gave Coral was genuine. Coral wanted to believe it, and so she did. For a moment, she allowed herself to bask in that expression, pushing away the dark voices that told her she was an awful judge of character. For a single second, she let her resolve weaken and she let herself believe that they were more than what they actually were.

"Friends." Zenara's hand closed gently over her shoulder. "I would like that very much."

"No, no, no. You are doing it *wrong*," Caspian lectured. It wasn't the first time. Zenara had been right about one thing. He was strict. The minute she'd set fin downstairs he was all over her like white on rice.

First, he began by listing rules. She was to be up at the crack of dawn every morning. She was to be dressed and in front of him at a certain time. If she was not, there would be punishment. He then laid out their schedule. Swimming lessons first, breakfast afterwards, followed by community service and helping around the queen's castle with whatever it was he did.

He was treating her like she was a soldier and he a drill sergeant.

Already her muscles screamed in protest at every move she made. He was *very* specific in his instructions. Apparently, training to be a mermaid wasn't *just* swimming. He'd made her feel her tail, feel the weight of every inch, stroke her fins, feel the warmth and strength of the current. She had to move with precision and choreograph her every movement.

It was madness.

"What did I do wrong that time?" Coral was breathing heavy, resting her palms on her tail and leaning over. God, her lower back ached, as did every muscle in her arms and shoulders.

Fitness had never been her thing and swimming required a lot of it. You could find Coral hiding under the covers, eating donut crumbs off her chest instead of running every morning. She wasn't a fucking masochist. The only exercise she did was from her bed to the fridge and back again. This whole thing was a special kind of torture.

"You undulate from the head and roll down your body. Like a wave." He demonstrated, placing his hands together in front of him and undulated his body, just like she'd *tried* to do.

"I thought that's what I was doing?"

"No. You bob your head and your shoulders. You do not undulate."

"I can't undulate! I'm not a belly dancer!"

Caspian looked at her. "Belly dancer?"

"Women who dance with their bellies?" Coral explained. At his blank look, she continued, "It's a form of art. They can move their stomachs and chests around and wear bangles and—"

"I do not see how that matters," Caspian interrupted with exasperation. "I have trained guppies better at survival than you."

"Guppies are born knowing how to swim! I've had a tail for, like, a day!"

"You have had your tail for a week and three days."

"And I was tied up for most of that week in a prison cell, now, wasn't I?" She threw that in his face, hoping to see any little smidge of guilt on his features. But there was nothing. He just glared.

"Again," he ordered strictly, tapping her tail with his own. "Remember: undulate."

"Undulate," Coral growled low so he wouldn't hear. "I'll show you undulate." Loosing a breath, she tried it again, placing one hand on top of the other like he'd showed her, arching her back and lifting her head. With a powerful thrust of her tail, she shot forward. She tried to undulate like he'd told her to do. He said it was best to do it that way to keep sailing through the water. She started with her head and her arms, concentrating on moving them like a wave, letting the motion roll down her spine and through her tail.

"Stop!" Caspian called out.

Coral groaned and tried rearing back, but she tripped over her own tail fin and spun in circles through the water. How embarrassing. *Just hit me with a bus already,* she thought, then wondered if there was a merfolk term for that. *Hit me with a beluga? Whack me with a whale?*

She straightened and turned. Thankfully, he'd taught her how to stay afloat before he'd taught her how to swim, and she was rather good at that, at least.

"What did I do wrong now?"

Caspian's cheek twitched. "Where do I begin? You lack

form and discipline. Your body is too tight. You are thinking too much instead of feeling."

Coral blushed at all her failings. "You told me to swim with my head."

"But you should also swim with your heart. Loosen your limbs. Feel the water caressing your tail, pressing against your body."

Coral closed her eyes and tried to imagine what he was saying. She felt the water all around her, obviously, she was submerged in it.

"You are still thinking like an *anthropos*," he accused.

"That's because I am an *anthropos!*" Coral snapped her eyes open and yelled at him. "You all never fail to remind me that." Frustration had been building in her chest for the past hour, clawing up into a rage-filled monster that wanted out, no matter how hard she tried to keep it tamped down. She swore, she'd never been criticized this badly in her entire life.

"By Neptune." Caspian rubbed a hand over his face. After he stroked his chin, he turned to her. "Again," he demanded. "And do it right this time."

"I've been doing it right this entire time," Coral complained. She turned to begin swimming again but was suddenly whipped back around. Caspian was gripping her by the wrist and pulling her against him. She fell to his chest and looked up into his blazing eyes.

The panic of the sudden aggression clogged in her chest. Her breath froze where it'd been. There was a brief flash of memory. One she'd buried deep and had only caught in flashes in her nightmares. Of fingers wrapping around her throat, pinning her body against a mattress. She felt the burn of her thighs as they were pushed open wide, and the rutting pain of someone drilling into her body, chests pressed tightly together until she felt like she was suffocating.

You're not there anymore, she reminded herself, but her stubborn body refused to cooperate. To pull her out of that moment of helplessness. It melded, the past and the present, making her weak. Maybe she'd always been weak. That pathetic, violated creature still lived inside her, enveloped her body like a skin she couldn't shed no matter how hard she tried.

Caspian shook her, breaking her out of the painful remnants of a past that she'd never escape.

"You have *not* been doing it right," he growled. "You have been disobeying me at every turn. You are insubordinate and uncoordinated. I am trying to *help you* and you do nothing but complain. Ungrateful little *anthropos*."

Rage built a steady nest in her chest, chasing away the breathless sensation from before. It was easy to direct those negative feelings to him. Perhaps they didn't make sense, these flashes of defiance that burned hotly inside of her. But something about it, about this new world, made her feel like the pieces of her were chipping away. This new body made her feel reborn somehow. Still broken, still carrying the weight of something terrible, but it was like she could no longer hide it or the emotions that came with it anymore. They were begging to break free of the confines she'd kept them in, demanding a voice. Fear and truth screamed over each other and came out sounding a lot like fury. And she needed that.

She tried pulling her hand back, but he didn't free it from his iron grasp. If anything, he squeezed tighter. "I suppose I should thank you then?" Coral said between gritted teeth.

"Yes, you should."

She glared up at him. "You're an arrogant bastard, do you know that? *Thank you*? What should I be thanking you for, exactly? For turning me into a mermaid? For throwing me off a hippocampus, tying me up, and dragging me through the streets to be lynched? For lying to me about your real name?

Oh, or maybe I should so kindly thank you for sparing me from death and instead condemning me to a life of slavery under that psychotic *bitch*—ow!"

Caspian flung her hand back at her, hard enough to hurt. He took a stroke back, away from her and turned his head away. Coral cradled the wrist he'd gripped. They were still raw from the ropes and he'd only made it worse.

"I never wanted to hurt you, Coral," he whispered sadly, but that sadness disappeared as soon as it came and he was turning back to her, his face set in a stone mask. This time, though, his voice wasn't as hard or as demanding, but cracked around the edges as he ordered, "Again."

Coral swallowed the lump in her throat and turned back around, placing her hands in front of her and thrusted to begin her swim. She undulated and undulated, going through the room in slow, steady strokes. She waited to hear him call out his criticisms, but it never came. At first, she'd thought he'd left the room but when she snuck a peek, he was staring at her with a look in his eyes that was so heartbreakingly vulnerable, Coral had to look away and keep swimming and hold back her tears.

Because if there was one thing she refused to do, it was cry for Caspian.

THE QUEEN'S DAUGHTER

"Whatever happened to the fearsome commander that could send even the most powerful of mermen screaming like guppies?" Zenara mused from the entryway of his office. Gilded in a clash of gold and obsidian, the mermaid's tentacles were a bright burst of color against what would otherwise be a melancholy space. Then again, nothing was ever dark when Zenara was near.

"Shut up," Caspian retorted. He sat behind a wide mahogany table he'd bought from a merchant's shop; they'd salvaged it from a shipwreck and had enchanted it so it would never rot. He was holding a glinting blade in his hand, the hilt was made of bright aquamarine, cobalt, sapphires, and gold. And the blade, the blade was Atlantean steel, mined in the caves of the underwater volcano.

A remnant of his old life.

One of the only ones he had left.

Zenara swam in without an invitation. Of all his servants, she was the only one who treated him with familiarity and a friendship he'd not find anywhere else. She sat at the edge of his desk, slapping her pink tail against his playfully. He sighed and rewrapped the blade with cloth and placed it back inside the desk drawer.

"Why do you look so gray, Caspian?" she asked sincerely. "Is it because Miss Bennett is not afraid of you? Or is it because you are a terrible teacher?"

"Did you come here merely to taunt me?" Caspian nudged her tail away from his. He was not in the mood for jesting. Not after that first horrendous lesson. He had pushed Coral hard, he knew, but it had been necessary.

"She is not a soldier, you know," Zenara pointed out.

"She has the spirit of a soldier. She would have made a good addition to the *Stratia*. With the proper training." It was an odd thing to admit, merely because it had been years since he'd last met anyone with the nature of the warriors of his home. It was a pleasant shock as much as it infuriated him. Perhaps because she reminded him of everything he could never have and all that he had lost.

"I am surprised you would admit that to me."

Caspian shrugged. "It is the truth."

"Well, you cannot treat her like you used to treat your soldiers. She will not learn that way."

Caspian glared up at Zenara. She just met his glare with a quirky smile of her own. Damn her. "It is necessary that I show her no affection. It will help harden her heart. She will need it for days to come."

"I rather like her soft heart," Zenara mused.

"Soft hearts are easily breakable."

Zenara snorted and began slapping at his tail again. "I do not know who told you such a lie. Drop something soft to the sea floor and it will float back up. Drop something hard and it might well shatter, even below the depths."

Caspian fought back a groan that had wanted to escape since that morning. Instead, he sat straight and tense and glared at his servant. "Stop with the pretend wisdom, Zenara," he warned. "I am not in the mood."

"My wisdom is very real, Caspian. It is why I came to give you advice for tomorrow's lesson. Be gentle. You have hurt her too much already."

"I cannot be gentle. You know that." His hands tightened into fists. He longed to put them through something, to *move*. But for so long he had kept a tight rein against his own emotions that he had long forgotten how to actually show them when they threatened to emerge. That was another thing he despised about Coral being here. She brought out emotions from within him that he would otherwise like to remain hidden.

Zenara sighed. "I know you cannot. I would just hate to see *your* hardened heart break even further." Before Caspian could protest that his heart was *not* broken, she was hopping off the desk and floating upright before him. "I must go back to her."

Caspian stared at her with affection, the only real feeling he would ever dare show anyone. Her tail was bright pink, hidden behind the ugly decorations of cloth and net, but nothing could hide her beauty or heritage, even if she tried. The tentacles surrounding her face were curling and uncurling, the color of pink flesh. It was unnerving. And he could not look at them without thinking of another. When a tentacle curled slowly around her cheek, Zenara pushed it away from her face.

Caspian could not help himself. He reached a hand up to rub his thumb across the curve of her cheek. "You are nothing like your mother," he whispered. Zenara was kind and compassionate. She always had been.

She smiled sadly at him. "Thank Neptune for small favors." She bent and kissed his forehead, much like an older sister would do to a younger sibling. That thought, however, was ridiculous. They were not related, and he was older than her by what felt like centuries. Still, he felt a deep connection to her. It was because of her Atlantean blood. Her copper skin and facial features betrayed her heritage, hinting she was descended from a great household, and the tentacles betrayed something else. She straightened and turned to leave but thought better of it, pausing. "Do not tell her, okay?"

"I would never reveal your secrets." Caspian frowned. If she thought he would, then he had not proven that he was trustworthy.

"Even if I reveal yours?" She looked at him with years of sadness in her eyes.

"Zenara—"

"I do not want her to know just yet. She trusts me, as much as she can trust anyone here, and I do not wish to change that. I wish for us to be friends."

Caspian's fists tightened. "Whatever she feels for you now would still remain if she discovers the truth—"

Zenara laughed softly, but there was no humor in the sound. "Oh, Caspian. No one ever feels the same about me when they learn that I am the queen's daughter."

A TOUCH OF KINDNESS

CORAL COULD BARELY GET UP THE NEXT MORNING. HER muscles quivered at the slightest movement. She'd over-worked them and now they were trying to refuse her commands. But it didn't matter that she was in pain. She swam through it, got ready with the help of Zenara, and made it downstairs in front of Caspian. He floated in that same turquoise and gold uniform, with his arms crossed against his chest.

"You are late," he accused quietly.

She mumbled a half-ass apology that she was sure he couldn't hear anyway. Patiently, she waited for him to give her strict commands and insults on her figure and form. But he was just staring at her, his red hair floating above his head. After a moment, he uncrossed his arms and swam up to Coral, close enough to touch. She tensed at his nearness. Caspian took note of that and didn't freeze, but approached her more cautiously, the way one would approach a frightened dog it didn't want to startle.

"Show me your form," he grumbled deep in his chest as he floated before her.

Coral tried not to let Caspian intimidate her, tried to focus on the swimming lessons. The sooner she learned, the sooner she could plot her escape. So, she got into familiar position and waited for the clicking of his tongue, the harshness of his words.

They never came.

His massive body swam in circles around her, powerful tail stroking the water slowly as he took in her form. She floated still as a statue, feeling her palms tingle with heat and her face redden under the scrutiny of his gaze.

He stopped behind her, and she felt her stomach drop when his big, warm hands palmed her waist.

"W-what are you doing?" she stuttered. Not out of fear, surprisingly, but of something else.

His fingers tightened ever so slightly against her, thumbs trailing small circles on her lower back. "Your form is wrong," he said in a low voice. "I am going to help you." Using his fingers, he guided her back into the correct position, arching her back. His hand splayed against her stomach, and with the other, he trailed a painful line down the length of her spine. She fought not to shiver, not to give in to that touch that scattered her every thought into a frenzy. Where his hand grazed only left tingles, instead of pain in their wake. "There," he whispered. "Perfect."

Caspian's hands left her stomach and back only to go to her shoulders. His fingers poked at her, massaged them until they drooped lower.

"There," he whispered, warm breath blowing against her neck. This time she did shiver. If he noticed, he didn't comment. He was closer now, so close she felt every gloriously hard inch of him pressed against her backside. She felt every detail in the scales of his armor, felt the smoothness of his tail against hers. A treacherous part of her longed for him to wrap his tail around hers like some strange craving.

One she thought had been long buried beneath the broken pieces of her, but it came to life beneath his guiding, gentle touch.

She pushed that sentiment aside and tried to *focus*.

Again.

But it was hard to focus when his hands left her shoulders and began traveling down the length of her arms, over bare skin, enveloping her in his warmth, in... well, in *him*. His hands grabbed her own, and he placed one of her hands on top of the other, fixing her thumbs so they were placed under, not out.

"There," he whispered against the back of her neck.

Coral nearly came undone then and there, and that unnerved her. Because she was resolved in her hatred for him. But this tingling spreading through her body didn't feel like hatred. It felt a lot like desire, and she wondered if the two lines had blurred somehow within the span of a few seconds.

"Is my form correct now?" she asked in a shaking voice. She mentally punched herself for it, too.

He didn't answer. His hands were now encircling her wrists so gently. He seemed to be staring at them. She felt his face next to hers, but he made no comment. His thumbs rubbed the redness of her skin tenderly, as if he were too afraid to hurt her. Coral swallowed past the lump in her throat as she watched his fingers move against her.

"I am sorry," he rasped.

"For what?"

"For hurting you. For everything." He let go of her immediately and took a few strokes back. Coral didn't dare move. "There, your form is perfect now."

Coral nodded and kicked her tail. She shot forward and then began to move her body. She didn't think about it, didn't concentrate. All that ran through her mind was the feel of his skin on hers, the way it had glided over with ease and practice. There had been nothing more torturous than that moment. Nor anything more exciting.

She swam, undulated, kicked, undulated, repeat. She moved her tail against the water, felt it pressing up against her skin. She didn't fight it, didn't try to push against it. She just flowed with it, moved her arms, her stomach, her hips, and tail.

Then there was slow clapping behind her, scattering her thoughts and causing her to drop her form and trip over her own tail. Coral cried out as she somersaulted through the water and landed against a nearby wall with a dull thud.

"Ow." She sat up and rubbed her head. The clapping had stopped. Coral almost dreaded looking up at Caspian, but she did, even if her face was on fire.

The side of Caspian's lip twitched. "We will work on how to stop immediately."

Coral shot him the finger.

COMMUNITY SERVICE

THEY WORKED ON SWIMMING LESSONS FOR ABOUT TWO weeks. She learned how to swim in a tunic, in a flowing gossamer dress, wearing heavy plates like armor and with nothing at all. That part of the lesson had been complicated, but Coral had finally gotten Caspian to agree that Zenara should teach her that part while he hid away in one of his rooms. He'd taught her how to swim backwards, how to swim straight-backed, moving nothing but her tail, how to swim up and down, how to curve through the water, how to swim against a current, how to stay afloat for hours and how to swim in a varying degree of temperatures.

Seeing each other never went beyond the lessons, though. Even if Coral was living under his roof, she rarely swam into Caspian. He began their lessons for hours every morning, and then he'd send her off to lunch while he went away. He never said where, but Coral had a pretty good idea.

The thought shouldn't have filled her with something that tasted acrid like jealousy, but for some reason it did. Caspian was nothing to her but a mentor and slaver. She should hate him, but deep in her heart she knew she couldn't bring herself to anymore. He hadn't even come close to redeeming himself for all of the cruel things he'd done and all of the lies. Coral still hadn't forgiven him, but after that day he'd successfully taught her to swim, after putting his hands all over her body and igniting something deep inside Coral, something had changed in her.

And he hadn't touched her again.

Instead, every day he rushed to his queen's side as if he were burning without her. Coral tried ignoring the feeling that swept through her every time she saw him swim away at the end of their lessons. He barely spoke to her beyond commenting on her progress and giving her swimming tips. They had nothing, *were* nothing. He'd not led her on, so why did she feel betrayed?

"You have mastered the art of swimming." Caspian swam back and forth in front of her that morning. "Now we will go out and you will have to clean the ocean of human filth." He paused, hands clasped behind his back. "You understand what the conditions of your temporary freedom are?"

"Cuffed. Cleaning. No escaping," Coral stated, her words bland and sarcastic. The truth was, she was dreading it. She was dreading being tied up like a dog and being yanked around. They would keep on finding ways to humiliate her for being human, and because of that she needed to find a way to escape.

"This is not a joke, Coral," he said sternly, gaze burning her. "If you make an escape attempt, we will both be killed. Do not think for a moment the queen will not have others in her Personal Guard spying on us. Do not think for a second they will not hesitate to kill you if you try to leave."

"I understand. I really do." It's not like she had anywhere to go anyway. She couldn't swim out in open ocean without any idea of where to go or how to fend for herself in the wild waters. This mission was about surveying the area. Maybe later, if she somehow managed to convince him, he'd teach her to defend herself against various creatures.

"You will have to be tied up again," he warned, eyeing her wrists where the red marks had once been. Even the bruises had long since faded from her skin, but the phantom whispers of the ache still lingered. She rubbed at them self-consciously. The idea of being tied up again gave her rising anxiety that she tried to swallow back down, but it was thick in her throat, a painful swallow.

Like choking on a fucking donut hole. She'd done it before. It wasn't pleasant.

"I know." Her voice was scratchy and thick with emotion.

Caspian eyed her for a grave moment before dipping his head into a small nod. "Then come on."

THEY RODE REDWAVE. It was a good rest for her muscles not to have to swim all the way to their destination. It was difficult keeping track of directions. Without street names, Coral was hopelessly lost.

She rode behind Caspian, her arms wrapped tightly around his waist. He was wearing his Personal Guard uniform jacket, and Coral had the urge to rip it off him and let Redwave trample it to the silt. How could the queen stand to see him in such ridicule when he obviously looked so much better in turquoise and gold armor? Instead, she had him looking like her own personal plaything. She supposed that was the whole point.

Her thoughts were cut off when they finally made it to their destination.

There was a lot of open water, coral reefs, families of different breeds of fish, and sea turtles. Coral would have been amazed by the sight, by being close enough to touch clownfish, dancing sea sponges and starfish.

If it were not for the trash.

She didn't know what she'd expected but it hadn't been this. Trash. Trash *everywhere*. Plastic bottles, cans, bags, and other disgusting things floated underwater and above the surface, expanding out for miles. And the smell... It was horrendous. She tried not to gag, but it was impossible. As a human, she hadn't thought fish or ocean animals besides predators really had a sense of smell, or that scents could transmit into the water, but it was very possible. The stench was overpowering and disgusting.

The waters down here were darker, looking a bit like cloudy muck. Coral looked around with a hand over her mouth both to block out the stench and to cover her shock. A school of seahorses swam by her; upon closer inspection, she noticed one of them carrying trash by its tail.

Tears sprang to her eyes at the sight, but they never fell.

"My god," she nearly sobbed.

This. This is what the humans had done.

It was no wonder they hated her so much. She didn't blame them for feeling the way they did. She had known that humans were polluting the ocean, that was no secret, but actually *seeing* the damage, actually *swimming* through it, *living* it was the real eye-opener. How much of this had been her own doing? How much waste had she unknowingly disposed of that had landed somewhere like this? Of course, she recycled and didn't throw her trash on the ground, but garbage was everywhere. In paper, in plastic bags from grocery stores, even in the things she ordered online.

This was where it all ended up.

"I—I don't know what to say." Coral felt the tears prickling behind her eyes; she blinked to keep them away.

"You see now?" Caspian held tightly to the reins on

Redwave. Maybe that was the only action keeping him steady. Coral really wanted to punch someone herself. Preferably a human. The government. Big corporations. Anyone.

"I—I'm so sorry." The merfolk deserved more than an apology. They deserved a better life. They deserved clean homes. While Coral abhorred her own blatant mistreatment for things she was ignorant of, while she still felt her capture to be unfair, another part of her could sympathize with their reasoning, even if she didn't agree with their methods. She didn't deserve what they'd given her, just like they didn't deserve this.

She turned to Caspian and took the saddlebag from his shoulder. She pulled out the fishnet he'd brought and a sea worm silk bandanna. She tied it around her nose and mouth, pulled on sealskin gloves, and started to go to work.

"Wait," Caspian called out.

Coral turned with impatience to find Caspian holding up rope. Her heart lurched, but she nodded and swam back over to him. She avoided looking into his eyes as he began tying complicated knots around her waist. She was afraid of what she might see in them. Pity? Humor? Jesus, did he think she *deserved* this?

When he finished, he tied the other end of the long rope onto his own wrist and gestured that she go. Coral swam up to the surface, pulling trash and shoving it into her fishnet sack. She repeated this action for what felt like hours. When the fishnet sack was nearly bursting, she went to secure it near a sleeping Redwave, got another net, and began the process all over again.

The waters started darkening by the time she was finished filling up the last of the bags. There were still miles to go.

"Can Redwave carry all of these bags back?" Coral began hefting them over Redwave's saddle; the hippocampus stirred at the interruption and whinnied.

"He can manage." Caspian lifted up a few more bags, securing them across Redwave's back. "We must leave now. It will be nightfall soon. The waters are dangerous at night."

Coral didn't argue. She hurried with her task and when they finished, made their journey back to Caspian's home. Halfway there, they were interrupted. A merman intercepted them on his own hippocampus. The merman wore a Personal Guard uniform. He didn't even have to speak for Coral to know what was happening. It was in the expression on his face as his eyes flicked to her.

The queen was summoning them.

"My, my." The queen lounged against her throne.

Was it possible that she'd gotten much more beautiful since the last time Coral had seen her? She wore a green gown with shining white pearls threaded through the waist and skirt. The sheer material of it flowed over her tentacles and hugged her tightly at her curvaceous chest. Her crown matched her dress, looking like glittering diamonds on fancy curved wire, with green stones of jade and amethyst and dangling bits of sea glass.

"How well you seem to be faring, *anthropos*. Tell me, how was your first day cleaning up your own filth?"

Her elbow was sitting casually on the arm of her throne, her chin in her upturned palm and her fingers tapped lazily against her lips. Two of her Personal Guards were lounging just as lazily as she against the sides of her two headed eel, smirking down at Coral and Caspian.

"What I saw came as a shock to me, Your Majesty," Coral bit out the words, keeping a straight face. Any unpleasant gestures on her part and the bitch queen might just kill her there and then. She wouldn't let that happen.

"A shock indeed." The queen sighed delicately and turned to Caspian. "My little merman..." Her bright red lips curled into a vicious yet sultry smile. "How I have missed you in my chambers. It just is not the same without you, is it boys?"

The mermen on the eel snorted.

Coral tried not to glare at *them*. Just how many did she have in her Personal Guard anyway? And she wondered if these were her favorite. They were both *very* beautiful but polar opposites physical wise.

One of them was muscular; not as muscular as Caspian, but he appeared to have a highly arrogant aura about him. His shoulders were crossed against his chest and he was smirking. His hair was light brown, curling against his forehead from the top but shaved on either side of his head. A sneaking spider web of bleeding ink stretched against his neck and on his hands, hinting at the presence of tattoos. He had a strong, square jaw, perfectly groomed eyebrows, and a tiny fishhook sticking through his nose like a piercing. A copper tail curled from underneath him, his fins flickering in the same lazy demeanor with which he leaned against the throne.

The other merman was skinnier, *leaner* than the other. He wasn't smiling; his face was set in a rather grave expression, but that didn't make him any less handsome. His hair was black and straight, not a strand out of place even underwater. His eyebrows were thick, cheekbones high, face long and thin, and his tail was light gray, near silver in color. There was something about this one that unnerved her, so she avoided his gaze.

"Not the same at all, Caspian." The brown haired one smiled widely. His fins flicked almost like they were echoing the sarcasm of his words.

The black haired one said nothing in response.

"Any time spent away from you is agonizing torture, my

queen," Caspian declared with affection in his voice. The only affection Coral had ever heard him show was when he spoke to his queen. When he spoke to Coral, his voice was stiff and cranky.

Jealousy seared into her like a hot rod, and it didn't belong inside her at all.

"Such pretty words..." The queen touched a finger to her lips in an overtly sexual manner that had Coral both entranced and disgusted. "...but so little actions."

Caspian sauntered up to the throne then. He didn't bow or use any formalities as he had when they first entered the throne room. He wasn't gentle either, when he gripped the queen by the back of her neck and pulled her to him to take her mouth in a hungry kiss.

Coral wanted to look away. She should have, but her eyes fell open as if hypnotized by the workings of his full lips devouring hers. It was an addicting, enchanting sight. The way their mouths worked against each other's in a dance that only they knew the choreography to. As if they had done it before.

Coral suddenly wanted to scream, to cry and rage. But mostly she wanted this over with. She wanted to go home. She wanted to stop hurting and stop feeling whatever it was she felt about a merman who didn't even care about her at all.

The queen gripped the lapels of his jacket, tearing the material apart to expose his chest just before breaking their contact with a loud smack. She gripped him at the shoulders and whipped him around in the water so that he was facing Coral. The jacket was falling off his shoulders, the squid hanging on by only a tendril. The queen looked at Coral, her eyes penetratingly deep and cruel. She didn't break the contact, but she stared back without defiance or any emotion showing on her face. Then, the queen smiled and slid the jacket from Caspian's body, letting it float to the floor, exposing him completely.

Coral stared. There, where the squid had rested on the shoulder of his jacket, was the black ink of a matching tattoo. Black outlining of tentacles stretched out over the massive expanse of his chest, covering his pectoral, shoulder, and even trailed a bit down his right arm.

The rest of his glorious form disappeared. Perfectly aligned abs marked in ridges and hard bumps down his chest, stomach, and on his sides became nothing compared to that tattoo. That tattoo was an insult to his form.

Queen Ulla traced her long nails against the figure slowly. "You see this mark, *anthropos?*" An answer wasn't needed. It was obvious, as Coral was staring at it as if her eyes were pried open and being forced. "It means he is mine. My property. All those in my Personal Guard have them."

As if she'd given a silent order, the two mermen by her throne swam down to frame either side of her and they ripped off their own jackets, discarding them to bare themselves before Coral. Indeed, they had the tattoos of squids, but these were more detailed than Caspian's, and their bodies were just as glorious.

The black-haired merman's tattoo was filled in with colors of black, purple, and strawberry pink to match his queen's pallor. But the brown-haired merman's tattoo was something else entirely. It didn't just stretch from his shoulder to his chest. It stretched across every inch of him. The tattoo curled and twined over abs, hard curves of arm muscles and even went up his neck and onto the shaved sides of his head. It was the detailed portrait of a sea kraken, tentacles stretching out in every direction to tear apart a ship in the water. Other images decorated his body as well, images that she couldn't make out beneath the attention the kraken demanded.

"Are they not beautiful?" the queen asked appreciatively, looking from merman to merman with awe and a dazed expression. She looked back to Coral, eyes expectant of a response.

"Very," she replied tightly, her hands curled into fists. She hid them behind her back. Why was she doing this? What was her purpose? To show off her *toys*? If Coral hadn't known what Caspian was to the queen, she knew now. She treated him like a common harlot, and he sat before her smiling as if it didn't matter, as if he didn't *mind*. She supposed he didn't. He seemed to enjoy it.

After all, what was a stupid *anthropos* compared to Dark Water royalty? Why should it matter that Coral felt humiliated on his behalf? That the queen's roaming, possessive fingers reminded Coral of the own touches she'd been forced to suffer through herself? Mer or human, evil breathed the same substance regardless, and Coral recognized it within the queen.

"When they offered themselves to my service, I marked them right away. How else was the world to know they were mine? That way, if any other mer attempts to seduce them, they will see the marks they bear and know that they cannot touch royal property."

Is that why she was doing this? Coral wondered. Was she warning her away from Caspian? If that was the case, she wished she could tell her to save her breath. There was nothing between her and Caspian, despite the sensual way in which he'd held her close, touching his breath against her skin. That had been one time and it had been to help her swim. Nothing more. He hadn't touched her again, anyway. Whatever the queen thought he might feel for Coral, or Coral for him, was all in her imagination.

"I can be ever so forgetful sometimes." The queen chuckled. Her nails still traced circles around Caspian's pebbled nipples. "Sometimes, when I receive new things, I forget to give them their mark to let the world know that they belong to me."

A bad feeling wound around Coral, the beginnings of a whisper of premonition.

Queen Ulla smiled mischievously. Then her gaze snapped to the mermen as she commanded, "Hold her down."

THE BRANDING

CASPIAN WANTED TO TIGHTEN HIS HANDS INTO FISTS, TENSE his body, do *something*, show any type of emotion. He could not. The queen was pressed tightly against his backside, her sharp fingernails scratching his bare skin. She could dig in a little deeper, leave a trail of split flesh and swirling blood and it would not hurt as much as the feeling of helplessness.

Matthias gripped Coral's wrists from behind. She screamed and thrashed her sapphire tail, bucking and disturbing the water with her frightened movements. He was smiling, everything about him manic. He loved violence. Relished in it. In it, he was powerful, unstoppable.

And Zalyn would not show his *gusto* in a smile but in his eyes. The dark gray depths were shining with vicious delight as he approached her, taking his time to smell her fear and taste it on his tongue. He pushed his black hair away from his eyes before reaching down and holding her tail in his crushing grip.

Coral didn't stop thrashing. She fought to get away from them with all the strength of a wild orca, but Caspian knew what a useless task that was. They were stronger than her, fiercer, and they thrived on this. There was nothing she would be able to do except wait for it to be over. Because once the queen had you in her sights, there was no escaping her wrath.

The queen lifted a hand, waved her fingers around in an enchanting circle, and sang. Caspian couldn't focus on the words. He was staring at Coral's body held tight in their crutches. When Queen Ulla finished her incantation, a steaming metal rod appeared, floating beside Matthias. The tip was hot with blue water fire, shaped in the image of an oyster shell.

Matthias grabbed it with one arm, keeping Coral in place with the other. At the sight of the rod, her screams grew almost painfully deafening, pleas ripping from her throat that would not be heeded. She kicked her tail, fins slapping against Zalyn's face, but his grip remained ironclad. Caspian longed to tell her to stop, that she was just wasting energy.

He could not.

He could do nothing.

The queen trailed her tongue along the lobe of his ear. He groaned, as he always did when she did that, even if he felt no stirrings, no lust. He could summon desire on command, make his cock hard from one second to the next whenever the queen needed it. He always did what was expected of him. Only that and nothing more.

"I want you to watch, Caspian," the queen whispered into his ear. "I want you to watch them brand the little *anthropos*. Later, you will apologize."

"Apologize for what, my queen?"

"Apologize for hurting her. For everything."

Then she claimed his mouth in hers at the same time she gave Matthias the signal.

∿

CORAL'S GAZE strayed to Caspian, her eyes pleading for help, but when she looked across the throne room at him, he wasn't focused on her at all. All of his attention was diverted to Queen Ulla Magissa as she dived in and devoured his mouth, tongue slashing and thrusting. Her groans of pleasure cut through Coral like a blade.

Then came the pain. Searing hot, unbearable pain. The brown-haired merman dug the rod into her side, and she screamed. Her flesh felt like it was on fire, the stench rising up in tendrils of liquid smoke to stain the water. Tears stung at her eyes and the merman just laughed, digging the instrument deeper into her skin, tearing over flesh and scales.

The pain shot over her, pulled her under like a violent riptide claiming her body. Stars and white lights danced behind her eyelids, making her head spin. She was sure, in her pain, she cried out names, though past the piercing agony, she couldn't be sure whose.

Olivia.

Caspian.

If she could have reached her hand out to him, she would have but the mermen's grip on her thrashing body was solid, unyielding.

Her eyes found Caspian of their own accord, but his image fell away when the merman tore away the rod, taking her flesh with it. Coral screamed, cried, but he only laughed while the black-haired one gazed on in silent delight. Then, the queen's laughter followed, high-pitched and cruel.

And then Coral knew nothing but blackness as the riptide of pain swallowed her whole.

CORAL DRIFTED in and out of consciousness. She thrashed and turned on her sea bed, crying out for someone named

Olivia, but it was Caspian who she cried for most of all. As if she were cursing his name even in sleep. Worse, as if she were begging for his help, even knowing just how impossible it was for him to offer it.

She burned with fever and exhaustion. Her body was not used to such pain, and the strenuous and barbaric violence they'd inflicted on her had caused her body to shut down entirely.

Zenara pressed cool strands of sea kelp against her forehead, hoping to absorb some of the fever into them. The action soothed Coral, if only in the smallest increments, until she finally settled into the cushioned sponges with a deep sigh.

Careful not to wake her, Zenara touched her fingers to her waist, against the unmarred scales on her side. They had branded her skin like they would a hippocampus. Charred skin, red and black formed the figure of an oyster. It was one of the queen's favorite symbols besides the octopus and squid. For, what did an oyster hold? The pearl had long since been a symbol of the royalty of the Dark Waters, and Zenara's mother had made a mockery of it, using it to brand those she thought were less than her, nothing but property.

Gingerly, Zenara reached out and touched her own side, feeling for the faint scar through her clothes. She was not thought of as a daughter to the queen, for Ulla Magissa had dozens of daughters, products of her lust and cruelty towards her Personal Guards.

Zenara did not know who her father was, and the queen would certainly never tell her. Oftentimes Zenara hoped it would have been Caspian, but that was impossible, considering they were nearly the same age. Besides sharing no likeness beyond the color of their skin, he had not been in her mother's service that long, fifty years at most. Zenara had been born long before the queen had accepted Caspian into her Personal Guard.

Her own branding had been painful, but Zenara had borne it with gritted teeth and no tears. Zenara had long since learned to live with the unpleasant things that came with being a part of the queen's court. Being the bastard daughter of Ulla Magissa had taught her how to smile through the pain, if nothing else.

Coral jerked in bed again, and Zenara ripped her hand away from her skin. Even though she was an *anthropos* and the merfolk were taught since they were guppies that humans were the pure definition of evil, Zenara could find no such darkness in Coral. She was gentle, shy with a heart softer than sea sponge. How could Coral be a danger to anyone?

"Caspian..." Coral croaked. Her eyes fluttered opened, and Zenara leaned forward to hear better. "Where's Caspian?" Coral whispered.

Zenara's heart broke for her. "He is not here," she said truthfully. After Matthias and Zalyn had branded her, they brought her here, only to dump her on the front steps like a sack of garbage. Caspian was with the queen, where he would be for hours, no doubt. When she was feeling particularly nasty, she liked to keep her Personal Guard at her side and demanded they pleasure her for hours until she grew bored with them. Zenara suspected tonight was going to be one of the crueler nights.

Coral's face opened into raw vulnerability and cracked. Zenara reached out to grip her hand tightly in her own.

"He's with the queen." It wasn't a question, but Zenara nodded anyway. Coral bit into her bottom lip. She looked as though she wanted to say more or to ask Zenara a question instead, she closed her eyes, took her hand away and turned to lay on her other side.

Zenara stared at Coral's bare backside. She'd taken her

clothes off, knowing that they would only irritate the wound further.

"Coral..."

"Could you leave me alone for a bit, Zenara? Please?"

Zenara stared at her for a while longer; she remained unmoving. Sighing, she left Coral alone. Sadness descended heavily on her shoulders as she closed the bedroom door behind her. If she knew her mother, and she did, Zenara knew that she would do everything in her power to break Coral in every way she could.

And there was nothing anyone could do to stop it.

CORAL SOBBED into the sponge that served as pillow. They'd branded her like a damn animal. They'd humiliated her, tying her to rope and tugging her around like a pet. She supposed that *anthropos* were nothing more than animals to the merfolk.

And that hurt. It tore a gash in her chest, bleeding her out.

She'd been so hell bent on staying alive, on escaping, but now she just wanted to die. What was the point of going on when she had no one? Olivia was dead anyway, so why was she still fighting to stay alive? She couldn't seem to conjure up an answer to that question, so she just sobbed endlessly on, hoping to release some of that pain, but without tears the agony just seemed endless.

They'd marked her white skin, just above the line of her hip where her tail began, tearing off scales with it. It was charred and fleshy and ugly, and it would live with her forever.

That thought boiled inside of her. She'd wanted to get out of here, but it seemed like this was the queen's way of saying that even if she escaped, Her Majesty would be with Coral forever. A mark she couldn't clean, a brand carved into her flesh that could never be erased. Just like Trent had been.

She wanted to claw at her skin, tear it off inch by inch and grow a new one, one the queen hadn't touched or tainted.

The worse part about the whole situation was when she'd glanced towards Caspian. She'd expected him to help, to at least defend her as he had at her trial, but when she saw his face, he wore a look that said he couldn't care less. He'd spent her branding making out with the queen, letting her tentacles roam over every inch of his body instead of pleading for her to stop torturing Coral.

She didn't know why she was surprised at anything he did anymore. He'd made it clear in the beginning that he hated her kind and he'd only saved her life to make sure she made up for her race's crimes. She meant nothing to him, and the simple act of letting his hands roam over her body and apologizing for hurting her meant nothing.

She'd been a fool to believe it. To believe *him*. She'd fallen for the softness of his expression, the brief glimpses of vulnerability he dared show while they were together. Like it had been his own brand of pain meant for Coral's eyes only. She'd recognized it, because it had matched hers.

She'd forgotten the faces liars could wear. They were manipulative and twisted what they saw in their victim's expression to mirror their own and to serve their own purpose.

A deep shuddering breath, and Coral felt brave enough to finally catch a look at her new wound. The brand itself was the outline of an oyster shell. What meaning did it have? Did it even matter? She was considered property now. It was a degrading and sobering thought. The wound throbbed and seemed to emanate heat in response to her thoughts.

A tentative knock at the door interrupted her observation. She didn't want to see anyone so ignored it, but not even a second later, the door opened. Caspian swam in, closing it behind him. In his hands, he carried a colorful, squishy tube of... well, Coral didn't know what it was.

Coral pulled the silk blanket over her body to cover her nudity. "Go away," she croaked, hating herself for how weak she sounded, but hating him even more for floating there and looking chagrined and contrite at the same time.

Caspian ignored her and swam beside the bed. "I need to tend to your wound," he said softly, as if nothing had happened. As if he hadn't floated there humping his bitch queen while Coral was tortured in front of him. "If we leave it unattended, it will get infected, and you will not be able to work tomorrow."

Coral's throat tightened. Of course, that's what he was worried about. Her ability to work. The bastard.

"I said go away."

He just looked at her with those odd eyes of his. Then his expression softened into one of sorrow, a brief flash of emotion that he left wide open for her to see. "Please," he rasped. "Just... let me do this for you. Please, Coral."

"No." She would not change her mind just because he pretended to be sad about her situation. He'd already proved time and time again that he was a fake. She wouldn't fall for his act.

"You will attract infection."

"I don't care."

"I do."

Coral narrowed her eyes at him. "Do you? Because it seemed to me like you didn't give a damn what happened to me."

He worked his jaw angrily. "You do not understand..."

"I understand plenty," she interrupted, feeling all her rage and hurt boil over. "You are as cruel as your queen, and you only keep me here for yours and her entertainment. I'm nothing to you but an animal you can torture as you please. So go away and let me catch infection. Let me die as I should have on that shipwreck. Leave me the fuck alone!"

As she'd shouted that last word, she suddenly felt herself enveloped in Caspian's arms. He was pulling her towards his chest, crushing her against his big frame in a hug that left her breathless. His hands stroked the back of her head, his nose buried into her hair.

"Do not say that. Please, Coral, there is so much I wish I could tell you, but I cannot. She... she has a hold on me that you do not understand."

Coral pushed away her surprise at his words and actions before pressing her palms against his chest and shoving him away. She'd heard that excuse before. Men's dicks had about as much sense as their brains, and it obviously wasn't even that much. She didn't know why she'd expected mermen to be any different.

"I think the hold she has over you is called 'lust'," she said angrily. "Stop pretending. Leave me alone."

His face was the perfect picture of heartbreak. Unfortunately, it was just another fake expression she was well versed in.

"Coral..." he breathed. "You do not *understand*..."

"Get. Out," she demanded, pushing at his chest with her fist. The movement hurt her wound, caused her to gasp and drop the blanket covering her chest. Caspian's big hands went to her waist. "No!" she cried out. She didn't want him igniting fire in her, making her doubt his true intentions and cruelty. "Just get out! *Get out!*"

Caspian looked at her one last time, his expression pained, before he picked up the discarded tube. "Very well," he whispered. "As you wish." And he got off the bed and swam away, closing the door behind him.

Coral stared at it for a long time after he'd gone, feeling

numb. Then a firmer, steadier knock came at the door. Zenara swam in without waiting for Coral's permission, carrying the tube that Caspian had earlier.

"Caspian told me you were being as stubborn as a little catfish," Zenara announced, swimming to her side. "Let me dress your wound, Coral."

"Why?" Coral demanded. "You'll fix me up right now so that I'm healthy enough to be tortured again tomorrow? Is that why you're doing this? To see me suffer? You're as cruel and as fake as Caspian is! I bet you hate the *anthropos* as much as everyone else in this messed up kingdom!" She couldn't help the words that spilled from her mouth. She didn't know who to trust, who was sincere and who wasn't.

"I am not your enemy, Coral. And I do no not hate you."

"How can I believe you when every mer I've met so far has just wanted to see me tortured and dead?"

Zenara stared at her a long time in concentrating silence. "There are things you do not understand..." she declared with inscrutable firmness.

"Caspian keeps saying that, but do you know what I *do* understand? I understand that I am hated and that I am now *property*. Something neither of *you* seem to understand."

"I understand perfectly what it is you are going through," Zenara replied. Then, she backed away from the bed to float before her. "You think we do not know what it is to be in the queen's service, Coral? We know more than anyone. *Caspian* knows more than anyone the burden of being property. Because to her, we are all property."

Then, Zenara began undoing her fishhook belt with ease, dropping it to the floor with a clank. She then reached for the shoulders of her fishnet dress and smoothed them down her arms until the material was nothing but a puddle at the end of her tail. She floated bare before Coral who could only stare at her lovely form. Zenara was muscular in all the right places.

Her skin was a lighter shade of brown than Caspian's and smooth all over except for the place she was now pointing out with her finger. The place on her hip that had the traces of a scar in the image of an oyster shell.

Coral gasped.

"So you see?" Zenara began dressing again. Her fingers shook as she pulled the dress back over her arms. Like she was reeling from that vulnerable piece of herself she'd given. "I understand perfectly how you feel."

"Zenara..." Coral longed to reach out to the mermaid, to clasp hands or something, but she kept them buried into the covers.

She felt herself charting into unfamiliar territories. For so long, she'd kept her own pain bottled in. Logically, she knew there would be others to have had suffered a similar fate such as hers. Pain had a way of bringing broken people together as they tried to fit their pieces in empty spaces. Though, Coral had never opened her eyes to look for someone who's scars mirrored her own. For so long, she'd felt blind in the dark until Zenara ripped open the curtains and exposed the truth of bleeding wounds that surrounded her.

"I'm sorry. I didn't know."

"Of course you did not know," Zenara said dismissively but not angrily as she secured her fishhook belt into place. "It happened many decades ago. I was six at the time. Merely a child."

A child. She'd been a *child* when the queen had—

"But now that you *do* know, maybe you will not judge neither me nor Caspian so harshly."

"But Caspian—"

"Just because he does not bear the scar of a burn does not mean that he himself is not marked. What do you think that tattoo is? A decoration?"

"But the queen said that the Personal Guard accept going

into her service. That they agree to it. I thought that Caspian had a choice and that he *chose* to be with her."

Zenara let out a bark of a laugh. "That is what she would like the mer to believe, that they have *choices,* but it is all a lie. She gives no one choices or free will. It is why Caspian was forced to watch your branding. To refuse would have made it worse for him and for you."

Coral was silent for a moment, mulling this new information over in her mind. Caspian had no free will? If knowing what being in her service would do to him, that it would take away any sense of freedom, then why had he gone into it in the first place? That was the part that didn't make sense to her.

"Why did he go into her service?" asked Coral.

Zenara stiffened. "It is not my place to say, and it is not your place to ask. Just know that he bears what he does with his head held high and a smile on his face, as if he truly loved being in her service and *servicing* her because he has no other choice. He bears the unbearable without so much as a complaint, and I expect you to do the same. Otherwise, you will not survive," she lectured.

He bears the unbearable...

Coral wondered why he was in her service, what she had used against him to get him to agree? Had she threatened someone he loved? A mate, perhaps? And then used him for her own amusement? He kissed her in front of everyone, and she openly mocked him about being in her bed. Like Caspian was nothing more to her than a whore.

The thought filled Coral with anger and apprehension, the emotions swirling together in a little vortex inside of her. The two mermen who had branded her were also part of her Personal Guard. Did that mean they were used as Caspian was? But if what Zenara said was true, then Caspian didn't enjoy it. She wondered if the other two felt the same but shook that off.

No, they relished in her cruelty. They loved it. It had been obvious from the smiling face and manic happiness in their eyes.

If Caspian really was shouldering a heavy burden, dealing with everything and pretending that it didn't bother him, how was he still alive? She supposed, she hadn't been so different, either. Hadn't she done the same? Hid away in her room and locked any sense of feeling away? Because to feel even the slightest was the greatest agony. In Caspian, Coral had found a kindred spirit, at least.

But what secrets was Caspian hiding? What reason could he have for all of this?

Coral was suddenly determined to find them out.

"Zenara," she inquired. "Will you please tend to my wound?"

SEA LEGS

"CORAL...." CASPIAN EYED HER WITH SURPRISE WHEN SHE swam into his office a few hours later.

It was a space built on both comfort and masculinity, with rich, dark tones that shouldn't have gone together but somehow worked. Blacks, golds, and rich cherries. Everything inside was arranged with an intricate perfection that made the ambiance seem... sacrosanct. Holy or revered, almost, in a way she couldn't explain.

It reminded Coral of swimming into a church. With its sea glass, mosaic windows that filtered through little beams of phytoplankton light. Light that expanded in shocking streaks and made the water look like it was filled with star dust.

She floated awkwardly before his desk, staring at him and seeing a totally different Caspian, a totally different merman. It wasn't him who had changed, though. Maybe it wasn't even her. Thanks to Zenara, she now knew the truth about him. It was like having a veil ripped from her eyes, and it changed the way she would approach him, because she now knew that truth.

That he was as trapped as she was; and while Coral

suffered physical abuse in the kingdom, he might be suffering another kind entirely. One that she was innately familiar with. That didn't excuse his behavior, but it made her understand. He was as much a victim to the queen as she had been to Trent. And maybe it didn't feel right to compare their pain, but she couldn't help but feel like his was infinitely worse than hers. She didn't know how breaking it would be, to be coerced into the act every night. To have to face her abuser. To smile. To pretend.

Just the thought of seeing Trent again made her stomach heave. Just like she couldn't ever imagine subjecting herself to that torture.

Coral didn't know what kind of hold the queen had over Caspian, over anyone in her Personal Guard, to keep them submissive the way that she did. A part of her wanted to know.

A larger part of herself feared the truth.

She feared the truth of his own story. And it kept her a silent observer in front of him for a moment.

"What do you want?" he asked, wary but not unkind.

"Um..." Coral tugged awkwardly at the flowing purple dress Zenara had helped her change into after dressing her wound. It was smoother than silk, with a diaphanous layer of loose skirts that would prevent her scales and wound from being irritated. Pearls were sewn along the straps of her arms, spanning across the juts of her collarbones and shoulders. It was very light and flowed over her body like waves themselves.

It was a simple gown, but still rich, and it also served as a distraction for her fingers while she tried to find the right words.

She hadn't thought about what she'd say to him when she arrived at his little office. She'd just asked Zenara where Caspian was and had swam in without contemplating the enormity of what she was about to do. But she'd wanted to see him, to look at him with new knowledge about his life in her mind. To empathize.

So she did.

She picked apart every interaction they'd ever had, every expression he'd ever made. How he could go from one expression to the next at the snap of a finger. Oftentimes, she found the slightest etchings of vulnerability in his gaze. A mirror of loneliness echoing through her own soul that she understood. But there was anger there as well. A rage against the world like he could break it apart with his own two fists, but just as he swung to do just that, he found himself chained.

Trapped.

"Hi," she whispered. Her voice was thick with emotion as realization began to set.

Caspian was pissed at the world, and he had a right to be. Just like Coral had a right to be. Because this cruel, underwater world had taken the fragile pieces inside them and broken them. The queen had wielded their innermost fears against them until they were little more than crumbled bits of broken glass without their matching pieces.

Caspian raised his eyebrows. "Hi?"

"Um, I just, I mean, I don't—" She blew out a frustrated breath at her sudden inability to form coherent words. She diverted her attention to his hands and found him holding a beautiful short sword that was about as long at her forearm. The hilt was golden and different variations of blue, and the blade was a scintillating silver. "What's that?" she asked curiously, swimming towards his table.

Caspian ran his fingers against the hilt in a soft caress that somehow left tingles down her own spine as if she was the one being touched. "It is an Atlantean dagger."

"It looks more like a sword." She stopped just at the edge

of the table and resisted the urge to run her palms against the cherry wood.

"It is a dagger used by the Royal *Stratia*." He twirled it adeptly in his fingers before handing it to her, hilt first. Coral hesitated, but his quiet insistence had her taking the weapon tentatively, feeling the heavy weight of it in her palms, and feeling strangely this pacifying moment between them. The colors of it matched the armor she often saw him in. She wondered if they were small remnants of his past.

"Zenara mentioned you were part of the *Stratia*."

"I was." His voice held a whisper of wistfulness and an edge of something darker.

"Why did you quit?" She handed the blade back to him, the same way he'd handed it to her. He took it and covered it with a swath of cloth before enclosing it in a desk drawer.

"Because I had nothing left in the *Stratia* to fight for," he said, much to Coral's surprise. The words sounded heavy and sad.

"What is the *Stratia*? I don't exactly know what it means," she confessed.

"The *Stratia* is a group of Atlantean *guerreri*, made up of the strongest, fastest, and bravest merfolk. We were an army, the strongest in all of the seas. Undefeated soldiers charged with the protection of Atlantica."

"That sounds like quite an accomplishment," Coral mused. "Better to be a commander of the Royal *Stratia* than a washed out wannabe author and librarian, anyway." The bitterness on her tongue was unexpected and made her face flush what she was sure was an unattractive shade of red.

Caspian reached across the desk to envelop her small hand in his large one. She looked at their hands then at his face. "Never underestimate your worth or your value, Coral. Knowledge Keepers are *very* valuable. Besides, your spirit is that of a *guerreri*, because you are a survivor and have dealt with things that would have broken lesser mer. Not everyone can endure such changes to their bodies and their lives. You would have made a good addition to the *Stratia*."

Coral blushed but tried with light humor. "Where I come from, librarians aren't that important anymore. And we don't really keep knowledge. We just shelve books."

"Why are you really here, Coral? I know you did not come to speak of my dagger or of the worth you think you do not have." His eyebrows rose, and she caught the brief flash of amusement in his eyes.

"You're right. I didn't." She stared at their joined hands; she couldn't help that her eyes were drawn to that particular spot. Like the touching of their skin was an addictive, hypno-tizing force that she was too weak to resist. Somehow, his fingers had filled the spaces between her own and held tightly. It was comforting and nerve-racking at the same time.

"Why are you here, Coral?" His grip tightened and his voice dropped an octave, filling her entire body with a tingling, nervous sensation. She was glad for his steady hand in hers, or else she would have visibly trembled.

"I don't know," she confessed. Everything she wanted to demand of him slipping between her fingers because it seemed too personal. He didn't owe her his story, no matter how entitled to it she felt. It felt wrong to ask him suddenly, but she still couldn't bring herself to be dishonest. "I—I wanted to see you. I wanted to look you in the eyes and try to find a trace of the merman that selflessly saved my life after that shipwreck time and time again. I wanted to see if *this*," she gestured at him, at the straight and tense posture, "was just a facade."

"Is that what you want?" he asked, his voice low. "For me —for my actions—to be a facade?"

"Yes. No. I don't know! I just want the truth, Caspian. I just want you to tell me the truth. And if you can't do that, if it's somehow too painful, then I want you to tell me that, too."

Caspian froze, and she was afraid she'd made some grave mistake, that he would again retreat behind that steel mask he wore. If he would push her away, go to his queen instead of looking at her. The thought hurt more than it should have, struck a spear straight at her heart. She started to pull her hand away, but he pulled it back.

"Say it again," he whispered, his voice little more than a broken, fragmented sound.

Coral looked at him. "Say what again?"

"My name. Say my name again."

"Caspian," she breathed.

That was all it took for him to pull her over the desk and into his lap in a single dexterous move, cradling her gently. The quick, unexpected movements had her heart pounding against her chest. Not of fear, but something she hadn't felt in so long.

Desire.

It clogged through her chest and mind, making her dizzy with his every touch. It felt like a drunk haze, but she reminded herself she was in control. That she wasn't drugged. And Caspian... he wasn't Trent.

His hands were tentative, yet firm. They slid up her sides, careful with her room. Touching, pulling away, then touching again like he couldn't help himself. Like her skin was an addictive force he kept gravitating towards but didn't quite know how to navigate her body.

She could understand that. The wanting, though not knowing. Of being curious of touch, of wanting to know if it was different now that they both were tainted with the touch of violence.

Coral knew she should push him away. Just hours before she'd hated him. But she had felt alone for so long. She craved this. To be vulnerable with another. Despite herself, she leaned closer towards him, silent in her permission.

His hands cupped her cheeks gently, his eyes warring with indecision. They both wanted this, though. His breath hitched as he leaned forward, his lips brushing against her own. Their every touch was explorative. First, a brush, then a firm press. His lips traveled to the corners of her mouth, to her chin.

Coral ached in every bit of her body for more. But she let him set his pace, and she accepted with deep sighs and sounds of encouragement. Her hands reached for his neck, holding him lightly so he could pull away or closer as needed.

That first brush of her fingers against his skin had him groaning and she answered with one of her own. It was like a dam burst between them suddenly. His kisses became more fervent, more eager, until it became an explosion.

His mouth opened her own and he was thrusting his tongue inside, caressing it against her own. He bent her head back, adjusting her angle so he could delve in deeper. He was all giving, all demanding and the ferocity in his kiss had Coral's nails raking against the back of his neck in her own attempt to hold on and match him stroke for stroke. She gave what he did, matching passion for passion, matching her own frustrated ferocity with his. Her tongue did a dance inside his mouth, causing him to groan low and deep in his throat.

He broke their kiss apart. "Say my name again. Please, Coral."

The desperate request wasn't lost on her. If anything, it made her feel sad.

Her lips felt bruised and swollen, and still tingled from the pressure of his mouth. "Caspian," she whispered like a much-needed daydream after all she'd known was nightmares. "Caspian..."

His grip on her body tightened, fists bunching the material of her dress. "You have never said it before."

Coral was going to comment on that, but he was devouring her again, and she couldn't help but fall into the bliss of his touch. His mouth was eager and impatient, but his hands were ever so gentle as they roamed across her back, finding their way into her hair.

She sighed into his mouth, only causing him to groan and pull her body tight against his. One hand left her hair and went between them to hike up her dress. It slid up her scales, the hem bunching against her stomach. A tingling sensation, like electricity or pins-and-needles, swept down the length of her tail. She pressed herself up against him, a tightening need demanding release. She opened her legs up to straddle him and...

Wait? Legs?

Coral ripped her mouth from his to glance down between them.

What. The. Fuck?

The words froze in her throat as she took in something she never thought she'd see again.

Where her bright tail had been, she now had legs. Twin legs covered in sapphire scales that expanded down thighs, over knees, and her calves. She lifted a foot and found it elongated, webbing between her toes. Her hands grasped at the tops of her thighs, fingers edging over the tendons located on the inner side of her legs. As she grazed those, a tingling sensation spiraled through her body, and a tendon lifted like a tentacle, reaching...

She felt herself gasp and brought her thighs together, watching the tendons lift up and knit her legs together like magic, forming a tail all over again. She experimented, opening and closing her sea legs, alternating between tail and legs, watching as the lines of muscle reached and released, hugging her together and pushing her apart again.

She hadn't had a chance to explore her body before, but she did so now with fascination, her fingers drifting over her every inch. When her legs opened again, she stared between them at the glistening folds of her pussy. That part of her body looked human enough, except it was hairless, and there was a smattering of scales in between the V-line of her hips.

Her gaze wandered to where Caspian's body met her own. The fabric of his long tunic had floated up at some point, to reveal that he no longer had a tail either. Thick, muscular sea legs were spread wide. His whole body was human-like, his thick cock bobbing between his legs. Even that was different from a human's. It was long, covered at the base with scales the same color of his rich green tail, though the tip was the color of his skin. Where a heavy sac should have been, there was a hard, scaled ridge instead, just beneath his cock. She knew if she reached for it, it would feel hard to the touch.

Coral blushed and shot back, away from him and on top of the table. She looked at one leg then the other, stretching it out to admire it.

"What? How?" She wriggled her toes and webbing.

"It is the way our bodies are built," he explained. "We swim faster with a tail, but the sea legs allow us to do other things."

"What other things?" She bent her knees, a giggle rising up in her chest.

"Things like riding a hippocampus at a faster pace as well as... mating."

"Why didn't you use them when we first met?"

"I was setting a leisurely pace, and I did not want to frighten you more so than you already were. I saw no need to mention them." Her thoughts went wild with possibilities, of what having sea legs could mean for her. Almost as if reading her thoughts, Caspian frowned. "Even with sea legs, walking on land is impossible as you are still merfolk, and this type of bodily magic will prevent you from breathing air."

Coral snapped her legs opened. "Magic?" she wondered.

"Magic," he repeated, then waved a hand and her sea legs suddenly became a tail again.

She looked down to find that his legs had closed as well. "How do you do that?" she asked in awe. She waved her own hand across her tail, but nothing happened. Fingering the right spot, just down the middle of those interconnecting tendons, however, made them open and then close again.

"All merfolk possess magic within our bodies, though not everyone has the ability to access it in its full form. This magic has evolved through our blood and allows us to alter our appearance out of a need for survival and procreation," he explained cautiously.

There were so many types of phenomenon out there that Coral couldn't even begin to comprehend. She'd filled her mind with random facts throughout her life. Like how if a female clown fish died, the male altered his gender. Or how star fish squirted semen at females because they were too lazy to have sex. Or how sharks had a pocket for their dicks. Or how sharks had *two* penises. Or how it was the male seahorse who gave birth. Or how sea turtles always found their way back to the beaches where they were born.

She supposed there was a little bit of magic in everything.

Especially in that shark dick thing.

"And do you think *I* could make magic?" she asked.

If there was magic in the blood of the merfolk, however dormant or miniscule, then maybe she could access it somehow. If she couldn't walk on land with her own sea legs, then maybe she could find some way to tap into magic and get her own legs back.

Caspian looked at her sadly. In that look, she got her

answer. And she didn't like it. "Humans that are turned into mer are without magic, Coral. Magic is a gift given from birth to us. You were created."

She swallowed past the thick lump that suddenly rose in her throat. "So, do you have magic?"

"Yes, I do. As a commanding officer in the Royal *Stratia*, we had to learn all sorts of magic. We relied on it as well as physical strength to get through battle."

"Magic is self-energy, and the most basic of it requires matter in order to work. You cannot expect something for nothing. It requires an exchange. The Knowledge and Magic Keepers of Atlantica schooled the *Stratia*. They knew which magic would benefit us best."

"Did they ever teach you to make human legs?" she asked longingly. She knew she sounded desperate because she'd already asked before. But she'd been hoping that he'd been lying before and now that there was a semblance of trust between them, he would be honest.

Caspian looked at her sadly. "I did not lie to you, Coral, when I said that I could not give you your legs back. I only learned to create human to mer, but never learned how to reverse it. I am sorry. Know that I did it to save your life."

Coral bit the inside of her cheek. "Why would the Magic Keepers teach you how to make a mermaid but not how to reverse it?"

"Because the queen had the Keepers killed before they had the chance to teach me. She learned all of the ancient Knowledge before destroying their great shell of secrets."

"Oh." Coral wasn't sure how else to reply to that, so she just sat there, flapping her fins for lack of a better response. She still had so many questions, but his face had grown grave, and she wasn't sure if he was ready to talk about it just yet.

The queen seemed to have taken more than just his freedom but Knowledge as well. So maybe she *was* the only one in the kingdom who could give her legs back. Her hopes of returning home depleted.

"About the queen..." Coral began uncertainly. She shouldn't ask, but she had to know. After that passionate kiss, it was obvious there was something between them, even if she didn't want there to be. "Do you think you could tell me the truth about your relationship with her? I mean..." She blushed when his eyebrows furrowed. "Is she your *mate* or something?" She hated saying the words, given all Zenara had told her and the conclusions Coral had drawn. But she didn't want to assume anything only to be hurt later.

"I am a part of her Personal Guard. That means I can have no mate and must be dedicated only to the queen," he said from between clenched teeth, as if it hurt to grind the words out.

Her heart deflated. "But... we..."

Caspian shot out of his chair and pulled her into his arms in another crushing grip. "Coral, please," he whispered, stroking her hair. "Please understand. I cannot promise you anything beyond what just happened. It should not have even happened, but I could not hold back any longer. I—I just do not want you to hold to hope where there might be none. I am her property. I am *hers,* and I will always be *hers* in body. That will not change, Coral. The queen..." He swallowed. "She uses me, and I let her. That is the truth. I do not like it, but it is something I must bear and pretend to enjoy. I must pretend to enjoy *her.* If she knew that any in her Personal Guard have strayed from her chambers..." He paused and tilted her chin up so that she was looking him in the eyes. "No one can know. We must pretend nothing happened. I will be forced to treat you like a worthless *anthropos,* and you must pretend to hate me. Do you understand?"

"But why? Why does she have this hold on you? Why can't you just leave her?" She knew her words were hopeful and foolish, and they were crossing a line she swore she wouldn't cross. Because it was his story, and she wasn't sure she had a right to it. Even if nothing ever came from her knowing.

The queen was insane.

If she thought any of her subjects had double crossed her, had left or betrayed her in any way, she would make them pay. And it would be cruel, and it would be violent. That much Coral knew for sure.

Caspian rubbed a thumb against her cheek and bent to press a kiss against her forehead. The gesture was melancholic, like it was the last kiss he would ever give her. When he looked at her, his steel mask was already sliding into place again, and she knew that their time was up. "Let us just say that she has something of mine. Something I intend to get back."

A LESSON IN FIGHTING

THERE WOULD BE NO REST FOR CORAL. THAT WAS MADE clear when Zenara awoke her the next morning despite her injury. She ate a speedy but hearty breakfast with Caspian, a meal that consisted of things she never imagined she'd eat. A thick frothy tea that looked like pink sea foam, a sea fruit salad with jelly fruits and things that looked like green watermelon, and crunchy leaves that resembled lettuce.

The only sound that filled the dining room that morning was the loud bites and chewing as Coral devoured her food, and Caspian brooded over his own like she wasn't even there.

When they finished, Caspian gestured at her with a flick of his fingers and an annoying swish of his tail. She hated this. Hated pretending like they meant nothing to one another even after his lips had been on hers the night before. As they ventured out into the trash-filled waters, she was forced to remind herself that this was for the best.

A merman and a human had no future together, anyway. Least of all one who belonged to the Queen of the Dark Waters.

Those thoughts beat a percussive rhythm in her mind as

she worked for hours, shoving trash into fishnet bags, while still feeling like she wasn't making any progress at all, in any aspects of her life.

When she finally finished, Caspian helped her secure the bags across Redwave's wide back. He hoisted her onto the hippocampus and sat behind her, caging her in on either side with his big arms. He was careful not to touch her skin or any other part of her, even when she was all too aware of his presence, even when his body seemed to brand her backside with such a close proximity.

She reminded herself all the reasons wanting him was a bad idea.

Because he was the queen's property.

Because he'd dragged her through the streets.

Because he hadn't let her die.

Because he'd taken away her freedom.

Because he treated her like she was trash.

Knowing he was pretending to be cruel so as to not draw the suspect eyes of his queen made everything worse. Only cowards bent to the will of a tyrant. Only cowards watched and participated in the torture of others to save themselves. Only cowards sat back and did nothing.

Her temper was rising, and by the time they made it back to the city, Coral was gripping Redwave's mane until her knuckles went white and grinding her teeth until her jaw hurt. Sweeping her gaze around the water, she realized he wasn't heading in the direction of his home.

It wasn't until those peaks and spires loomed above them that she realized he was taking her to the queen's castle.

Her anger faded, replaced with fear. She wanted to ask him what the fuck she was doing, but bit down hard on her tongue. She didn't bother questioning him. Not here where anyone could listen in on their conversation, but she did tense up, gripping even tighter onto Redwave's mane for support. Nothing could prepare her for another encounter with the queen.

She remembered the schedule Caspian had set up for her that first week during her swimming lessons. After she mastered the art of swimming, she was supposed to live the life of the dark mer. She supposed he was taking her to do just that.

After handing Redwave over to a groomsmer, he gestured that Coral follow him through the castle. She tried to keep her gaze straight ahead on the back of Caspian's black jacket, but her eyes kept wandering.

The interior of the castle was bare of any furnishings, portraits and light. There was nothing to give the place a personal touch, nothing but a few of the queen's Personal Guard in their black jackets with squid shoulders or other guards carrying spears and floating in front of doors. It was rather empty and made the hairs on the back of her neck rise. The entire place was bereft of warmth, and it filled her with apprehension.

Finally, they came to a stop before a set of double doors. The guards took a look at Caspian and immediately parted, opening the door behind them to give him passage. Coral followed and stopped short in the entryway.

The room was a massive expansion of violence and weaponry. Sparring swords, spears, and tridents made of strong wood and coral hung decoratively over the walls. There were what looked like boxing gloves made of seal and shark skin and training armor made of orca teeth and tortoise shells. In the center of the room, floating through the water to form a square fighting ring, were bioluminescent jellyfish, and within the ring two mermen were engaged in a boxing match. One merman pummeled the other with fist and magic, sending a small vortex of water spinning his way. It slammed into him and he fell back on top of the jellyfish.

They stung him, and he let out a yowl before falling to the floor.

Coral didn't feel herself freeze because nearly a dozen mermen turned to stare at her entrance. She didn't stop because they sneered or hissed at her.

She stopped short because there, at the edge of the room, leaning against the obsidian structures were the two mermen who'd branded her.

Fear seized her up, making her limbs go immobile. She stared at them, heartbeat accelerating with every inhalation of their dangerous figures. Hatred roiled in her belly, but terror was the stronger of the two.

The black-haired merman who'd held her tail down was wearing a sleeveless black tunic, the material flowing down past his waist. He was thin, hardly a muscle in sight, but the way he was twirling daggers dexterously through his fingers made her shudder. Just because he wasn't stacking muscle upon muscle like Caspian did not make him any less deadly. If anything, she felt more wary of him because of the perfectly blank expression he wore. There were secrets in his eyes. Like finding yourself trapped within the gaze of a serial killer that had marked you as his prey.

The brown-haired merman, the one who'd branded her with manic laughter pushing past his lips, was shirtless. His tattoo was like a badge of honor standing out against the ridges of taut-muscled stomach and chest. He wore a loose garment of red tied firmly around his waist that accentuated the copper of his strong tail. He was leaning against the wall, wrapping what looked thick rolls of kelp around his knuckles. He tucked a strand under and bent down to take it between his teeth, giving it a sharp tug to keep it in place.

The moment the brown-haired mer looked up and saw her, he gave her a lopsided grin that crept through to the marrow of her bones.

She hated how beautiful the both of them were. Why was evil always so goddamn *pretty*? It was hardly fair.

"Hurry up, *anthropos*," Caspian snapped.

His voice was an awakening. She tore her gaze from the merman who'd branded her to look at Caspian. She gave a small nod and swam cautiously inside to where he was floating near the wall where all of the sparring tools hung.

"You are to take these down and clean them," Caspian ordered tightly. Gone was the sweet voice he'd used on her just last night. He looked at her with no gentleness, his lips in a hard line. Lips that had desperately tried to devour her own. Coral remembered that this was supposedly a facade. That he meant none of his anger and hatred. But it felt so fucking *real*. She reminded herself of the thoughts she'd been sitting on before they arrived. That he was a *coward*. "After you clean them, you will take inventory. When everyone is done training, you will clean up after them. Do you understand?" His voice and eyes were irritable.

Coral swallowed. "I understand." She nodded her acquiescence. Inventory was easy. It was safe. More importantly, it was something she knew how to do.

"Then hurry up. The supplies to clean the weapons are there." He pointed to the far side of the room at a little door. "And if anyone has need of you to carry their things or bring them their weapons, you will do so." He looked her over once to make sure she understood the rules and then swam away to join the brown and black-haired mermen.

Coral watched him leave, watched him swim right up to the mermen and fall into easy conversation. She couldn't hear what he said, but it made the black-haired merman's lip quirk up the side and the brown-haired one to throw his head back in boisterous laughter. Then the brown-haired mermen's gaze found Coral's and he winked.

Feeling nauseous, she tore her gaze away and went to the

wall and began pulling weapons down. She had to swim back and forth carrying the heaviness in her arms, but she piled all of them next to the supply closet. She took out a small jar of what looked like coconut oil—but was slimier and smell like lemon cleaner—and a sea sponge and got to work.

Some of the weapons were carved out of coral, others out of stone. She noticed that none of the weapons had the clanking metal steel or sharp points. Everything was dull, merely for practicing, she assumed. But it still polished and gleamed as she rubbed the sponge across it.

She looked up from her work to find Caspian stretching his muscles both in his arms and his tail. Her gaze lingered on him for a moment, watching the flex of his biceps as he pulled his arm over his head and then the other.

Her breath caught at his movements, so graceful and strong.

And then the brown-haired merman swam up next to him and the picture shattered. Coral sighed and kept on polishing until her fingers were raw and she'd finished. By the time she was done, Caspian had moved on to target practice.

He hit the target with a blade every time.

Aim, fire, *thwack*.

It was enthralling to watch his whole body move with the throw, his fingers gripping the knife, gracefully letting go. He'd been born for this, Coral realized. Born for the structured control the blades brought while in his hands. Born to wield them. It was an art, and he was the master.

Caspian let loose the last of his knives. It hit the center target, knocking down the ones already embedded into it, tearing a hole straight through it. Coral's breath caught. What must it be like, she wondered, to be a warrior?

"You have done enough dawdling, Caspian." The brown-haired merman snickered from the wall where he lounged, his arms crossed leisurely against his bare, tattooed chest. "It is time to get in the ring."

Caspian gave him a long, hard look. His features revealed nothing but an air of arrogance. His lip twitched. "And who would my opponent be?" he asked nonchalantly. As if it mattered little to him. Maybe it did. Maybe he could best any of them. He certainly looked like he could, with his massive frame compared to the others.

"If you were hoping to toss me around, I am afraid you will be disappointed." The merman turned, smirking at the black-haired merman who suddenly swam up, adjusting kelp wrap around his knuckles.

Caspian looked at them both before smiling. "Fine," he said. "To the ring."

The jellyfish hummed as they floated, their long vibrating tentacles looking like the bars of a prison. At their approach, the jellies parted. As soon as the mermen swam through, they were enclosed in a glowing cage. Caspian swam to one end while the other male swam to the other.

Coral gawked at them openly, wondering if it was even possible for that lithe merman to take Caspian down. Perhaps his size was an advantage and meant he was faster. But Caspian had been commander of the *Stratia*. Surely that meant he had skill in abundance and wouldn't be bested so easily, right?

Before the thought even fully left her head, the match began.

It was a dance, slow and prowling, predator after predator. They circled around each other with powerful tail strokes, sizing each other up. And together they struck. Their fists connected with a deafening crack that vibrated through the water, sending a tremor all the way down to her tail fins.

Caspian sent his other fist flying to the male's side. He bent over with a grunt but swept his tail out as he did, twining it with Caspian's to send him twirling through the water, away from him. Caspian let out a low growl and charged, stretching a fist out, meeting flesh with magic. A little vortex of water spun around the male, sucking him in.

Coral held her breath as magic clashed together in whirlpools and balls of light. The sound of flesh pounding against flesh reverberated, making Coral's own bones shake.

"What happened to taking inventory, *anthropos*?" The voice was smooth and deadly, curling around her every nerve like the promise of a threat. She snapped her gaze up and saw the heavily tattooed merman looming over her, arms crossed against his chest and a smile splayed widely across his face.

Coral sucked in a breath, fear clenching tightly at her. Nervous, and with her hands shaking, she began piling spears into her arms and straightened. He was close enough that she could feel the warmth emanating off of him. The heat of his body made her uncomfortable. She took a stroke back, but his eyes sparkled with a challenge, and he eased forward until the hard panes of his tattooed chest pressed against her arms.

So close.

So dangerously close.

He bent his face down to level with hers. She recoiled at the sight of him. At the cold, calculated cruelty in his golden-brown eyes. His nose, up close, was slightly crooked as if it had been broken before, his lips full and sensuous and grinning.

His smile unnerved her.

"Frightened little thing," he muttered, pressing even closer to her. She bent back, hefting the spears up higher to use as a shield between them. It did little good; he dominated the whispers of space between them, as if it didn't exist there at all.

"What do you want?" She couldn't help the way her voice shook. Not when she saw his handsome, deadly face and thought of the glee in his eyes and the tip of the rod digging into her side. Her heart thundered. She was sure he heard it because his eyes flicked to her chest, then to her pulse and lingered there. His gaze only made it beat harder.

"What a curious thing you are," he mused wickedly. His hand came to her face, and she flinched when he took a strand of hair between his fingers. The touch felt like an all-new brand. Painful and overwhelming. "Are you worried about Caspian? Is that why you watch him with light in your eyes? Do you think he is a fit match against Zalyn?" He let go of her hair and tore his gaze away to look at the match going on in the ring.

They were both breathing hard but seemed far from exhausted. Now she had a name to go with the face of the merman who had held her thrashing tail. The two mermen threw punches at each other, sweeping their hands up and bringing forth waves and light and water fire in blue, flickering waves.

"Caspian *is* an expert fighter. Born and bred for battle," he continued. He was still so close to her. She tried taking a stroke back, but his tail fin wrapped around hers, pulling her forward. His touch was nearly painful. Not because he put pressure on it, but because she was nearly choking on her own fear of him, and her mind registered the pain of his touch with every graze. "He is everything a fierce commander should be," he went on, his voice hypnotizing her to turn back and watch the fight.

He was right. Caspian was a fierce and commanding fighter. He struck and struck true, anticipated Zalyn's next move and countered with his own. He fought with what seemed like years of experience. It wasn't just awkward fists flying and landing. There was more to it than that. There was a certain finesse about them.

"And that is why he will lose," he murmured, a smile on his lips.

Coral snapped her attention to him. "Why?" she asked, despite being uncomfortable around him, her curiosity won over.

He looked at her, lips curling even higher. "Because he underestimates those who were not raised in the ranks of the *Stratia*. You see, Zalyn likes to cheat by poisoning his hidden blades. And," he added, bending down to whisper in her ear, "Caspian is distracted."

His hand shot to the back of her neck and *squeezed*. Coral cried out, dropping the spears in surprise. She put her palms on his bare chest to push him away, but he wouldn't budge. He kept his grip locked around her neck, holding her in place.

"Watch," he commanded.

Caspian, upon hearing Coral cry out, had turned, momentarily distracted. It was enough time for Zalyn to produce a hidden dagger from the inside of his tunic. He lunged, making a swipe for Caspian, who let out a curse and jerked back. The blade snagged his clothes, but the reckless impact of him shooting away from it sent him falling backwards.

Straight on top of the line of jellyfish.

There was a flash of bright white light, blinding the water, and then a zinging. Caspian grunted as he floated to the floor of the ring, his body still twitching from the pain of the sting. Coral was distracted from the sight the minute the merman let out low laughter and released her neck.

She glared at him, all fear dissipating. "You did that on purpose," she hissed.

He stroked his golden-coppery tail down the length of hers, making her fins curl. "I did," he confessed. "And I enjoyed every second of it." His eyes danced to the rhythm of his wide smile. There was a challenge there, daring as if to say, *What are you going to do about it?*

There was a lot she wanted to do. Not one option that would end well. She bit her tongue to keep from replying; she even dimmed her glare to a look of neutrality, though she was sure her eyes were blazing. He seemed to notice it. His lips curled even wider, if that were at all possible.

"Do you care so much for your captor, *anthropos?*" he asked sarcastically. "Does it hurt to see him bested by the likes of us?" He pulled at the edge of her own tunic until she fell to his chest. She tried to pull away, but he wrapped his arm around her waist to hold her in place. "Do you like it rough, *anthropos?* Is that why your eyes burn for Caspian? Maybe I should have branded you thrice over so you would look at *me* with awe—"

Coral slapped him.

He let go of her immediately, probably more from surprise than from pain. Even so, Coral bent to pick up a discarded spear and quickly straightened, brandishing it before her in warning. "Stay away from me," she demanded through gritted teeth.

He looked at her with brilliant eyes. From the weapon to her face and back again. Maybe he hadn't expected her to use a weapon against him. She hadn't expected to do it, either. Instinct had screamed at her to defend herself from the bastard, to put space and a shield between them. His hands on her made her skin crawl, made the back of her throat clench unpleasantly. She'd needed to do this, even if it ended badly.

Because Coral would never be that vulnerable again.

"If you are going to pick up a weapon, you had better be prepared to use it," he whispered with wicked delight. To her surprise, he swam forward until the dull tip of the spear pressed tightly against his chest. "And if you threaten me with it, at least cut me *a little*."

Her grip tightened on it as she contemplated his face, the

glee in his eyes at this, at just another challenge. This wasn't even about the fun of torture for him, she realized. It was about the chase, about the fight she could put up. He seemed like he was getting off on it. He was a masochist and a sadist, and he was pushing her.

"Is something wrong here?" a deep voice demanded. Caspian.

Coral loosened her grip on the weapon and dropped it to the floor. She didn't take her eyes off of the merman, though. She imagined he'd lunge like a snake, striking while her back was turned.

"I was just telling your beloved *anthropos* that it would be a pleasure to fight her in the ring." He smirked, crossing his arms against his chest, barely sparing a glance at Caspian as he did so.

"Fight?" Coral glared at him. Surely he wasn't serious.

"Yes. Fight. You and I, *anthropos*. Indulge me." His voice was the sarcastic musings of a challenge, his eyes a dare that raked over her body. It felt like he was undressing her, inch by slow inch until she felt naked, her soul bared for this stranger.

"No."

"You are mistaken if you think you have a choice."

Bastard. Bastard. Bastard.

She *knew* this would end badly. She never should have picked up that spear. Why was he doing this? He could tell just by looking at her that she had no fighting experience, that she couldn't *win* against him. So why? Just another way to torture her?

Her fists tightened at her sides. He eyed the movement, lip twitching. "Save it, *anthropos*," he said and turned away.

Towards the ring.

She finally managed to look up at Caspian. Maybe hoping for a warm look to reassure her or maybe his intervention. Would he really just let her swim into the middle of dozens of jellyfish and *fight* him? It was a challenge that could only end one of two ways. Coral, broken and beaten down yet again.

Or dead.

But when her eyes roved over Caspian, begging for that sliver of compassion, he wasn't looking her way. She didn't know why she was even disappointed.

~

CORAL FLOATED NERVOUSLY in the middle of the ring. All around her, enclosing her in a box, the jellyfish hummed. Their tentacles vibrated in a strange little dance that sent off tiny sparks. She stayed as far away from them as she could, all the while trying to stay away from the merman as well. He was cracking his knuckles and sizing her up like a hungry shark would its prey.

Keeping her hands steady—even though they wanted to tremble—Coral pulled on fingerless sealskin gloves. Apparently, they didn't believe in boxing gloves. They liked having scars on their knuckles and bodies, evidence of hard battles fought. After buttoning the gloves, she tightened her hands into fists and placed them in front of her, in a laughable version of a fighting stance.

The merman chuckled. "Your stance is wrong," he offered. "Fists like this." He demonstrated, and she copied his movement begrudgingly. She hated how helpful he sounded when it contrasted with the manic look in his eyes. Once she was appropriately positioned, his lips twitched in a low smile. "Good," he said, and then he charged.

If Caspian had been born for battle, *this* merman had been forged from it, molded into a weapon of destruction. Caspian had been structured order and calculation. But *he* was a dance of savagery, and violent grace thrummed off of him in terrifying whorls and waves.

Coral yelped and swam aside as his fist nearly collided against her face. Her tail was close to the jellyfish so she brought it forward. How was she supposed to dodge him *and* the edges? The merman turned back to her, eyes dancing with delight.

"Very good," he snickered. "Unfortunately, not good enough." He struck again with his fist, but this time she couldn't dodge it. His knuckles connected against her face in a movement that was so sudden, she didn't feel the pain at first. She fell to the side, twirling in circles through the water, coming to a halt just inches from the line of laughing jellies. Her head spun and her jaw pulsed in agony. The coppery tang of blood swirled inside her mouth and she spat it out, watching it rise in wisps like smoke. She was getting her ass kicked. Dodging would obviously do no good, so she'd have to put up her best fight, with whatever she had left in her. Even if she was no good.

So when the merman came forward again, she tried to focus on his movements, focus on where his arm was aiming. She took it all in, his left arm arched up above his head and swung down towards her. She dodged, twirling through the water in a quick burst of speed. When he followed, she brought the heel of her hand up and aimed for his nose.

The blow was well-placed and strong. Too bad he seemed all too familiar with pain. He didn't care that blood swirled out of his nose. He just smiled an encouraging smile before sweeping out the end of his tail, tripping her on her own. With a cry, she fell backwards, straight towards the line of jellies.

But the merman was there, pulling her up by the tunic before she could fall. She breathed a sigh of relief that was short lived. He whipped her around and held her in his crushing grip.

"With the proper training, you could be an excellent

fighter, *anthropos,*" he mused in her ear, causing the hairs on the back of her neck to curl. "I could make one of you yet."

Coral jerked her head back, skull clashing into his face. His arms slackened around her and she broke his hold, spinning around to catch his face in her fist. She pounded them into him, hoping to push them back, to trip him up, *anything.* There was nothing beautiful about her own movements. Just wild and untamed with desperation.

And he, he was chuckling at her punches which only served to fuel her anger even more.

Bastard. Bastard. Bastard.

His hands were crossed in an X in front of his head, blocking her every blow, leaving his stomach completely exposed. She switched directions there. Her knuckles screamed as she punched the hard ridges of his abs.

When she felt him tug at her hair, she cried out for a split second before biting down on her lip in an attempt to take the sound back. Stars danced behind her eyes at the pain. She ignored it—or tried to. He brought her face inches from his own. Her body struggled against his, but he tightened his grip, pulling her against his every crevice.

"You need to think before placing blows," he advised. The homicidal gleam in his eyes never dimmed. "Do not just waste your energy on panic and ill-aimed punches. Aim for the vulnerable spots." He placed a finger to her temple, her throat. "Aim with precision. For if you do not, you die." And then he slammed his head into hers.

The last thing Coral saw was his wide smile following her into the darkness.

~

WHEN CORAL CAME TO, she was lying beside the pile of polished spears. Her head pounded in an unsteady rhythm and her jaw was aching. She put her hand to face and winced.

"I did not even hit you hard," an amused voice drawled. She looked up and glared at the merman floating leisurely before her. He'd put on his red shirt in the time she'd been knocked out, hiding the muscles underneath. "I went easy on you... *this time*."

Though her face throbbed and she longed to rub a hand against it to ease the pain, Coral didn't. Not with him observing her like some sort of viper waiting to strike at the first sign of weakness. She couldn't shake the feeling that this was some type of test to him, and it was imperative that she pass. So Coral ignored both her pain and him and looked to the weapons. She hadn't even been able to finish what she'd come here to do, and it was all his fault.

Hissing low, she began piling spears into her arms and got up to go place them back on the walls. To her disdain, he followed close beside her.

"It looks like you could use some help." He smiled.

"I think you should go away and leave me alone," she retorted.

"Now, where is the fun in that?" Then without permission, he reached over her and took half of the weapons into his own arms. "Training is over. Soon they will be calling you over to pick up their equipment."

Coral fought back a groan and looked around. Sure enough, they were all tossing aside gloves, unwrapping their hands and dropping the kelp to the floor. Spears were left against walls and near the ring even though the wall to hold them up was a few strokes away.

Pigs.

They made it to the wall, and he leaned the spears against

it. Coral eyed him suspiciously. "Do you want *me* to clean up after you, *too*?"

He snorted as he began hanging the instruments up onto the wall one by one. "There is a certain contentment to be had at having servants at your beck and call." She rolled her eyes at the pompous way he said that. "*But,*" he added, "I can clean and secure my own weapons. Now go; your precious Caspian is calling you."

She turned to see Caspian waving her over. How had the brown-haired merman known when he hadn't even taken his eyes off of the wall? She looked back at him one last time. He was smirking.

"Just leave the spears here, *anthropos*. Go pick up Caspian's filth."

She shot him one last glare, deciding that she *really* didn't like him, before she turned and swam away. Even as she did, she felt the heavy weight of his gaze boring into her back.

THE WHISPERS OF AN UPRISING

ULLA MAGISSA SAT AT THE END OF THE TABLE IN THE Council Room. It was an obsidian structure, the surface of it so immaculately polished, her cruel, beautiful reflection stared back at her. The crown adorning her head was made from mother of pearl. This particular piece, designed to look like the overlapping scales of a fish, accentuated her green, low-neck, long-sleeved gown.

Her sharp tipped nails slowly tapped against the table, the noise slow and menacing, and it frightened every member of the royal court currently present. Each tap had one of them flinching, looking upon her warily.

The tendrils of her magic pulsed around her dangerously, waiting impatiently for the release of her fury. But the Queen of the Black Kingdom waited, and she did not unleash it.

Instead, she looked to her magistrate. The old mer's eyes faltered, his bent fingers trembled nervously before him. He clasped them together.

She smiled. "You have read the reports, have you not, Magistrate?"

"Just this morning, Your Majesty," he replied, every word trembling past his lips.

"Hmm..." She tapped her nails against the table, and he flinched. "And you were the one who chose which soldiers would go to Atlantica?"

Tap. Flinch. Tap. Flinch.

"I did, Your Majesty."

"So tell me, dearest Magistrate, why is it that they were *ambushed* and my shipment of Atlantean slaves *stolen*?" Upon that last word, Queen Ulla unleashed her power. It was a lightning whip striking down at the table, forcing it to split in two.

Her council gasped, cried out, and whimpered in fear. *As they should,* she thought cruelly. Because the queen was *not* happy with this turn of events.

"Your Majesty, *please,*" the magistrate begged.

Beggars annoyed her.

"Please *what?*"

He faltered at her tone, body seeming to physically shrink back and away from her. Any other time, Ulla would have smiled. But she did not. "You are aware that my brothels need filling, Magistrate?" she asked with an infinitesimal amount of patience.

Unable to voice a reply, he merely nodded.

"And who am I to fill them with if not Atlantean sea scum?" Then an idea occurred to her, that had her twisting her features into a cruel smile. "Perhaps your *daughters* could make fine work of pleasuring my noblemen? Or maybe they would be better suited as housemaids?" She tapped a finger-nail against her chin.

The magistrate tensed, old face paling. The room had gone quiet. No one would dare interfere lest they find their own children slaves and whores.

These nobles of the Dark Waters were as spoiled as the

Atlanteans, blanching at the slightest whisper of a threat of discomfort. No one could endure half of what the queen had, so long ago.

"Please, my queen." The magistrate trembled. "It was the rebels."

Ulla froze mid-tap and slowly lowered her hand to the broken surface of the table. Her hand curled into a tight fist before her, but before anyone could get a glimpse of the tight rage of her white knuckles, her tentacle slipped around her hand, shielding it from their view.

"Rebels," she repeated softly, as though she were not bothered at all.

"There are whispers, your Majesty, that there are Atlanteans rising up in the name of their true king and are building an army against you."

Her rage boiled high and hot. The tension in the room was as palpable as waves, and she knew her subjects were assessing her every move, digesting her every reaction. And she knew she could not let her worry show.

"I would hardly call a few entitled, renegade Atlanteans an 'army'." She flicked his words off with a wave of her fingers. "But I expect you to send out more soldiers at once. Unless you would rather offer up your children..." He shook his head back and forth. She smiled cruelly. "I thought not. Send some of my Personal Guard with your own men and bring me back my slaves." She rose, her tentacles curling and weaving around her. "Oh, and if you hear any more whisperings of an uprising... cut off the heads of those who speak of it and stake them to the front gates."

MATTHIAS

"Lord Matthias is here to see you," Zenara announced at breakfast the next morning.

Coral sat at the beautiful table made entirely from sea glass and stone. On chipped vintage china, salvaged from a shipwreck, there was a breakfast feast of smoked sea slugs, hard boiled fish eggs, sea cucumbers, pickled fruits, walrus milk and cheese, and a light frothy tea that looked like sea foam. It was all surprisingly delicious. Coral was rubbing seaberry jam onto a piece of scone made from deep fried catfish skin, or so Zenara had told her when Coral had asked.

Caspian was at the table with her, on the opposite side, of course, digging into his own meal when Zenara had announced Matthias' presence. The merman in question swam through the entry behind Zenara, who floated with her head bowed obediently, and Coral tensed at the sight of him.

He wore his Personal Guard uniform like a badge of honor, and he swam in like he owned the place. His brown hair curled over his forehead and even that seemed arrogant in manner. The black ink rose out of the collar of his jacket, twining around the cords of his neck and over the shaved sides of his head. It was the merman who had branded her, the merman who had *fought* her. Matthias. The fake name Caspian had given himself when they'd met.

Coral clutched the butter knife tightly in her hand when he swam past her.

"So you allow *anthropos* scum to break their fast at your table, Caspian? How about calling all the servants in for tea? I saw a stray salamander in the streets, maybe he would like to dine with us as well." There was a malicious smile on his face as he kicked out a chair with his tailfin and sat in it.

"I'm not an *anthropos*, you know." Coral found the words out of her mouth before she could stop them. Caspian froze, teacup halfway to his mouth. Matthias turned to look at her, smiling as if nothing she could say would faze him or make him frown. He just looked like he was demanding an explanation. "I have a tail. I can breathe underwater and swim like you. I'm not an *anthropos* anymore."

Matthias' smile widened into a full toothed grin. "I reckon you are still as useless as one, though." Then he turned his attention to Zenara, who still waited by the entryway. "I do not know what you are waiting for, half-breed," he said viciously, manic grin still firmly in place. "Bring me food."

Zenara dipped a curtsey and left the room. Coral glared at Matthias for his rude behavior. What a bastard! He'd taken great joy in permanently marking her flesh and beating her around in the training room the night before. She would take joy in sticking a knife through his eye.

"Why are you here, Matthias?" Caspian asked, calmly digging into his food.

Zenara came back and placed a tray of foodstuffs in front of Matthias and then backed away, ignoring the way he flashed his teeth in a mockery of thanks. Before answering, Matthias began shoving hard boiled fish eggs into his mouth, chewing obnoxiously. He licked his fingers one by one, making annoying popping sounds. "Her Majesty sent me," he said. Despite his awful table manners, he still addressed the queen respectfully.

"Why?" Caspian eyed him warily.

Matthias sucked a sea slug into his mouth, chewed and licked his fingers again before answering. "I am to accompany the *anthropos* today while you are to see to the queen's *personal needs.*" He eyed Caspian, as if daring him to argue, and Coral held her breath. If Caspian showed any sort of emotion, gave any sort of protest, then they would know. They would know he didn't really hate Coral. But he seemed to have years of masking his true self to his favor. Caspian shrugged and went back to his meal.

It nearly hurt her to see him so nonchalant, but Coral had to remind herself that it was a lie. That the lies were necessary for their survival. Even if she didn't like it. Even if she thought he was a coward.

It took Coral a moment to realize that Matthias was staring at *her* as she stared at Caspian. Quickly schooling her features, she glared at him. Hopefully, she hadn't given anything away in her face.

And if she had...

God help them both.

"Hurry along, *anthropos*. This place reeks of shit and I want to leave." Matthias tugged at her already bound-tight wrists, nearly causing her to be jerked backwards and fall into the silt. She kept her balance and shot Matthias another glare before bending over to pick up trash and place it in the fishnet. As she bent over again, Matthias let out a low, vulgar whistle. Coral shot straight up and spun around to glare at him—again. "It is no wonder Caspian has been panting after you. You are all curves, *anthropos*."

Coral snorted. "Caspian has *not* been panting after me."

Matthias shot her a knowing look, one of his perfectly groomed eyebrows lifting in mockery. And he smiled. He was *always* smiling, and it was starting to grate on Coral's nerves. There was no possible way he was that happy all the time. "Of course not."

Coral rolled her eyes at him. Ever since they'd left, he hadn't shut up. He was probably just trying to bother and get a reaction out of her so that she would let slip information. Well, it wouldn't work, and he was just wasting his time. She refused to give him anything to use against her. Nothing she could possibly have to say to him would serve the queen's purposes.

They'd proven themselves at breakfast that there was nothing between them. It had been proven the night before as well, after she'd woken up from unconsciousness. Caspian had ordered her about quite loudly that she hurry up and clean the entire training room. It had taken her hours, but she eventually finished. Caspian hadn't helped her at all—though it was still strange that Matthias *had*—and he'd made a point to ignore her on the way back to his house. He didn't even glance at her swelling cheek the entire time, just pulled her along like a dog on a leash. When they made it to the house, she'd expected the mask to fall away, for him to take her in his arms and cradle her injured face. Instead, he'd commanded her to go to her room and sent Zenara to tend to her instead. Even at breakfast, he ignored the bright purple bruising along her jaw and ate silently.

"Are you almost done?" Matthias complained once. "I want to leave."

A low growl rumbled in Coral's chest. "We *just* got here."

"And I want to leave."

"Maybe if you actually helped me instead of floating around complaining, this would go faster," she snapped, her patience already frayed. "Just a thought."

Matthias snorted. "Yeah, that is not going to happen."

You helped me last night. "Then stop fucking complaining!" She started to bend to pick up more plastic when her bonds were suddenly jerked and she flew back in the water, her back landing heavily against Matthias' body. She grumbled and started to swim forward but was suddenly wrapped in the circle of his arms. She stilled, her body shuddering with awareness. "What are you doing?" she demanded in a low whisper.

Matthias pushed aside her hair to expose her neck, the action caused her to tense up. He trailed his nose against her skin and inhaled as if memorizing her scent. She felt the warm rasp of his tongue against the most sensitive part of her flesh.

Coral thrashed against him and tried to pull away, but his vise-like grip was unbreakable. He chuckled against her skin, and then she gasped when the end of his tail curled around her own, wrapping them close together and snuggling her against his hard chest.

"Let go of me," Coral squeaked, suddenly too breathless to move. She recalled the moment he'd held her down to brand her, how she'd fought as hard as she could with all of her strength, but it had done no good. He was too strong, and she couldn't fight him off. He'd proven that the night before.

"I want to see what the fuss is about," Matthias whispered. "I want to see if you taste as good as you look..." He grazed his suddenly sharp teeth against her neck and dug them in. It felt like knives piercing past her flesh. Coral cried out, going slack in his arms. He held her up, arms resting just under her breasts. The pain was nauseating. She groaned and counted down the seconds until he extracted his teeth. When he did, he slid his tongue across the wound. "You taste better than I imagined, *anthropos*."

With a cry of rage, Coral straightened and shot her head back, slamming it into Matthias. He let out a curse from the surprise of it and released her. Momentarily blinded by stars, she swam without direction until her bonds came up short.

Matthias gave them a jerk and spun her around so she was facing him. She glared, a feral snarl ripping past her lips. He exposed his teeth, as sharp as a shark's, before they shifted and became perfectly straight and normal. Blood flowed from his nose and swirled in with the water.

He was smiling. "You have a burning spirit within you, *anthropos*. I like it." He ran his tongue across his teeth, cleaning any traces of her blood that may have been left there. Matthias gave another hard yank on the rope, but this time, she didn't let herself fall forward. She struggled back, even as he easily pulled her close until she was in front of him. His hand went to her neck, thumb caressing her collarbone in fast, excited movements. He leaned down, so close she felt his warm breath against her lips. So close, only a centimeter separated their lips. He opened his mouth and whispered, "Now get back to work."

BY THE TIME CORAL FINISHED, she was exhausted. Her tail muscles ached, her back felt heavy, and her wrists were throbbing. She finished lifting the final bags over Mathias's massive orange and white hippocampus, with no help from *him*, and she was just ready to get going.

"I'm done," she announced to a bored looking Matthias who had started to entertain himself by twirling a gold and black coin between his fingers. At her statement, he nearly dropped it in relief.

"Thank Neptune." He got up and stretched his arms over his head, the movement sending his jacket riding up to reveal the perfect shadowing of a V along his hips, and with it, a smattering of golden-copper scales. Coral eyed his figure involuntarily, then blushed when he said, "My eyes are up here, Knowledge Keeper. You will do well to keep them here, for the queen does not take kindly to those with wandering gazes."

"The queen doesn't seem to take kindly to anyone," Coral mumbled and regretted it immediately. It was one thing to *think* insulting things or to say them to Caspian, but Matthias seemed fiercely loyal to Ulla, if his exaggerated tattoo had been of any indication. He'd probably gut her for even saying that.

Matthias swam beside her, and she tensed as his hands went to her waist. "Easy, mer," he said as if he'd startled a frightened hippocampus. "I will not smite you where you stand for speaking the truth." He hoisted her up on his enormous hippocampus and hopped on behind her, reaching around her body, caging her in to grab the reins. Unlike Caspian, he didn't try to avoid touching her. He didn't seem to care that his skin brushed along hers, or that his heart was a steady beat against her back. He had no qualms about roaming hands or stolen smiles. While she didn't exactly welcome his touch, he didn't make her feel like she was some dirty secret to be hid away in the shadows.

Don't feel so fucking happy about that, she warned herself as he nudged the animal with the end of his tail. They were off, going at a steady pace through the water. He seemed to be in no big hurry.

"Why are you in her service?" Coral boldly asked. If she was going to ride with him, she could at least find out all she could about the queen's preferred Personal Guard. It may serve to her advantage later on.

"Because the sex is fantastic," he replied. Coral tensed, and he laughed at her. "Not the answer you expected?"

"I was expecting something more inspiring and emotional."

Matthias laughed. "You will find no such sentiments with me, Knowledge Keeper. I am not Caspian. There is no sob story in my past, no manipulation or heartbreaking emotions to get you to cry over me. I do what I do because I love it. I love power, riches, and mermaids. That is enough for me."

Definitely not what she was expecting, but she could see no other reason he'd be there. He was right; he wasn't Caspian. He wasn't gentle or quiet or spiritually strong. He wasn't hesitant with his touches or unsure in caresses. He was no coward. With Matthias, what you saw was what you got. A violent, honest psychopath.

Coral had known his type. Had been broken by them. Yet there was something infinitely more comforting about an honest crazy person rather than one who lured others into a false sense of security.

"You claim to love mermaids, but in her service you aren't allowed to stray."

Matthias roared with laughter. "You do not think I follow that rule, do you? Although I am very discreet in all matters, I have no doubt that the queen knows. Why do you think Caspian is her favorite? Of the three of us, he is the only one who has never been corrupted." His hand trailed down her bare arm. "Until now."

Coral fidgeted in her seat in an attempt to get his hand off her. "I've not corrupted anyone," she said firmly.

Matthias chuckled, and she felt the rumble in his chest vibrate against her back. She scooted forward on the hippocampus to put as much space between them as she could.

"Right." Matthias splayed his palm over her stomach and

pulled her back against him until she thumped against his chest. He kept his palm firmly against her and bent his head down to bite the lobe of her ear. Not with his shifting shark teeth, thankfully. Still she flinched, and he chuckled. "Do not worry, *anthropos*," he whispered. "Your secret is safe with me."

"What secret?" She jerked her shoulder up to nudge him off of her. He just laughed at her pathetic attempts in fighting him off and leaned back, giving her the space she desired.

"Do not play dumb, Knowledge Keeper. It does not suit you."

"I thought to you mer all *anthropos* were stupid."

"Ha! You said yourself earlier, did you not? You are no longer an *anthropos*. You are one of us now." His hand found her waist, fingering lightly over the material of her dress, right where he'd branded her. "One of the lost, the forgotten of the sea." He dug his fingers cruelly into her wound and she cried out, gasping against the hippocampus' mane. The pain sent a throbbing fire down her entire side.

"Let go of me," she gasped, jerking her elbows back.

"You are not one to be giving me orders, land scum." He dug his fingers in even harder. Coral sobbed. "Come on, Knowledge Keeper. *Fight back*. Where did the earlier burning spirit go?" He sunk his fingers in deeper. Coral screamed, arching her head back, gasping. "Fight back, Coral. I want a glimpse at the warrior in you. You hide behind glares and shy words, but when it comes down to it, you are as tough as one of us. I know you can do it." His other hand trailed up her stomach to grip beneath her breast. She whimpered. "*Fight back*."

Coral brought her elbow up, crashing into Matthias' temple with all of her strength. He cursed and released his hold on her. When he did, she gave a powerful thrust of her tail and fell off the side of the hippocampus and towards the silt below. But Caspian had taught her to swim with ease and before she crashed, she angled herself and kicked her tail, and *swam*. The rope binding her wrists snapped with the force of her fall.

She swam through the open expanse of blue ocean; fish dodged her as she darted past. She jetted freely, swimming away from Matthias and the delight he took in her torture. Away from the kingdom of the Dark Waters. Away from the psychotic queen and away from Caspian.

The slapping of hooves and fin against water only had her swimming faster, putting more power into her tail. He was gaining on her, catching up...

The heavy weight of a powerful body crashed into Coral, knocking her face-first into the sand. The breath was knocked from her body from the impact. She lifted her head up and coughed out the silt from her mouth, felt the warm trickle of blood swirl out of her nose.

Coral was whipped around harshly, staring face to face at Matthias. His grin was nearly manic with glee. "It seems Caspian taught you a thing or two." Coral grit her teeth and brought her fist up to punch him in the jaw, but he caught her wrist and slammed it down against the sea floor. She tried with the other one, but he did just the same thing until she was pinned beneath his heavy weight. "Maybe I could teach you a thing or two more." And then he brought his lips crashing down on hers.

Coral struggled against him, but his tongue forced her mouth open. He explored every inch of her mouth, tongue demanding a violent kiss. He sucked on her bottom lip and pressed his whole body into her. This kiss was so different from Caspian's. His had been desperate, nearly frantic with unchecked desire, his hands gentle. Matthias' kiss was savage and untamed. He didn't worry about hurting her, about pressing too hard on her wrists or nipping her lips with the tips of his sharp teeth.

Every press of his body felt purposeful. While it was violent, she felt her fear dissipating at the words he'd said. At the *intent* behind them and every aggressive touch. Almost as if...

Almost as if he were teaching her a lesson, in his own sick way.

On instinct, Coral bit down. Hard.

Matthias yowled and jerked up. Blood flowed from his mouth. Coral used his surprise to her advantage and swung her tail up, smacking his own. He loosened his hold, and she brought the palm of her hand against his nose, cracking it. Coral slipped from beneath him and backed away, wiping a hand across her mouth to rid herself of his taste.

Matthias grinned through the blood. "You are a fighter, Coral, like me."

"I am nothing like you," she spat, her chest heaving with her anger.

"Keep telling yourself pretty lies, Coral. No one believes them but you."

"Why would I even want to be like you? Slave to a psycho queen?"

Matthias swam towards her, and she took a few strokes back. "You are more like me than you know. We are both the queen's property." He yanked aside the lapels of his jacket to reveal the black ink of his tattoo. Then, he shot out like a jet and was in front of Coral before she could even blink. His hands gripped the material of her dress and he pulled, tearing it to bare her skin and the wound he'd given her. "You are as much the queen's as I am, Coral. Never forget that because she never will."

Coral grabbed for the torn dress and brought it to her body, covering her bare skin and the top of her tail. Heat stained her cheeks at what he'd done, at another humiliation to make her suffer. She turned her face away, feeling the stinging press of tears at the back of her eyelids. Because this? The torn clothes, the pain? It threatened to remind her of something else.

"Do not cry." Matthias took her chin in his fingers and turned her face back up to his. "Fighters use fist and sword to take out their frustrations. Never tears."

This, too, felt like a lesson and a dare. She realized then that he was right. Even before Trent, she'd always been shy. She'd always hid behind books and glasses, using them as excuses to not stand up for herself or what she believed in. Even afterwards, she'd never had the bravery to confront the problem. To fight.

Matthias had given her a gift she didn't even realize she'd needed. It was a confounding thing, the way he penetrated her defenses. The way she hated him, but also... for some asinine reason, Coral also felt herself respecting his particular brand of crazy.

What did that make her?

Coral couldn't help herself. She brought her hand up and slapped it across his face, leaving a red mark in its wake, answering his dare with violence of her own.

Matthias grinned down at her. "Does that not feel better, *my little fighter?*"

She smiled. "It does."

"Good."

And then he picked her up and threw her over his shoulder. He kept his hand firmly planted on her bottom and chuckled as he swam back to their hippocampus, all the while with Coral's fists pounding into his back.

THE ATLANTEAN SLAVES

"WHERE ARE WE GOING?" CORAL'S VOICE CUT THROUGH the ever-darkening waters. It sounded harsh and percussive in its echoes, and as soon as the words left her lips, she flinched.

After that fighting fiasco between them, Matthias had retied her bonds and sat her in front of him on his hippocampus, his fingers forcing her sea legs open so he could slam her down on the saddle with a satisfied grunt. It still unnerved her, that gaining access to her legs and intimate areas was so easily obtained; with just a glide of fingers down connecting tendons. Luckily, her dress was long enough to cover everything as they rode on. She'd eyed their surroundings, noticing he wasn't taking the right turns and path that would lead them back to Caspian's house.

She'd ignored it, but after a while of traveling and after the scenery around them had so drastically changed, she'd grown wary. The open blue of the waters had bled into darkness and shadows that might have had something to do with the reflective surface of the obsidian buildings and homes. But even so, she'd seen the castle, and she'd seen bits and pieces of the city in that terrible drag through the silt.

This wasn't a nice place.

It was like an abyss, where creatures lurked behind dead bits of coral and stone, waiting for them to come close enough so they could gnash their splintered teeth. Merfolk slummed against buildings in tattered rags that looked like they belonged on the bodies of homeless people. Perhaps they *were* homeless. She wasn't sure, and she was too afraid to break the silence to ask.

Beady, glowing eyes peeked at them from lower waters as the hippocampus glided through the desolate streets, only to sink away with Matthias' brightening, feral grin. Her own fingers dug deeper into the hippocampus' mane for support as the nerves threatened to overpower her.

As they left the seedy place behind, they approached a more crowded area. There were more merfolk swimming through here, female and male alike. There was something innately different about these merfolk in comparison to others Coral had seen swimming about only moments before.

They didn't have strange, fish-like features at all. In fact, their tails looked like they could be beautiful, had the colors not been dulled to a grimy sheen. Her eyes swept over faces and dead eyes of female mer clad in skimpy clothing that left nothing to the imagination. They didn't swim on tails, but instead kept their sea legs wide open as they flapped their legs, swimming leisurely in circles.

One of the female's caught Coral's eye, her skin an unhealthy pale shade, with dark circles under her eyes and a haunting look about her that would be burned in her retinas forever.

"Who are these merfolk?" Coral whispered. She was almost sure Matthias wasn't going to answer her at all.

"They're the whores of the Black Kingdom's infamous brothel."

She twisted to look up at Matthias' face. Surprisingly

enough, he wasn't grinning, though his eyes seemed to dance with some unknown emotion.

"They look so empty."

"That's because they are. Like you, they are little more than Atlantean slaves, here to serve the queen's purpose."

She turned back around to look at them, but the hippocampus was picking up speed, leaving them and their brothel behind.

She fixated her gaze ahead, but she couldn't shake the building ache in her chest or the way it spread throughout her body. Those mer were Atlantean. They were Caspian's people.

And they were enslaved.

"What happened between the Dark Waters and Atlantica?" she asked.

Matthias' hand dug into her hip, right over the mark of her brand. It didn't hurt, though. "Don't ask questions you are not ready to hear the answers to."

She huffed with annoyance, wishing she could kick him. Who was he to tell her what she was or wasn't ready for? That was her business and hers alone.

"Where are we going?" she asked again. "Why are you showing me all this?" She couldn't help but feel like he was showing it all for a reason, one that obviously alluded her.

He didn't reply, though. He dug his tail into his hippocampus, and the creature went faster through the water. When he finally stopped, it was at what seemed like the outskirts of the city. They'd stopped in front of a house. It wasn't as grand as Caspian's, and it wasn't made of cracked obsidian either. It was still beautiful, though, and rather endearing with its colorful, mosaic walls that appeared to be made of driftwood and thousands of fragments of sea glass that gave it a rainbow shine. The only thing black was its base, sitting on four legs like an underwater bungalow. The rest of it was a stark shine of brightness against the darkness Coral had become familiarized with.

Matthias hopped off his hippocampus and led it towards a black pole sticking up from the ground. He tied the reins there before he reached up and in a swift, almost gentle, move, pulled Coral down from it.

Her sea legs snapped closed, the tendons connecting into a tail. He steadied her as her body began sinking towards the sand, his fingers encircling her wrists. He was staring at her, and she found that she couldn't look away even if she wanted to.

He was a hypnotizing merman, almost as much as Caspian, if not more so. His eyes were the color of copper, the same golden-brown as his tail. His brown hair floated and curled over his forehead and she hated that it did.

That fucking Superman curl was a weakness that made her fins furl and her stomach tighten.

Jesus, what was wrong with her? Did she have a thing for bad boys? For men who would break her body as much as her heart? She couldn't fathom why said heart suddenly started beating faster in her chest. She was delusional, cracked out on all the salt water. That had to be the only explanation. Though, she had to admit, there was something charismatic about him, regardless of his flaws.

Matthias smirked as if he could hear her thoughts loud and clear. She frowned at him, wanting to scream. Just because she found him attractive didn't mean she didn't still hate him. It was her weak ass bookworm heart. Always crying for the hot villains with tragic backstories. Always wanting to wrap them up in a blanket and protect them, even if they could kill her while doing it.

Fucking villains.

Fucking authors.

Fucking Matthias.

He pulled away from her, and she felt the tightness on her wrists ease. A quick glance down, it was to see that he'd freed her of the confines of her bonds. Her brows pulled together as she looked back up at him.

"You won't try and swim away from me," he said, amusement twinging his tone.

Her fins flared at the hint of a challenge in his voice. "Is that so?"

"You wouldn't get very far."

She wanted to prove him wrong, but she knew he was right. She may have been burning for the opportunity to escape, but she wasn't an idiot. She was closer to the open ocean now, and who knew what kind of things lived out here that would turn her into lunch meat.

"Good *anthropos*." He patted her head and she jerked away from him.

"I'm not a damn pet," she hissed.

"The brand on your side begs to differ." He nodded at her hip.

Her own face flamed as she realized it was on display. He'd ripped her dress earlier and she'd forgotten all about it. The tatters on the side had it slipping from her shoulder, showing the top of her breast, while the hem at the bottom had risen to display her scales. She quickly settled it all back into place with a huff.

Matthias laughed and jerked his head towards the house. "Come on." He swam and Coral followed warily, her eyes roaming over every inch of the place.

"Where are we?" she asked as he swam to the door and pushed it open.

She stopped shy of the threshold while he swam inside.

"Don't just float there, *anthropos*," he called out from inside.

Taking a deep breath, she didn't contemplate how it felt like she was swimming to her execution and went in.

And she was immediately attacked.

She screamed as something flew towards her face. She tried dodging it, but sharp teeth grazed across her arm, like the slightest swipe of a knife. The thing was a blur through the water, and she couldn't see it as it zipped around her in a threatening circle. Her breath came out erratically as her eyes tried to zero in on the thing. By the time she found it, it was too late. It zapped towards her face and she barely had time to dodge. She screamed, cowering back...

Then Matthias was there, his hand clamping down on the thing. It wriggled ferociously, snarling and snapping, trying to get a bite out of the merman.

"Got you, you little shit." Matthias gave it a firm shake, and it stopped struggling enough so Coral could make out what it was.

"Oh, my—"

"He's been hiding in here for days," Matthias explained. "Fucking runt."

Coral slapped her palms against her cheeks, all her fears forgotten as she caught sight of it. "He's so *cute!*"

Matthias looked at her like she was crazy, but she couldn't help it. Her heart felt like it was about to burst at how cute the thing was.

It was a salamander.

Slick, bright blue skin encased the small thing, its lips pulled back in a sneer to reveal sharp teeth. Its stubby little legs kicked, its tail swaying wildly beneath it. He was about two feet long, as big as a dachshund but *cuter*, she thought.

"Oh, aren't you just the cutest thing?" She knew her voice pitched high like she was talking to a baby, but she couldn't help it. She swallowed the space between them, holding her hand out.

"What the fuck, *anthropos*—"

She didn't listen to him and grabbed the salamander's face in between her hands. It didn't make another swipe at her, obviously adoring her voice as she murmured kind things to it. It relaxed as her fingers glided along his skin and let out a low, almost purring noise that sounded broken. Unable to help herself, she pulled the creature from Matthias' hands and into her arms, cradling it to her chest, where it burrowed against her with contentment.

"Aw, he's just the cutest little salamander. Aren't you? Who's the cutest? Huh? How long have you had him?" She looked up at Matthias to find him staring at her like she'd suddenly grown a second head. "What?"

"That thing is no pet, and you have me questioning your competence as a Knowledge Keeper with the way you keep rubbing yourself over it." His lip curled back. "Filthy, disease-ridden creature."

Coral's eyes rolled. "You're the only filthy one here, *dick*. He's so cute!"

A crater of a frown formed between his brows. "Did you just call me a dick? Is that an insult in your realm? Here it is little more than an invitation for dangerous proclivities." His eyes danced down her form suggestively, and it made sparks trail across her exposed skin. "Anyway, he's a pest," he argued. "He got inside somehow and won't fucking leave. But now that I've got him, I'm going to make salamander stew."

As if he understood what Matthias was saying, the salamander wriggled in Coral's grasp, but she just hugged him tighter to her chest, jerking back from Matthias. "You can't eat him! That's barbaric!"

"I can do whatever the fuck I want, Knowledge Keeper." His brows raised, like he was amused at her audacity.

"He's a pet. You can't eat him. I—I won't let you."

He threw his head back and laughed. Any other time, she

would have been hypnotized by the workings of his throat, but she was too breathless and full of adrenaline to do so. "Like you could stop me?" The dark and dangerous gleam in his eyes was back, and he was inching closer towards her.

"He's a pet," she pleaded. "You can't cook him if he has a name."

His feral smile returned, and he was so close, she could feel the heat emanating from his whole body. "It just so happens he doesn't."

"He *does*." She looked down at the pitiful creature. "His name is Gibby!" she blurted.

If she'd hoped he'd stop coming near her, he didn't. He inched closer until they were pressed tightly together, Gibby all but squished between them.

Matthias bent so his lips were near her own. This, too, felt like a test. Like he was waiting for her to jerk back. Like he was just waiting for her to prove how weak she was, how frightened she was. And her heart was a wild thing in her chest, beating so hard it felt like it would burst, and she *was* afraid of him. But not so afraid that she would let him take this poor creature's life.

She tilted her chin up higher and felt the soft brush of his lips linger near her own.

"I won't let you kill him," she whispered.

Something dark flashed through his eyes, and she swore it fragmented across his whole face for a moment. Pain. But it was gone in an instant, and that smile curled up even higher. He pushed away from her, his fins sliding against her own as he put space between them.

"You would disregard your own life for this creature's? *Fine*," he conceded, so quickly that she almost wasn't able to read the awe from his previous sentence. "But when we leave, he's going back outside."

Feeling like it was a small victory, she breathed a sigh of

relief and loosened her grip on Gibby. As she did, he wriggled out of her hold and darted up to crawl against the ceiling.

Matthias glared at him as he scuttled away into another room.

"Little bastard," he growled. "Next time I won't let you get in the way of my revenge."

Coral chuckled without meaning to and found herself observing the merman. In this new light he seemed less... vicious somehow. Like maybe he wasn't all that bad?

The brand burning at her side begged to differ, so she quickly shook that thought off.

"Why are we here?" she asked instead.

Instead of answering, he disappeared into another room, and when he came back out, he was wearing a new jacket and long tunic that covered half of his tail. It was the same style as the one he'd been wearing before, but cleaner.

"I wanted to change. That jacket reeked like those shit-infested waters. And so do you."

The barb struck her straight in the chest. She sniffed discreetly, noting that she *did* smell bad. Her face flushed with embarrassment, but Matthias didn't pay attention to it at all. He was already moving about the space. It looked like a living room, with a plush couch with anemone edges, and yet almost every corner of the place was crammed with things.

She hadn't noticed before, but she took it all in now. Treasure chests were filled with jewels and coins in gold and obsidian, sapphires and diamonds, rubies and jade. There were so many things, objects that looked all too valuable like marble statues that shone brightly, paintings that somehow remained pristine beneath the depths, collections of things that looked to be pilfered from an old pirate ship.

"Why do you have so much stuff?" Coral asked.

"I think the better question is why would I not have so

much stuff?" he teased as he dropped himself onto his plush couch. The frame of it was made of pure gold.

"You live in little more than a shack," she pointed out. "And you fill it with a lot of valuable artifacts. Why? What if someone comes and steals your stuff?"

His teeth flashed, and she watched them elongate into sharp points like that of a shark before her eyes. Her own neck burned at the sight of them, remembering the feel of the bite. She'd felt it, but it was still a shock to see them grow like that. Though, at this point, she wasn't sure why anything surprised her anymore.

"They can try," Matthias said, his voice lowering with a dark edge. "Like you, they would not get very far. And if they did, then I would cut off their hands with my blade and rip out their throats with my teeth."

Her throat closed, and the back of her neck prickled. She believed his every word, and that made him so much more frightening. To know he'd come so close to doing the same thing to her.

Her fingers grasped at her neck and the tender wound there that still throbbed.

He tracked her every movement. "That was a mark of affection. Trust that anyone who robbed me would suffer pain, not pleasure."

Coral's eyes widened. *"Pleasure?"* She snorted. "Is that what you're calling it?"

His arms widened at his sides. "It is what it is, whether you are willing to admit it or not. That is how my kind shows..." He paused, tilting his head a fraction. "Admiration."

"Your kind?"

"Part shark, part siren, part merman. Hybrids of the sea." He flashed his teeth. "Biting is our form of admiration."

She wasn't surprised that for him, pain and pleasure went hand in hand. She could shove a blade into his chest right now and he'd probably get turned on by it. "You're crazy," she whispered. "Like, there's something seriously wrong with you."

He planted his tail firmly on the ground, leaning forward. His eyes sparked with curiosity. "Is that so?" he echoed her earlier words. "Pray tell why you have drawn such a conclusion about me."

"I just can't fathom how you think that *this*," she gestured at her neck, "is a sign of affection. I mean, maybe some people like it. There are BDSM communities, and people who lean towards being sadistic or masochistic, but this wasn't pleasurable for me."

"The only word I heard in that entire explanation was 'pleasurable'." He smirked.

"Of course you did."

"Come now, *anthropos*."

He swam up and was in front of her in a flash. Her breath caught in her throat, and a startled yelp pierced past her lips. His fingers reached out and caught her shoulder, his thumb brushing against the edge of the mark he'd inflicted. As he stared at it with eyes the color of whiskey, she felt it pulse like the brand on her hip. He'd marked her twice, she realized with a start. The first for his queen and the second...

"Tell me this does not feel good." The slow, steady sweeps of his thumb had her arching her head back, almost involuntarily. The gentle touch of his fingertips near the pain did something to her she didn't know could be done. He leaned closer, the edge of his sharp nose brushing against hers. "Tell me you do not like it, that you do not feel your pearl vibrate with every caress."

"I... I..." Her eyes fluttered closed, then opened again. "My pearl?" she questioned.

His grin was feral, the glints of his sharp teeth biting against his bottom lip. "Shall I show you?" He pressed against her wound, and Coral felt a slice of discomfort in her neck, but that feeling was quickly replaced with desire the moment his fingers glided up the tendons of her tail and pressed to her mound.

"Oh, my God." Her head dropped back, her hips jerking closer to his touch. She hadn't meant for that reaction, but it had been almost instinctive to do because it had felt *so good*. Even when she knew it shouldn't feel that way.

"Feel my fingers slide against you and feel how my bite heightens the experience." His knuckles brushed against her center just as his other hand pressed to her wound. She gasped. He was right. It felt like the two were... connected by more than just muscles; by magic and nerves and the secret where want and need met. "Your pearl..." Then his fingers pinched her clit and she gasped.

That's what he meant.

"So, what do you feel?"

The smugness in his voice irritated her as much as her body's reaction to him did.

"I think you're deflecting." Her fingers grasped his shoulders, and she shoved him away. He went surprisingly easily, pulling away from her a fraction and letting her straighten. One hand still remained on her neck, but the other disappeared from beneath her skirt. She still felt his heat, could still see the glow in his eyes.

"Deflecting?"

She swallowed and knew he could feel the move against her throat. "Yes," she rasped. "You don't want to answer the questions about your confounding living space. You live in a place that looks like shit on the outside but is crammed with riches on the inside. You could live in a house like Caspian's since you're one of the queen's favored."

"Could I?"

Annoyance flared. "Stop answering a question with a

question. Why do you live at the edge of the kingdom with no neighbors but with all this stuff? It's like you're trying to hoard it all. For what purpose?"

"Maybe I live at the edge of the kingdom so no one can hear the screams." His thumb pressed into her collarbone. "And you *will* scream if you keep asking questions you are not ready to hear the answers to."

Her chin tilted in defiance, but it only made him gleeful. "Why do you live in such a shitty house, Matthias?"

His fingers wrapped around her throat, and Coral gasped as she was lifted higher in the water. Her fins flared as she grasped his wrist. He wasn't choking her, not really, but his touch was firm and demanding.

"You are mistaken if you think you can give me orders and make demands. I have nothing to explain to you that would be any of your business." Both his eyes and nostrils were flaring, and for once she didn't feel the wickedness in him.

She felt the anger.

She feared it more.

"I think I hit a sore spot." Coral wasn't sure why she was taunting him. Maybe it was to break past the smiles. To see if there was more to him than just that cruelty he so relished in. It didn't matter. At least, it shouldn't. But it was like poking at something in the sand. It filled her with gross curiosity. "You seem upset, Matthias. Is it because I'm right?"

He dropped his hand and reached instead for a dagger.

But still, she couldn't stop.

"Why do you live here instead of a mansion? Does this place mean something to you?" His eyes flashed dangerously, and she knew she was right. "Whose house is it? Yours? Your childhood home—"

The blade kissed her throat but didn't pierce deep. Even though Matthias looked like he was prepared to use it against her, out of anger instead of for diversion. He never got the chance.

He yelped and jerked away from her, the dagger sent clattering from his hand. Coral watched with fascination as his tail flailed, dangling from the ends of his fins was Gibby.

The salamander clung to his fins, his stubby legs clawing at them, a threatening growl emanating from his throat.

"You fucking *beast*." Matthias reached for Gibby. "Let go of me!"

But Gibby didn't relent. Even as Matthias tugged, all it did was cause the salamander to dig his teeth in deeper and his claws to rake more profound wounds against his scales.

"Fucking Neptune..." Matthias breathed heavily. "I will cook you over a spit of water fire if you do not release me, cretin."

Gibby did not move.

And it was so comical to see him battling against a two-foot salamander that Coral couldn't help herself.

She laughed.

The sound burst past her in uncontrollable shakes of her shoulders and a sharp pain in her belly that had her doubling over and wheezing.

"Glad you can find this amusing," Matthias grumbled.

"Oh, it is! You should see your face." Laughter bubbled and didn't stop until Matthias stopped flapping his tail around. He stilled, watching Coral as her amusement abated and was replaced with the slow curl of self-consciousness.

Only because Matthias was staring at her in a way she'd only read about in books. He was staring at her with awe and admiration. He was staring at her like she held the stars of the sky in her eyes and the sun in her smile. But that was absolutely ridiculous.

This wasn't a story.

Matthias wasn't a hero.

He wasn't even an antihero.

And no one had ever looked at Coral that way, so why would he?

Yet she couldn't shake the feeling that there was something more in his gaze. Something she didn't understand but wanted to. Maybe he wasn't all sharp edges and brittle words like he'd have her believe. Just like Caspian wasn't just quiet pain with miles-long walls.

"Gibby," she whispered, though unable to break contact with Matthias. "Come here, boy."

The growling stopped, and only then did Coral find it in her to turn away. Gibby released Matthias' tail, then swam out of reach and raced towards Coral, hiding behind her billowing skirts.

Matthias made an impatient noise. "Figures. Broken creatures flock to you."

Her frown was question enough.

"It's your eyes. They beg for companionship." He swallowed and looked away. When he looked back, he was smirking again. "Why do you think Caspian is so enthralled with you?"

Her nose wrinkled. "You're disgusting."

"I never claimed otherwise. Now, let's go, *anthropos*. I have things to do that do not involve an interrogation. We should get you back to your precious Caspian before he worries."

She wanted to argue and ask more questions but held her tongue. She didn't have a right to know about him or his life, and she'd poked at it any. She understood all too well what it meant to have wounds you let fester in quiet, and she wouldn't begrudge him for it. All she knew was that the dark mer of the Black Kingdom weren't all black or white. There was more to this place, and to Caspian and Matthias, than she knew. It was in the poverty-filled waters, in the eyes of the

Atlantean slaves, in Caspian's attitude, and in Matthias' house.

Whether he'd admit it to her or not.

Gibby followed outside as they swam to his hippocampus. Matthias grabbed her waist to lift her up and sit her down. Gibby swam up to her eye level, and Matthias swatted him away. "Go away, pest."

"I'd take him with me to get him out of your hair, but I think Caspian would be angry if I did."

Matthias snickered and hopped on behind her. His lips were hot on her ear. "I don't think you understand that Caspian would forgive you anything." Before she could come up with a retort for that, he was turning to Gibby. "Besides, he is a wild animal, not a pet. Do not attempt to tame it, because you will be sorely disappointed."

She couldn't help but feel like his words had a double meaning.

Then he dug his leg into the side of the hippocampus and they were off, leaving Gibby behind in the silt. A crushing weight pressed to her chest at leaving him behind. It was always like that with animals. You could meet one for thirty minutes and feel like you'd known it all your life. She felt like she was leaving a child behind, but he was right.

Gibby belonged in the wild. Not locked up like she was.

"By the way," Matthias purred. "You did not seem so surprised with your sea legs." Her body tensed and he was so in tune with her reactions, that she felt the rumbling chuckle against her back. "Well, well, well... Has Caspian taught you to explore your body already?" His hand slid down the side of her thigh.

"I—I discovered it for myself," she defended weakly.

"You are a terrible liar, Knowledge Keeper," he whispered near the lobe of her ear. "I hope you know that."

They rode the rest of the way in silence, and Coral felt

entirely too sick to her stomach, knowing that all this ignoring Caspian had been doing, all this pretending, had been royally fucked up within a matter of a few innocent words.

Because she had no doubt that Matthias would take this information straight back to his queen.

KEEPERS OF KNOWLEDGE & MAGIC

THE DUNGEONS WERE HIDDEN WITHIN A LABYRINTH OF massive stone walls covered in thick layers of algae and clumps of barnacles. The years had begun crumbling away at the stone, and it looked like they were standing in a maze of ruins. The only illumination came from bioluminescent spots mottled on the walls.

The water down in this part of the castle felt heavy and warm, suffocatingly so. It was uncomfortable to swim through, but Caspian would never let his discomfort show. He swam at a steady pace next to Zalyn, the only sound around them the slow slapping of their fins against the water.

Caspian had memorized the way towards the *calabazos*. He visited them often enough, he could have swam through this maze in the dark.

His mind swam from thought to thought. He thought of Coral, alone with Matthias and what he might be doing to her. Matthias thrived in violent acts, and Coral would have been like a fresh new toy for experimentation. He was a rock fish waiting to strike his awaiting prey. He hoped Coral would be fine, that she could survive Matthias' cruel acts. She had the spirit of the *guerreri*. She *would* be alright.

The queen had sent him with Zalyn and Matthias with Coral to unnerve him and get a reaction. But Caspian had been playing this game for years. He had long ago mastered the art of hiding his emotions in plain sight. Even if he cared, even if his heart twisted without Coral in his sight, he would reveal nothing.

They rounded the last turn and came to a halt before massive iron bars. They dug deeply into the ground and rose to touch the ceiling. The bars had very little free space between them to avoid escapees.

Guards floated at attention before the massive doors; they saluted Caspian and Zalyn when they saw them. Caspian ordered them to open the gates and when they did, both him and Zalyn, ever his watchful shadow, swam through.

This *calabozo* was a wide and long rectangular room with cells aligned on either side. The end of the room displayed a cleanly polished assortment of torture devices. Iron chains, collars and bindings for wrists and tails, sharp razors, knives, and head gears with iron spikes poking out of them. It was the queen's own personal torture chamber. Caspian knew she relished in the screams of her victims. Atlantean rumors said that she bathed in the blood of her enemies, bottling it up with her sand scrubs because it helped her stay young and beautiful.

An exaggeration, but she did love torture.

"The prisoners have been restless tonight, my lords," one of the guards said from his post.

Caspian stole a quick glance at Zalyn and saw his lip twitch in a semblance of a smile. It was his cold gray eyes that flared a delightful silver at the prospect of punishment. He was only glad the queen had not sent *him* with Coral. It would have ended with her death.

Caspian turned to the guards. "I will deal with the prisoners." He waved a dismissive hand and swam forward.

He passed occupied cells. The mer inside them wailed or hissed at the sight of him; he glanced into each cell but ignored them. He passed a lone cell, where a bent old and wrinkly merman huddled in a corner, hugging his tail to his chest. The man looked at him with golden eyes and smiled.

Caspian quickly carried on.

He came to a stop in front of a cell that held about ten merfolk. He peered in at them. A lot of them were huddled naked in pairs. There was a mermaid in the corner of the cell, holding a child in her arms. They saw him and Zalyn, and they sank deeper into the shadows fearfully. All of them but one mermaid. She swam weakly up to the gate; her thin and frail form jerking through the water. Her blonde hair was ratted, dark smudges framing her darker eyes. There was anger in them.

"Let us out," she croaked, fragile hands gripping the bars tightly. "We've done nothing wrong. Let us out!"

Caspian schooled his features into neutrality. "Quiet down," he commanded and began to leave.

"Let us out, you bastard!" she shrieked, pulling at the bars.

Caspian let out an aggravated sigh and turned to give her the command to swim back. Zalyn beat him to it. Silently, he reached between the bars and took her neck in his hands, cutting off her cries. She gasped and clawed at his hands, but it only caused him to squeeze harder. Zalyn's eyes sparkled in delight at the violence. His hands tightened white at the force in which he gripped her.

"He said to quiet down."

Instinct told him to reach out and pull Zalyn's hands away from her neck. He could not give in to that instinct. He just rolled his eyes at Zalyn and turned. "I will be down the hall if you need me." He started to swim away, and as soon as he did, Zalyn released the mermaid's neck. She fell back, coughing.

"Always ruining the fun," Zalyn muttered and turned to follow Caspian towards the end of the *calabazo*, towards the mer he really wanted to see. Towards the one he came here for.

Her cell was well away from the others, hidden behind a wall of stone. There was nothing but a simple circular bar window near the ceiling, not even wide enough to fit a body through. Caspian swam up to it and peeked through the bars.

There was little illumination in the cell. Only two small windows on either side of the cell, and that was barely enough for the light to glimpse through. There was bioluminescent algae on the ceiling and a single little beam of it shone down to the floor below. And just underneath the dull glow, there she was, sitting in the silt, running her hands through overgrown kelp.

His heart clenched at the sight of her. Where once she wore silk gowns in gold and pearls, rags had taken their place. Her hair, once long and threaded with the rarest of jewels, was now chopped disproportionately and threaded through with seaweed, silt, and tangles.

She did not notice his arrival. But he noted everything about her. Her skin was deathly pale and sunken in to mark the shadowing of her bones. So frail, so weak. She moved her hands wildly through the water, shoved them in silt and threw the stuff over her head, letting it shower over her.

She started giggling. *"I am as pretty, as pretty as a queen. Come see! Come see! I rule a castle in the sea! A castle made of gold, a castle made of blue. A castle brand new, new, new!"* She fell to the silt and laughed, thrashing her arms about. She sounded like she was breaching the line of insanity. Caspian had dreaded this day, the day he would find her this way. Her shrill voice continued to speak in sing-song, *"My son, have you seen him? He's trapped, trapped, trapped! Trapped in the web oh, drat, drat, drat! She keeps him by her bedside, oh yes, she does! And I'm locked away. Where? No one knows!"*

Caspian pushed himself away from the bars. He never should have come to see her. It was not as if he could even speak to her anyway. Not with Zalyn shadowing his every move, watching his very gesture and expression to take back to the queen.

Even though it hurt to turn his back, to leave without even announcing his presence, as he had to do every time, Caspian turned and swam away. He drowned out the sounds of the prisoners crying, begging for mercy and help. He could not help them.

No one could.

And they were wasting their time asking for it.

Because it would never come.

"Zenara, can you tell me what you know about the Keepers of Knowledge?"

Zenara nearly dropped a shell she was rearranging in Caspian's office. She sighed and placed it back on the shelf. The mermaid had been dusting the algae and particles off of the many nautilus and conch shells in Caspian's collection when Coral had barged in after Matthias had dropped her off.

She was feeling a bit confused about him. Coral hated him, that much she knew for sure. He'd branded her and had taken immense joy in doing so, but she had the strange sensation that he'd been testing her earlier in the day, that maybe he'd always been testing her. And she had the strangest feeling that she'd passed and had earned his stamp of approval.

That really shouldn't have mattered to her, but to be

considered a warrior, a *guerreri*, a *fighter* was something she'd never experienced before, and it felt good to be thought about as such. He hadn't gone easy on her and she'd managed to best him.

It was their goodbye at the entryway of Caspian's home that left her confused and strangely... tingling...

He had retied the bonds after her faux paus regarding her tail, and by the time they'd arrived at Caspian's house, her wrists were aching once again.

"Untie me," she'd demanded.

Matthias had rolled his eyes and let out an exasperated groan of complaint, but he still reached for a dagger at his hip. "A real fighter would know how to rid themselves of these bonds." Matthias placed the tip of the blade at the rope, and with a strong jerk, they came undone.

The bastard. Coral wrinkled her nose at him, rubbing her wrists. "A real *Knowledge Keeper* would know how to give herself legs and get out of here."

Matthias play-nudged her in the chin with one hand and sheathed his dagger with the other. "Chin up, fighter." He smiled. "You are both. Smart with the will to live. A real fighter *and* Knowledge Keeper would never let anything hold her back from discovering what she wants."

The comment surprised her into a gaping silence that had her merely staring up at him. Who was this surprising merman? The thought flittered through her mind before he pulled her against him by the tattered remnants of her dress.

"To be clear, that is not permission to start plotting your escape, but if you do..." He grinned, wide and radiant. "I *will* come after you." He bent down and trailed his tongue against the lobe of her ear before whispering. "And I *will* enjoy the chase."

"Whyever do you wish to know about them?" Zenara asked, moving on to the next shell.

Coral plopped herself into a chair, her muscles aching everywhere after the trying day. "I don't know," she confessed. "It's just that, everyone is calling me a Knowledge Keeper, and I really don't know anything about them or anything else, really. I just want to know what a Knowledge Keeper *is*."

Zenara kept working efficiently. "It is a little difficult to explain."

"Could you at least try?"

The mermaid sighed and placed the last of the shells into place, then swam over to sit opposite of her. "Why the sudden interest?" she asked cautiously.

Coral shrugged. "I'm a librarian, a lover of books and *things*. I'm curious." She couldn't exactly tell her that she wanted to know more about them, discover more of their magic, investigate if there really was a way she could give herself back her own legs and get out of here.

"Curiosity can be a dangerous thing, Coral," Zenara said seriously.

"Curiosity killed the cat, but satisfaction brought it back," Coral retorted. At Zenara's blank look, Coral said, "It's a human saying. It means that even if something you discover is dangerous, the satisfaction of knowing the truth always trumps any negative aspects of it."

"Fine." Zenara crossed her hands in her lap. "I will tell you what little I know, but as I am not Atlantean, my knowledge is limited to the Dark Water teachings." She settled comfortably in her chair. Coral did the same, ready to grasp onto anything that may have been of use.

"A long time ago, Atlantica prospered and thrived in riches and decadency. Their army was strong and near invincible, their people were happy and well-fed, and their merfolk were said to be the most beautiful in the entire ocean. But their kingdom only thrived with the aid of the Keepers of Knowledge and Magic."

Coral thought about the Atlanteans she'd seen earlier. At what they'd become. They certainly hadn't looked like thriving beings, but that was because of what they were now forced to do by the queen.

"I cannot give you details of them, as I do not know much. I know whisperings, what everyone else in the Dark Waters grew up knowing," Zenara warned. When Coral nodded, she continued, "The Keepers were said to be the most powerful magic casters in all of the ocean. They said that the Royal King of Atlantica scoured the waters for powerful mer and brought them back to Atlantica to train in the Keepers' Temple. There they learned the magic and secrets of old, but they kept that Knowledge to themselves. They would give certain Knowledge to the king when he needed it. Knowledge of when best to battle, what magic to use to enhance strength, and where best to dig for wealth, or when to plant crops."

It sounded to Coral as if the King of Atlantica was a massive cheater. She supposed it was true what they said, that knowledge was power, and it seemed as though the king had a lot of it.

"No one was allowed entry into the Temple but the Keepers themselves, and even they seldom left their home. It was said they kept the darkest secrets hidden of the darkest magic known to mer. The Atlantean king thought they were invincible and well protected. He thought wrong.

"The Dark Waters were perishing under the tyranny of the power hungry Atlantean King. He invaded, stole away children for his Temple, for his castle, and for his brothels and gave nothing in return. So the Black Kingdom devised a plot to go to war. It knew it had no chance to defeat Atlantica by attacking directly, so Queen Ulla Magissa herself led an assault against the Keepers' Temple. They had not been expecting it, and she destroyed their greatest resource and killed every last one of the Keepers."

Coral sat entranced in the story. Caspian had said as much; that the queen had murdered them all and destroyed all of their Knowledge. It seemed unlikely that she would have destroyed such valuable knowledge unless of course it truly meant nothing to her. But, knowing the queen as she did, Coral knew that the lust in her eyes was a lust for power.

Zenara's story was wrong somehow. Coral mulled it over in her mind. She thought of everything she'd ever read, every villain she'd ever encountered in a story, every history text, every battle, and every story she'd ever dreamed up in her head, and she *knew*.

Queen Ulla hadn't destroyed the Knowledge.

She'd only kept it for herself.

The queen knew that keeping the Knowledge would have made her vulnerable. What was to stop anyone else from attacking her the way she'd attacked Atlantica? So, she'd done the only thing she could do. She'd lied and had made it seem as though she'd destroyed everything.

Heart thundering, Coral leaned back in her seat, already devising a plan in her mind. All she had to do was *find* this Knowledge. She imagined the Keepers had kept records like library books. There was bound to be one on how to get her legs back.

But where would the queen keep the Knowledge? The obvious answer was in her castle chambers or her throne room. Which meant that Coral had to look for the less obvious answer. She was done being a victim. If her day with Matthias had taught her anything it was that. She needed to start using her brain and her own knowledge of things and be a *fighter*. She *would* survive.

"Did that answer your questions, Coral?" Zenara asked, mistaking her silence for something it wasn't.

Smiling, Coral nodded and got out of her chair. "It answered my questions perfectly." She feigned a yawn. "Oops, sorry. I've had an exhausting day. I'm going to take a nap." She wasn't sure Zenara bought it. When the mermaid's eyes traveled to her tattered dress and her neck where Matthias had bitten her, Coral blushed and unconsciously placed her hand over the spot. "Later!" she said quickly and swam out of the room and into her own.

The minute she got to her room, she closed the door behind her and flopped onto the bed, batting away the anemones that reached to suckle her tail and sinking into the delicate sea sponge.

If she were a villain, where would she keep the ocean's most precious and valuable Knowledge? Certainly she'd place it somewhere close, somewhere she wouldn't have to travel far to find. Somewhere easily reachable in case of an emergency. Her chambers were too obvious, as was the throne room. She wouldn't risk the prying eyes of servants searching through her things and finding or stealing it. So... where?

Coral sat up in bed, her floating wildly around her. What she needed was someone on the *inside*. But who? His face swam into the front of her mind, his thin brown hair curling in a simple wave over his forehead, sides of his head shaved and tattooed, the arrogant smile... She halted her thoughts right away. She couldn't even trust him! What made her think he would help her betray the queen he so obviously adored?

Unless...

Coral chewed her bottom lip. *Unless* he didn't know he was betraying his queen. Coral had read enough books of protagonists who tried at the art of seduction to get information they wanted. It never really worked out for them, and wouldn't Matthias find it suspicious if she suddenly threw herself at him? He wasn't an idiot. An arrogant bastard, maybe, but not an idiot. She would have to manipulate him into hinting at the Knowledge's location. But how? How could she manipulate a violent, faithful servant to the queen? The task seemed near impossible.

But it wasn't.

Nothing was impossible.

She was a human-turned-mermaid. That alone should have been impossible, but here she was in a kingdom she hadn't even known existed, living beneath the roof of an Atlantean warrior, slave to an evil queen.

Stealing back the Knowledge of the Keepers was possible.

She just needed to find out how.

A SECRET IN THE DARK

CORAL THOUGHT LONG AND HARD ABOUT HER PLAN. According to Caspian, *anthropos*-turned-mer had no magic. So even if she was able to find the Knowledge, she would need a mer to reverse the magic on her. But who? A part of her wanted to confide in Caspian this discovery, but what then? Would he agree to her maddening plan, stealing from the queen? And if he *did*, what *then*? If he got her legs back, she'd leave and then he would be stuck in the aftermath of it. The queen would know what he'd done, and he'd be number one on her hit list. Could she really leave him behind to face that on his own? The answer, however treacherous, was simple.

Yes, yes, she could.

He was a *guerreri*, ex-commander of the Royal Atlantean *Stratia,* for god's sake. Besides, if they got this Knowledge, he could have something that she wanted. He could bargain anything, even the precious object of his that the queen had hidden away.

It still felt like a betrayal to leave him, after everything they'd shared. Granted, a kiss hadn't been that much, but it still had been *something*. Coral didn't go around kissing strangers. Ever. And if what Matthias said was true, then Caspian had never strayed from the queen. She meant something to him as well.

Which made it harder to confide in him with this. But who else did she have? Zenara? No. Zenara was not a warrior, however strong willed she may be, and Coral wouldn't put her in jeopardy.

She was so torn. Whatever strands of a plan she began piecing together unraveled at the slightest bit of doubt entering her mind. Logically, there was no other choice. She needed Caspian. She needed him and the information he could provide. He knew what went on inside the palace. He knew the guards, knew the queen's habits. Because she worried for him, she wouldn't tell him everything. She would confide her suspicions regarding the Knowledge and nothing else. She wouldn't tell him of her plans until she was sure he would be willing to help her and risk it all to do it.

"What do you think so hard on?" Caspian's deep voice drawled from the entryway to her room. She couldn't see him —it was the middle of the night—and no lights shone in her room save for the phytoplankton glowing directly over her own head. But she felt the stirrings in the water and the sudden nervousness pound frantically in her chest.

"Caspian."

There was a dip in the bed that announced his proximity. How he'd gotten there so fast, she wasn't sure, but his warmth enveloped her in a swirling cloud, making her head spin. "Do not say my name," he rasped. "When you do, I find I cannot resist..." His fingers trailed lightly over her bare arm.

"Caspian..."

He groaned and bunched the blankets into his fist. "Coral..." He sounded as though he were in pain, riding the line of desperation. His hand touched her waist and slid down to the length of her tail. As it did, there was the tingling sensation of electric sparks down her muscle and bone. The tendons disconnected and he was parting her legs, dipping his knee between them against the bed.

His heavy weight was on top of her, elbows digging into the cushioning on either side of her head. Coral looked up into his face, now illuminated beneath the floating lights, into those brightly lit eyes with irises like the blue-green scales. His full lips curled into a sensual smile that left her breathless. Reverently, he pushed aside her hair and his fingers went to her neck, right where Matthias had bitten her.

His hand stilled.

"I'm fine," she said. And strangely enough, she was. The wound didn't hurt, and she knew Matthias had done it as some strange and demented lesson. And her day with him had been full of them. It had served to help her find what it was she'd needed to do. Like he was teaching her to fight, to be stronger. He'd helped her realize that she would need that strength to survive the Dark Waters.

"I should have been there," he whispered vehemently, taking his hand from her neck and digging it into the bed. His eyes flared in barely concealed anger.

"It doesn't matter," she reassured him. "I can take care of myself." Or, at least, she was learning to. She tried not to scoff at her own words. A few moments with Matthias and already she thought herself a warrior. She was aware of how ridiculous the words sounded, but she had to believe them somehow.

He chuckled, the sound low and soothing, and he bent to press his lips to her wound, sending warmth trickling through her entire body. She arched beneath him when he began kissing her lower, on the sharp jut of her collarbone and lower still, pulling down the neckline of her dress to kiss the tops of her exposed breasts.

Coral's thoughts evaporated against his caresses, against

the attentiveness of his tongue and soft lips on her flesh. This was a terrible idea, that much she knew for certain. They had no future and were irrevocably wrong for one another. They didn't *fit*. Even so, she understood his pain, his loneliness. The broken pieces of him called out for the broken pieces of her, and she was too weak to resist that kind of temptation.

Neither of them knew the kind touch of a body or one that wasn't forced. She wondered if that was why they gravitated towards one another, believing it was something it wasn't or couldn't ever be. Perhaps deep down she knew that integral truth, but she craved the kindness anyway, when all she'd ever known was cruelty.

Caspian was ever so gentle as he tugged her neckline to the side to expose her breast, and Coral nearly came off the bed when he took her nipple in his mouth. Any thoughts about rejecting him died as soon as they were formed. A part of her wanted to push him away because she knew how wrong using one another was, but his seductive touch silenced everything but her own whimpers of pleasure.

"Ssh," he whispered when she moaned, threading her fingers through his hair to hold herself steady. "Quiet, Coral."

She bit her lip and nodded, but it was difficult to keep that promise. Not with his mouth working wonders over her. Not with the wonderful way he grinded against her. His mouth moved to her other nipple and tortured it to a painful peak. She scraped her nails into his scalp, silently urging him on, urging him lower. And lower he went. His tongue traveled down the valley between her breasts, pulling the loose silk dress down with his hands as his head went lower. He bared her like a feast before him, her head spinning at every touch of his lips. His tongue dipped into her belly button and then trailed lower... lower...

"Caspian," she rasped. Her whole body was trembling

with need. She needed friction to ease the ache he'd built steadily through her system.

"Ssh," he whispered.

"Caspian..."

"I said, *be quiet.*"

"Shut up, you stupid cunt."

Her fingers clawed, though the very blood pumping through her veins felt sluggish, and she could barely lift her arms. Still, whimpers and cries for help came out in moans that were met with a violent push between her thighs.

Through the fog, she could make out his handsome features, twisted in cruelty. She reached for him again, trying to push him away. His fingers closed around her neck and squeezed. For a moment she couldn't breathe, and his laughter was followed by the violent rutting of his hips against hers. Her thighs screamed like her throat couldn't.

"Ssh, Coral, baby. Be quiet."

But she didn't want to be. She didn't want this. Didn't want him.

And he was taking by force what she hadn't wanted to give.

Coral gasped for breath as the memory tore through her mind. It was so vivid, that for a moment she feared it was Trent above her in the darkness. It took her minutes to realize it was Caspian, though his words echoed the terrible memory of her past.

To be *quiet.*

The circumstances had been different then and now. Now, she gave herself freely to him, and yet humiliation at his words burned her cheeks. Her brows furrowed. She didn't *want* to be silent, and for a moment she couldn't figure out why he was trying to keep this a secret. The haze of desire cleared as reason slammed back into her. She tensed against him, her hands going to his shoulders to push him away. How could she have been so stupid? How could she have let him seduce her into this?

How could he treat her like a dirty little secret? Because that's what she *was*. What they'd become the moment he'd pressed his lips to her own in that fucking office. And in the end, a few moments of kindness were not worth the suffering that would surely follow.

The blame felt like a heavy, crushing weight on her chest that she quickly pushed away. Caspian was the one who had decided they could never be, and she'd agreed. Because they *couldn't*. So why was he coming into her room now, kissing down her body like he owned it when he'd been the one to push her away in the first place?

Was this some sort of *power play*? Was he using her to get rid of his own demons? Or, fuck, was he trying to wipe the memory of Matthias' touch from her body as if it was his to do so?

She pushed against his shoulders. "Caspian, I—I—"

Ignoring her, his hands went under the dress to caress her calves and smoothed up her thighs. He parted them wider. Coral tried to fight back the moan, but her body was already buzzing on edge.

"Caspian, wait, stop—"

His fingers slid against her folds...

Then the door to her chambers burst open.

"You see, half-breed? It does not look like she is sleeping," a lazy, amused voice drawled from the entry.

Coral and Caspian split apart, Caspian swimming out of the bed, his tail already in place. Coral frantically pulled her nightdress back into place, face heating with mortification and *anger*. At the situation, at fucking Caspian. Because she'd told him to stop, and he hadn't listened.

Matthias floated in the doorway, his broad shoulder leaning against the frame. Behind him, Zenara was holding a glass globe with a bright blue jellyfish inside that probably had illuminated the entire scene before them. His face lit up with wicked delight as he glanced between Coral and Caspian, but his eyes sparked with an emotion that Coral couldn't quite decipher.

"The queen has need of the Knowledge Keeper. Now," Matthias said. "Unless you wish I tell her you are otherwise occupied?" His eyebrow raised in mocking. Caspian, tense, began swimming past him. He paused when Matthias gripped his arm, tightly from the looks of it. Dangerous energy pulsed between the two mermen, like a violent eruption just waiting to happen. "Do not worry, Caspian." Matthias smirked, his voice dripping with malice. "I shall not tell the queen that you've strayed."

Caspian merely jerked his arm away and left the room. Never once did he look back at Coral. She couldn't say why that flayed her.

Zenara shot Coral a sympathetic look before swimming after Caspian.

And then Coral was alone with Matthias.

He stayed in the entryway, staring intensely at her, so intensely it felt as his gaze was a brand of its own. Coral looked away and slid off the bed. She floated in the water with legs and webbed feet. Sighing, she swam over to the intricately carved armoire off to the side of the room and pulled out a simple dress in black.

When she turned, Matthias was still in the doorway. Still staring.

Coral gestured to the dress. "Turn around."

Matthias smirked and shook his head.

"Ugh." Coral turned her body and began stripping. Having sea legs was different from having a tail. It was almost more human, in a way. With a tail, there was no intimate exposure like there was with the sea legs. With a tail, her vagina was well and truly hidden behind scales. With sea legs, it was visible, hairless, and fuck, it was goddamn *pretty*.

Once she slipped on the new dress, she turned back around. She ignored Matthias and started to swim past him, but she stopped short when he gripped her by the upper arm. He whipped her back into the room, slamming her back against the door frame.

She winced but didn't make a sound; she looked up into his eyes and glared. His eyes glared back, but his face was set into a terrible smile that curled down her spine in a way that made it impossible to discern if it was from fear... or desire. He pressed his forearm just above her head to lean down until she felt the warmth of his lips near her cheek.

"What do you want, Matthias?" The words trembled out of her mouth. It was the look in his eyes and the twist of his mouth that made her stomach curl into knots. It made her heart pound in her chest.

She didn't know how to navigate the situation. She told herself she *wasn't* that kind of person. That she didn't feel the pleasure that was pulsing between her thighs for Matthias. That they were just leftover remnants of what Caspian had done. She wasn't just some horny bitch—okay, maybe she *was*.

It had been so long, and the stale memory that Trent had left behind had kept her legs tightly locked until today. Until Caspian took and fucked with her emotions. They were probably still fucked. Either that or she was dizzy with the heady presence of Matthias and how daring and strong she felt in his presence.

With Caspian, she felt delicate, broken, *lost*. When she was with Matthias, he made her feel a strength she never thought she possessed. He made her feel normal. He brought out something deeply buried within her and didn't shame her for it.

Matthias pressed himself up against her, pushing her back even more firmly against the frame with his body. He bent closer so his soft lips grazed against the lobe of her ear. It was that single touch that ignited the spark in her body all over again.

"I would have made you scream," he whispered.

Coral's breath caught in her throat at his words and the implication of them. Caspian *had* been hiding her. He'd come into her room for a quick fuck, knowing he'd leave the moment he pulled out. The queen could never find out about them because she was so obsessed with Caspian that it would have been a slap to the face.

And he'd *put* her in danger for his own needs.

Anger burned in her chest, becoming a slowly spreading ache through her that she tried so hard to ignore, but couldn't.

"I would not have covered the sounds of your passions. I'd never make you hide in the shadows." He waved his hand, and a ball of light illuminated the room, illuminating *him* in all his dark danger.

Her breath caught. He was the bad boy of all bad boys. He was corruption and violence and darkness. He was the sin good girls wanted to commit and risk purgatory for the rest of their afterlife. He was Coral's every twisted fantasy that she'd never admit to wanting out loud.

And his eyes gleamed as if he knew it.

"I would have watched your every gasp with wicked delight." His fingers grasped the hem of her skirt, his movements slow but firm. His eyes glistened with daring energy as the dress slowly went up her scales. "And I wouldn't give a *fuck* who heard, and I certainly wouldn't let anybody come between us."

The words were almost too much. Her face flushed and her next word came out as a breathless whisper. "Matthias..."

"Tell me you don't want this," he whispered, urged her, *dared* her.

More importantly, he gave her a choice. She could tell him

to fuck off and he would drop her skirt and swim away. Somehow, she knew he would respect that. The truth shone in his eyes. A psychopath, but an honest one.

"I—"

"Tell me no, my little fighter." His hand had paused halfway up. Waiting for permission she knew she shouldn't grant, but his eyes held her hypnotized and she couldn't pull away.

"I—I can't."

She didn't want to. She wanted control. That's what this felt like. Even if he was taking the lead, even if he was dark and dangerous, she still held her own power at this moment. That gave her a rush of emotion, of desperate need.

His smile was triumphant, and then her skirts were shoved up to her waist, and he pressed the heel of his palm into her center. She gasped at the immediate contact. In surprise and unexpected pleasure. Then, his hand began moving against her.

"Matthias," she gasped, gripping the wrist that was torturing her. To move it away or press him tighter against her, she didn't know. All she knew was that his hand was there, and she didn't put up a struggle as his fingers dipped inside and moved against her. She gasped at the sensations he caused and jerked her hips forward, her body betraying her, wanting him to let go, wanting him to go on. She moaned when his thumb ran over her clit.

"Yes," Matthias rasped, thrusting his fingers in faster. "I want to *hear* you." Coral's breaths were coming out in gasps now, her whole body trembling with the need for him, her treacherous need and attraction to this dangerous merman. She teetered on the edge, her body tightening into a painful coil...

And she fell.

Coral cried out, coming apart in his arms. She sobbed into

his shoulder, biting down on the crook of his neck. He shuddered, gripping her hip, digging his fingernails into her skin roughly. Coral trembled in the aftermath, arching her body, breathing heavily and opening her eyes to look at Matthias, at what they'd done. At what he'd done to her.

He was smirking down at her. For once, his face wasn't set in mocking or sarcastic lines. It was knowing. He whispered, "I would have watched you come."

Her breath hitched as the cold bite of reality settled over her. She closed her eyes momentarily, taking in deep breaths to compose herself while her thoughts stormed within her mind.

So, that just happened, she thought wryly. And who was she kidding, she'd *wanted* it to happen. What she couldn't understand was why she'd let it happen with Matthias so readily, but she'd been prepared to push Caspian away.

What was the difference between them? Caspian wasn't bad, but he wasn't exactly good either. He was a good merman made bad in a shitty situation. He was confusing, broken, and her heart ached for the sadness and vulnerability she caught in his eyes. Matthias... He was psychotic, pushed her boundaries, had branded her, and had acted violently to teach her lessons of survival that he'd known she would need.

But in the end, they were both the queen's property.

She took his wrist and pulled him from inside her, letting the dress billow back into place. Regret, an ugly poison, spread through her veins. What had come over her, to become prisoner to his seduction? To drop her inhibitions like that for a single moment of bliss?

"We shouldn't have done that," she said breathlessly.

Matthias smirked, while something dark and threatening slashed across his expression. As quickly as it was there, it disappeared. "Afraid Caspian will find out? Sound travels through water, you know. But do not worry, *my little fighter.*

We share the queen, I am sure he would be willing to share you, too." The words were cruel, leaving his mouth tight and clipped, like they were meant to punish her.

Coral's hand shot out before she could stop it, slapping his face with all of her strength. Matthias' head jerked to the side with the force. He looked back to her, smiling. Then his hands trailed up the sides of her thighs and slammed them together. There was a tingling sensation as the tendons connected and she knew that if she looked down, she would find that her sea legs had become a tail once more.

"One more thing, Coral." He brushed aside a lock of hair, his touch almost tender, so at contrast with the manic flashing of his eyes. He bent so their mouths were only a breath apart. "I would have *never* swam away without looking back."

WEAPON OF WAR

"My most gracious queen, what honor do I have to be called before you once again?" Coral swept into a low bow and waited with bated, nervous breath.

"Rise, Coral Bennett."

Coral straightened. The queen was sitting straight backed on her throne, looking as grave and as murderous as the two-headed eel canopied above her head. She wore her long white hair down, a face without makeup or lipstick, and she was wearing a pink silk robe. Even without makeup she was beautiful, but she looked as though she'd been roused hastily out of bed.

"It seems that the opportunity to prove your worth has risen," she said harshly. Matthias floated beside her throne, as did Caspian and Zalyn. They weren't leaning casually against her throne, nor were they smiling. Coral knew this meeting was serious, if the queen had been willing to present herself crownless and in nothing but nightclothes before Coral.

"I'm grateful for this opportunity, Your Highness," replied Coral.

"I received word that a strange *anthropos* ship was spotted a few leagues east of here. It is not one we have seen before..."

So that's why they'd called her here. They didn't know what the ship was and were hoping she could tell them. Coral's hands trembled. She worked in the library, had read a great many books. She only hoped she was able to help them. Because if she didn't, she'd die.

"What did it look like, Your Majesty?" Coral asked.

"A large metal ship with no deck that can completely submerge within the water." The queen snapped her fingers at Matthias. "What did the sentry say it looked like?"

"A large metal whale, Your Majesty."

The queen nodded, her malicious gaze eyeing Coral. "So, enlighten us, Knowledge Keeper of the realm of Colorado. What is this ship?" There was something almost jesting in her tone. Coral's eyes narrowed, and she chewed the inside of her cheek before she answered.

"Based on the information you've given, Your Majesty, I'd say that it is not a ship at all but a submarine." At least, she hoped it was. She couldn't be entirely sure until she saw it first.

"A submarine?"

Coral nodded, her suspicion at the disbelief in the queen's tone only heightening. This line of questioning felt like a trap. She couldn't believe that they'd never seen a submarine before. Maybe they had and just didn't know its proper name. Or maybe, maybe this was a test. To see if Coral would offer up the truth to them. So she did.

"The submarine is a warship that carries missiles and torpedoes and is designed especially with the ability to help humans submerge into the water."

"A warship to submerge humans into water?" The queen's fingers tightened on the arms of her throne. Her anger seemed genuine, at least, if not the questions. "They will discover our existence, take our merfolk captive." She turned to share a look with Zalyn and then Matthias and Caspian. They looked back at her worriedly.

The four mer seemed to come to a silent understanding.

The queen nodded at them. "You know what to do," she said gravely. Then, she looked over at Coral. "Take the *anthropos* with you. Her *knowledge* may be of help."

The mermen saluted their queen and sprang into action. Caspian gestured that Coral follow them; she bowed to the queen before swimming after them. They led her into a weapons room. There were paraphernalia of all types: spears and golden tridents hanging on the walls as well as daggers and swords. Shields made of orca teeth and the hard exterior of turtle shells. Bows in the shapes of seahorses and thinly sharpened arrows, staffs, axes decorated with the spikes of a lionfish, spiked teeth of sharks, and gauntlets with long claws sticking off the sides.

The mermen began stripping off the clothes they were wearing, dropping them to the floor, exchanging them for decorative jackets in black with red trimming. Zalyn grabbed a bunch of short knives and began strapping them into a holster at his waist. He went shield-less, instead opting for a short sword that he strapped to his back and a shark tooth tipped spear. Matthias grabbed his own daggers, a short sword that he attached to his waist, and a longer, black sharp sword and a shell shield that he attached to his forearm. Caspian grabbed nothing but a handful of small daggers and a golden trident from the wall.

He looked at her and she looked away, biting at her bottom lip. She hadn't met his gaze since they'd left his house. The door to her bedroom had been wide open when Matthias had made her come. She didn't doubt both he and Zenara had heard her cries. When they'd met up to leave, she'd searched his eyes to find—what, she wasn't sure—but he'd merely clenched his jaw tight and turned away, giving her the cold shoulder.

He may as well have ripped her heart out.

Because, seriously, how fucking dare he ignore her?

He didn't get to treat her like she was his side piece, his dirty secret from the queen, and expect Coral to be at his beck and call, but then get pissed because of what had happened with Matthias. How hypocritical.

Matthias swam up to her, pulling her from those thoughts. "Ready for battle, my little fighter?" he asked with a smile. Coral flushed at the sight of him in gear. The tattoos spiraled up from the collar of his jacket and around the sides of his shaved head.

"I don't know how to fight. I'm just going because I'm the Knowledge Keeper, remember?" She couldn't seem to meet his eyes, instead stared at his hands. Even the backs of them were covered in sprawling ink that looked like cresting waves. He brought the hand she was staring to her chin, lifting it so she was looking him in the eyes.

"I think it is time for you to learn." He produced a smaller, matching black jacket that had an attached holster at the bottom hem, and wrapped it around her shoulders. Coral put her arms through it and secured up the pearl buttons and the belt. "A dagger." He pressed the hilt of a dagger into her hand. "A word of advice: always keep an extra weapon hidden, somewhere it will not be easily found." His eyes wandered to her cleavage.

"Ugh." She scoffed, pushing him away. "Don't be a pervert."

"I did not mean there." He chuckled. "That is the first place an enemy will search. Keep it somewhere easily reachable but well hidden." He gave her a short sword that she took and secured at her waist. When she looked back up, he was pulling a small bit of rope out of his pocket.

"Please don't tell me you're tying me up." She frowned at it.

"No. Come here." He leaned over her and pulled her floating hair away from her face, securing it with the rope into a tight bun on top of her head. He leaned back to admire his work. "Better?"

Since her long tresses weren't flowing over her face and getting into her mouth and she could actually *see*, she nodded. "Yes."

"Then fight well, Coral." And Matthias swam away.

Coral stared at the dagger in her hand before hiding it in the lapels of her jacket. The weight of it pressed against her breastbone and bounced as she swam towards Caspian. She knew it probably wasn't very wise to do it, to be seen talking to him in front of Zalyn and Matthias if he was so dead set on keeping her at arm's length, but... Well, Matthias had already caught them in bed together, and she knew nothing about Zalyn. She didn't know if he would betray that information or not. Hell, she wasn't even sure if Matthias would keep the secret as he'd promised or if he'd give it up if it benefited him.

Coral just had to speak to Caspian. Just once before they went out to meet whatever danger they'd face ahead. He probably hated her for what she'd done, not that he had any right to.

She shook her head of those thoughts and looked up at Caspian. "Will there be danger?"

Caspian didn't look at her as he buckled and secured the last bits of his gear around his waist and chest. "There is always danger," he said curtly, stabbing another dagger into his holster.

"I know that, but—"

"Look, *anthropos*, the queen commanded you go with us. Either go beg her to stay or suck up your fear and *be quiet*."

Coral's heart gave a pang. He'd said that they'd have to put on a show, but Coral didn't know if he was acting or not. There was a real harshness in his tone that froze her solid, and only the pounding of her heart was her awakening.

She tightened her hands into fists. "Don't talk to me like that," she whispered lowly between clenched teeth. "And don't call me *anthropos!*" She was sick of hearing that word like a poison coming from the mouths of mer. At least Matthias had stopped referring to her like she was beneath him. It hurt that Caspian still did.

Caspian's hands stilled on the buckle of a belt. He looked down at her, his expression very hard but his eyes very soft. It melted her. "All will be fine if you follow orders." He looked beyond her, then back. "Matthias is waiting for you." He turned and swam from the room.

"DO NOT FRET, MY LITTLE FIGHTER," Matthias said in her ear. She rode in front of him on a hippocampus, holding on to the animal's mane while Matthias took the reins to guide them fast and sure through the water. They'd ridden hard for what felt like hours, and the closer they approached their destination, the slower they went.

Coral turned in her seat to look up at him quizzically. "Fret?"

"Over his *royal* pain in the fins, Caspian." He gestured to said merman, riding his own hippocampus way ahead of them at a faster pace. Zalyn brought up the very rear. "He will brood and pout as he always does until he comes swimming back into your opened, waiting arms." He snorted.

Coral didn't know what to respond, so she decided falling into easy banter was as good as anything. "You sound jealous," she joked quietly, though her face and tone of voice weren't laughing.

Matthias laughed. "Maybe I am," he said jokingly, nudging his chest into her back. "But at least I am the one who made you come."

Coral whipped around to glare at his smiling face. "Stop that," she said angrily. "This isn't some stupid competition."

Matthias was acting like some giant male gorilla banging his chest at his rival. The thing was, there was no competition. None at all. At least, not to Coral. There may have been feelings between her and Caspian, however tentative those might be, but her main objective was finding the Knowledge and going home, leaving this place for good.

"It is always a competition between us, my little fighter. I am surprised Zalyn has not tailed in to vie for your affections yet. It is always like that with the queen."

Turning back around, Coral grumbled, "I am not the queen."

"No," Matthias admitted. "You are not." He bent down to her ear. "You are much, much sweeter."

"Stop it." Coral nudged him away again. "I'm not a toy you can all play with. Stop treating me like one."

"I can assure you, my little fighter, I do not see you as a toy."

"So what do you see me as, Matthias?" she asked impulsively. She wasn't even sure she wanted to know the answer to it. A part of her did. Was she just a stupid *anthropos* to him? A game to play? Someone he meant to spy on for his queen?

"I see you as..." He kissed the back of her neck. "...a worthy opponent."

She shivered. "I wish you'd stop thinking of me like that."

"Like what?"

"Like we were in a UFC match and you're waiting for me to tap out!"

He paused then asked, "UFC?"

"It's a sport—a game—that humans play. They wear gloves

on their hands and fight in a ring. The first to tap out basically loses."

She felt him smiling, as if that was the kind of thing one could *feel*. With Matthias it was true. He radiated smiles, delight, and violence. "My favorite kind of game."

"I'm serious, Matthias. Answer me."

He sighed in annoyance, hands tightening on the reins. "You will not give up, will you?" Her silence was answer enough. She almost expected him to reply with a 'does it matter?' as Caspian had so many times before. He surprised her. "You intrigue me, my little fighter. I long to see you succeed because I *know* you can. You have a strong heart, stronger than what I have seen in a long, long time." He gave a small pause and then whispered almost tentatively, "And I like you."

His words curled around her heart and seemed to squeeze something out of her. "You branded me," she whispered, feeling the wound throb at the words.

His hand went to her hip, just over her wound, where he trailed his fingers lightly across it. "I will not lie to you, my little fighter. I did not care for you then because you were nothing but a useless *anthropos* to me. So, I did what I did because my queen demanded it of me." His hand tightened ever so slightly against her before easing his grip. "And then you slapped me, challenged me. You were willing to forfeit your life for a fucking salamander, who will still not leave my house and wails for you constantly. I saw the spirit in the depths of your pretty little eyes in those moments. Any violence I inflicted afterwards, I did because I knew you could take it, because I knew you would learn how to fight back." His hand left her side and went back up to grip the reins. "Stay strong, my little fighter. You will need that strength for what's to come."

~

THEY RODE in near silence the rest of the way. Coral had a feeling they were getting closer to the submarine because even Matthias had stopped joking, smile disappearing and body tensing. It seemed even he could be serious when the occasion warranted it. Still, it was strange that the ocean was so... still...

She'd gotten used to the noise of the sea, of passing fish, of idle chatter, laughter, the swaying of seaweed and kelp against coral reefs. Everything was so empty. As if the ocean was holding its breath. It was unnerving.

And then Coral heard it.

And she knew why there was no life around her.

The churning of an engine, the whirling of blades, metal pushing through water.

Caspian held up a hand and the hippocampi came to a stop, scaled hooves pawing through the water nervously.

"It is time," Matthias whispered in her ear. It wasn't nerves she heard in his voice. It was that familiar delight that she'd thought had evaporated.

He threw a sea leg over and slid from the hippocampus, Coral following after him. Caspian and Zalyn slid from their own and gave them quiet orders to stay put. The mermen didn't even unsheathe their blades. Before they got into a strange formation. Caspian gestured at Coral to follow them. There was the crest of a hill and they swam low, pressing themselves against the silt and crawl-swam up it to peer over the edge.

A submarine floated steadily about two hundred feet away and was slowly approaching. The sentry hadn't been wrong when he said it looked like a large metal whale, just without flippers and a tail. It was thick, gray metal with thick glass windows. There were markings on the sides of it that Coral couldn't quite make out.

"It *is* a submarine," Coral whispered to them. She was between Caspian and Matthias, closed in against the press of their strong arms. She ignored the feel of them and squinted to get a better look at the markings. "It looks like a naval sub." The three mermen looked at her with confused expressions. She sighed in exasperation and explained, "It's like a ship that belongs to the *Stratia*—soldiers. They're trained to be on water and to handle that submarine, but..." She looked closely and cursed. "I can't see inside it. We'd need to get closer or wait for it to—"

Caspian waved a hand in front of her face. She felt the crackling of magic over her skin and suddenly, her eyesight was better, perfect. She squinted and saw *everything*. She saw the exact design of the ship, saw through the thick windows to the inside. A lot of buttons, levers and flashing lights that she couldn't even begin to comprehend. She ignored that and focused on the people instead.

There were a few men and women in uniforms, handling monitors and buttons, presumably steering. "I think it is a naval sub, but—" She looked at the other people. "Something's off. They aren't all in uniform. I'm pretty sure if they were in the navy, they'd all have to be in uniform right now."

"Do you think it is a trick?" Caspian asked, his gaze focused intently on the submarine.

"No, I think the ones driving really are officers." They had a strict demeanor about them, whereas the ones in the back wearing regular jeans and long-sleeved shirts appeared slightly less professional. "But I can't tell what the ones in the back are." They had clipboards in their hands. They were looking over the shoulders of the officers and jotting notes down. "Perhaps scientists?" she said.

"Right. Let it begin," Caspian said gravely.

Matthias and Zalyn fanned out in different directions, disappearing into darker shadows of the water. Caspian stayed where he was, quiet as if holding his breath. Coral waited as well. There was a strange prickling sensation at the back of her neck that she fought hard to ignore.

Then she felt a stirring in the water. It was light, like a current swaying her side to side but then the force of it picked up. It was the equivalent to wind slapping violently at her face, like a storm tearing through the water. Coral dug her hands into the silt, squinting her eyes as they began to burn. The water started to lift her tail up and she brought it slamming back down.

Caspian had no such trouble. He straightened and began swimming through the storm with ease until he was nearly in front of the sub. Coral could see the people inside, see their surprise, disbelief, their *awe*.

Then Caspian lifted his hand.

The water and silt began to coalesce into a small vortex that started from the bottom and swirled and swirled. The engine to the submarine sputtered and gave a loud shriek before silencing completely.

And then it jerked to the side.

Coral watched as Caspian twirled his fingers round and round, as the water and silt vortex picked up speed with his movements, whirling around the submarine, jerking it in violent circles.

He'd done the same with the sharks that had tried attacking them. She'd been grateful back then, but seeing the extent of his power now, seeing him use it on humans, on an enormous metal machine, was frightening. It twirled like a plastic toy in a draining bathtub and then gave another shriek.

Matthias and Zalyn swam out from either side of the sub, their hands out, and the metal began twisting. Energy flowed through the water, and it felt similar to static electricity on land, making the hairs on her arms stand up on end. They were using all of the magic they had. Matthias and Zalyn *pushed* with their bodies and their magic, using the water around them as an adamant wall against them. It groaned and creaked and started to indent and twist in on itself.

Coral looked through the glass at the people in it being thrown about like rag dolls. They were being jerked back and forth, screaming as the walls of metal got smaller and smaller around them. Matthias and Zalyn gave a loud cry as they pushed water, the crushing pressure of it smashed into the metal, flattening it together in that last forceful shove.

A shower of metal and blood crumbled through Caspian's dying vortex of water, settling calmly down to the floor below.

Coral stared at the remnants of the submarine. Nothing but broken bits of metal and blood already disappearing in pink swirls. Crushed. They'd *crushed* them, leaving nothing but bits and chunks behind, like ashes in a dying fire. Nothing more than gnarled, metal bones. Coral bent over and heaved onto the sea floor, but nothing came out.

The queen had sent them to slaughter those humans. She'd damn well knew what a fucking submarine was, and she'd sent Coral to watch. To make Coral feel like a traitor as she'd gladly given away information against her own people. Regardless if they'd already known what it was, she still felt used. Though she should have expected this. They'd said it in her trial. Coral was a weapon of war against the humans, and this had been her first test.

"Coral..." Caspian's hand clamped down on her shoulder. She whipped around angrily and slapped his hand away, glaring at him.

"Stay away from me!" she screamed. "Murderers! All of you!" Matthias and Zalyn had swam up behind Caspian, Zalyn staring with a blank, neutral expression and Matthias' lip twitching as if he found her amusing.

Caspian was looking at her with hard features but soft, sad eyes. "We did what had to be done."

Her stomach heaved, but she forced the bile down. "You *murdered* my people!"

"And your people murder ours every day," Matthias interjected with disinterest. "This was nothing compared to the havoc the *anthropos* wreak on the ocean daily. You saw for yourself."

"You bastards!" she yelled. What he was saying was true, she knew. She'd witnessed the human's terrible deeds herself, and yet she couldn't unsee the cruelty and ease with which they'd murdered them. They'd crushed the sub so easy, as if crushing together a Styrofoam cup.

"Coral, we have to go," Caspian said carefully. "We need to get back."

"Why?" she demanded. "So you can tell your bitch queen that you murdered innocent people? So you can tell her that the deed is done?"

She saw the dagger zip towards her before she felt the pain in her tail. Coral screamed at the embedded hilt surrounded by scales and blood. She looked up to see Zalyn balancing another dagger in his palm, his face calm but his eyes blazing like lightning.

"Insult Her Majesty again, land-scum, and the next dagger will find its way to your heart."

Coral glared and ripped the dagger from her tail. It hurt like hell, but she bit her lip to keep from screaming. She had a feeling that Zalyn liked when his victims screamed and thrashed about. Though it hurt, she straightened. Her tail cried in protest, but she vowed not to let her discomfort show. Not to him. Not anymore.

She threw the dagger to the silt and glared at Zalyn. "Your queen is a *psychotic bitch!*"

Because she knew it was coming, she gave a painful but powerful thrust of her tail just as the dagger zoomed past, missing her. But Zalyn didn't stop with the dagger. He lunged forward, tackling her to the ground. She was vaguely aware of Caspian shouting for both of them to stop acting like children, but she ignored him. The breath was knocked from her when she went down, Zalyn's heavy body on top of hers.

She'd been in this position before and had gotten out of it just fine on her own. Zalyn brought his fist back and crashed it into the side of her face. Stars blinked behind her eyelids, but she didn't let the pain cripple her. She kicked her tail up, tangling it with his and pushed him off of her.

Zalyn rolled at the same time she did and then they were up. Coral reached for the short sword at her hip and wielded it in front of her. She knew nothing about the weapon, but she refused to cower before him or any other mer. The pain throbbing in her face made her dizzy, but she managed to stay afloat and hold the sword with steady hands.

Zalyn's lip twitched in a smile, and he pulled out his own weapon—the spear. Then he lunged. Coral gave a grunt and dodged the pointy end, slapping it aside with her own blade. As she did, it left her side completely exposed to his fist. He punched her and she went down to the ground, coughing.

He used the dull end of his spear to hit her, sending her sprawled on her back. Silt swirled up in a cloud of smoke around her. Zalyn swam up and kicked the sword from her hand with his tail fin. Coral tried to sit up, but he pressed the end of the spear into her chest bone, digging it in until it hurt.

"Never insult my queen again, *anthropos*," he snarled savagely. His eyes flashed and flared with a mixture of anger and glee.

"Screw you," she gasped, "and your *bitch queen*."

He growled low in his throat and hit her with the end of the spear. Coral's eyes stung and she coughed out blood, having bitten the inside of her cheek. Her hand gripped her chest. Zalyn bent down low so that he was smiling in her face; he gripped her chin roughly in his hand and jerked her head forward.

"I have longed to kill you for quite some time," he whispered gleefully. He opened his mouth to say more, but the words never came. Coral didn't give him a chance to.

Because she plunged her dagger into his chest.

Zalyn coughed blood and looked down with surprise at her hand wielding the hilt of the blade. Coral pulled the blade out and watched as he fell to the side.

Coral floated up and looked down at the merman with disgust. "Too bad I got to kill you first," she whispered and turned.

Caspian was staring down at Zalyn with wide, surprised eyes, but Matthias was looking at her with delight. She placed the dagger back inside of the jacket and redid up the pearl buttons.

"An extra weapon, right?" she said mirthlessly.

Matthias burst out laughing and began clapping. "Well done, my little fighter."

Caspian shot Matthias a look. "Do not encourage this!" He swam to where Zalyn lay. "The queen could have you killed for this! Zalyn is one of her favorites." He bent down to check for a pulse and the wound. "You missed his heart," he said with relief.

"Too bad," Coral said, though she wasn't sure if the ease in her chest was relief or something else. Her eyes were still locked on Matthias, and he was still looking at her with an expression that said he meant to devour her completely.

"Next time aim up and to the left. Or stab him in the

back between the fourth and fifth ribs," he advised. "And then twist for good measure."

Coral glared at him but saved that advice for later. Just in case. She looked to Caspian. He was bandaging up Zalyn's wound. When he finished, he gave out a shrill whistle and a moment later, the hippocampi rode forward. Caspian hauled Zalyn up and threw him across the back of his black hippocampus and secured him down with a bit of rope.

"We should get back to the castle before he dies on us. That would not go down well with the queen." Caspian mounted Redwave, his tail splitting into sea legs in a moment, and reached out for the reins of Zalyn's black beast.

Coral swam forward and hauled herself up onto the remaining hippocampus, and Matthias was right behind her. He gripped the reins and dug his webbed feet into the animal's side, and then they were off.

Coral winced with each bounce through the water. Her face ached and burned, her tail was on fire, but she kept her head held high. She was done cowering before the mer like some wounded animal. They treated her like she was nothing, but at the same time used her against her own people. They pushed her around and talked down on her and Coral was *done* with sitting around doing nothing.

She was going to steal the Knowledge back and go home.

Or she would die trying.

SECRETS UNVEILED

"AND WHERE, PRAY TELL, IS ZALYN?"

The queen was sitting before them in a dress of gold, the skirts embroidered with hundreds of shining blue shells and pearls. Her neckline was low and tantalizing, a golden necklace embedded with turquoise stones hung just above her collarbone, and her hair was coiled tightly behind a beautiful heavy crown in matching colors.

Caspian, Matthias, and Coral bowed low on the throne room floor. "He is indisposed at the moment, your Majesty. You see, there was trouble and—"

The queen waved off Caspian's answer with an annoyed flick of her hand. "Never the matter," she snapped. "I shall deal with him later. Were you successful?"

"The submarine was found and destroyed your Majesty."

"And what of the *anthropos*? Was her information helpful?"

Coral's hands tightening into fists on the floor.

"Her information was faultless, Your Majesty," Caspian replied.

"You may all rise."

They did as she commanded, floating tall before her. She

looked at Coral, her gaze scrutinizing her swelling cheek, the throbbing wound in her tail. Coral stared back, trying not to let anything in her features show.

She wondered why Matthias hadn't told the queen that Coral had stabbed Zalyn in the chest. Caspian, she knew, did it to protect her. She suspected Matthias didn't because he'd actually enjoyed the show. Crazy bastard.

Anyway, the queen would find out eventually, once the healers knitted Zalyn's skin back together and he made his way back to her side. It was worse, in Coral's opinion, to hide this from her than it would have been to just come clean. All Caspian was doing was dragging along her inevitable punishment, and Matthias' willingness to keep secrets from his beloved queen was highly suspicious.

"Very well done, my little mermen." Ulla smiled at Caspian and Matthias. "As always, you get rid of the threat in order to protect our home. Go, celebrate this victory in the castle kitchens. Even you, *anthropos,* have proved useful. Go feast and drink with Matthias. Caspian..." She looked to him. "I have need of you." Her voice was sultry, leaving no doubt just exactly what her *needs* truly were.

Rage swept over Coral as she imagined those black and pink tentacles curling over Caspian's body, drawing him close enough to kiss, to fuck. The queen used him in the vilest of ways and Caspian allowed it, allowed her to touch his body, kiss him, to *use him.* Coral watched Caspian swim up to the throne and take the queen's hands in his own, kissing the backs of her knuckles gently. He murmured low things to her, causing her to laugh.

Matthias whirled her around before she could see more and led her out of the throne room. As soon as the doors closed behind them and they were down the hall, Coral let her anger show and she went to the nearest wall and began slapping her tail angrily against it until her fins hurt.

"Calm down, my little fighter," Matthias's voice soothed. "Why hurt yourself when you can take it out on another?"

Coral stopped, her fists curling, ready to let loose. "You're right," she whispered, just before whipping around. Catching Matthias by surprise, she punched him across the temple. He gave out a low grunt just before sinking to the floor, eyes fluttering closed.

She tried not to gasp at what she'd done. Instead, she bent down to press her fingers against his neck. The pulse at his throat was steady, so she briefly checked for a head wound or blood. There was none. Sighing with relief, she looked around to find the hall empty and swam away.

Coral was afraid the thundering of her treacherous heart would give her away as she went down the otherwise silent halls. There were little guards about, a small blessing. She honestly had no idea where she was going, but right now was the perfect opportunity to scour the castle in search of the Knowledge.

There would be hell to pay later for what she'd done to Matthias, but Coral had no doubt that she could handle him easily. It seemed he wasn't as tough as he thought he was if she'd been able to knock him out.

She rounded a corner, and then another, and another. The castle was so large that the hallways soon became a blur in her mind. Already she'd dodged a couple of guards, wandered around in a circle, and finally she found a set of enclosed stairs. It was unguarded, thankfully, and she went down them.

There was no telling where she was going, what she was swimming into, but she had to risk it. She had to find the Knowledge that would get her out of here. The end of the stairway was dark and dank. The only illumination that came from down below was the occasional bioluminescent algae and phytoplankton covering tall walls of stone. Coral looked around. Her eyes, thanks to Caspian's earlier magic, adjusted well in the dark.

This didn't seem like just some other part of the castle. For starters, there wasn't perfectly polished obsidian. These walls were made of stone and were dirty with algae, and seaweed flowed back and forth steadily. It looked to Coral as if the castle had been built just over this maze of walls.

She swam between the crumbling structures only to come to a dead end. She back tailed and turned right. It was a total labyrinth, Coral sighed. What was the purpose of this place anyway? Sighing, she started to turn...

But strong arms came around her shoulders, locking her in place. Coral started to scream, but a big hand clamped down over her mouth. She tensed. She hadn't heard anyone swimming down this way, hadn't felt vibrations through the water to alert her of another presence. Had she been so entranced in her thoughts that she hadn't heard?

The hand wrapped around her body suddenly traveled down to her hip, then to the front of her body, down her stomach, to the front of her tail. A single touch of the tendons holding her legs together made them open. When her captor's rough hands gripped at her inner thighs to spread her sea legs, Coral thrashed in his grip. She kicked out at him with her webbed feet, jerked her head back until it connected with her attacker.

He roughly whipped her around, slamming her back against a stone wall. Coral gasped as she looked up into Matthias' face.

Shit.

His eyes were blazing with barely concealed rage. Rage that was directed straight at her. She didn't flinch away from the look in his eyes. She met it with one of her own. She pushed him away from her but he didn't budge.

"Anyone could have snuck up on you," he said angrily. It

was the angriest she'd ever seen him. "Anyone could have taken advantage."

She lifted her chin at him defiantly. "What do you care? It's not like you mind sharing me with everyone."

Matthias worked at his jaw and slammed his fist into the wall beside her head. That time, she flinched. "You think I do not *mind*? You think I was not filled with murderous *rage* at the sight of Caspian's filthy hands all over you today?"

"You said you wouldn't mind sharing me," Coral reminded him.

"I never said I did not mind. I said Caspian would not mind. I am not your keeper, little fighter. You can kiss and *fuck* whoever you want. I do not have to like it, but as I told you before, I *like you,* and I would hate to see anyone take you against your will."

"You mean like you just tried to do?" she snapped.

Matthias reeled back as if she'd slapped him. Hurt and anger seemed to bleed together over his expression, and her heart pounded. She didn't know how to feel about that, didn't know how to deal with a Matthias who looked hurt by her words. She could deal with his brand of crazy, she could fight back and clash the hatred with desire easily enough, but everything else was like swimming into foreign territory.

"You think I would force you?" His jaw clenched tight. "You think I would take what you would not willingly give?"

"I—" She clamped her mouth closed. She didn't think that. Not really. The truth was, he'd been rough up until now, and while she'd been angry and afraid, she'd never felt truly threatened in Matthias' presence, the branding notwithstanding. Even earlier, he'd asked for her consent before he'd dipped his fingers between her thighs to make her come. "I don't think you would."

"Others are not like me," he continued.

"I thought you said I was a fighter." Maybe he'd lied this

whole time. Maybe he didn't think she was capable of defending herself.

He squeezed her upper arms. "You *are*, but you do not have much fighting *experience*."

"I stabbed Zalyn earlier and knocked you out." She tilted her chin up with confident defiance.

Matthias snorted. "Zalyn is a fool. And you do not really think your little punch knocked me unconscious, do you?"

She flushed.

"I pretended to faint so I could follow you and see what you were up to. It is a good thing, too. This part of the castle is more dangerous than open waters. Any guard could have found you wandering about."

Coral, still flushing, tried to muster up some scraps left of her dignity. "I could have fended them off."

Matthias raised a brow. "Really? Then fend *me* off." And he was gripping her wrists tightly, pressing them above her head and against the wall. He pressed every inch of his body against her own and she shivered at the slick hardness of his cock she felt pressing against her belly. He bent his head down, lips gently touching her cheek. "Fend me off, Coral," he demanded. "Prove that you can." His words blew warmly against her neck, and he trailed his tongue just behind the lobe of her ear.

Coral shivered. Why did Matthias do this to her? Why did he make her lose all reason, make all logical thought fly out the window? She melted under the warmth of his lips, his tongue.

"Fend me off, my little fighter," he rasped against the nape of her neck.

Coral could hardly think. She could hardly breathe when he called her that. A nickname meant just for her. Not *anthropos*, not human, not Knowledge Keeper. She was a fighter when she'd never been before. And Matthias gave her the confidence to *be* one.

She had the urge to thread her fingers through his short hair, but her hands were pinned tightly at her sides. She ground hips against him and groaned. "What if I don't want to fend you off?" she asked breathlessly.

Her words had him stilling briefly against her before he lifted his head, looked down at her, eyes flaring with desire. His lips twitched into a smile right before he bent down to claim her mouth.

Coral melted into the kiss. She opened her mouth to him, twining her tongue with his. It was a well-choreographed dance, fitting so perfectly and so in tune with each other. He demanded and gave, never stopping, never slowing. She kissed him back with equal fervor, roughly nipping her teeth on his bottom lip.

He groaned, grinding his hips against hers. She felt a strong thigh wrap around her own and pull her close. He shifted her position, angling her so she felt his cock against her sensitive center. She broke the kiss.

"I want to touch you," she pleaded. "Let me touch you."

He chuckled and released her hands to trail his own down her hips, reaching behind to grip her bottom. He pulled her closer to him, as if they could never be close enough. As if there were hardly any space between them already.

Gently, she trailed her palms up and down his hard chest, up to his neck to finger the curling edges of his tattoo, to the back of his neck, up to grip his hair between her fingers. He was smiling down at her, triumphant in his seduction. Coral leaned up to kiss him again, framing his face in her hands, letting them travel freely over nearly every inch of his body. She gripped the lapels of his jacket, and with strength she didn't know she possessed, switched places with him, twirling him so that he was pressed tightly against the wall.

He laughed. "Easy, my little fighter."

Coral smiled. "I don't want to go easy." And then, quicker than he could blink, Coral whipped the dagger from her coat and pressed the tip of it against his neck. Matthias blinked in disbelief at her, then at the dagger she had tightly against his throat. Coral smiled sweetly at him. "I told you I could fend you off."

Matthias laughed, his throat bobbing against the blade. "Well done, little fighter. I was not expecting that."

"I know you weren't. You think I'd throw myself at you just because you're an attractive merman?" Her breathing was rapid and erratic, as were her emotions. They suddenly erupted. The stress, the memories, the fear. It all exploded. "All men, no matter the species, seem to be alike. They think more with their dicks than anything else."

Matthias held his hands up in surrender as each word was punctuated with her digging the knife deeper into his skin. He stared down at her warily.

"All they want is to see how many women they can get without a care for *our* feelings. You and Caspian have your perfect and beautiful queen, why would you want me? Is it because I'm a challenge? Trent was the same way." She felt the hot tears pour out of her eyes, invisible as they blended in with the water, and she didn't even know why. She was frustrated, she was scared and *alone,* and she wanted to go home. She'd just seen humans slaughtered by the queen's Personal Guard. She was sick of being treated like an animal, of being pulled around on a leash and of being treated like nothing by everyone. She was *tired.*

"Coral," Matthias whispered. Her hand was shaking, and a low sob escaped her throat. Matthias' gaze softened. He took her wrist lightly in his hand and brought it down in front of them and gently pried the knife from her. She let him because she found she no longer had the energy to fight him. "Coral, who is Trent?"

Coral sobbed. "It doesn't matter," she whispered. She didn't even know why she'd brought him up in the first place. Neither Caspian nor Matthias were anything like Trent. Yet, she couldn't stop the memories of the past from coalescing with the present. Cheeks burning with shame, she tried to look away, but he forced her face back to his.

"It matters. Who is he? I will find him and kill him for bringing tears to your eyes, little fighter."

"I'm not a fighter, Matthias. I've never been. I want to be, but…"

"You are a fighter, Coral. Never doubt it." He stared at her with such an intense look that she found herself believing the words. "Now tell me, who is Trent?"

Something clogged in her throat that she wanted to choke back. The denial and the lies sprung to her tongue so easily. Things she'd been so used to saying after it had happened. Things she'd forced herself to believe.

I'm fine.

I'm okay.

It's over now.

She'd hid behind the words so she wouldn't have to face the truth or the judgment it would bring with it. But one could never escape the truth. It was there in her nightmares. Because even if she didn't remember wholly, her nightmares did. He was always there. His hands jerking open her thighs and breaking past the barrier of her virginity…

She'd never told Olivia the truth. She'd lied, said Trent had cheated. Because beneath the pain of what happened, there was also shame. Like maybe what had happened had been her fault. Like how could she have been so naïve to believe that someone of his status actually wanted her? So when he invited her on his yacht for the weekend, she'd gone.

Only to wake up drugged and with blood and semen dripping from between her thighs.

She'd stumbled out on shaking legs, and he'd laughed in her face. She'd winced then, had fled and cowered. It was like he knew she wouldn't turn him in. He'd been right.

And he'd gotten away with it.

"Trent was my boyfriend." The words hurt as they exited. Not even Olivia knew, but she was telling Matthias. She didn't want to understand why. Was she stronger now? Or was it simply time to let the truth breathe? "He was my mate," she amended, when she caught Matthias' quizzical look. She hated that word even more than boyfriend. It seemed more permanent, when it wasn't.

"What did he do?" he asked, his voice low with murderous rage she had come to associate with him.

"He slipped something into my drink. A drug. It dulled my senses, but I remember." In flashes. In nightmares. In the pain from the next day. "He forced himself on me. He raped me."

If she'd expected to feel relief at finally telling the truth, she didn't. She just felt hollow. Like she'd been carved up one too many times and there was nothing left of her.

"The queen reminds me of him," she whispered angrily. "Only, she doesn't have to drug her victims to fuck them. She holds things over you. Promises you things, manipulates you. Uses you." Her eyes flicked up to his face. She realized she hadn't been looking at him as she told her story, but at the space between them. "Like you and Caspian both use me."

She knew, in a way, those final words might have been unfair considering the queen used her Personal Guard for her own pleasure. But sometimes it felt like Caspian and Matthias were using her, too.

"You have your queen. Can't you just leave me alone?"

Matthias looked at her with what she wanted to assume

was guilt. She wasn't sure what she'd been expecting of him, or what kind of a reaction he would give. It wasn't this silence. Maybe she'd expected a war path, his anger and violence, as he'd been so happy to display. At least he wasn't smiling and laughing at her.

"I do not know what to say," he confessed quietly after a moment.

Tears prickled at the back of her eyelids. She wondered if he would see her differently now. Perhaps the real reason she'd never told anyone was because she didn't want them to see her differently, even if she was. She didn't want them to know just how tainted she'd become.

That's why she'd drifted towards Caspian. Because the calls of her pain recognized his. At the same time, it was why she'd drifted towards Matthias. He didn't treat her like the fragile, broken thing she felt she was.

She hoped that wouldn't change now that he knew the truth. She feared it did.

"What strength you have. You truly are a little fighter." His fingers gripped her chin, and she didn't flinch away from the touch as he tilted her head up. There was violence in his gaze. There was also awe.

"I wasn't. I didn't fight back. I didn't turn him in. You're the first one I've ever told."

He took in a deep breath, his fingers caressing lightly at the ends of her hair. "Then that makes your secret precious to me, little fighter."

"Matthias..."

"Don't," he interrupted. "Do not think you are not a fighter. I see it in you every time you speak, every time you snap at me with that pretty little mouth of yours. You may have not turned him in, however I've no doubt that one day you will get your revenge. And I will watch. And it will be the sweetest sight to see."

Coral scoffed. "Revenge. Not likely, as I'm trapped in the queen's service." Though the prospect did sound sweet, she knew it was impossible. Another thing that sounded sweet was the fact he wanted to witness Coral get her revenge.

Matthias wasn't treating her any differently now that he knew.

Maybe she'd never been broken, after all.

"As am I," he replied. "And yet there is no such thing as impossible. Be confident and hope for that vengeance and you will receive it. Of this, I am sure."

Coral laughed and to change the subject asked, "Why are you in her service? Caspian had no choice, but you? Do you love her?"

"Love her?" he asked with horror dripping in his tone and over his features. "No one can love the queen. Except maybe Zalyn. What she and I have is a contract. That is it."

"But *why*?"

"I do not wish to lie to you, but the story is not a pleasant one."

"Tell me anyway."

He searched her face; if he was looking for doubt or fear, he would find none. "Do you know what it is to go hungry?" He didn't wait for her to answer. "Of course you do not. You are quite plump." His eyes roamed to her chest before he continued. "I was not in the Atlantean *Stratia* like your precious Caspian. I was born and bred in the slums of the Dark Waters. I killed and stole to survive. I fought and fucked my way through life because it was what I was good at. I was young and thought I could conquer the world. So when someone dared me to steal from the queen's palace thirty years ago, I did. I stole jewels from her chambers. I was nearly out, too, when Caspian and other guards caught me. I was brought before the queen and all I could do was laugh. Why cry in the face of death? But Queen Ulla took one look at me and saw nothing but a pretty face. She offered me a place in her Personal Guard. She offered me power, riches, sex, and my life. All so she could fuck me every night and so I would do her bidding. So, tell me, little fighter, as you look upon me in judgement, would you really have chosen another path?"

Coral felt more tears in her eyes. She pressed the heels of her hands against them before they could fall. "I'm not judging you," she whispered, slowly lowering her arms. She chose to ignore the fact that both Caspian and Matthias had been alive longer than she had, their lifespans longer, stranger.

"No?" He smiled. "I am not so noble as Caspian and now you know. I have no *Stratia* training, I have no inane story to make you pity me, and I certainly have nothing to regret. I live in the wealthiest castle of the sea, fuck the most powerful queen every night and morning. Enemies look away because to face me would be to die. What more could I want?"

"What about someone who actually cares and loves you?" Coral placed her hand lightly on his arm, as if that could project her warmth, her sadness for him into his bloodstream. He'd been born into a life of violence and poverty, had thrived in it and had made his way up, at least in his eyes. He was all powerful, invincible. But it still seemed a lonely life, to be in service of the queen and to no one else. To never be able to marry, to have children... To be free.

Matthias looked at her hand then into her eyes. "Love does not exist for me, little fighter. And I refuse to seek it out. Loving another is the surest way to self-destruction, and I am a survivor. Just ask Caspian. Love has crippled him enough."

Coral removed her hand from him as if his touch were painful and backed away a few strokes. "I guess I understand why you'd think that about love. The one person I loved more than anyone has only brought me heartbreak."

"Who?"

"Olivia."

"Who is Olivia?"

Coral smiled, the image of her best friend swimming into view. Her blonde hair, brown eyes, and tall, willowy form. Her opposite. The *yin* to her *yang*. A tightness squeezed at her chest. Her best friend was dead and she'd taken Coral's happiness with her. "She was my best friend," she confessed. "She died in the shipwreck."

Something flashed in his eyes, gone so quickly that she was sure she imagined it. "I am sorry, little fighter." Matthias swam forward and pulled her into his arms. "I am not so good at comfort," he said, "but if it will lessen your grief, you are welcome to punch me until you are satisfied."

Coral giggled, wrapping her arms around his waist. It was comforting, even if he couldn't give her reassurance, it felt good to be held. It felt good to be held by someone who wasn't constantly looking over his shoulder, waiting to be caught and punished for what he was feeling. To be held by someone who'd kept no secrets from her, who didn't have to hide who he truly was while hurting her in the process.

"So why are you really down here, Coral? Why did you try to swim away from me? Escaping?" He smoothed her hair back from her face. At some point, the rope holding it together had snapped and she hadn't noticed at all.

She looked up at Matthias. He'd been so open and honest with her, but could she trust him with the real reason for coming down here? He said himself, he was with the queen for power, money, and sex. That had to mean he was loyal to her. If Coral told him, would he go to the queen and have Coral killed? So far, he'd kept her every secret but how long would that trust between them last?

Her gut was screaming at her to confide in him, in *some-one,* but her mind was conflicted. She had to play it safe. She couldn't afford to end up locked away in a cage again for what she was doing. But she needed help. She needed someone on the inside.

"Matthias, you have the queen's confidence, don't you?" she asked tentatively. She was going to have to tread very, very carefully with him.

"She is confident I will protect her and do as she pleases. However, I am not one she shares all her deepest secrets with. The queen is a very private mer." He looked at her with raised eyebrows. "What are you thinking?"

Coral took a deep breath. Could she do this? Could she trust him?

Sighing, she took the plunge and prayed he would not betray her.

She told him everything. Told him about her talk with Zenara, how the queen had claimed to have destroyed every Keeper and every last scrap of Knowledge. She told him of her theory and how much sense it made, she told him of her desire to get home, of her need of a mer who could do magic and give her her legs back. She confessed everything, baring her mad soul and plans to him without pausing once. When finally she finished, she looked up at him expectantly, holding her breath.

After a long moment, Matthias said, "Your theory is quite sound. I had never thought to doubt the queen's word, or the proof of the destroyed Knowledge. Nobody did, as those were difficult times. If I could help, I would, but I have not heard of the queen sneaking off at all hours or any whisper-ings of hidden Knowledge. She visits the dungeons often, but that is because she likes to mock the prisoners."

Gripping the lapels of his jacket, Coral pulled him down to her desperately. "Will you help me, Matthias? Please?"

"Why do you wish to go home so badly? You said it yourself, your best friend is gone. There is nothing left for you there."

"I'm an outsider, Matthias. The mer treat me like an anomaly, like a murderer. I have no freedom. You may like being property of the queen, but I don't. I know Olivia is gone; I know I'll never see her again. I may not have anything left to live for, but I'd rather die standing than live the rest of my life on my knees."

Blinking down at her in surprise at the passion in her voice, at the words, he opened his mouth and closed it again. He ran a hand through his hair then smiled. "Fine, little fighter. I will help you. I will be your eyes and ears in the castle. But you must promise me one thing."

Coral's heart thumped. "Of course," she agreed too quickly. "Anything."

His smile was sin itself. "If you find this Knowledge and manage to get your legs back, say goodbye to me before you leave." He chucked her softly in the chin with his fist.

Joy overwhelmed Coral. She was one fin closer to getting her legs back. Impulsively, she pulled Matthias down into another hug and pressed her lips against his in a quick kiss. He groaned when she pulled away.

"Sorry," she apologized. "I was so excited!"

"If you are going to kiss me, at least do it properly." Matthias frowned at her. She rolled her eyes and opened her mouth to reply, but their conversation was interrupted.

"What are you doing here?" came Caspian's harsh voice. She pulled away from Matthias and turned to look at Caspian. A small ball of yellow light floated above his palm, and he was looking suspiciously at them both, eyes narrowing in anger as he took in their set of sea legs. Because having their legs out could only mean one thing.

"Relax, your Royal *Highness*," Matthias sneered mockingly.

Caspian tensed. "We needed to get away from prying eyes. You know how that is, do you not? Hiding in the shadows?" As he spoke, he trailed his hands lightly over Coral's bare skin.

She knew he was teasing Caspian, riling him up to make him upset, to get a reaction out of him. It was precisely why she didn't move. Maybe it was selfish and cruel of her. She knew Caspian's feelings, knew he had something at stake and that showing emotion was to risk it all, but she desperately wanted to know what she was to him. An adventure? A quick lay in the dark of the night? Or was he like her, drawn to Coral because he saw something that matched him there?

Caspian's eyes followed Matthias' movements. Coral held her breath, waited for a chip of anger to slip past the heavy armor he wore. His eyes were hard, the pupils narrowed into thin slits, the scales of his eyes glowing green in the light on his palm.

"Come, Knowledge Keeper," he said simply, tightly. "We are leaving."

Coral's heart plummeted at his words, at the vile, hurtful nickname. He couldn't stop pretending? Even once? It's not like Matthias was *blind*. He'd caught them in bed together and had kept their secret. She sighed a little and turned to give her goodbye to Matthias.

He was looking down at her angrily, and she had to take a stroke back. Was he angry with *her*? Was that look in his eyes directed at her? It was unnerving. But in a second, it was gone, and he grabbed her arm, pulling her to his chest. Coral gasped, but the sound was swallowed by his mouth when he crashed his lips onto hers and took her tongue between his teeth.

She groaned, closing her eyes. This was wrong. It felt so wrong somehow to kiss like this, to do it so openly in front of Caspian. It was one thing to let his fingers graze along the skin of her arm, but another entirely to do this. It was another level of cruelty that Coral couldn't bring herself to do. She pushed against his chest, breaking off the kiss.

"Stop," she demanded breathlessly. Matthias' eyes fell from humor. For a moment he looked as he had when they'd first met, when he'd crossed that throne room to hold her down for branding.

Murderous.

It chilled her.

"So I am good enough to fuck in the shadows, little fighter, but not under the light of watchful eyes? You have no problem kissing me as long as no one else knows it, right?" He smiled cruelly. "You and your precious Caspian have more in common than you realize. Or maybe you want what the queen has? Willing mermen that way you do not *have* to choose?"

Her hands tightened into fists, the urge to punch him strong. But she looked at his smiling face and realized that that's what he wanted. He thrived in violence and made an ass of himself so that he could fight, so that he could hurt and be hurt. Because he'd rather do that than actually *feel*.

And who was she to punch him when what he had said was right? As much as they were playing with her emotions, she was playing with *theirs* with all this back and forth. She thought that she would be the one hurt in all of this. Caspian, touching her in the shadows, pretending to hate her in the light of day. Matthias was more consistent; he did not care who saw or who knew, did not care for the consequences because he seemed convinced there would be none. But she'd done to *him* what Caspian had done to *her*.

Coral turned silently to Caspian and swam over to his side. She could feel Matthias glaring at them both, could feel his anger like a palpable thing. She wanted to hold him and reassure him. But she couldn't. How selfish of her. After everything he had done for her. He'd taught her to stay strong, to conceal a weapon, he'd held her when no one else had through her pain, kept her secrets.

Caspian was still looking at him with hard lines over his every feature. "Do not bother her again, Matthias."

Startled, she looked to him. The ice in his eyes had seemed to have finally chipped, staring at Matthias with murderous intent. Coral looked at Matthias.

He smirked. "I think that is for her to decide. Not you."

"If you do not want the queen to know about this, you will leave her be," Caspian ground out.

Matthias smiled wider, wickedly. "If the queen finds out about *us,* you can be sure I will let slip of *you.* And we all know who the queen will favor and who she will punish. We all know who would die for their indiscretions." In a flash, he was in front of Caspian. In the closeness of the light, his eyes gleamed like hell's fire and his wickedness was that of the devil himself. "Do not make idle threats to me, Caspian. I will forgive it this time, but the next you may not find me lenient."

Caspian looked as though he were going to throw a punch at the other merman or stab him through the chest. Matthias must have noticed the look in his eyes as well, for he chuckled darkly.

"You can try, Caspian. You know what will happen. There will be no one to stop me from killing you." A sneer pulled at his lips "And I *will* kill you. You may have been someone in Atlantica, but here you are *nothing* but the queen's whore."

"Okay, *enough,*" Coral interjected. It wouldn't do good for them to try and kill each other here. She didn't want either of them to die, especially on her behalf. "Let's go, Caspian." She tugged on his arm, but her gaze was on Matthias, even if he wasn't currently looking at her. Finally, he managed to tear his gaze away from Caspian to offer her a cocky smile.

"See you soon, my little fighter." He winked.

Caspian growled and pulled Coral away to swim out of the stone maze. She dared a glance over her shoulder before rounding a corner with Caspian. Matthias was still staring after them, but the smile on his lips had vanished, replaced instead with a deep frown. Before Coral could wonder on it, Caspian was pulling her away.

MATTHIAS SWAM slowly and leisurely into the queen's private chambers, as if he had not a care in the world. She was lying against a mound of colorful, spongy pillows with silk blankets in bright colors strewn off the sides of her grandiose bed.

Her hand was propping her head up, her long hair flowed like white waves crashing to a shore, her skin flushed red in satiation, and there was a lazy smile on her mouth. Caspian seemed to have made the most of his time with her.

The black and pink of her tentacles curled and unfurled invitingly. He stared at them, licking his lips, then looked up to her bare and generous chest.

"Oh, how your eyes wander so, my little merman," she teased.

Matthias smiled that delightful, cocky grin he was known and loved for. "Only for you, my queen," he said lazily and slipped into bed with her. He trailed a rough hand over her bare body and enjoyed as she shivered in delight. Her nipples were bright and puckered. Caspian's doing, no doubt. Matthias was sure he could surpass him in bed sport. He could make the queen scream, make her shake the very waters of the kingdom with his tongue and teeth.

Coral had called it a competition. When it came to the queen, there was no contest. They all knew where they fell, what purpose they served, and who she favored. Caspian was her favorite pet to torment; he always had been because he was the most unattainable. He pretended to love her, to enjoy every moment with her when they all knew that Caspian despised her. And that, to Ulla Magissa, made it sweeter.

Sometimes the queen would take them to bed one by one, but others she took them all together. There had never been any jealousy then, either. They relished in her attentions, in her endless well of power. Matthias could not care less if she took him first or if she took him last or not at all. He did not care that she made him watch Caspian take his time with her. He did not care that they had all tasted that delicious mouth —sometimes one right after the other.

Because she was the queen.

And Matthias felt nothing for her.

But when he had opened the chamber door to find Caspian kissing his way down Coral's body, he had wanted to rip the other merman apart. He had heard him shushing her in the hall when all she had wanted to do was cry out, and Matthias *knew* that he could give her a much more pleasurable time than Caspian ever could. He would never silence her. Never force her to hide what she truly felt.

So, when he'd lifted her skirts up and pressed his fingers inside her, he'd wished it was something else instead. He wished he could lay her down over her bed and make her scream. And what a lovely scream it had been. He loved watching her face as he moved inside her. The way her eyelids fluttered ever so slightly. How color heated the curve of her cheeks when he'd run his finger over her clit. How her breathing shallowed when she was close. How just before she fell apart in his arms, she bit her bottom lip and sunk her teeth where his shoulder met his neck.

He even loved how shocked she had looked afterwards at what she had done. She could deny that she wanted it for the rest of her days, but Matthias knew the truth. She had not stopped him. If she had, he would have done as she wished, but she had given him permission. And in her desperation, she had grabbed his wrist and pulled him tighter into her body. She had wanted him with her every fiber.

And she still did.

Were it not for Caspian.

Never before had Matthias felt any stirrings of jealousy until Coral. He wanted her almost more than he wanted power and riches, and he could not exactly explain *why*. His little fighter was strong. Even while she was crying, her strength shone like a blinding, scintillating light through her tears. He wanted her. In every way he could think of. But he knew he would have to let her go. It was what she wanted.

How could he let her go when he knew the truth? When he knew that the empty sadness deep in her heart was for naught? He had not placed the pieces together until after she had left him to go with Caspian.

"You seem distracted, Matthias," the queen said with annoyance.

Matthias smiled at her, at the mer who could give him life or condemn him, and he gripped her breast in his hand. She arched beneath his touch. He could not help noticing that her reactions did not seem as genuine as Coral's. Coral's reactions were far, far sweeter. She held nothing back. Her cries weren't practiced; her movements weren't calculated.

He began pulling off the pearl buttons of his jacket. Usually, he went fast with the queen because he knew she liked the rougher edges of sex. He wanted to take his time. Her black eyes fixated on him, but he imagined them different, imagined them rounder, bigger, and the color of blue gems.

"Let me help you." The queen sat up and ripped the rest of his jacket off, scattering the buttons across the water. She pushed it off his shoulders and trailed her ever-sharp nails down his chest, over the dark lines of his tattoos.

He remembered when he'd gotten every single one of them. Many believed his tattoo was in honor of his queen, and he let them believe it. The truth was, he'd gotten them all before he'd known her, in the slums. The queen allowed him to keep it because it reminded her of herself. But Matthias had gotten it because he loved the power it radiated. He hadn't cared that the tattoo stretched over the entire expanse of his chest and stomach or that it ran down the length of his arms, to the backs of his hands and up his neck and sides of his head.

"Come play with me, Matthias," the queen commanded, lying on her back against the cushions, raising her arms above her head.

Matthias stared at her but did not see her. Instead, he saw a curvaceous little fighter with blue eyes and black hair floating steadily around her. He smiled and covered her body with his own.

The queen fell asleep instantly after he'd satisfied any lingering needs. She had not dismissed him, so Matthias lay at her side, hand sprawled over his chest and thought of *her*. She was a plague on his mind, and it was only spreading. He found he did not mind it, even if he wanted to be rid of it. He'd meant what he told her about love. He would not look for it, for it only led to unhappiness in the end.

If she took a good long look at herself, she would realize that what he said was true. She grieved over her human friend so much so that she had cried in front of him.

Matthias tightened his hands into the sponge mattress, heart clenching at the reminder of her unseen tears. Could he really allow her to continue feeling that way? Could he really allow her to swim away without certainty? Could he really let her go away, knowing that she would forever wear that expression?

He cast a glance at the queen. She was in such a deep sleep that his movements as he got out of bed did not disturb her. He quickly got dressed, picking up discarded weapons as he went. He had to get to Coral.

He had to tell her the truth.

~

"WHAT IN THE name of Neptune were you doing with Matthias in that part of the castle?" Caspian demanded angrily as he practically threw her into her bedroom chambers.

Her mind flashed back to the ardent kiss, to running her hands over nearly every inch of him. Her face flushed. To the secrets she'd confessed to him and the truths he gave in return. "Nothing," she replied.

"Do not lie to me!" Caspian shouted. Then he checked himself, but the hold he had on his anger wasn't very strong before he let it loose again. "What were you doing with him, Coral?"

"Am I Coral now?" she asked sarcastically. "I thought I was *anthropos* to you."

"Do not change the subject. You know why I cannot be kind to you in public."

"It seems like you can't be kind to me in private, either." She placed her hands on her hips, like she imagined Olivia would do, and glared at him. She noticed for the first time the markings trailing up his arms and on his neck like dark reddish-blue bruises. Her own face flared in anger at the sight of his hickeys.

At least his cheeks flushed at her words. "You cannot *trust* him, Coral. He is in league with the queen."

"So are you," she pointed out, though not unkindly, and he still flinched at her words. "Maybe there's more to Matthias than you think."

Caspian snorted. "You have let him poison your mind with his manipulations. Is that all it takes to convince you, Coral? Just the quick touch of his hands on your skin and you are his for the taking?"

Coral didn't know how she swam up to him so fast. All she knew was that he was across the room one moment and the next she was in front of him, slapping her hand against his face. "Don't speak to me like that."

Caspian rubbed a hand across his jaw. There was raw fury in his eyes that truly frightened her. For all of Matthias' violence, for all the thirst for danger, he had never scared her as much as Caspian did in that moment. She tried backing away a moment too late. His large hand reached for her, pulled her forward by the front of her dress until she was crushed against his chest. His arms circled around her waist to keep her in place despite her struggles. Then he bent down to kiss her.

This kiss was different from the others she'd experienced. It wasn't giving. It wasn't a hunger that thrilled her. It wasn't even that silent desperation that he'd so deeply hypnotized her with that first time. This kiss was about possession, about taking whether she wanted him to or not.

Coral pounded her fists against his chest, pushed her body away from him, but his arms held in place like a steel lock. She went to reach for the dagger, only to realize that Matthias had never given it back. So, Coral bit down as hard as she could on his lip.

Caspian let out a curse and backed away, slamming into the wall. Coral put as much distance as she could between them, her breathing uneven and harsh. "What the hell is wrong with you?" she demanded.

Caspian looked at her frantically, apologies began sputtering out of his lips. "I am so, so sorry, Coral. Please, I do not know what—" He let out a frustrated groan and turned to bang his fists against the wall, the entire room shuddering with the force. When all sound in the room subsided, Caspian whispered sadly, "I *heard* you. I heard your every moan, your every passionate scream. I heard what he made you feel right after *we*—" He cut off and turned around to look into her flushing face. "I wanted to stop him, but you *enjoyed* him. And that filled me with rage. I wanted to murder him where he floated, but I have so much to lose..." He broke off with a curse and ran a frustrated hand through his long, floating red tresses. "I cannot stand to see you with him because a part of me says that you are mine and only mine. Please, Coral, *please* stop seeing him."

As he spoke, another voice rang in her ear. *You think I do not mind? You think I was not filled with murderous rage at the sight of Caspian's filthy hands all over you?*

She squared her shoulders and looked him in the eye. "Will you stop seeing the queen?" she asked.

Caspian stared at her incredulously. "Of course not. You know that I cannot."

"Then how can you ask me to stop seeing Matthias when you will not even stop seeing the queen, Caspian? I will not be that girl. I will not be asked to sit and wait patiently on the sidelines while you bounce back and forth between the two of us. I will not hold only a part of your heart while the queen has the other half."

"Coral..." He let out a frustrated breath, tugged at his hair. "*Please*," he begged again. "Please wait for me to sort this out."

"While you pleasure Ulla at night and then come back to try and lie with me?" She was offended by the very idea. "I will not, Caspian. I will wait for neither you nor Matthias.

And I will not stop seeing him, either. He's a friend, and I need his help."

Caspian jerked his gaze up at her. "His help? With *what*?" He glared at her suspiciously.

Coral sighed. She hadn't been sure whether to trust him or not, but... looking into those sad eyes, hearing the desperation and helplessness in his voice roused sympathy in her. If she could get him to help her as well, they'd have a higher chance of finding the Knowledge and besides getting her legs back, maybe Caspian could take back whatever it was the queen was holding against him.

So, Coral explained her theories to Caspian, and she explained why she was really in the stone maze with Matthias and how he'd agreed to help her. By the end of it, she'd expected Caspian to smile, to agree, but he was just looking at her with fury.

"Are you *insane* Coral? Why would you trust Matthias with this information? He will betray you to the queen as he sees fit. You cannot see him anymore. I *forbid* it. This crazy theory will do nothing but get you killed!"

Taking a stroke back, she gaped at him with disbelief. How could he *disagree* to such a brilliant plan? How could he refuse the opportunity to get back whatever the queen had taken from him?

"My plan is smart. I may have gained information that could change your fate and you tell me it's stupid? What's *wrong* with you?"

He went on as if Coral hadn't even spoken. "So that's why you were with Matthias in the stone labyrinth? Of all the idiotic... You must stay away from that place. It is dangerous! You have no idea what lurks there."

"Save your lecture. Matthias already told me that." And he'd given her a lesson on fending off attackers, too.

"This is not a joke, Coral. You are meddling in things you

do not understand. Stay out of it. Finish out your sentence and if you prove useful to the queen, she may just let you go free."

"You and I both know she has no plans of releasing me, Caspian."

He looked at her sadly. "You do not know that. The queen may be a lot of things, but she keeps her word."

Coral rolled her eyes before snorting. "Right, because she's so trustworthy. The mermaid who has whatever you care so much about and is using it to manipulate you into her service and her bed is very honorable. Right." Her fins flared and she slapped her tail. "This is something I have to do. I have to go back to my own world. I can't stay here anymore."

"Why?" His voice cracked. "I thought you had no one left."

"I don't! But that doesn't mean I want to be her slave forever! Why can't you see that?"

"Because I do not want you to leave!" he shouted. Coral froze. Caspian's breathing was heavy, his massive chest heaving up and down. "I cannot bear the thought of you leaving. I—I know I should not feel this way. You said the queen has one half of me while you have the other? That is a lie. The queen may have my body but you, my Coral, have my heart, my *soul*." He swam forward slowly and bent to press a soft kiss on her forehead. There was a certain finality in the gesture, a broken vulnerability that hurt her heart. "Get your rest," he whispered, the words cracking. "You're just confused. Tomorrow will be better. Tomorrow we will speak more of this, but heed my words, Matthias is not to be trusted."

And then he was gone.

IT WAS WELL into the night when Coral heard a strange tapping.

Tap, tap, tap.

On and on it went. She sat up in her bed, hair loose around her face and looked around. There was dark stillness in the water, the only illumination came from behind the bedroom window where there was a small, floating bubble of light.

Coral rubbed her hands across her eyes and stared at it.

Tap, tap, tap.

Then his face appeared in the window.

Sighing, she slipped out of bed and swam over to the window. She gave it a strong but quiet jerk, lifting it up to let him swim through. The waters outside were chilly and she quickly closed the window to prevent the cold current from getting in.

Turning to Matthias, she said, "I hope you didn't come to catch me with Caspian. As you can see, he isn't here." She swam past him and went to sit back on the edge of the bed. He followed silently. Surprisingly silent. She looked at him curiously.

His face was set in deep concentration, brows furrowed, eyes distant. His usual smile wasn't in place and that worried her. She placed her hand over his. He was ice to the touch as if he'd just come back from swimming through the arctic.

"Matthias?" she asked worriedly, pressing her other hand to his cheek. That was cold as well. "Matthias, are you okay?"

He blinked, coming out of his trance and turned to look at Coral. "My little fighter," he whispered, leaning his cheek into her warm palms. "I need to know something of great importance." His voice was urgent.

"What's wrong?"

He took a deep breath. "Do you trust me?"

She looked at him quizzically. "Matthias?"

"Do. You. Trust. Me?" he enunciated very carefully.

She swallowed but found herself nodding. "I do." She didn't know why. She shouldn't even be within a couple strokes of him. But she *did*. And she hoped she wouldn't regret it.

"I was thinking about what you said earlier. About dying for freedom instead of living on your knees and about the only person you ever loved breaking your heart."

"Olivia," she breathed.

Matthias nodded. "Olivia. There is something I have to tell you. Or rather, something I must show you." He took her hand, threading his fingers through hers. "Get dressed," he said urgently. "Wear something warm. It is cold where we are going."

Her heart beat faster in her chest. "What is it, Matthias? Where are we going?"

He looked around warily as if expecting someone to be spying near the shadows. Satisfied, he leaned in to whisper, "Survivors." Coral looked at him in questioning. "The cruise ship you were on, little fighter. There were survivors."

PRISONERS OF WAR

CORAL HAD NEVER GOTTEN DRESSED FASTER IN HER LIFE. She didn't care that Matthias was there, that he was watching her as she stripped. She did it in record time, dawning a long-sleeved gown and throwing a seal skin jacket with a fur collar over it.

When she'd finished, Matthias had thrown open the window and dived out of it, Coral right at his tail. They swam through the darkest alleyways, kept a low profile, and somehow Matthias managed to sneak them into the queen's castle without being seen.

"Do exactly as I say, fighter," Matthias whispered quickly to her. They'd hidden in closets, floated noiselessly above the ceiling as guards and courtiers swam by until they made it to the lone staircase, descending down to that same stone maze. Coral kept track of every turn and direction they made, following closely beside Matthias the entire time.

Her heart beat more erratically every stroke closer towards the end. Towards the survivors. Matthias hadn't guaranteed that Olivia had survived; he said he didn't know her to confirm such a thing, so he'd brought her down to the queen's *calabozo*.

It was a different area from where she'd been held that first week she'd been in the castle. Her own cell had been tiny and dank, and there certainly hadn't been a maze. Her nerves hummed through the entirety of her body, causing her hands to tremble. In her eager rush to get to the prisoners, she'd tripped many times over her tail already. Each time, she got up and kept swimming.

Her mind wandered through so many different scenarios as they swam. What if she got there and Olivia wasn't there? What if she *was*? Coral couldn't leave her there to suffer. And why had Matthias told her about this anyway? She looked warily up at him. His face was a stone mask, grave and serious. She focused her own gaze ahead and vowed to ask him later. She had to know why he would risk everything for her.

Coming towards the end of the hall, Matthias put his hand to her chest, forcing her a few strokes backward. She looked at him in questioning. He pressed a finger to his lips. Gulping, she nodded.

Matthias swam out beyond the hallway, smiling. Coral listened attentively, heard the salute of guards. They spoke in low murmurs and hushed tones. Then, there was silence. Coral strained her ears and let out a small yelp when Matthias appeared before her again, gesturing for her to follow.

She swam behind him and came before looming iron gates with bars that dug deep into the ground and rose high above the ceiling. There was no way out, as the bars were separated only enough for a hand to get through. The guards manning it were piled on top of each other, unmoving.

"Did you kill them?" Coral gaped.

"No, they are only sleeping. That magic will not last long so we must hurry." He produced an enormous iron key from one of the guards and placed it in the lock, turning it and pushing it open to gesture her through. Once they were inside, he left the door slightly ajar and guided Coral down a long, long hallway of cells.

The *calabozo* was enormous, but not every cell was occupied. The ones they passed that were occupied filled with suspicious-looking mer that squealed and howled and whistled as they swam by. Matthias growled low in his throat at them but kept moving beside her, drawing her closer with every passing second.

They passed a cell with a bent old man inside. His scales were dull and dirty, his skin wrinkled beyond saving, but his eyes when he looked up and smiled at Coral were pure gold. She shivered and went on.

"Here," Matthias whispered, nodding at the next cell. Coral's heart nearly exploded with nerves as she swam up to the bars to grip them tightly. Inside the cage there were at least ten mer, including a small child of about seven. At the sight of her and Matthias, some of them whimpered and shrank back into the shadows of their cell.

Coral looked from face to face. Some of them were so haggard and dirty, she couldn't even see their features clearly, and others she didn't recognize at all. Her heart sank to her fins; tears began to swell up in her eyes.

"Olivia?" she whispered.

There was silence and the humans-turned-mer just stared at her. She half expected them to hiss or begin clawing at her through the bars. None of them came forward. None. Coral fought down a rising sob. She wasn't here. Her best friend wasn't here. It felt like losing her all over again.

Turning to Matthias, Coral shook her head sadly. His own face was grave, but he nodded once and went to take her arm, presumably to lead her out of there, but then there was a voice.

"Coral?" It was scratchy, low and tentative. But Coral

would have recognized it anywhere. She turned back to the bars and watched as a mermaid with a dull brown tail swam out from behind the mass of people. Her blonde hair was tangled through with seaweed and broken bits of shell. Her naked body was covered in a mess of algae, her face was pale, and her lips were cracked. Her brown eyes devoid of hope looked at Coral suspiciously, as if she didn't quite trust her mind was being truthful. But Coral knew the truth.

Olivia was here.

Olivia was alive.

Coral pushed her hands through the bars and reached for her best friend, pulling her in an uncomfortable hug with the bars between them. Coral pulled away, gripping her friend's haggard face in her hands. The tears that spilled forth were genuine tears of happiness. Happiness that her friend was alive. That she was here.

"I thought you died," Olivia rasped. She was sobbing, too. "I thought you were killed in the shipwreck!" She touched her face as if to prove to herself that she wasn't dreaming, that Coral was solid and in front of her.

"I thought the same about you," Coral said. She ran her hands over her friend's head, down her cheeks, over her lips. "What happened?"

Olivia snorted, almost sounding like her old self. "The ship exploded and I went under. I thought I was going to die since a metal piece had pinned me to the sea floor. I remember drowning, forgetting everything and then..." She broke off with a cough. Coral gripped her shoulders tightly until her fit subsided. "I woke up with a tail. There was a merman there; I thought I was dreaming or crazy. But then I saw him kissing the sinking bodies, and one by one they turned into mer. He rounded us up and put is in a carriage pulled by a hippocampus—those are *real,* if you can fucking believe that shit. We thought we'd be safe with him, but he locked us in *here*." She sobbed. "They barely feed us, they torture us by poking us with spears. They call us anthro— whatever. That first night..." She broke off to sob again. Coral rubbed her shoulders in comfort. "There were more of us, but that first night, the guards had had too much to drink. They decided it would be fun to play with some of us for sport. They took them away and... and they never came back. We could hear their screams down the hall. We could hear them laughing with the women they took."

"Oh, Livvy." Coral stroked her head sadly. It felt so odd to be the one on the other end of comfort, as Olivia had always been the one to look after Coral, but it also came so naturally. Her heart ached for them, ached for what her best friend had to endure.

"Where have you been?" Olivia asked. "How did you get away?"

Coral recounted her story, about a merman who had saved her and brought her to his queen because he thought she was a Knowledge Keeper, how that might have been the only reason she'd been allowed to live. How they'd thrown her in the dungeons, given her a trial to be executed but decided against it, her community service, all of it. When she was finished, she hadn't realized she was crying until Olivia touched her cheek.

"How did you know where to find us? How did you know we were alive?"

Coral smiled. "I didn't know. *He* helped me." She gestured to Matthias, who was floating behind her, looking a little awkward. As if calling out his cue, he smiled at Olivia. "Olivia, meet Matthias."

Olivia shot back in her cell at the sight of him. Coral stared after her, confused but her friend's eyes were focused solely on Matthias. They were filled with distrust, anger, and hatred. "It was *him,* Coral," she hissed. "*He* put us in this dungeon. Him and that black-haired devil, Zalyn!"

Coral whipped around to face him, her heart constricting with the beginnings of betrayal. "Is it true?" she asked.

Matthias looked at her unblinking. "It is true," he confessed. Coral's hand itched to reach out and punch him for it. For what he'd done to her best friend and these people. He must have read it in her face. "I was under the queen's orders," he reminded her, though his brief smirk said he wouldn't mind if she got rough with him. "She told us it was for the good of the mer." His eyes spoke of a challenge, a dare to doubt him or argue or do *something.*

Coral gripped tightly at the bars. "Olivia," she began, "did he ever hurt you?" She didn't think she could forgive him if he had, so she had to know, though she figured she already knew the answer.

"No, but—" Olivia hesitated, still eyeing him warily.

Matthias shrugged. "I do not enjoy playing with other mer's things."

"They aren't things!" Coral snapped, but then reined in her anger. Did it really matter what he'd done then? That was in the past. He'd brought her to her friend now and that was what mattered most.

"It's okay, Olivia. He isn't going to hurt us. He's the one who told me you were alive. He brought me to you."

Olivia swam back over warily. When she was close enough, she whispered, "You can't trust him, Coral. You can't trust any on the queen's Personal Guard."

"I could have easily let you rot in here, land-scum," Matthias interjected with a smile. Apparently, he *had* heard. "But I brought my little fighter to see you instead."

Olivia glared at him, then turned to Coral. *My little fighter?* she mouthed.

Coral sighed. "It's a long story. But we can trust him. He's on our side." She shot him a glance. He smiled widely at her, and she rolled her eyes at him.

"No one on the queen's guard is trustworthy," Olivia said. "Look at what they did to me." She pushed aside her hair and lifted her chin to reveal her long, slender neck covered in black bruises in the marks of fingers. Someone had choked her.

"Who did this to you?" Coral demanded angrily.

Olivia glared at Matthias. "The black-haired one. Zalyn. He took great joy in it, too."

Coral gripped tightly at the iron bars. "I should have stabbed him harder."

"You *stabbed* him?" Olivia asked with disbelief.

"I did." Olivia smiled and raised her hand. Chuckling, Coral high-fived her best friend and it almost felt like old times. "Now come on," Coral said. "We have to get you out of here."

Matthias laid his hand down on her shoulder immediately. "I am afraid we cannot do that."

Coral turned to glare at him. "What do you mean we can't? Look at them! They're dying, Matthias! They're naked in a cold cell. We *have* to get them out!"

Matthias glared steadily at her. "And where will you take them? How will you get away when they can barely float? The queen will know if we help them escape. That is why we cannot. Not until we have a plan."

"But Matth—"

"Have you found the Knowledge yet?" he demanded on interruption.

"No, but—"

"Then how do you plan on helping them? They would not survive in the ocean and neither would you. You need to find the Knowledge, Coral. Find the Knowledge and then come back for them."

"He's right," Olivia rasped begrudgingly. "We've been trying to learn to swim in this cage, but without a proper teacher, we're useless. Besides, we're starved. We wouldn't make it a mile."

Coral bit her lip, pushed away the tears and sadness that threatened to overpower her. "I can't leave you here," she whispered sadly. "*I can't.*"

Olivia took Coral's hand. "You *can*," she said fiercely. "*And you will.* Find a way to get our legs back and then get us out of here. I have faith in you."

Tears began swelling in her eyes again. She sniffled and began unbuttoning her jacket. "At least take this. You can take turns using it against the cold."

"You cannot leave that, either," Matthias said softly.

She wanted to shoot him a look, but Olivia placed her hand on hers. "He's right. They threw us in here naked. You'd be found out if you left anything."

Nodding, she buttoned it back up. She dreaded having to leave her best friend in this awful place. She suddenly felt so privileged, to have lived for the past few weeks in a mansion, to have Zenara dress her, comb her hair, feed her, and have a warm bed to sleep in at night. Not to mention all of the mermen she'd already kissed. She was a selfish friend.

"Stop that," Olivia snapped. Coral raised her eyebrows. "Stop wishing our places were reversed. Stop feeling guilty about whatever it is that's going on through your mind."

"But—"

Olivia shook her head wildly. "Stop. I don't want to hear it. I don't care what you've done. Just find the knowledge, whatever that is, and come back for us. Okay? Promise?" She held out her pinky. Coral sniffled but gave her own pinky, interlocking them, sealing the promise.

"Time to go, my little fighter." Matthias' lips brushed across her ear. Coral nodded and reluctantly let go of Olivia.

"I'll be back. I promise." She took a few strokes back.

Olivia took the time to glare at Matthias. "You." She pointed at him, her voice the stern one that Coral remembered. "Take care of my friend. I'll kill you if you don't."

Matthias chuckled. "You are in no position to be making threats. But, in any case, you need not threaten me for *that*. She is a fighter and can protect herself. However, if it will help ease your mind, then I will protect her with my life."

That being said, he turned away, and together they left the *calabozo* behind. Matthias reclosed the door, placed the key back into the guard's pocket, and they swam away into the quiet waters of the night.

～

CORAL COLLAPSED ONTO HER BED. There was worry in her chest, but unbending happiness as well. She was alive. Olivia was *alive*. She had an opportunity to find the Knowledge and save the survivors of the shipwreck. They all had the chance to get out of here. To go back home.

Matthias laid on the bed next to her, his hands sprawled out on his sides. His eyes were closed, and he'd made no sound, had said nothing, had not advanced on her once. The quiet was disconcerting.

She reached for his hand, threaded her fingers through his. "Thank you," she whispered. "Thank you for giving me my best friend back."

"Anything for you, my little fighter." He squeezed her hand back gently.

Coral sat up in bed, hugging her tail to her chest. She looked down at him, at the short tendrils of brown hair floating over his forehead, at his sharp nose with the small fishhook ring poking through and square jaw and that mouth... Her eyes lingered on it for too long, taking in his every detail. The perfect heart shape of his upper lip, the smooth curve of his bottom one. They'd been so rough on hers, so violent but not in a way that had been meant to harm her. He'd taken her mouth in his lips to *push* her into fighting back, into pushing him back with equal force. Ever the fighter, he was, and in pushing her, he'd made her stronger. And for that, she would be eternally grateful.

"Why did you do it?" she asked. He opened his eyes. "Why did you betray your precious queen for me?"

Would he tell her? Or would he just say, '*Does it matter?*'

"I thought the answer to that would be obvious." He smiled, lifting his hand up to lightly knock her chin in a joking manner. She caught his wrist in her hand. Her eyes said, *I'm serious*. He looked at her for the first time with open and vulnerable eyes, the expression shuttering just as quickly. "Because I want you." He said the words almost painfully, his fingers sliding down her tail.

Coral's breath caught. "I cannot give you what you want. Not while you are tied to the queen. I won't be second to her."

"I know that, Coral." He sighed and took his hand away from her. "I knew that the moment I decided to tell you the truth. And even now after you have confirmed what I knew, I will *still* help you."

Her heart clenched at his words, at the raw honesty at this new layer of Matthias she was starting to peel back. He was definitely more than he seemed. He wasn't just violence, rage, sex, and power. He was also kind, gentle, and caring.

"I ask nothing from you in return except for your good-bye, before you leave this world forever."

Throat clenching, Coral bent over him. Her hair floated like a curtain around their faces. He was smiling, not in mocking or sarcastic cruelty. His lips were upturned gently for her. Only for her. "Thank you, Matthias. I may not be able to give you what you want, but—" She bit her bottom lip, drawing his eyes to her mouth. "I want to give you one last thing. Just one."

He stared at her curiously and nodded his assent. Coral released a nervous breath and bent down to him and pressed her lips shyly to his.

He didn't move, so she would have to. She pressed her palm to his cheek and delved in deeper, opening her mouth in his, shyly touching her tongue to his. Coral worked her mouth against Matthias', his warmth enveloping her core in a small fire that lit a trailed path down her veins. Matthias groaned when she bit his tongue.

It was his undoing.

He grabbed her by the back of the neck to pull her closer and held her in place as they devoured each other. Coral was careful not to touch any other part of him, not to let the flames consume them both. She kept her hand on his cheek, and he kept his hand on the back of her neck. Steady, their hands were so steady, but their mouths desperate and rough. As if they knew that this would be the last time, the last promise they would ever share.

It ended all too quickly.

Coral broke it off first but didn't pull away. Their lips were still a whisper away from each other, and heat crackled between them like a palpable current. "A kiss," she breathed against his lips. "Willingly given and shared between the two of us."

Matthias smiled sweetly and reached up to push aside her hair. "I should go." He took his hand from her hair and it went into the lapels of his jacket. He pulled out her dagger. "This belongs to you. Hide it well." He ruffled her hair playfully and then got up, swimming over to the window. "Until tomorrow, my little fighter," he said before diving out the window and leaving her in the cold.

A CHANGE IN PLANS

"Where did you go last night?" Caspian asked at the breakfast table the next morning. Coral paused with the fork halfway to her mouth, set it down then cleared her throat demurely.

"What do you mean?" she asked.

Caspian dropped his own fork into his bowl, the harshness of it making her flinch. "Do not treat me like a fool. I know you left."

She broke off a piece of fruit and nibbled on it nonchalantly. "How would you know that unless you went into my room?"

Caspian growled lowly and turned to Zenara who was in the middle of refilling his empty plate. "Leave us, please, Zenara." The mermaid flicked her curling tendrils from her face and left, not before shooting Coral a small, nervous smile. It was like she knew Caspian was about to blow up into full lecture mode. As soon as she was gone, Caspian's voice softened. "Coral, *where* did you go last night?"

Coral wiped her mouth on a spongy napkin and looked

him in the eye, expression serious. "What were you doing in my room, Caspian?" she demanded quietly.

He waved off her question. "It does not matter."

"It does." She was sick of him answering every question that way. Why couldn't he be honest for once? "I told you I wouldn't wait for you, that I wouldn't be second to your queen or hidden in the shadows. I'd made myself perfectly clear, and still you sought me out in the middle of the night. I'm not some nighttime entertainment. I'm not some whore."

Caspian's expression hardened into angry lines. "I do not think you a whore or entertainment. I just wanted to see you." Then he narrowed his eyes. "You will not let me into your chambers, but you will go out with Matthias in the middle of the night?" His voice bled with suspicion.

Coral rolled her eyes and pushed the plate of food in front of her, suddenly at a loss in appetite. "I never said I was with Matthias. But hey, let's talk about something else, shall we? Let's talk about the fact that there were survivors from my shipwreck. Let's talk about the fact that my best friend is *alive* and that you didn't tell me anything!" She raised her voice to a shout.

Caspian's eyes widened and he was up, out of his chair and swimming towards her. Without warning, he grabbed her arm and began pulling her out of the dining room and into his office where he shut and locked the door.

"What are you saying?" He whipped her around so that she was pressed up against the door and he was looming over her. "What do you mean there are survivors? How do you know this?"

Coral glared up at him, at the merman she'd trusted since the beginning. The one who had made her what she was and who was constantly turning his back on her.

"I found out last night. I went exploring again in that maze. Olivia is *alive,* and you never bothered to tell me.

You're a bastard!" She punched him in the chest. Her fists dug into the hard metal of his turquoise and golden scale armor. It didn't matter that it hurt, that it split open the skin at her knuckles. She punched his chest for every betrayal, every lie.

"Coral. Stop." He grabbed her wrists and brought them down gently to her sides. She growled at him and tried pulling her hands away, out of his icy grip. He held on tight, looking down at her with an expression that she couldn't quite decipher. "Coral," he repeated. "What are you talking about?"

"As if you don't know!" she snapped.

"I do not."

Coral looked into his face, trying to find some hint of a lie, some tell, but he'd had years of practice at being unreadable. She didn't know what he was thinking, what was going through his mind. She didn't know what to believe.

"There are survivors in the *calabozo*, hidden within the stone maze. Olivia is there. She's alive. Why didn't you tell me?" Her voice broke, chest aching as she said those words. He'd claimed to be so trustworthy, but he'd lied. He'd let her believe that Olivia was dead.

He looked at her now, his eyes, mouth, every feature on his beautiful face the perfect semblance of surprise. "There were survivors?" He sounded genuinely shocked. "How many?"

She looked at him suspiciously. "Ten, including a small child and Olivia. I thought you *knew*."

Releasing her wrists, he ran his hands over his face, through his hair in an attempt to clear his muddled thoughts, to process what she'd just told him. He soaked up this new information, swam back and forth across his office in hurried movements, Coral's gaze following his every stroke.

"You are sure they are alive? You are sure there were survivors from the shipwreck you were on?" He stopped to ask.

"I'm positive."

He loosed a breath, and a swarm of bubbles rose and danced around him. "Coral, I swear to you I did not know there were survivors. If I had, I would have told you. You have to know that."

Coral didn't know what to believe. She looked at him, *really* looked at him. He wore the golden armor in the house and nowhere else, she noticed. When he went beyond these walls, he was always in his Personal Guard uniform or a black jacket. Black, to match this dark kingdom. His scaled eyes were distracting in their sadness but could shutter into a whole new feigned expression in a moment. His soft features were so perfect, no scars marred his skin as if he'd been sculpted for royalty. His long, dark red hair flowed like gentle waves behind his head, his long, powerful blue-green tail and darker fins flapped to keep him afloat.

He was perfection.

His face was all soft, plump lips and cheekbones, eyes and nose rounded. As she stared, she couldn't help but compare him to others she'd seen in this kingdom. None other had the coloring of his skin except perhaps Zenara, even if hers was lighter toned. Nearly everyone in the Dark Waters was some type of hybrid creature with strange, animalistic features.

Caspian looked like a Greek god.

But what really mattered was if this was a deception or not. She couldn't read past the distraction of his good looks and grim face. He looked at her innocently, and she found her heart thundering with each passing second. His eyes seemed to scream *believe me* and she longed to. He'd saved her life. He'd taught her how to swim. He'd shown her his vulnerable side. In him, she saw herself.

Surely, if he'd known that her best friend was alive, he would have spared her the heartbreak. He seemed to read the doubt in her eyes.

"I had a best friend," he began slowly. "Back when I was in the Royal *Stratia*. We had been friends since we were children and then..." He broke off to take a deep, shuddering breath. "His name was Killian." A smile tugged at his lips at the name. "I do not know what happened to him when Atlantica fell, but I would give anything to know the truth. You have to believe, Coral, that I would extend that truth to you, had I known."

There was a long pause. Coral stared at him, weighing his words. "Fine," she whispered finally. "I believe you."

Relief relaxed his body, and he swam over to her to place his hands on her shoulders. "I am glad to hear she is alive, Coral."

She nodded. "But she's in the dungeons. They're being tortured and starved to death while I'm practically at a five-star hotel. I have someone to dress me, to feed me. I'm living in luxury while my best friend suffers." She shook her head to clear her thoughts. "I need your help, Caspian. Help me find the Knowledge. I beg of you. Help me find it and help me set them free."

He stiffened then, his entire body going taut. Coral immediately regretted asking him, but she needed help. More help than just what Matthias could provide. She needed a second pair of eyes and ears within the castle. She needed him to look out for any evidence to the whereabouts of the Knowledge. She *needed* him.

"I cannot help you, Coral," he replied gravely. "Do not ask me again. And I would advise you to steer clear of both Matthias and the *calabozo*. Nothing good will come of this plan."

"Why?" she demanded. "Why won't you help me? What if it was Killian in that prison? Wouldn't you do anything to get him out?"

Caspian tightened his hands into fists. "No," he whispered angrily. "I would not."

Coral had to take a stroke back from his words as they nearly staggered her. Shock rippled through her. He wouldn't save his best friend from the queen? She supposed knowing about his friend's life or death was different from actually *saving* him, but why? Why was he like this? "What does that queen have over you, Caspian? Tell me."

He shook his head. She saw how his body seemed to physically begin locking all of the doors she'd tried opening. "Just heed my words," he said. "Olivia is as good as dead."

As he swam away, closing her door behind him, she realized, with a sort of sad clarity that Caspian would never, ever be willing to help her.

CORAL SAT before the gilded mirror in her bedroom, staring at her reflection. Blue eyes hardened by life stared back. Once they'd been round and afraid, and though they still were, they were no longer filled with timid uncertainty. For once in her life, she *knew* what she had to do. She had a purpose. Someone who needed saving. Someone relying on *her*.

She knew she could do it.

With or without Caspian's help, she would break the prisoners out. She would find the Knowledge and she would leave this ocean forever.

Zenara ran a comb through her hair. The movements were steady, calm. Coral relaxed in her hands, watched as her adept fingers began separating strands and weaving them together expertly to form a crowned braid around her head. Coral had asked for the braids. It was annoying having to push her floating hair from her face.

She watched Zenara work in the glass. Her fingers were long and thin like a musician's, and not one of them faltered as they wove strand after strand into place. Her tentacles were surprisingly still today, falling down her back and over her shoulders. The tentacles reminded her of the queen and unnerved her, but when she found herself feeling uneasy, she just looked back into Zenara's beautiful face and all that faded away.

Zenara had been a true friend to her ever since she'd arrived. The only one of the mer who hadn't battered and abused her, lied or betrayed her. She would miss her the most.

"Why do you stare at me like that?" Zenara asked with amusement.

Coral chuckled. "Sorry. I'm just thinking about what a good friend you've been to me since I got here. And how I've never even thanked you for treating me so kindly."

The mer chuckled, securing shell pins to hold her hair in place. "Being a decent mer warrants no thanks."

"It *does*, though. Here it does."

She secured the last pin in her hair and smiled at the finished product before answering. "The Black Kingdom is a hard place to live, Coral. Being the smallest Kingdom in the Water Realms and being so close to human territory, it suffers the brunt of human cruelty. You have seen for yourself the garbage-filled waters..." Coral nodded solemnly. "Please forgive the dark mer if they are reluctant to trust you or have treated you unkindly."

Coral didn't know if she could. She supposed she understood what Zenara was saying, and she *had* seen with her own eyes the terrible conditions they lived in, from trash to excrements to shipwrecks. It had all impacted them terribly. If she were a mer, she would probably hate humans, too. In fact, being a human and seeing the extent of the damage made her angry with her own. For all that they'd done. For all they would do.

"Do you like it?" Zenara asked, pulling her slowly out of her thoughts.

Coral looked into the mirror. Small shells of all kinds were woven through the braids. It kind of looked like a small crown nestled across her hair. She'd never worn her hair so fancy before, especially not for picking up garbage.

"I love it." She smiled.

Satisfied, Zenara placed the comb back onto the lovely vanity table—a solid structure made of colorful stone, the top bursting with white and red coral, a gilded mirror in front of it—and took a stroke back.

She observed Coral a moment longer in the mirror, a look she couldn't quite decipher clouding her eyes. When she opened her mouth to speak, she was interrupted by someone suddenly bursting into her bedroom door.

Coral turned to see Matthias floating in the entryway. He wasn't smiling. Zenara took one look at him and bowed her head in obedience before taking her leave, closing the door behind her. Coral swam out of her chair.

"What's wrong?"

His eyes weren't dancing, his mouth wasn't smiling. He looked far off and distracted. He looked at her then and her heart sputtered with fear at what she found in his gaze. "There has been a change in plans, my little fighter." He hands moved with quick urgency. "The queen has given orders. The survivors, they will all be executed tonight."

CORAL FELL BACK to her chair as if her tail had been too weak to keep her upright. Her eyes burned like the bright blue of water fire. Gone was fear and dread and in its place, determination. She was a fighter now. A survivor. So different from the timid creature she'd been before

"Why?" she demanded.

Matthias shrugged. "The queen grows bored with them. She always executes prisoners on a whim."

Coral placed a hand to her chest. Her breathing had grown frenetic with rage and worry. Matthias gave her a moment to compose herself, to work through the thoughts that flashed so openly over her face. Finally, she sat up straighter, lowering her hand and tightening it into a fist. She looked up at Matthias. There was trust there. So much trust.

"You know what this means, don't you?" Coral breathed. "We can't look for the Knowledge now. We have to get them out without it. We have to break them out before their execution."

Only then did Matthias smile in that savage and malicious way he did. He swam towards Coral, but she didn't flinch back from him. It was as if he no longer frightened her. As if something had grown between them. Something only the two of them could see. He bent at her tail and took her hands in his own, kissing the tops of her knuckles.

The act was so intimate.

So *frighteningly* intimate.

He smiled up at her as if Coral were his queen. His every-thing. "Then we will break them out, my little fighter. And we will kill anyone who gets in our way."

The image faded as Zenara took her hand from the door to Coral's bedroom. Her magic had allowed her to see and hear through it. To hear their every plot and plan. Her heart tugged painfully, and she placed her hand against her chest, as if that could stop the terrible feeling that worked its way up her breast.

It didn't.

So, Zenara took a stroke away from the door. And

another. And another. Until she reached the end of the hall, she turned and swam away, wishing she could un-see and un-hear the events that had transpired in Coral's room.

But no matter how much she wished those words would exit her mind, she knew they never would. Like the scar at her waist, Coral's and Matthias' betrayal to the queen—to Zenara's *mother*—would be branded on Zenara forever.

And there was no magic strong enough that would ever be rid of it.

CASPIAN HAD EYED them suspiciously when they came out of Coral's room. His eyes roamed over her from head to tailfins, as if searching for signs of moussed hair, reddened cheeks or heavy panting. Her cheeks were red but with rage, and her panting was from much the same reason. He would find what he was looking for, but his reasoning behind why would be wrong.

Matthias noted his look as well and smirked at him then threw his arm lazily over Coral's shoulders. He was playing his part well, she thought, as Caspian's eyes flared mutinously for a brief second before dying down.

"You can go back to brooding, Your *Highness*." Matthias snickered. Caspian's fists tightened. "I will be escorting her to her duties today."

Caspian's eyes narrowed suspiciously between them, noting how she didn't pull away from him or cower shyly away from his gaze. Before she would have, but she was tired of his games and antics when there were more important things to worry about. Like saving the survivors before the queen could execute them. And she would accomplish them, whether he wanted to help her or not.

"Does the queen have need of me today?" was all Caspian asked.

"No. Not today. Today you are free to roam about as you wish," Matthias said cheerfully and tugged at Coral, pulling her away from Caspian. She didn't look back. She couldn't bring herself to do it, to say goodbye. Her heart ached because of it, because it may very well be the last time she saw him, and she couldn't thank him for saving her from drowning, for being kind to her within these walls.

She kept her shoulders straight and her head held high as Matthias led her away. Far away from Caspian.

He was preparing his hippocampus when Zenara swam down the front steps. Coral turned to her just as the merservant hurtled for her, pulling her into a crushing hug. Startled, Coral gripped the other girl tightly before letting go.

"What was that for?" Coral asked tentatively.

Zenara just stared at her knowingly. Coral's heart dropped. She knew. "Stay safe, Coral Bennett," she whispered so no one could hear. Then she embraced her again. Her arms were comforting, causing tears to well in Coral's eyes. This would be the last time she saw Zenara. The moment she broke the prisoners out, she would swim away from the Black Kingdom and never look back. Even if they never got their legs back and had to live in the ocean for the rest of their days, they'd do it. Knowledge or no, she was getting them out. Choking back a sob, Coral gripped the mer tightly one last time before pulling away.

"Thank you, Zenara," she whispered. "For everything."

Zenara nodded and turned, swimming back up to the house.

"Come, little fighter," Matthias said softly from behind her. "It is time to go."

∾

They had a plan. As good of a plan as they could make, under the circumstances. They were short on time, had no allies, and would have to accomplish their goal based on wits alone. Matthias had given her a detailed layout of the queen's castle, all entrances and exits, the names of the guards that would be on duty and at what time they switched.

It was too dangerous for them to traipse through the castle together, so Matthias had suggested they split up. The thought of swimming alone made her nervous, but she swallowed it down. She'd brave it. For Olivia, she'd do anything.

He said they'd have to rely on the cover of darkness, a mere two hours before the execution. He told her that the queen oversaw the executions herself. She liked to witness the cruelty, liked to watch the prisoners bleed out beneath her vile magic.

"I will keep her busy before it is time for the execution," Matthias said.

"How do you plan on keeping her distracted for two whole hours?"

Matthias shot her a knowing look that sent her face flushing the bright red of coral with embarrassment and yes, a twinge of jealousy. She bit the inside of her cheek and looked down, focusing on strapping a seal skin leather belt around her waist and shoving daggers through it.

"Jealous?" Matthias tapped her chin with his forefinger. She rolled her eyes at him in response, causing him to chuckle. The situation didn't seem to make him nervous. His body hummed with anticipation of action and adventure. "I am doing this for you, little fighter." He went weaponless, merely straightening his uniform. "And there is no need to be jealous of the queen. When I am inside her, I think only of you."

Coral scoffed, face flaming. "Yeah, right. Also, too much information. Can we just focus on what we're supposed to be doing, please?" This was serious and he was making jokes. He didn't even seem the *least* bit afraid that they were about to risk their lives.

"Whatever you say," Matthias said. He bent over her to help crisscross a set of belts against her chest, securing them tightly. He procured a hidden dagger and placed it into her palm, hilt first. He was still so close to her. "Remember to hide it well," he reminded her, face now solemn.

Coral swallowed and nodded, taking it from him. She'd hidden it in the lapels of her jacket last time. This time, she tied it with a strong piece of kelp on her upper arm. It rubbed against her skin, but she ignored it as she put on a jacket over her tunic to hide the weapon.

"You remember the plan?" Matthias asked her. She gave him a grave nod. "You have no magic, so stay close to the ceilings and only on the paths I provided."

"I remember them."

"Good." He sighed in relief. Already the rays of sun that pierced through the surface of the water were dying down, the shadows made stronger by the obsidian castle and buildings. Nighttime was approaching. Hours. They'd spent *hours* going over the plan, memorizing every tunnel, every hidden doorway, every empty hallway. Hours since that morning, teaching her how to snag the keys from the guards, how to put them to sleep without the use of magic or strength. And now, they'd put it all to the test. "Swim carefully, my little fighter. Eyes are around every corner."

Gone was his smile. In the place of sarcasm and teasing, there was a seriousness that had never been there before. They would not rendezvous. He would distract the queen so she couldn't give the order, and she would get them out on her own. He had arranged a bag full of necessities—clothes, supplies, maps, compasses—and two hippocampi to aid them on their journey. Far, far away.

Her heart clenched. From now on, she'd be on the run. And Matthias had helped her. He'd helped her more than Caspian. He had betrayed his queen to help get Olivia out, to help Coral find her freedom. She owed him her life. She owed him a great deal. Because of him, she found the strength that had lived burrowed within herself.

"I guess this is goodbye." She hefted a small bag full of necessities for the breakout around her shoulder. Her throat clenched as she took him in, one last time.

"It was a pleasure to know you, little fighter." His golden eyes scanned her face. He looked as though he'd say more. She *wanted* to say more, but the words caught in her throat and she held them back.

"Thank you," she whispered, "for helping me."

He gave a small nod. "I would do it again without hesitation."

A part of her wanted to reach on the tips of her tail fin and press her lips against his. A final farewell to the unsuspecting merman who'd managed to steal away part of her heart. But she couldn't bring herself to do it. He wanted her to. She wanted to. But her body did not move.

"Goodbye, Matthias." She placed her hand on his chest. His eyes flicked to the movement, but her hand was already gone and she was swimming away.

Towards the castle.

BREAKOUT

CORAL FOLLOWED MATTHIAS'S EVERY INSTRUCTION IN careful silence. In her nervousness, her mind struggled to remember directions but determination, the image of Olivia's haggard and bruised face, was what kept her going. She had no magic to cloak herself in darkness, so she stuck to the shadows in the ceiling.

She lay her body flat against the stone and tried not to stir the water in her eagerness to get to the *calabozo*. She went down abandoned hallways, only pausing when a sentry or a guard swam by below. As soon as they'd pass, she continued her journey on. She took a left. A right. Another left.

Going through the halls was the easiest part. Matthias had told her as much. The difficulty lay in getting past the guards, managing through the stone maze, getting the keys and actually getting the prisoners *out*.

No fucking pressure or anything...

Coral crawled along the ceiling like a salamander, channeling her inner Gibby, pulse thundering in her ears. She was near the stairwell that would take her to the stone maze. Last time she'd come around here, there had been no guard. Now, there were two. Apparently before executions, the queen liked to stock up on security. Likely to prevent this moment exactly.

Matthias had said it would be easier to sneak in when it came time to change the guards. So she waited in the corner above their heads. The two mer were in uniforms of black with the royal insignia of an oyster on their breast. They held spears at their sides and tortoise shell shields on their forearms.

Coral tried waiting patiently. Seconds passed. Then minutes, and they still hadn't moved. Had Matthias given her the wrong time? It felt as though she'd been waiting forever, yet they were as still as statues. She loosed a quiet breath and leaned her body down slightly to look through the hall.

As she did, her tail slipped and she lost her balance. *Shit. Shit. Shit.* Her upper body fell forward, suspended through the water above the tips of their spears. She tightened her tail against the ceiling, holding herself steady.

Shit. Shit. Shit.

Don't look up. Don't look up.

She quietly fought to right herself, trying not to stir the water and alert them of her presence. But all her wriggling around only made it worse. A knife sheathed at her side began to slide out. She didn't notice until it was out and floating down...down...

Giving a silent cry, she reached out for it, catching it by the blade. It dug into her palm and she bit back a cry, but with her balance forgotten, she started to fall forward...

Then she was pulled up by the back of her jacket. Her cry was muffled by an enormous familiar hand going over her mouth. A tingling sensation swept through her entire body. The tingling of *magic*. Her body shuddered with the feeling just before the guards below looked up.

Straight at Coral.

She stilled and waited. Waited for them to sound the alarm.

But they just glanced in her general direction and went back to their watch.

It felt like hours before the guards left their station. Meaning, Coral only had a ten second window before the other guards showed up to take their place. As soon as they'd left, her captor released her. The tingling sensation of magic swept over her again, and she made a zip for the door.

"What are you *doing*?" Caspian hissed in her ear.

She'd known it was him by the feel of his hand, by the hard press of his chest against her back. As if her body had memorized his form, his warmth and the sensation his magic left over her body.

Coral ignored him now, though, and pried open the door, swimming through it. Caspian let out a curse and followed close, closing the door behind them. Coral had memorized the path and turns when she'd gone through with Matthias. The night she'd learned the truth about Olivia. The night everything changed.

Caspian was silent until they reached the bottom of the stairs and found their way into the maze. "What are you *doing*, Coral?" he demanded, tugging at the hem of her jacket. She waved him off with an annoyed gesture and kept swimming, counting down the rows and turns. "Coral, *stop*!" Caspian pulled her back, whipping her around.

She glared up at him, annoyed, heart thundering. "What?" She was in a hurry. She didn't have *time* for Caspian. Their goodbye had already passed. He wasn't even supposed to *be* here.

"You owe me an explanation." He crossed his arms over his chest.

"I don't have *time*," Coral cried and turned back around, swimming.

Caspian followed. "I just saved your life. Again. You owe me. What are you doing here?"

Five, six, seven, turn left. "How about you tell me how you knew where I'd be?" she asked him suspiciously. He was always demanding answers of her yet gave none in return.

"I followed you."

"Why?"

"You really think I believed Matthias' earlier claims? You were both acting suspicious. I *figured* this was where you were coming. I came to stop you from this foolishness."

"You can't stop me, Caspian," she said determinedly. "I'm getting them out. Whether you like it or not." She gave a sharp turn to the right. She was almost there. She was so much closer to freeing her friend. *So close.*

Caspian stopped her by pulling at her upper arm. "Listen to me," he hissed. "You cannot save them. The queen will *kill* you if you even try."

She jerked her arm away and glared up at him. She realized, looking into his scaled blue-green eyes, that he wouldn't let her get through this. He wouldn't let her finish her task unless she *convinced* him. And she had little time to do it.

"Why?" she demanded. "Why are you so against me saving them? Why don't you want me to be free?"

"Because I do not want the queen to hurt you as she has hurt so many others before you."

"I have an opportunity here, Caspian," she tried. Her voice was desperate, her heart beating a wild drum. "Wouldn't you give anything, *anything* to save the one you loved?"

His face up until that moment had been nothing but stern linings, but at those last words, something in him crumbled. Physically. She saw vulnerability in his eyes, saw something shatter within them.

Coral held her breath for a moment. Just a moment. If he was against her, she'd knock him out and make a swim for it.

She'd give him a chance... just one to decide if he'd be on her side or not.

Finally, Caspian loosed a breath. "Fine," he conceded softly. "Do what you must. I will not stop you. But nor will I help you."

That was something at least. She gave him a gratified nod and turned back. When he followed close behind, she shot him a look over her shoulder. "I thought you weren't going to help me."

"I will not help you break them out. But I will come with you just in case your flawed plan goes awry. Perhaps I could convince the guards and the queen that you were doing nothing untoward."

She nodded her thanks and kept going until she made it just around the bend. One more turn and she'd be face to face with the looming iron gates. And the guards. This was the tricky part. Pulling the sack Matthias had given her over her head, she reached inside the bag and pulled out tiny vials with swirling red liquid.

As Matthias instructed, she swam up to the very top of one of the ledges and discarded the bag into a tight crack in the stone. When she was done, she gave a look to Caspian that said *stay here* and kicked her tail, swimming to ceiling quietly. She crawled above it until she reached the gates just below were the guards. She eyed them, noting the keys hanging from the belt of one.

All she had to do was open those vials. The potion would knock them out.

"Ink from a venomous squid," Matthias had supplied when he'd handed them to her. "One sniff will render anyone useless. But have a care," he'd warned. "You do not want to ingest it yourself."

Holding her breath, she reached for the cork to uncap it. Her trembling fingers slipped against the glass and

Coral despaired as it slid from her grasp and floated below.

The rest of the scene played out slowly before her. Heart beating in her throat, she could only watch as the guards turned their faces upwards and caught sight of her.

"Hey!"

They attacked and she wasn't quick enough. She was yanked down by the tail. Her back hit the silt and a cloud of it blinded her. She was hauled up again. Arms reached for her, pressing and angry. Blindly, she fought back. The panic fueled her moves as she struggled against the merman's hold.

A fist connected to her stomach, and she doubled over gasping. A burning sensation pricked behind her eyelids, and she nearly toppled into the silt once again. Her fists tightened and it was then she realized she was still holding the potion.

She just needed an opportunity.

Lowering herself to the silt, coughing and wheezing, her other hand scooped up a fistful of the grains. As she was hauled up a second time, she reacted fast. Her hand shot out and the silt clouded her attacker's eyes. He coughed and her fist shot forward, crushing the glass against his nose before she shot back.

Ink clouded with the silt in front of her, expanding in a cloud that both guards inhaled. Coral held her breath, fins pushing her backwards to put distance between them.

Within moments, they drifted towards the ground, their bodies twitching as the poison went into their systems.

Coral held her breath until she felt she'd explode, and even then she held it longer. For as long as she could, until she was sure the poison had subsided and it was safe to breathe the water again. When her body didn't crumple, she knew it was safe to continue.

Her ribs screamed at her, but she didn't have the time to wonder if one had been cracked. She darted forward to yank the keys off the guard's belt. Caspian came out of hiding then and looked down at them then up at her, his eyes wide. With fear or appreciation, she didn't care. All she cared about was the mer on the other side of this gate. Close. So close.

Hope, a dangerous thing, flooded through her veins even as she tried to keep it at bay. Her hands shook as she went through the keys. Being so close to her goal made her clumsy and forgetful. Which key had Matthias said? Which one *was* it?

"This one." Caspian pointed to the largest one.

Sighing, she gave him a nod of appreciation and took the key and opened the gate. It gave a loud creak. She winced at the sound, but hurriedly swam in. She passed prisoners who hissed and clawed through their cage. She passed the old man with the golden eyes and then stopped in front of Olivia's.

The human-turned-mer were huddled together as they had been the night before. "Olivia?" Coral whispered. Her friend broke free from the protection of the group and swam to Coral. She gasped. Her friend looked even worse than she had yesterday. Her face was nearly unrecognizable, bruised in all different colorings of purple, green, and red. Her nose appeared to have been broken. "What did they do to you?" Coral gripped the bars, as if she could bend them in half with the force of her rage.

Olivia smirked. "The guards don't like when you talk back." She looked Coral over. "What's wrong?" she asked. "Why are you here?"

The question snapped Coral out of her anger. She flipped through the keys and unlocked her friend's cell. "I'm breaking you all out. Right now." The door swung open, causing the mer inside to flinch.

"What?" Olivia looked at the keys then the unlocked door. Her brown eyes clouding with disbelief.

"Listen, Olivia," Coral began urgently. "The queen has

ordered your execution tonight." She looked around the cell. "All of you are supposed to die." The woman holding the child whimpered and pulled him closer. "I know it's going to hurt, but I need all of you to try and *swim*, okay? We're going to get you out of here!" She turned to look at Caspian for confirmation, but he wasn't looking into the cell. He wasn't looking in their direction at all. His gaze was focused on the far end of the *calabozo*. He stared so intently at it, his gaze so open and... broken... "Caspian?"

He broke out of his trance and, with a sharp shake of his head, turned back to her. "What?" he asked absently.

"I said that we are going to—"

"*You!*"

Coral started, turning to look at Olivia who had practically shrieked the word. She was staring at Caspian with recognition and fiery rage. "Olivia, what—" But Olivia didn't listen. She swam forward on her jerky tail, pulled a knife from Coral's waist, and charged for Caspian with a feral cry. She arched the blade over her head and brought it crashing down towards the merman. He dodged it easily enough, knocking her arm to the side and sending the blade flying. Olivia began hitting her fists across his chest. He only took her wrists in his hands and pushed her away.

"Olivia, what's going on?" Coral demanded.

"*You!*" she shrieked again. "You did this to us! It's *your* fault we're here!"

"Olivia, what are you talking about?" She reached for her friend to try and soothe her, to calm her down, but Olivia just shook her off. "What's wrong?"

"It's *him*, Coral. It's *Caspian de Magissa* of the queen's Personal Guard! He is the reason we're here." She glared at him menacingly and cautiously. Her whole body was shaking. Coral reached for her then, wrapping her arms around her shoulders.

"It's okay," she soothed. "He's with me. He *helped* me, Olivia. He's the one who saved me from drowning."

Olivia pushed her away and *glared*. She sounded almost manic, almost insane. "Don't you *understand,* Coral? It was him. Him and the Personal Guard. They sunk our ship. They tried to kill us!"

BETRAYALS AND LIES

CORAL STAGGERED BACK, HAND GOING TO HER CHEST. IT didn't stop her heart from beating holes against her ribcage. It didn't stop the confusion or the betrayal from withering at her insides. She looked at Olivia, but her friend had her entire focus on Caspian. Coral looked to him instead.

His face was flushed, and he was looking down at her friend with heavy eyes. He said nothing. Olivia did. "The Personal Guards in here like to talk," she ground out. "Usually it's to make fun of us. But last night, after you left, they were extra cruel to us. What good is censorship when we're all as good as dead anyway? They spoke so freely. They spoke of you, her favorite in the Personal Guard. They said it was *you*. *You* and *Zalyn* and *Matthias* who tore our ship down. You followed us and then destroyed our ship! You bastard!" Olivia lunged for him again, but Coral was fast, pulling her back.

She tried to think, tried to organize her thoughts. They didn't have much time. They *had* to get out of here before the guards woke up. Before the queen came down to oversee their execution. But the betrayal was lodged into her. She wanted to doubt that Caspian had had anything to do with that... with the killing of innocents. But Olivia spoke with such surety, and Coral would *never* doubt her friend.

Images came to her like a flood. Images she'd never been able to piece together before now. She'd thought she'd imagined it on the cruise ship, the hand splayed across the window. A tail of blue-green. The flashes of red through the water. And the ship... just before it'd exploded...

Coral recalled how easily the three of them had destroyed that submarine. As easily as if they'd crunched a paper cup. There'd been nothing left but scraps of metal and blood swirling through the water. And the ship, the ship that *she'd* been on, had exploded into nothing but scraps and chunks.

"*Why?*" Her voice broke as she looked to Caspian. "*Why* would you do that? There were *children—*" She broke off as a sob tried to rise in her throat and forced it down. She wouldn't cry. She was a fighter. Fighters didn't cry.

Caspian looked at her steadily. His face, his body, even his words were tense. "I was following orders."

"Is that the bullshit excuse you came up with when you and your black-haired friend came to choke me?" Olivia snapped. She pushed aside her hair to show the black and blue markings along her neck.

"Wait..." Coral held up her hands. "You *knew*? You *knew* Olivia was alive and you didn't *tell* me?" His reply was to remain silent. "Is that why you never wanted me down here? Is that why you refused to help me? Because you *knew* my best friend was alive and you didn't want me to know?" Coral whipped out a dagger and shot forward to press it against his neck. "You're a liar, Caspian. A traitor and a liar. I can't believe I trusted you."

In her rage, she dug the blade in deeper. It all made so much sense now. The secrets, the lying. He'd been furious with her when he'd caught her in the maze with Matthias. She'd thought it jealousy, but now she realized it was much more than that. And when she'd told him that Olivia was alive, he'd played *dumb*. And Matthias—*Matthias* had been the one to confess. He'd been the one to tell her the truth. She'd expected the truth from Caspian. Of all mer, she'd expected more from *him*.

"I did help sink the ship. I helped kill innocents because the queen wants all humans dead for what they have done to the Dark Waters. It is her own personal war against them, but I swear to you, Coral, I only did it because she *forced* me." His voice rose to a panic, as if he could explain, give reason for his despicable actions.

Coral scoffed. "Oh, right, because the queen has something over your head. What is it, exactly? What is this mysterious object she has of yours?"

His jaw tightened. "If only I could tell you."

"It doesn't matter what the queen has over your head," Olivia said angrily from behind them. "No object is more valuable than the deaths of innocent people. Of *children*."

At this, Caspian chuckled low and soft, causing Coral to press the blade tighter to his throat. A trail of blood swirled from his neck. "If only you *knew*."

Olivia scoffed and put her hand on Coral's arm. "We're wasting time, Cor. If what you say is true, then we have to get out of here. Fast."

The blade shone, giving her a small wink. The siren's call of the tip called out to her, hypnotized her in an enchanting melody, bade her to take blood, to take her revenge. One life gone for all of those he'd taken. It would have been so easy to do it. He wasn't fighting back. He looked like he'd welcome the sweet kiss of steel. If it was at her hand, he would take it. The itch was there, her hand trembled with the need to do it. Trembled with the need for revenge.

"*Why* did you go through such lengths for me, Caspian?" she asked in a steady voice. If they'd destroyed the ship, if they'd taken hostages and she was one of them, why had he treated her as if she were special? She had to know. And she wouldn't accept a 'Does it matter?' as an answer. Not anymore.

He seemed to read that in her eyes because he sighed. "I saw you," he whispered. "I saw you from below." She flushed. "I saw you laugh and joke. I saw you *read,* and I saw your sadness—and I knew I could not let *this*," he gestured at the prison cells, "become of you. Because, Coral, since that first moment I saw you, I loved you."

The weight of the words settled over her like a soft nestling blanket. She'd wanted to hear him admit those words for so long. That was before. Now that she knew the truth, they just cut a deeper wound into her heart, made her all the more infuriated, made the betrayal cut deep. She tightened her grip on the knife. Coral could kill him now. She could kill him now and make a swim for it with the prisoners. It's what he deserved.

Coral lowered the knife.

"That is no excuse," she whispered, "for all that you have done." She turned to the prisoners. They were staring at the scene as if it were some sort of theatre play. When she glared at them all, they flinched. "Let's go. We don't have much time left."

Coral and Olivia began ushering them out of the prison cell. They swam slowly, some in jerky movements. They were useless on their tails and slow, too slow. Coral didn't know if they'd make it on time.

Olivia swam behind the prisoners. Her movements were a little smoother, but she was still almost lethargic. Coral stayed behind for a second, watching Caspian. His gaze had gone back to the end of the *calabozo* and stayed there. She looked too but saw nothing except instruments of torture.

Her heart ached with his lies, his betrayal, but the broken, vulnerable look on his face still hurt to see. She'd thought so highly of him and it had all crumbled down in a matter of minutes.

"Goodbye, Caspian," she whispered and turned to swim away. She didn't wait to see if he looked back at her, if he'd say his own final farewell. She started forward and froze when Olivia shrieked.

Her best friend was by the bars of a cell, a wrinkled hand clasped tightly onto her forearm. "Let me go!" she shrieked. Coral swam forward to help her friend. The old merman with the sagging skin and bright, golden eyes had his arm through the bars. And he wouldn't let go, no matter how hard she pulled.

The old mer's head was shaved entirely, a bristle of white hair poking out from his scalp. His hands and face were mottled by purple spots, and his brown skin was sickly pale, losing the tone of its color. His eyes *glowed* like gold peeking out in mining caves. His pupils were practically tiny specks against the brilliant glittering iris.

He smiled at Olivia to reveal pink gums. "You," he whispered in a voice that sounded like the eerie blow of a soft wind. "My vessel." He chuckled, the sound of wind blowing through leaves. "I have finally found you."

"Let go of me!" Olivia pulled at her arm again. This time, Coral went to help. When she touched the merman's arm to pull it away, he was burning to the touch. She yelped and pulled her hand away.

The merman kept smiling and reached his other hand through the bars to caress Olivia's cheek. She flinched at the contact and tried to jerk away, but when he said, "I have waited for you for a long time..." Olivia stopped struggling. She stopped moving as she looked into the old mer's eyes, entranced by them and whatever she saw in his golden gaze.

When he finally pulled away, her friend turned to look at her, a dazed, glossy look over her eyes.

"We have to take him with us," she said breathlessly.

"What?"

"We have to get him out."

"Olivia, we have to go, *now*."

"We can't leave him here to suffer, Coral."

Coral threw up her hands in exasperation. "Fine," she grumbled. "What's one more?" She made quick work with the lock, and the old mer fell forward, his body covered in algae, starfish, and barnacles. Olivia grabbed him, throwing his arm over her shoulder. "Now let's *go*," Coral demanded.

And they were off.

ATONEMENT

Determination was the only thing that kept the group going. If one would fall, another would help them up and continue their trek. Matthias had given her specific instructions for hidden cracks, doors, and rooms throughout the castle. Easier to get in than out. Matthias had said as much to her.

"Let me help." Caspian followed them out. She had expected him to stay in the dungeon, staring off at nothing, but he surprised her by following them out and begging to let him help them all.

She stared at him distrustfully as she replaced the keys back onto the unconscious guard. "Why should we trust you?" He'd done nothing but lie to her the entire time. His words meant nothing, no matter how pretty.

"I can help you camouflage yourselves. Without magic, you are useless."

She shot him the finger as she led them down the maze. Matthias had told her of another way they could escape the castle undetected. Another way with holes in the walls. The stone-like structure had been the original foundation of the

320

castle, he'd told her. But when Queen Ulla Magissa had won the war against Atlantica, she'd reconstructed the entire kingdom and built an obsidian castle over the original structure. There had been a part, hidden deep inside the maze, that they'd missed. The structure was too poor to add heavy obsidian over it. The whole castle would have toppled down.

Coral counted the turns, slowing down only occasionally to make sure everyone was following her. She'd tried to ignore Caspian, tried to push aside the boiling rage and heartache that came up with him next to her. There would be time to feel later. Right now, she had to lead these people to safety and get out of the Dark Waters as soon as possible. Caspian wasn't making it any easier.

"We don't need your help. We don't trust you." She gave a sharp right, counted the turns.

"Let me atone for what I have done," Caspian begged. "Let me help."

Funny how people wanted to beg for forgiveness and *atone* after the deed was done when they shouldn't have done the terrible thing in the first place.

"Come on, guys, hurry up!" She ushered everyone to move faster. Olivia tripped on her tail under the weight of the older mer. What he'd done to convince her to bring him along, Coral didn't know, but she hadn't had time to waste arguing with leaving him there. The old mer looked like he'd keel over any moment, but Olivia pulled him along despite her own pain.

They swam and swam. It was minutes. Minutes that felt like hours.

"Almost there," Coral urged them. The mother holding her seven-year-old tripped and sent the kid sprawling through the water. He let out a soft cry, and Caspian was there in an instant, hauling the kid up into his own arms and pulling the mother up. She looked at him warily, but the desire to be helped shone in her eyes. She was weak. They all were. They were all tired, hungry, and battered. But they were almost there. Almost to that hole in the wall. "It's just around this corner!" Coral said, relief swamping through her. She rounded the turn and stopped short.

Matthias had given her the exact number of turns, the exact number of hallways and strokes. Where the hole should be, a solid wall of stone stood in its place.

"No. No. *No.*" She pounded her fists against it, only succeeding in scraping her knuckles. "Where *is* it? He said it would be here! Did I take a wrong turn? I *couldn't* have. I counted them exactly as I should have! So *where is it?*" She slapped her tail against the stone. Hysteria muddled with the worry, the desperation. Time snapped at their tail fins. They had so little of it. This couldn't be the end. It *couldn't.* She couldn't let them down.

"It has been closed off." Caspian muttered a curse. Then turned to her. "Please, let me help you. Let me camouflage you."

Coral slid down to the floor. She didn't have the luxury, but her tail had gone weak, her hands shaking. She looked to all of them. To all of the human-turned-mer. Their faces were dirty and scared. She'd given them hope only to take it away from them.

Her gaze found Caspian's. He was looking down at her. Worried, sad, and *begging*, begging to be trusted again, begging to be forgiven. But what if she trusted him again? She'd done that already and it had been a mistake. But if she didn't... they'd all die, either way.

"Fine." She gave a resigned sigh. "Caspian, please help us."

∼

HE CAMOUFLAGED them in a matter of seconds. They couldn't even see each other, but they could feel one another's body heat, feel the stirrings in the water. They held on tightly to each other's hands, swimming in a slow line.

Caspian aided them with magic the entire time, pushing tiny vortexes and bursts of light to distract the guards as they passed them. Everything went smoothly, but even so, Coral's heart didn't stop thundering until they'd made it outside. Until the glamor of Caspian's magic fell off and made them all visible again.

They were hiding in the shadows outside the castle. Out. They were out. Now they had to get to the hippocampi. "Stick to the shadows. Do not draw attention to yourselves," Caspian ordered. They glued their bodies to the buildings and swam away.

Coral lugged behind. "You aren't coming?" She only asked because maybe they'd have need of his magic again, she told herself. Not because she cared.

He shook his head. "The queen will be furious. She will likely punish or kill me for what I have done here tonight. I can draw her away from you, if only for a bit longer." He looked at her then, his eyes sad and full of regret. "I truly am sorry, Coral. For everything."

Coral didn't know if she accepted his apology, if she could find it in herself to forgive him. But he'd helped them get out, despite the risk to himself, despite whatever it was the queen had over him. Coral opened her mouth, to say what, she hadn't planned, but then there was a shriek. Loud and deafening, like a piercing whistle through the water.

The foundation of the castle shook back and forth, the waters slapped all around them violently like a storm wreaking havoc.

"The queen," Caspian said. "She knows the prisoners are gone."

Shit.

Coral turned. The prisoners were openly crying now, waiting for her for direction. "It's time to go. Swim fast!" she told them. Olivia grunted as she hauled the old merman through the water, kicking her tail to try and keep up with everyone else. Caspian handed the small merman back to his mother and told him to be brave. The kid nodded firmly before gripping tightly to his mother's neck.

"Goodbye, Coral," Caspian said and then he turned away.

To face the storm alone.

TRAITOR

T HEY SWAM TO WHERE THE TWIN HIPPOCAMPI WERE tethered. Just like Matthias had said. Saddlebags were thrown over their backs with provisions—clothes and food. "Two minutes," Coral heaved, holding up her fingers. "Two minutes to throw on clothes, eat, and then we are off."

They all got to work at lightning speed. Olivia tended to the old merman, pulling a tunic over his arms and handing him a canteen with energy boosting tea. He took a sip and capped it again. She hurried and pulled a shirt over her own head and then swam over to Coral.

"You okay?" Olivia put her hand on her shoulder.

"I should be asking you that." She eyed her bruises and broken nose.

"Don't worry. It looks worse than it feels. And I meant about Caspian."

Coral tensed. She didn't want to talk about Caspian now. Not even to her best friend. "What about him?"

Olivia rolled her eyes. "I'm not blind or deaf. I heard him tell you he loves you. Was there something between you two?"

"Was." Coral straightened and began adjusting her knives and belts tighter. It was a dismissal. One Olivia didn't seem to get.

"What happened between you?"

"Nothing," she grumbled, pushing aside the strands of hair that had fallen out of her braids. They were just two broken things trying to find comfort in one another. She had cared for him, maybe she'd even seen him as a friend, maybe more.

"I'm calling bullshit." Olivia crossed her arms over her chest and gave Coral the look. The look that would always have her flinching, always have her confessing, telling her everything with tears in her eyes in exchange for comfort. Now, she just met the look with a cold stare.

"It doesn't matter. Not now, anyway."

"It does to me."

"Do you hear that?" Coral asked suddenly. She strained her ears to hear. There was something... something in the distance...

"I don't hear anything."

"Ssh!" She waved a hand at her friend and listened harder. Everyone had gone silent now. The sound of the current breezing, that was normal but beyond that, beyond that there was a stirring... a growling.

Shit.

Coral shot up like a rocket. "They're here!" The queen's mermen. They'd followed. The pounding of fins on water and shouts were getting closer. Close enough that Coral could already feel the hot breath of their fate down the back of her neck. "Split the hippocampi. Hurry!" She helped them all on, weakest first. The animals were massive enough that they all fit to ride between the two. Olivia was the last to get on. "Ride hard and fast," Coral advised. "Stick to back roads. Hippocampi can scare away sharks and other predators, so that's a comfort. There's a map in the bag and a compass."

"Wait, why are you telling me this?" Olivia demanded, gripping her wrist. "Come on, let's go."

The hoof beats against water sounded closer. They wouldn't make it in time. They were after them and they would find them. Unless Coral did something to stop it.

She smiled sadly up at her friend. "Keep each other safe. I wish I could've found the Knowledge to get you out of here."

"Coral, no!" Realization dawned on Olivia's eyes. "You can't!"

"You've always protected me, Olivia. And I always cowered behind you. I'm not that person anymore. I'm a fighter now. And it's *my* turn to protect *you*."

"Coral, *no!*"

But Coral didn't listen. She gave the hippocampi hard pats on their rears and they tore off through the water. She watched them go. Watched them until they were tiny specks silhouetted in the distance. Only when they were out of sight and the shouts a slight distance from her ears did Coral turn around.

THEY'D HERDED her with tiger sharks on leashed chains, pulled her roughly by the arms and placed her in cuffs. Coral faced them bravely, satisfied that at least everyone else had gotten away. Everyone except her.

That didn't matter. She tried pushing those thoughts from her mind, instead focused on the road ahead. They'd taken her back to the palace, hauled her back towards the throne room. Coral braced herself. Braced herself to look into the eyes of death.

Into the eyes of Queen Ulla Magissa.

The guards opened the doors and hauled her through it. She didn't struggle against them. Not this time. This time her head was held high, her eyes defiant. Gone was the scared creature they'd tried to break. In her place was someone else entirely. Someone they'd made her into.

A fighter.

A warrior.

The queen was not on her throne. She wasn't in a colorful dress with an ostentatious crown to match. For once, she didn't look regal and commanding. She paced back and forth in front of her two-headed eel throne, all eight of her tentacles tightening beneath her. A robe was thrown hastily around her body, her makeup was smudged across her face, and her hair floated like a wild flame of white fire around her furious face.

For once, she looked so out of place, so *unbeautiful* that Coral felt a swell of triumph.

And fear.

Because when the queen turned to look at her, her black eyes were filled with killing rage. Coral faltered a stroke as they dragged her into a kneeling position at the bottom of Ulla Magissa's throne. She didn't bow her head down this time. Didn't offer kind words of greeting. It appeared as though the queen wouldn't tolerate them anyway.

Surrounding her throne, floating in a straight backed and obedient positions were Matthias and Zalyn. She flicked her eyes to Matthias, but he was staring solemnly at the queen. She avoided looking at Zalyn altogether, obviously healed after she'd stabbed him and no doubt wanting revenge for that little act. She was afraid his gaze would undo her and instill fear into her heart.

The queen finally stopped pacing and turned to glare at the guards who'd brought Coral in. "Well?" she asked them, gritting her sharp teeth together.

The sound of one of the guards gulping filled the room.

"We could not find them, your Majesty. This *anthropos* was alone."

"You mean to tell me," she began slowly, "that you let my prisoners *escape?*" The words curled something inside Coral, gave her a bad feeling.

"No, your Majesty, we——"

The queen let out an angry scream, waving her hand as she did. The guard's words were cut off by an agonizing choke. Coral couldn't see him, but the sounds were vivid enough to paint a picture in her mind. He was clawing at his throat, gurgling and gasping for a watery breath that wouldn't come. The queen watched him struggle, hand still pointed in his direction. With a wave of it once more, the sounds stopped. And the guard died.

"Send dispatchers out to find my prisoners, Matthias. *Now!*"

Matthias bowed low. "Yes, my queen." He swam out of the room without sparing a glance at Coral.

The queen resumed her pacing, ignoring her completely. It was as if she didn't exist. At the moment, at least. Ulla's hands were shaking with rage, and she tightened them into fists. Anxiety roiled off of her. The freedom of the prisoners had riled her up so much, she'd let go of all her royal facade, was finally discomposed. She began muttering to herself in a frightening manner. Magic cackled like static through the water, emanating from the queen, begging for release. Coral feared she'd soon be on the receiving end of it.

Everyone in the room was tense. No one dared breathe lest they hitch a wrong breath and find themselves dead on the floor like the guard immobile near her tail. Even Coral bit the insides of her cheeks in anticipation for what was to come.

Minutes later, the throne room door opened. The queen's attention snapped up and her lips thinned out into a sneer, cruel eyes cold and calculating. A moment later, more of her guards were pushing Caspian into a kneeling position next to Coral. He was bound in steel shackles just as she was.

Her heart lurched at the sight of him. They'd gotten him. They'd gotten them both.

"My little merman," the queen sneered. In that instant, the sight of Caspian seemed to perk her up. She fixed her composure, straightened, head high, and once again became the fearsome queen instead of the desperate one. "How nice of you to join us." Her lip twitched.

"My queen," Caspian went into full-on flirtation mode, his smile curling with warmth despite his position. "How lovely you look this evening."

The wave of magic that shot towards him was unexpected. Coral flinched, nearly falling as a wave of heat singed at Caspian's chest. He cried out as the hot blue water fire burnt through his clothes and scorched his flesh. His forehead fell to the marble floors lightly as he took in the pain, tried to swallow it down. When it finally became bearable, Caspian sat up and gave a small, painful chuckle.

"Do not mock me, Atlantean," she spat.

"Never, my queen. Do you not know that every word I speak is the truth?" He smirked.

Coral stared at him like a new merman had taken his place. He was being flirtatious in the face of death. Gone was that subservient merman. His words were icy cool, eyes dancing with hatred. Hatred at the queen. Coral would bet anything he'd never looked at her like that before. Even Ulla seemed taken aback by the sudden change.

The queen composed her expression back into one of soft rage. Her tentacles began moving, dragging her down the steps of her massive throne. She glided before them until she was just three strokes away. Behind her, Zalyn reached for the dagger at his hip.

"We had an agreement, Caspian." She placed a hand on her arched hip in an empowering gesture as she looked down at him. At her favorite in the Personal Guard. "And you have broken my every rule."

Caspian looked up at her through innocent eyelashes. "Whatever do you mean?"

In her growing rage, she shot forward, slashing her hand out so that her sharp nails swiped across his cheek. Blood oozed from the fleshy wounds and she slid back, dragging her fingernails across her tongue. "Do not play stupid with me, Caspian. I know everything. I know of your secret and disgusting *interludes* with the *anthropos*. I know all about the way you caress her skin and kiss her mouth—" She broke off with a glare aimed at Coral. She wanted to flinch at the sight, at the murder in Ulla's eyes, but she stared back defiantly. Ulla chuckled in her face. "I know you have feelings for her. I know you *conveniently* looked the other way when she escaped your home to free my prisoners." Coral must have made a gasping sound because the queen turned to her and smiled cruelly. "Yes, *anthropos*. Did you think I would not know? Did you think I do not have my *informants*?"

As she said this, the throne room opened again, and Matthias swam up to the queen's side. Coral looked at him. He stared back at her and he smiled, the sight of his mouth twisting was vicious and full of secrets.

Coral's heart dropped.

No.

No. Matthias. There was no way the queen could know those things. No way she could know unless someone had told her. And someone *had.*

It just hadn't been who Coral had expected.

He'd fed her every scrap of information, spun pretty lies into it to make both her and Caspian culpable. All the while, he remained innocent. Untouched. Beside his queen with all the powers and riches and sex he could want.

He had warned her, too. He had *warned* her that he loved those things more than anything else in the world. More than her.

And somehow, she'd pushed away all the warnings, and in doing so ignored who he truly was, had left her with a broken heart and a stain of betrayal that could never be removed.

THE SECRET PRISONER

"*No!*" Coral shrieked and *lunged*. She gave a powerful kick of her tail and focused all of her rage, all of her hatred on Matthias. The merman just looked at her with amusement in the quirk of those lips. Lips that had touched hers. Lips she'd given herself freely to.

And he was a traitor.

She didn't make it within inches of him before the queen sent another wave of magic directly at her, sending her flying back. She thumped onto her back and gasped. Pain, rippling pain like a shockwave jolted her entire body, made her scream. The crushing weight of it was suffocating. It was drowning. It was being trapped within a riptide and being pulled under into blinding darkness.

"You see, *anthropos*, perhaps in the future I would have forgiven you for crimes against my people. But now…" She flicked her hand, and the pain subsided. Coral still writhed on the floor from the aftereffects of it. "Now, you have stolen from me, and that is an offense I will never forgive. I will take great joy in killing you, Coral Bennett." Her lips twisted into a horrible parody of a smile. "I will kill you for taking my prisoners, but first, I will find them. I will find the one you love most, Olivia, and I will peel her skin from her bones. Slowly. And I will make you watch."

"B-b-bitch queen," Coral spat out between her tremors.

The queen straightened, flicking her hands as if shoving away a pesky fly. "How tedious and mundane, your insults. And *you*..." She turned her ugly gaze to Caspian. "You have betrayed me in every possible way. I brought you into my inner circle, I have made you one of the most powerful mermen in the realm, and this is how you repay me? By falling in love with human *filth*? Atlanteans are so ungrateful. They have everything and still want more. It is why your kingdom *fell*."

"My kingdom fell, Your Majesty, because a peasant queen with no idea how to rule threw a *tantrum* and tore to the ground what she could not have. *That* is why Atlantica fell."

The queen's eyes went from angry to murderous in a split second. "Is that what you think, Caspian?"

"It is what I have always thought! Every day for the last fifty years I have been forced to lie with you, to smile and feign happiness at the side of the mermaid who brought *my* kingdom down! I have awoken every morning beside your body and thought of all the ways I could kill you for everything you have done. I *despise* you, Ulla Magissa, *peasant queen*, ruler of *nothing*."

Ulla froze. Everyone held their breath as the queen stared down at Caspian. Finally, her lips curled into a smile as she took him in, as she took in the rage he'd kept bottled up for so long, his disgust, the very burning he held inside of him. "Congratulations, my little merman," the queen said sultrily. "You just killed your own mother." Her head snapped to her other guards. "Take them to the dungeons. Their executions will be swift, for I have grown tedious of these fools already."

So Coral and Caspian sat in their cells—they'd thrown

them together—and hadn't said a word. Coral's body was still sore from the queen's magic. It hurt to move. It hurt to lift her tail. She could barely even nod her head without feeling pain. She wondered briefly what type of magic that was. If the Knowledge had given her the means to use it.

Caspian sat in a corner of the cell, his tail curled up to cushion his forehead. Coral had observed him for the better part of an hour. The queen's words replayed in her mind.

Congratulations, you just killed your own mother.

"Your mother?" Coral asked finally, her scratchy voice echoed in the quiet dungeons. Caspian finally looked up. The look in his eyes broke her heart. He nodded slowly. "That's who the queen has over you, then? She has your mother prisoner?" Again, he nodded. "Why didn't you just tell me that?"

He glared at her. "You would not have understood my struggle."

She fought not to roll her eyes. "Maybe not. But burdens can be lessened if shared."

He snorted unkindly. "Not this one. It is my burden to face alone."

"Where is she?" Coral whispered. "I mean, how do you even know she's alive?" Caspian turned his head to the wall, but his eyes were looking beyond, and Coral realized in an instant. "By the torture things..." she whispered with realization.

He chuckled, though there was no humor in the sound. "Hidden in plain sight."

She recalled the far off look he'd gotten when she'd been breaking Olivia out. The longing as he stared at the end of the dungeon. At what the other side of the wall held. His mother.

"Why didn't you tell me? I could have used a key; we could have gotten her out as well."

He shook his head. "There is a powerful enchantment on

the bars, as well as in this entire *calabozo*. Only by queen's blood can it be undone. To try and free her would have alerted the queen and done no good in the end."

"But why? Why finally lose the facade?" she asked.

Caspian sucked in a breath and looked up at her. "Because it was finally time I do something to save the ones I love. *Both* of them. This place has changed her." He gave a long pause before bowing his head low.

"Why go through such lengths?" Coral demanded. "Why put her there and not in one of these cells?" She looked at her surroundings. So uncomfortable, but at least she would have been *seen*.

"Where a better place to keep a secret prisoner than in a secret cell?" he said sarcastically, dropping his head back to his tail. "And everything I have worked for all these years, everything I suffered to keep her safe. Gone." His shoulders shuddered up and down as he cried. "Sometimes," he continued, "I imagine she is the same mother who raised me from a guppy to a merman, but this prison... it has poisoned her mind."

Coral was about to get up and swim to him, to offer him comfort, when the large screech of the doors opening stopped her. Had they come for their execution? A moment later there were guards in front of their iron bars, looking in with smiles on their faces.

"Ready for the show, Your *Highness*?" one of them asked Caspian. He ignored them, keeping his head buried in his tail. The guard chuckled. "Once she starts screaming, we will get your attention." And then they swam away.

Caspian's body tensed, but he did not look up. "What are they talking about?" Coral grunted as she swam near the bars. She wished her head fit through, wished she could see what they were doing.

Then came the singing.

"I am a queen. A queen. A queen of the ocean blue, blue, blue. Freedom! Freedom! My dream has come true, true, true." The voice was female, deranged with insanity. A voice that was familiar, for it had haunted her for days when she'd been locked in her own cell. *"My little merman, how I miss thee! Last time I saw you, you were but a wee thing! Teeheeeeeee!!!"*

Coral turned to Caspian. His shoulders had hunched more, his hands dug so hard into his tail that the scales started to come off, leaving trails of blood flowing behind. Coral went to him, grabbed his wrist but he didn't let go. His grip was vice.

"Caspian," she whispered. He ignored her.

"Have you seen my son? He has hair like his father. Last I heard he was too busy with the queen to even bother! Heeheeeeeee!!!" The voice dissolved into a fit of giggles. *"The queen's whore! The queen's whore! My son is now the queen's whore!"* Caspian flinched at the song, at the words. Coral held onto him tighter. If only she could shield his ears, protect him from this.

"Shut up!" one of the guards barked. There was the loud sound of flesh being slapped. Caspian sobbed. Coral wrapped her arms around his shoulders.

The singing continued, and the guards slapped her again. Soon, the singing turned into sobs, and she cried out Caspian's name over and over, begging him to help her. There was the sound of metal scraping stone, of guards laughing.

And then there was nothing but pain.

Caspian sobbed harder, and Coral could only hold onto him, trying to drown out the sound as Caspian's mother screamed.

And screamed.

And screamed.

THE QUEEN'S SPY

"I KNOW WHAT YOU DID."

The voice startled the mermaid into yelping. She dropped the bag of gold, black, and silver coins that she had been in the process of securing the side of her newly purchased hippocampus. She picked up her payment, holding it tightly in her hands as she turned to face the owner of the voice.

He wore the perfectly polished uniform of the queen's Personal Guard. The squid was a ridiculous addition, sticking its bulbous head next to *his*. She took a stroke back, only to run into the side of her hippocampus. The animal stirred restlessly.

"Are you going to reply, half-breed?"

"What do you wish I tell you, Lord Matthias?"

The brown-haired merman with the shaved sides of his head and whorls of tattoos threw his head back and laughed. There was no humor in the sound. None at all. There was, however, a cold cruelty in it. And *that* is what frightened her.

"Oh, Zenara, Zenara, Zenara," he purred, gliding closer to her. She made herself smaller against the hippocampus but nothing, no animal or magic, could save her from the wrath that roiled off Matthias. He placed his arms between her, caging her in. "Ze-na-ra," he brought out the syllables of her name. "What do you think Coral would say if she found out that her *friend* betrayed her to the queen?"

Zenara broke into sobs at her treachery spoken aloud. It had taken everything within her to fight against what she had planned to do. It had taken every ounce of her strength to try and *forget* what she had heard and seen ever since Coral had arrived.

But her queen had called.

Her mother had wanted information.

And Zenara had betrayed them to give it to her. Just like they'd betrayed her for putting her in that position.

"Be *quiet!*" Matthias shook her arm, and she clamped her teeth onto her bottom lip. He was looking at her with open disdain now, the smile completely gone. "Pathetic little thing," he judged.

Zenara glared at him then. "I would think you of all people would be thankful."

"Thankful?"

She nodded. "I could have condemned you along with them. But I did not. I *did not.* I kept your name out of the information I fed Her Majesty. Like the fact that you were the one who warned her about the prisoners' execution. Or about the fact that you and Coral kissed, but not only that, you—" He let out a growl that shut her up immediately.

"Full of information, are you not?" He smiled, revealing the lengthening of his teeth into sharp points. She flinched at the sight of them. "You fed Caspian to the sharks. Why? I thought he was your friend."

"Because the queen asked it of me."

"No, no, no," he *tsk*ed at her. "Why?"

Zenara sighed. "Caspian knew I was giving information to the queen," she confessed. He had guessed it the moment the queen had put Zenara in his services as a spy. She was supposed to report back on *everything* he did because she had not trusted him. She had believed he was working with Atlantean rebels, trying to aid in the restoration of the rightful Atlantean heir on the throne. He had not been, as far as Zenara could tell. She fed the queen small bits of information here and there. It had not been much. Not much treachery went on behind his walls. He wore the colors of his old kingdom and often took out an old blade to be polished. Other than that, there had been nothing. Nothing.

Until Coral came.

And he had been so gentle with her—at Zenara's request. He had taught her how to swim, had worried over her wounds, had literally *begged* Zenara to treat her. And they had kissed and Zenara—Zenara had been jealous. Not jealous of the obvious love that had been beginning to blossom between them, for she had no feelings towards Caspian, and Coral was quite lovely. She was just *jealous,* and she could not explain why when she loved them both so dearly.

"I am sure he did. I am sure he thought you fed her *lies*. You fed her half-truths and have condemned Coral in the process. What exactly did you tell Ulla?"

"I do not—"

Matthias shook her then and rattled her brain against her skull. "Do not *lie* to me, Zenara. I am not in a lenient mood."

"I told her that Caspian had feelings for Coral, that he visited her chambers in the night. I told her that they had been intimate—" Matthias growled. She continued, "I told her that she had discovered the prisoners were alive and that she had a sudden interest in the Knowledge. I think that is why she demanded their execution."

"And did you tell her that Coral planned on freeing them?"

She paused and then. "Yes. You know that."

He had been present when she had called for an audience

with Her Majesty. Zenara had tried to keep that information to herself. She really had. But the queen had promised, she had *promised* that if Zenara had brought her worthwhile information, that she would earn herself a bag of gold and her freedom. So Zenara had waited until the last possible minute; she had wanted to give Coral a fighting chance to escape before she went to tell the queen.

It had not been enough.

"I am to believe you conveniently left my name out," Matthias said suspiciously.

She had, whether he believed it or not.

"I believe the human has put a plan in motion to break the prisoners out tonight," she had told the queen. The queen in her rage had believed Caspian to be the culprit, the vendor of information. Zenara had not contradicted her. She had already condemned two lives. Why condemn Matthias, a third?

"If I had not, you would find yourself in a prison alongside them."

Matthias grunted and took a stroke away from her. He stroked his chin in thought and then turned to her, smiling. "Well, here is how we are going to make you pay for your treachery."

Her fist clenched against her chest out of fear.

He noticed and shook his head. "No, I will not kill you, Zenara. You value your life, and I will grant you many, many years of your future if you atone for what you have done to Coral."

It was as if the guilt was tainted on her face. She had bought her freedom, but at a great cost. She looked at Matthias and wondered, not for the first time, *why?* Why was he going through such lengths for Coral? The answer dawned on her.

"You love her," she whispered. He glared at her. "You do,"

she realized, stupidly too late that Matthias—Matthias who was faithful to the queen, who loved riches and power above all else had betrayed it all for Coral. Because he *loved* her.

"I cannot love." His eyes narrowed at her, warning her to be quiet.

Somehow, she could not silence herself. "If you could not love, you would not save her." He just gave her a menacing look. She swallowed. If Matthias of all mer could turn from his dark path, if he could betray the most powerful mer in the Dark Waters, then Zenara would, too.

The thought was almost overwhelming.

All her life, she'd known she meant little to the queen. She'd known that her worth was measured by the information she could provide. No love existed between Queen Ulla and any of her children, yet she expected their blind loyalty regardless.

Zenara had been such a coward that she'd given it.

Because she'd wanted her freedom from what the mark at her hip implied she was. And she'd sold out her friends to get it. The queen had tossed her a bag of coins for her trouble, and they'd weighed heavily in Zenara's hands as she picked them up, and that ache had spread through every crevice of her body. Not even the soft caress of her tentacles against her cheeks could make her feel better.

"What do you need me to do?" she asked quietly.

Matthias smirked. "The queen sent me to dispatch a group of guards to follow after the prisoners. Conveniently, I came to warn you first. Hide them well and then come back for my little fighter. If you do not," he smiled, revealing his shark teeth, "I will send the sharks to drag your body back."

ZENARA

THE SCREAMING LASTED HOURS. IT ECHOED THROUGH HER mind even after it had stopped. The crying, the sounds, the laughter, sobbing out her son's name. All the while, Caspian had kept his head bowed, had dug his hands into his tail and mutilated it while his mother suffered. Because there was nothing he could have done to stop it.

A part of Coral blamed herself for all that was happening. If she hadn't involved Caspian in this plan... If she hadn't found out about Olivia... If she hadn't wanted so *desperately* to save her friend...

She shook those thoughts away. This, this atrocious act was no one's fault. Not hers and not Caspian's. It was no one's fault but the queen's. After the sounds had subsided, there was more laughter, rustling and then the guards swam by their cell, stopping. One of the guard's, an ugly merman with a scaly face and spikes running from his forehead down to the back of his neck, had an enormous sack thrown over his shoulder. Coral swallowed her rising bile. His mother. His mother was in that sack.

"She put up a fight." The guard smirked. Coral's hands

tightened into fists. Caspian tensed at the words and let out a sob. The guard laughed at the sound. "Pathetic Atlantean scum," he spat and then turned away with his partner, taking their laughter with them.

But leaving behind the broken echoes of her torture.

Caspian sat in numb silence afterwards. It frightened Coral, but she understood. She understood how those sounds would live forever in him, the blame he would forever carry. Coral didn't push. She didn't try to rouse him from his position in the corner. Even if she wanted to shake him, to force him *awake* and help her find a way to get out of there.

But Coral searched through every inch of the cell, had tried picking the lock with her hair pins. She'd slapped her tail against it, tried fitting through the bars. She didn't stop until Caspian reminded her in an empty voice that the prison was magically warded against any escape attempt. That only a key or the queen's magic would free them.

It was hopeless.

The queen would come, and they would die here.

A sob rose to her throat, but she pushed it down. At least Olivia had gotten out safely. That was what mattered. Her best friend was safe, or at least she hoped she was. With the queen's mer out looking for her, Coral prayed that they'd gotten away.

Matthias had betrayed her to the queen, and that tore wounds that she felt would never heal inside of her. Perhaps he'd given the queen the same directions he'd given her, the directions her best friend and the prisoners found themselves riding towards. He'd helped her only to condemn her. Because Matthias was all about the chaos of the game.

After everything that had happened, Coral hadn't given herself enough time to process the situation with Matthias. When the echoes of Caspian's mother's screams faded from her mind, she thought of him. Of the merman who loved power and riches, of the merman who had come to mean something to her.

She'd told Caspian and Matthias that while they were with the queen, she wouldn't be with either of them. The truth was, she had wanted both. And she hated that she did. She hated that her heart ached for Caspian's gentle caresses, ached for Matthias's rough ministrations.

In a matter of hours, she had lost everything she cared about.

She supposed it didn't matter anymore. Death had been inevitable. But now she wouldn't cower before it. Now, she would stare the queen in the face and she would curse her name. And she would die with her head held high.

Just as she accepted that fate, the gates to the *calabozo* screeched open and the regal, angry voice of the queen floated towards them. Coral swallowed her fear. It was time. She sank next to Caspian and took his limp hand in her own, threading their fingers together. He held her as tightly as she held him. He knew their doom was upon them and lifted his head. His eyes were rimmed red, the only sign of what he'd suffered. Now, though, his eyes burned like blue water fire. He would die, head high as well.

The voices floated closer and closer. Her pulse jumped and she felt his own at his wrist, penetrating into her and making her nervous. She only hoped the queen could not hear her erratic heartbeat.

The cackling sensation of magic rose the hairs on her arms and she waited...

Strong hands gripped her shoulders. Familiar hands. She whipped around and stared into Zenara's solemn face. Coral gasped. "Time to go," she whispered to the both of them. Her body, much to Coral's amazement, was poking through the prison stone wall, as if her front half had become transparent to get through it.

Caspian stared at her with wide, surprised eyes. "How——?"

"I will explain later," she whispered before tugging at them both and pulling them through the wall.

Just as Queen Ulla Magissa stopped before their cell.

The echoes that followed them then was the sound of her shrieking in fury as Zenara stole her prisoners away from right under her nose.

"FIND THEM!" the queen shrieked. "Find them and bring them to me!"

Matthias hid his smirk behind a low bow to his queen. She had done it. Zenara had come through. Of course, the queen had not been able to tell that it was her own daughter who had pulled Caspian and Coral through the wall. All they had seen as they approached the cell were tailfins disappearing.

A strange thing, Zenara's magic. But not surprising. She was descended from the most powerful queen, after all. Magic within the prison cells did not work for anyone but the queen—and those who shared her blood had the same magical handprint as she. A fact that seemed to have slipped her mind when she had first put the wards up.

"We should split up," Matthias suggested to Zalyn as they swam out of the castle. "We will cover the waters better."

Zalyn gave him a curt nod and swam off. Matthias smirked at his back and hurried his own way. He knew where Zenara was headed. Because he had told her where to go after aiding the prisoners.

Already, she was making her way for bluer waters. Away from the Black Kingdom.

And Coral would be safe.

Matthias smiled as he swam and swam.

Away from the Black Kingdom.

And towards his little fighter.

Z‍ENARA SANG AND SANG, projecting her magic for miles as she pulled both Caspian and Coral through the water. The crackling of it spread throughout Coral's entire body, making all of her hairs and even her fins stand on edge.

She didn't stop even as they abandoned the darker waters of the Black Kingdom. She only started slowing down when the blackness faded and the ocean expanse became bluer. Finally, she stopped for rest, sinking slowly to the sea floor and into the silt. Her breathing was ragged, her energy spent.

Coral sank into the floor next to her and pulled her into a hug. Zenara tensed up at the contact briefly before melting into Coral's touch. "Thank you," Coral whispered to her friend. "Thank you, thank you, thank you. You saved us."

"Zenara." Caspian sat on the other side of her. He reached for her hand and squeezed it. "How did you do it? Magic is not supposed to work within the *calabozo*."

Coral pulled away so Zenara could answer. The mermaid smiled, a small twist of the corner of her lip. "Magic in the *calabozo* works only for the queen. I share the queen's blood, and the signature of our magic is similar."

Coral glanced at her. "What do you mean 'queen's blood'?"

Zenara chuckled and pushed back a stubborn tentacle that had strayed onto her face. "The catfish is out of the bag, I suppose." She grimaced and turned to Coral. "I am daughter of the queen."

Coral felt herself gasp. "Wh-what?" She stared at her. At the regular pink tail, at the matching pink tentacles curling protectively around her head. A strawberry pink. Pink like the underside of Ulla Magissa. "But... your father? I mean... is there a king?"

Zenara laughed. "No. My mother would not be willing to share her power. She keeps her Personal Guard as entertainment." She winced and looked at Caspian. "Sorry," she apologized. Then turned back to Coral. "All us dozen of her children are bastards. Daughters of the Personal Guard."

The queen had daughters with the Personal *Guard?* She took in Zenara and took in Caspian beside her. Their coloring was so similar and so different from anyone else in the Dark Waters. His a darker brown than hers, yet they shared similar facial features. Her heart clenched unpleasantly.

"And are you two—I mean..."

"No!" they answered at once.

She breathed a sigh of relief. "Okay." She looked around at their surroundings. Blue water stretched out for miles and overhead near the surface a shoal cast a shadow over them. "What do we do now?" she asked.

Zenara answered, "We wait."

"Wait for what?"

"My little fighter." The sudden words sent a familiar chill down her spine. She turned and found herself looking into the golden eyes of Matthias. Her whole body tensed as she took him in, floating little ways away from her, still in his guard uniform. Smiling.

Coral shot up in her place and reached instinctively for her weapons only to realize that she had been relieved of them when the guards had captured her. They'd been thorough in their search and had taken the one she'd hidden in her arm as well.

She tightened her hands into fists. "What are you doing here?" she demanded angrily. Caspian was up beside her as well, glaring menacingly at Matthias. He pushed Coral and Zenara behind him, shielding them with his own body.

"What do you want, traitor?" Caspian snapped.

Matthias spread his hands out to the sides. "Traitor? Is that what you think?"

"It's what we know!" Coral shouted accusingly. "You betrayed us to your queen. You sold me out. I—I thought we were *friends*."

Matthias scoffed, crossing his hands against his chest. His eyes flashed, but his smile never faltered once. "You really believe I betrayed you, little fighter?" He directed the question at Coral, but his eyes flickered to Zenara.

"Are you here to take me back to the queen?" Coral asked defiantly instead of answering.

"No."

Coral scoffed. "Why do I find it hard to believe the word of a traitor?"

Zenara who had remained quiet this entire time, gripped Coral's arm. "Stop," she whispered. "Matthias is no traitor."

They turned to look at their friend. Her gaze wasn't on them. It was on Matthias. She was chewing ferociously on her bottom lip and suddenly, a sob escaped from deep within her chest as she turned to Coral.

And in her eyes there was regret.

"He was not the one who betrayed you to the queen. The one who betrayed you... it was m—"

Zenara didn't get to finish her sentence.

Because at that moment, a spear shot through her chest.

A LOST VOICE

BLOOD SPLATTERED AGAINST ZENARA'S LIPS ONLY TO SWIRL in a red cloud and disappear. Her eyes went wide with shock before looking down to the massive spear protruding from her chest. Blood swelled from the wound.

Coral screamed as she fell to the ground.

Zalyn floated in the water across from them. His eyes smiled as they beheld the scene before him, as he beheld Zenara's fallen body and the blood swirling in large tendrils above her.

Coral dropped next to Zenara and gripped her hand, already going cold. No. No. *No.* She had a feeling she knew what it was the mermaid had been about to say, what she was about to confess. But the minute the spear had pierced her chest, the slate had been wiped clean.

"F—f—forgiv—"

"Ssh." Coral rubbed a hand through her tentacles. One curled around her hand and held her with all the remaining strength she had left. "It's okay, Zenara. I forgive you."

She coughed, blood flying from her tongue. "Don't—deserve—forgiveness."

"It's okay." Coral sobbed, feeling the tears sting at the backs of her eyelids. "It's okay. You'll be okay."

Then Zenara smiled. "You were always—kind—to me —too."

And Zenara took her last shuddering breath.

And died.

Her entire body slacked, tentacle falling from her hand. Coral sobbed. No. *No*. She looked up. Zalyn had rolled his sleeves up to his elbows and was circling Caspian. "Get the *anthropos*, Matthias," he said. "I will take care of *him*." And then he charged.

Their bodies collided with a deafening *thud*. Fists and magic flew, unforgiving vortexes of water and air, balls of light and blue water fire. They were nothing but blurs through the water, a clash of color and elemental sound.

"Coral..." She turned to Matthias. His hand was on her arm, gently but firmly, his eyes never straying from the fight. "I am sorry, little fighter."

"She betrayed us." Her words were empty.

He squeezed her arm. Coral kept her eyes on the fight as well. They sprang apart and threw magic at each other. A water vortex swirled towards Zalyn and he threw his own bright blue ball of water fire at Caspian. They dodged, giving a powerful thrust of their tails and flying upwards. They got close to each other and began slamming punches anywhere they landed.

This dance was different. It wasn't a simple training exercise from within a ring. This was a fight to the death. Matthias' words swam into her mind. *Zalyn tips his hidden weapons with poison.*

Her stomach lurched with that knowledge. She couldn't let Caspian fight this battle on his own. He needed help. They needed to get rid of Zalyn once and for all. Coral jerked her arm out of Matthias' hold and jetted up after them.

Matthias gave a shout and followed her.

She was up, going up higher and higher so close to the surface, so close to the shoal that darted back and forth. Caspian's powerful muscles rippled as his arm swung, clocking Zalyn in the face. Zalyn went with an undercut, a silver shine on his knuckles catching her eye. Coral cried out to Caspian. Her warning struck home and he dodged, falling forward. Caspian slapped him with his tail, and Zalyn twirled backwards through the water. Caspian followed. Punches blurred before her eyes. Bodies flashed, magic rained down like streaks of fireworks. When their figures finally stilled, Coral's heart dropped to her stomach.

Zalyn was behind Caspian, forearm against his throat. Caspian was going slack in his arms as Zalyn's muscles tightened in a crushing grip around his throat. Coral screamed at him to let Caspian go. His gray eyes sparkled like the edge of a blade as he tightened his hold. Caspian writhed in his grip, but he was already weak and Zalyn was too strong. There was a loud cracking sound that nearly shattered her eardrums.

"Caspian!" Coral sobbed.

Zalyn laughed at her desperation.

Coral swam up to him, to fight, to save him, but Zalyn's body suddenly tensed before she got there. He slackened just before he released Caspian and floated down to the seafloor. Coral stared after him. He didn't get back up.

She looked up to find Matthias floating where Zalyn had been. He held Caspian up. Coral swam up to them. Caspian's eyes were half lidded. He was still conscious but barely. "Caspian, are you okay?" she breathed.

His eyes fluttered and opened. He opened his mouth to reply, to answer, but no sound came out. A guttural noise came out instead. He slammed his mouth closed as if speaking hurt him. She recalled the crack. Zalyn had done something to him, had *cracked his throat*.

"Oh, Caspian," she whispered.

"We must go now," Matthias urged. "It is not safe so close to the surface."

Coral nodded. "Go make sure Zalyn *stays* down. I'll help Caspian down." Matthias handed Caspian off to her, one arm over her shoulder before swimming down to check Zalyn's pulse. He was heavy, but it was comforting. It gave her purpose. "I've got you, Caspian. I've got you."

He tried replying, but guttural sounds emanated from his throat. Her heart tore at the sound. How many times could her heart break? How much could it take?

They began swimming down, slowly at a steady pace for Caspian's benefit. From below, Matthias looked up and even from the distance, Coral could see his eyes widen. He opened his mouth and, "*Coral!*"

She narrowed her eyes at him, confused when he started swimming wildly towards her.

She soon saw why.

A shadow loomed over her body. *The shoal.* She looked up. The shoal was above her, the voices of hundreds of fish rising in panic.

Because falling over them was a net.

And it was heading straight for Coral and Caspian.

MATTHIAS HAD NEVER KNOWN true fear. Had never felt the ugly jaws of that emotion dig into him. When the Personal Guard had taken him to be tried before the queen, he had laughed at the possibility of death. He was used to it. Mer died all of the time in the slums. He had killed and fought and never once had he felt afraid.

Until now.

He put speed and whatever bits of magic he had left into

every thrust of his tail as he sped up, up towards the net that now held both Coral and Caspian ensnared. They fought as hard as they could with the fish to try and get out. But Caspian was only half conscious, his magic and energy depleted in that fight. Matthias was there himself, after swimming with the aid of magic to catch up to them. He had nothing left.

He made it to the top of the net and gripped it, pulling it down. Bodies covered in scales pushed against each other from within the entrapment. Cries and echoes called for help and he tugged with all his might but the human boat pulling it up.

Coral's face pressed against the net and in her expression, raw fear.

"Help!" she screamed. She tugged at the net herself, clawed and whacked her tail against it. Matthias did much the same. He had no weapons, had swum towards her without them. He cursed himself for that foolishness. He never left without weapons, but in his eagerness to get back to her, he had forgotten.

"Help us, please!" she sobbed.

He held on until his fingertips bled, but the machine was too strong. It lifted them up and Matthias lost his hold against the wriggling bodies and fell back into the water. His heart lurched as it was pulled above the surface.

And with it...

"My little fighter."

And then Matthias, slowly, heart breaking, sank to the sea floor.

MERMAID

THE NET WAS HAULED ABOARD, THE STINK OF FISH reaching the fishermen on deck. But they were used to the smells. They were used to the beauty and ugliness of the sea. There wasn't a life they'd prefer than the one they had.

There was something about the salt permeating the ocean air. Maybe it was the way it stuck to eyelashes or the way the sea sometimes called out as if there were sirens beneath the surface waiting for them to take the plunge.

Whatever it was, they loved it.

The net was flurried with activity. The fish this time around were lively things, flopping against the pull of the net, fighting for their survival. It was hauled up... up...

"What the hell?" one of the fisherman called out.

The movement became violent, the net swung back and forth, back and forth.

"Reckon we caught a shark?" another one asked.

They all took cautious steps backwards as the net was deposited in the center of the deck. It flopped open, fishes bouncing up and down, begging for water. The men all gasped at what came tearing out from under the net. Some of them rubbed their eyes, pinched themselves thinking that no, this couldn't be real. But it was. And she was there.

Her black hair strung like a spider web over her beautiful face. Blue eyes glared at them. Her chest, decorated in a black tunic and jacket rose and fell rapidly. And there, just below the waist, a long blue fishtail.

A thing out of legends and myths sprung true. On their ship. Something only young girls thought existed. But here she was. Real and frightened and struggling for the breaths she needed to survive.

A mermaid.

GLOSSARY
RIPTIDE TERMINOLOGY AND CHARACTERS

Anthropos: The mer equivalent to 'human'.

Atlantis: The ancient city of old. Home to scholars and bright minds, originally a mer kingdom that was destroyed.

Atlantica: Caspian's homeland, located in the Atlantic ocean. A mer city rebuilt to honor the fallen city of Atlantis.

The Black Kingdom: The capitol city of the Dark Waters. This is where the queen's palace is located.

Calabozo: Mer word for 'dungeon'.

Caspian di Magissa: Ex-commander of the Royal Stratia and Personal Guard to Queen Ulla Magissa.

Coral Bennett: A librarian, wannabe author from Colorado.

The Dark Waters: A mer kingdom near the human lands of Greece and Italy.

Hippocampus/Hippocampi: Mythological creatures resembling horses.

Knowledge Keeper/Keepers of Knowledge: They were the librarians of Atlantica. They kept the secrets and knowledge of magic from all around the land in their temples before Queen Ulla Magissa slayed them all.

Magistrate: Queen Ulla's right hand merman and royal advisor.

Matthias: A merman in the Queen's Personal Guard from the slums of the Dark Waters.

Merfolk: Mermaids and mermen.

Neo Limani, Greece: A docking port in Greece.

Olivia: Coral's outspoken best friend.

Personal Guard: The queen's most favored body guards. They can be told apart by their uniforms, as the Personal Guards all have bulbous squids on their jackets.

Redwave: Caspian's hippocampus.

Royal Stratia: A league of Atlantean warriors. An army composed of the strongest and best soldiers in the kingdom of Atlantica.

Trent: Coral's human ex-boyfriend.

Queen Ulla Magissa: Queen of the Dark Waters and current ruler of Atlantica.

Zalyn: A vicious and quiet merman who forms part of the queen's favored Personal Guard.

Zenara: Caspian's friend and merservant as well as daughter to Queen Ulla Magissa. Father unknown.

ACKNOWLEDGMENTS

When I started writing this book, I never knew how much it would mean to me in the end. And like any other book, there are people who helped me immensely along the way. This book was written as a challenge, a NaNoWriMo challenge I was never able to complete until a few years ago. It took a lot of brain power to write it, fix it, and make it presentable to the public. So, without further adieu, I'd like to thank the following people for believing in my mermaid dream.

Thank you, Gennadiy, for your help and expertise regarding oceans, ports, and what little you could supply about submarines. You were the first I bounced this idea off of and your encouragement inspired me to go on. Thanks AK Koonce and A.L. Kessler. You were the first people to ever read this book when it was still in its first stages of awful and encouraged me to publish it anyway. (And I will be forever grateful for the mer jokes!) Thank you to Silviya for my beautiful cover. I knew when I finished writing this that you were the one I wanted to bring the cover to life. Thank you to Dina, Desiree, Natasha, Stacey, and Crystal for being such wonderful and helpful beta readers. Thanks to Elle, the best

P.A. an author could ever have. And last, but certainly not least, a big thank you to my editor and best friend for fixing the errors I never would have found myself and for dealing with what a mess this first draft was.

I would also like to take a moment to remind everyone that the ocean, no matter how scary or vast it may be, is also very beautiful and mysterious and it is our job to protect it, as well as the creatures who live in it. As a race, we need to do better and *be* better. That means reducing as much waste as we can, cleaning up trash and oceans, recycling or passing knowledge on to our children. One small ripple can make a wave. Never forget.

ABOUT THE AUTHOR

Aleera Anaya Ceres is an Irish-Mexican mix who enjoys reading, writing, art, and heavy fangirling. When she's not dreaming up stories about mermaids, she's daydreaming about all sorts of fantasy creatures. A proud Slytherin from Kansas, she currently lives in Tlaxcala, Mexico with her husband and son. Visit her website and join her mailing list for updates on her writing!

Triton's Prophecy

Triton's Legacy

Dr. Hyde's Prison for the Rare

Escaping Hallow Hill Academy

Surviving Hallow Hill

Paranormal Romance Series

Deep Sea Chronicles

Fall in Deep

Siren Queen

The Blood Novels

Love Bites

Blood Drug

My Master

Last Hope

Young Adult standalone

The Last Mermaid